Tide's Reach

Annie Salter

Copyright © 2017 by Annie Salter.

All rights reserved. No part of this publication may be reproduced or transmitted without the express permission of the author.

ISBN: 1548444510
ISBN-13: 978-1548444518

This novel is entirely a work of fiction. The characters and locations in this publication are products of the author's imagination. Any resemblance to people, living or dead, or existing establishments is purely coincidental.

First Edition

Annie Salter was born in Portsmouth, England. A third generation nurse she still works part time as a cancer nurse but has always enjoyed and dabbled in all things creative.

Tide's Reach is her first novel and was inspired following personal loss and a rejuvenating holiday to the Isle of Skye.

For my Mum and Dad who proved that true love exists and who always told me I could achieve anything.

1

Pimples' Grand Adventure

644.1 miles, 11 hours, 16 minutes.

Excitement was dissipating into good old-fashioned cold fear as the miles clocked up, and low cloud and black skies weighed down oppressively on Kitty and her trusty camper. The dawn was much anticipated, and with it a boost to the traveller's mood.

She had tried very hard to travel light but was almost overwhelmed by last minute panic, and had managed to cram every available space. She laughed out loud as she looked into the passenger foot well and saw the stone she had packed. It had no sentimental attachment, and she now recalled the day she found it in the front garden and brushed it off. It was only ever used to wedge the gate open when she struggled in with arms full of shopping. Hopefully before the bloody traffic warden would sneak up and give her a ticket for parking outside her own house! Where she was headed stones would be the one thing she would have plenty of.

Kitty had fended off offers to help pack. People from work had said they would help, and although they weren't what she would call good friends – it would still have been upsetting to say good-bye to them. Her true friends, from childhood and from University were definitely barred from being there the day she left.

Beaconsfield, 584miles to go.

Sobs that started on the M25 hadn't really stopped until the M40. Turning the music off as it only increased her sadness, Kitty used her memories to keep her company on what was going to be a monumental drive.

The miserable bitch next door had managed a half smile and brief eye contact, just long enough for a "Hope it goes well." Five years, five sodding years she had lived in the little cottage in Southborough. The front doors were at the side of the houses and opened immediately opposite each other, and many a time she had opened the door and stood face to face with Susan. For the first couple of years Kitty and her husband had tried to engage her in conversation. It became a sort of game, "See if you can find out a fact from the misery next door."

Only separated from the neighbours by one brick's width private conversations had to whispered, and for extra assurity the shelter of the under stairs cupboard was required. Listening to next door had made for interesting night time entertainment and they knew more than they wanted about their attached neighbours sex life. Less about the act of sex but the fact that Jenny considered she didn't have enough of it, and poor Jeremy was always too tired. Stephen had pulled her into the cupboard one spring evening.

"Well I've done it! I think she likes me - maybe that's it, maybe she doesn't like you," nodding his head and standing straight he pushed out his chest. "Maybe she fancies me!" His eyes gleamed; yes he liked that idea.

Stephen's nine-inch height advantage meant Kitty had to lean back, his slim face edged with glossy black hair made him look a little sinister in the cramped, dim confines of the cupboard. Looking very smug he was obviously waiting to be interrogated.

"Miserable bitch, I don't care what you know, I'm not interested" said Kitty, knowing full well how this would infuriate him she sniffed and looked away.

"You know you do!" he laughed now and began tickling Kitty's neck. "You don't know and I do! - You don't know and I do!" Stephens tickling and singing soon broke Kitty's resolve.

"Oh alright tell me!" she shouted, then whispering "Come on tell me, what, WHAT?"

That was the day that they learnt after eight months as her neighbour what her name was – the miserable bitch's name was Susan, it was never used again by Kitty. For the five years they lived six foot apart she avoided all contact and was forever known as Sue by Stephen. A term, in itself a form of derision as he hated his name being shortened to Steve. As he hated it he assumed Sue would too. But to Kitty, the ever constant, she remained just plain bitch. At first Kitty thought it was their misfortune to live next door to an unusually morose neighbour, but the longer she lived in Royal Tunbridge Wells the more it dawned on her it was the norm.

M6 West, 485.2 miles to go.

Kitty had grown up in Wimbledon in a quiet road, like so many around it, Victorian terraces neatly joined. Number 87 was special, as her mother had been born there. It seemed to a young Kitty that her mother knew everyone within an at least a ten mile radius. Lillian, her mum, never stopped or walked the streets without nodding, smiling, even hugging an endless array of people – old, young, male or female. When Kitty was small her mother would always squeeze her hand and when safely out of earshot would stoop down and whisper.

"Went to school with her, horrible brother."

Kitty would always delight in their secret little exchanges and was always rewarded with an interesting fact or anecdote; her favourites were always the otherwise insignificant hunched old men or women who all else passed unseeing.

"He taught my friend Gladys to play the piano, apparently smelt funny and had a lot of stuffed cats!"

Or Mr Grace the butcher – "Always fancied me at school, but my mum knew he wet the bed."

Never able to make eye contact with poor Mr Grace as if her knowing his darkest secrets was written all over her face. She never outgrew this and despite her hatred of supermarkets Kitty would have to buy any meat there so as to avoid the blushes at seeing Mr Grace – AKA the bed wetter.

Stephen had grown up in Rochester; he was a Kent boy through and through. He revelled in the snobbery of living in Royal Tunbridge Wells, albeit just outside in Southborough. Kitty couldn't deny the town was beautiful, surrounded by the "garden of England" – she smiled then, sniffing away the last of her tears as she headed ever further away, on her grand adventure to the "garden of Skye" – ironic she thought.

Behind the facade of the grand houses with their beautiful white and cream painted exteriors lurked a dark secret. Kitty had never met so many miserable, superficial and materialistic people, keeping up with the Jones's was not only rife she feared it was contagious.

Never before had it mattered quite so much what car you drove, where you holidayed and how old your sofa was. Kitty would bemoan this fact but could tell her husband was a lost cause. Not only did she see his eyes glaze over, but when she was saying what ridiculous sum someone at work had paid for curtains, she knew he was looking at theirs and wondering if they were up to par. He was a Kent boy to the core - she used to joke if he were sliced in two in a magic show it would read "Made in Kent" right through his middle.

When they were both students at Wimbledon college and dating, it was obvious the discomfort he experienced when she would stop and chat to people she had known all her life. At first she would share the little gems of information her mother had imparted to her. Stephen would frown down at her, disdainfully asking, "Why do I need to know that?" It took all the fun out of a much-loved pastime and Kitty soon determined not to share these pearls of wisdom with him – he was not worthy. Instead Kitty would silently say them to herself and smile and occasionally giggle when they were out of sight and earshot. Refusing his entreaties to share the joke Kitty silently kept her mum's secrets alive.

Knutsford services, 414.5 miles to go.

Kitty now thought about her mum. It had been 4 years since her death and she was so pleased that she now could think of her and the good memories flooded back and not the lingering, excruciatingly painful ones of her last days and the wicked end. Anger always reared within her if she did think of this – anyone denying euthanasia should have to watch someone they love endure as her dear mother had. Shaking off the image of a tortured face, Kitty once more saw the beaming smile, and it was true after all, time does heal. People often said it even if they didn't truly know the reality of it. When it came to loss Kitty knew her fair share.

The first experience of grief was when Fluffy her beautiful lop eared rabbit died. Much to her parents dismay Kitty insisted on Fluffy living indoors, even trying to house train her bunny. With a shoe box lid in the corner of the lounge Kitty would dutifully tear up strips of newspaper and repeatedly carry the unimpressed ball of fur, placing her in aforementioned box with pleas of "Here Fluffy, go here!" After two years of futile hours putting the rabbit in the lid Kitty would spend just as long picking up the small brown nuggets from all over down stairs and putting them in the lid herself. For all of Fluffy's life Kitty was happy under the misapprehension that everyone else in the house thought she had a beautifully housetrained pet, when in fact her parents had also spent two years putting droppings in the lid without their daughter seeing so Kitty wouldn't be disappointed.

This was the sort of family the Harris's had, each individual willing to do what made their family happy and wanting only harmony and contentment. When Fluffy died Kitty cried for a week solid, staying home from school as the waves of tears prevented her sleeping. Despite the best efforts of her parents, Lillian and Leo, and even the pats on the back from a bespectacled little brother Tommy there was no consoling her.

Burton-in-Kendal, 314 miles to go.

As the miles clocked up so too did the ache in her back and legs. The dull throbbing resulted in frequent adjustments in her seating position and giggling dances to keep her circulation moving. Halfway – was she really halfway – this knowledge was a super tonic to tired muscles.

Kitty felt guilty and quite frankly stupid for this outpouring of grief when two years later it was Tommy she lost. The twelve-year-old Kitty looked at her mum and dad then, and was so shocked and aghast at the devastation the sudden death of her brother had on them. Kitty herself cried less for Tommy than she had for Fluffy.

Both her parents shared a pact, be brave for Kitty. But she knew, she heard when they thought her safely asleep. Lillian wept every night for months and Kitty always knew when her father could hold it in no longer, as it would make him cough and Lillian would rush past Kitty's door wiping away her own tears to fetch Leo a glass of water.

It had been a freak accident on a school trip, it was a glorious summer's day and Tommy, never one to win prizes for his balance, slipped and fell and smashed his head on a rock. Kitty had been on the same trip two years before and had nothing but fond memories of running through thick pine needles, revelling in the scent of crushed pine and the feeling of isolation. Whenever she thought of that day and conjured images of Tommy, white and still, the blood pooling over the pine needles her brain remembered the smell, the lovely fresh smell of pine.

A bench bearing Tommy's name sat immemorial now. His big sister never liked to go there with her parents as she could never process – never equate the loss of her little best friend and her parents raw grief with that lovely place. Kitty knew however from early on, that her parents found peace and solace sitting there on that bench, and she understood their need to go but thankfully this was usually when she was at school.

Losing someone, especially a sibling in your early teens is very hard to process. In later years after some grief counselling Kitty reflected that teenager hormones and loss equals a whole lot of anger. Selfishness coloured all her emotions and she bemoaned Tommy's thoughtlessness at going, and how it materially affected her and spoilt forever her own life. Too immature, too self absorbed, Kitty merely gave her bereft parents more to worry about. As a damaged family they were just beginning to see the light at the end of the tunnel. The second anniversary approached and it was fractionally easier than the first. Kitty was for the main, behaving and both parents had learnt to laugh again – some times. But two years nearly to the day the next blow decimated them in the form of a burst aneurysm. Wednesday Leo went to work but never came back.

Lockerbie, 255 miles to go.

Now here was a place that had had its share of loss, and Kitty shivered at the thought of bodies falling from the sky on such a simple small looking place. One man's political beliefs and a plane full of people who's families were forever shattered, lost amongst the debris of an exploded plane.

Now six hours into her journey she found herself reliving the bombshells of her life. If losing Tommy was a dream – or more like a nightmare, the loss of her father was devastation. For her mother it was simply too much. Surviving and forcing herself to keep getting up, keep talking, keep functioning had taken every ounce of resolve and determination after the loss of her son. She had only managed this with the support of her partner, friend, and soul mate. The snatching of her other half, was just that, leaving Lillian bereft, cleaved in two and she never really recovered.

Leo had been hearty and fun and Kitty always knew how truly and madly her parents loved each other. She wondered now, as the last of the repaired roof tops faded in the rear view window - was this the reason she always questioned the depth of her love for Stephen, her husband. Was it a very clever self-preservation device – depth of love correlates directly to depth of sorrow? She guessed a psychologist could have a field day with her.

Kitty should never have left Wimbledon and moved to Kent. She had stayed at home for University so as not to leave her mum, but like all before her in her twenties was too caught up in her new plans. With a persistent boyfriend and fuelled by the inherent selfishness of youth, she had gone. She always regretted that decision and the guilt of it tinged her memories of her mother's subsequent years.

Annandale Water services, 248 miles to go.

Shaking off the urge to sleep, her heavy eyes drooped and she wound down the window and sucked in a great lungful of chilled air. "Come on Pimples, services in two miles, WE CAN DO THIS!" She slapped the steering wheel of her new van, it was the first vehicle she had owned that she had felt the urge to name – but it suited him so well.

Consulting her Satnav she was cheered by the ETA of 4.39pm, having set off at 4.30am. This was firstly so she could make the drive in one day and secondly, and more importantly, she could leave without anyone seeing her or risk them waving her off. All her possessions were safely crated in storage having left the day before. Kitty had spent weeks busying herself labelling and cataloguing all that had to go with her – all that was not destined for six months storage. Many an item was moved from storage to essential only to be relegated back to storage – her van was only so big. It was too late now and anything wrongly locked up in Sevenoaks was there until October.

Kitty pulled into the services patting the leather steering wheel, "Well, well done Pimps!" As the engine was shut off it blurted and spluttered, a trait which Kitty liked to attribute to character and communication, and didn't dwell on the effect 644.1 miles might have on his engine.

Like many things in Kitty's life over the past few years her van had been bought on a whim. Having always loved VW campers she had aspired to own one as a student when she owned a very unreliable Beetle. A keen Internet shopper, or more accurately Internet window shopper, she always looked but never bought, and the dream continued never to be realised. The night before Kitty found Pimples she had enjoyed the mindless distraction of online auction sites and her favourite campervan site.

But it was on a trip to the library that she spotted the van, the unusual colour and the classic style caught her eye. He, (for he definitely was a he!) was navy blue with a shadow of turquoise with round head lamps and chrome visors that looked like eyelids.

Ignoring the faint drizzle Kitty felt herself drawn and walked purposefully over to it. As she approached, squinting and straining her eyes, it wasn't until she was within reach that she could make sense of the strange markings. The spots she had struggled to understand were in fact textural, and running her fingers over the bonnet were regular lumps – like chicken pox in paint. Kitty laughed but was quickly crestfallen as she realised the driver was seated only feet away behind the wheel, ironically, with very bad skin himself. The lank haired lad in his twenties lowered the window, Kitty retracted her hand quickly. Aware of her own blushes, and not wanting to risk looking at his pimply face she glanced down.

"Oh I'm sorry I didn't mean to laugh – I love bugs." She said lamely trying to dig herself out. "He's lovely, what happened to his paint work?"

"Well..." looking embarrassed himself, "I tried a respray, but it was really dusty... and well it ended up like it."

"Well I really like it; you want a van with character don't you!"

"I want a new one, you know something with banded wheels, ya know, slammed. Went to the Vdub show, there was some bare swag there."

"Oh... that's nice, I suppose you would." Although she knew no such thing as she didn't understand any of what he had just said.

"Yeh I've seen a really sick one but I need to get a proper paint job on this thing before I can sell it."

Kitty winced at the word "Thing" and again at "It" and aware then she was stroking the bonnet she heard herself say "How much do you want for him?" This was how they met and two weeks later they were a good way into their adventure.

It was just how things happened now. She didn't question it, for there was no one to discuss it with anymore. By nature Kitty was indecisive, and had all her life sought reassurance and advice before even the most trifling decision and usually could still talk herself out of any solution. Now throwing caution to the wind, and for the first time acted on impulse, reiterating her new mantra "Sod it, it will work or not!"

Guessing it may be unhealthy to anthropomorphize her trusty steed but Pimples now felt like her best friend.

"I know I said we could have coffee together but there's a Costa will you forgive me?" She heard herself say these words out loud as she patted the door as she locked it. "Now this is a worry, I may well be going mad but no need for everyone to hear it!" Kitty looked around and was reassured no one was listening as she hurried out of the wind and shivered into the services.

Sitting longer than necessary on the toilet, revelling in the warmth, the modernity of stainless steel, and who would have ever thought – the luxury of motorway services. There was one photo of the toilet at her new home, and she had seen the facilities that awaited her. Kitty found herself stroking the clean wall of the stall. Lingering under the hot tap, not for the first time today Kathleen Harris was having misgivings.

The property her trusty companion headed towards was bought on yet another whim. No full structural survey, actually no survey what so ever. In fact she had never seen it, but by the photographs on the Internet the plumbing was basic and the heating limited to one open fire. What would Stephen say? – Shuddering, she knew exactly what he would say and decided not to dwell on that. "Sod it! It will work or not" – this is what she had to say.

Suddenly anxious to be back in her van she clutched the milk, chocolate, crisps and biscuits and a latte to go. Balanced diet no, but food to keep you driving, hell yes. Upbeat and revitalised, the music was turned up, coffee and too many biscuits eaten; Kitty The Brave drove on towards Glasgow, pushing on ever further North.

Others had expressed their opinions on the plan, varying from complete madness to mild eccentricity. Not one person had thought it was a good idea and Kitty had borne months of pitying gazes. But all the people that had known her well were gone, she was an orphan and brotherless. Now Stephen had left, Kitty held true to her new mantra, and decided no-one else's opinions were valid, so paying no heed she was following her instincts.

The older she got, the more two things really rang true. One – what doesn't kill you does make you stronger. In which case why take the easy road when you can do what is difficult and grow by that; she figured she must be very strong now. Two - was the idea that what is meant to be is meant to be. By some twisted hand of fate after all her loss, and with Stephen abandoning her Kitty was supposed to do this, this was meant to be.

Loch Lomond, 164 miles to go.

The traffic lessened and Kitty suppressed the urge to stop and drink in the view at Loch Lomond. Her backside was beyond numb and her hands and arms ached from clutching the wheel on the evermore-winding roads. Eyes itched from tiredness, and not for the first time this journey she was relieved at her decision not to wear make up as she rubbed her eyes hard with the heel of her hands.

As the landscape changed, the reality and scale of her plan was becoming real. She had invested too much, and come too far now to turn around. Kitty puffed out flushed cheeks and tried to focus on deep breathing in an attempt to quell the nausea that now threatened to resurrect the too many biscuits she had eaten.

She had Pimples, she had a camping stove, a collection of her cuddliest blankets and a duck down duvet plus numerous thermal under garments. But if all that failed there was a fine selection of alcoholic beverages stowed in the back. The knowledge of this kept her from crying out in fear and terror at the potential folly of her cunning plan actually turning out to be a nightmare.

Glencoe, 104.4 miles to go.

Glencoe and then Fort William were the epitome of Highland Scotland - the images of heather and highland cows in subtle watercolour paintings captured it so well. It felt very real and even more terrifying now. Her level of dread seemed to correlate to the scale of the landscape.

The road wound ahead of them like a grey stream. The ochers and muted moss greens of the valleys were topped by the giant craggy greys of the undulating mountains to both sides. A small patch of bright blue sky tantalised on the horizon, peeking out from the blanket of cloud that hung ominously, obscuring the tops of the highest mountains.

One minute of bravery, that's what her dad used to say. Kitty had repeated this phrase more in the last few weeks than ever before in her life. It had served her well when she had shouted it in her mind with every stroke the first time she swam without armbands. Or the summer day, aged just four with pig tails flying she had squealed to Leo's cries, "One minute kitten, just one minute – be brave – good girl, brave girl – WELL DONE!" His words had carried her forward as surely as his large hand that had pushed but then let her go, laughing as she rode without stabilisers for the first time.

This was certainly one of those moments. Kitty pulled an idling Pimples into a lay-by. Closing her eyes she allowed herself a brief respite and rested her forehead on the steering wheel. Faded but clear enough, she relived the memory of her fathers beaming smile as she had turned and peddled back to him. Although he had been gone for more than half her life that guiding hand was still there. She smiled at his proud face that she could still see, safe and constant in her memories.

"Come on Kitten, you can do anything!" Kitty now spoke his words and got out of the van. She felt close to her dad here and remembered stopping in this very spot on their holiday. Stretching and filling her lungs, she stood long enough to marvel at a shaft of sunlight pan across the valley as the clouds moved swiftly across the sky.

Stretching and rubbing her aching buttocks for a few more minutes, the weary traveller then climbed slowly back into the driver's seat. Taking a few large gulps of a disgusting tasting energy drink she rolled up her sleeves and once more pushed on.

The last time Kitty had visited Scotland was with her family the year before Tommy had died. Amazed that the vistas and landmarks were familiar to her now, all these years later was proof she decided, that the awe she had felt then, as now, was a good sign. She remembered it as one of the happiest holidays that she had ever had. Based in Applecross on the mainland Kitty had been mesmerised by the sunsets over Raasay and Rhona, the small islands in front of their cottage, black against the richest orange skies she had ever seen before, or since.

She could still remember the utter delight and wonder at watching the circling of a pair of golden eagles at the "Pass of the Cattle". The road that rose with its stark warning of 1 in 5 gradients and hairpin bends was still there but the addition since her childhood of bold warnings against learner drivers, very large vehicles or caravans. Kitty promised herself that she would soon revisit it, her only reservation being Pimples ability to cope with the rough terrain. She could even recall the anxiety and anticipation. At the summit, the last of the winter snow had still filled the gullies and her father's old Volvo had slowed into one of the passing spaces and they had all sat open mouthed at the view before them.

Kitty clearly remembered her mum grabbing the wheel when her dad was straining his head out of the window to see the eagles. Also, everyone's obvious relief when her dad finally pulled over. She could even now remember the exact colour of Tommy's conker and carrot hair, shimmering in the sunshine. They all sat on a boulder and watched the scale and elegance of the birds circling overhead as they held their silent revelry.

Quite unexpectedly this day had opened many memories Kitty was practiced in hiding away. She had anticipated how physically challenging the drive would be but it was proving to be an emotional rollacoster as well. The magnitude and scale made Kitty feel safe and yet insignificant at the same time. In her later years she had craved that feeling too many times and that was part of the reasoning behind her latest whim. The house in Southborough was rented out for a year, forever for all Kitty cared for it. She had now purchased a dream, a dream of peace, a dream of hope and a new start.

Kyle of Lochalsh, 14.9 miles, 20 minutes.

Only twenty minutes and Kitty, near hysteria with fatigue, she bounced in her seat and cheered at the bright beautiful sight of the white arch stretching between the dark masses of land either side. The late afternoon had welcomed her with blue skies and a scattering of billowy clouds, the bottom edge of each dusted in an orangey pink. The reflection on the sea below was mesmerising and Kitty took her aching foot from the accelerator to breathe in, inhaling the beauty before her. She had driven the long way around to Skye, and although it had added considerably to the journey the idea of negotiating the ferry was a step too far. Pimples was coping well with the roads and Kitty some how felt more secure that way.

The bridge to Skye felt like the last leg of a marathon. This was it, this was home. The last few miles were a relief; physically as she hurt in so many places, but also emotionally for it was truly beautiful here. After the rashness of her purchase she had researched Skye and the area as best she could using the Internet and the library. The phrase "Purchase in haste repent at leisure" playing over and over in her mind. So with no small amount of relief Kitty liked what she saw. Darting looks all around her whilst trying to watch the road, endeavouring to not miss a thing. There were a dozen or so properties near her turning, many of which were Bed and Breakfasts so if plan C needed implementing she wouldn't have to travel far.

Plan A; The inside of the cottage was better than the photos suggested and so she could snuggle up in a brass bed in front of a roaring fire – likelihood = slim.

Plan B; Unpack, have a light dust but settle down in Pimps until bed arrives – Likelihood = hopeful.

Plan C; Despair at state of cottage, uninhabitable and when smell of living in Pimples too great move into B&B for soft bed and bath – likelihood = probable.

Well she was here, the Satnav told her she had reached her destination. The entrance was to the right; an old plank of wood marked her turning. Set at a rakish angle with barely decipherable lettering that read; "TIDE'S REACH."

The small tarmac road sloped steeply down with a sharp bend that had Kitty clinging to the wheel, arms outstretched bracing back into her chair and pushing hard on the brake. Possessions slid forward and she closed her eyes and waited for everything to settle – thankfully nothing crashed or smashed.

"Oh bugger! Well they didn't mention that on the details – arhhhhh, sorry Pimps."

Everything ached, and her knees and hips complained as she tried to straighten. Satisfying clunks came from her back as she arched backwards and yawned loudly. Kitty was very happy to be at journeys end, especially before dark. Leaning on the open van door waiting for some normalcy to return to her limbs she looked out at the view – her view – Kathleen Anne Harris, landowner, her own piece of Skye, her very own piece of heaven. Well that was the dream.

So she was here on the 14th April, her parents anniversary and the first day of her new life. Twisting the thick band of dark gold that was her mother's wedding ring on her right hand, she said out loud.

"Well we've done it Mum, Dad, Tommy! We always said we would come back to Scotland and we're here."

A little known fact that Kitty hadn't felt the need to share with anyone was that the ashes of her family were one of the essentials that had travelled with her today. Never wanting to scatter them before, she hoped they could wait together here for her to join them.

2

Tide's Reach

The area Kitty now stood in comprised of a gravel turning circle thirty foot across; behind her a steep bank of wizened birches and shrubs obscured the road. West facing it was rich with emerald moss, the brown of last year's bracken with the small early promise of vigorous fronds uncurling. Primroses shone from the vivid shades of green, their cheerful bright faces an exquisite welcome.

"You're mine now, all mine!"

A large tear rolled unhindered down each check, relief and joy and fear, topped by one overwhelming feeling – exhaustion. Taking a deep breath and wiping away the tears on her sleeve, scanning from left to right trying to take in every detail. Too soon her eager eyes were on the house, sitting close to the shore of a small bay with a smattering of houses on the opposite bank. She looked along the trodden grass path with the breeze from the water chilling her left cheek. Alright not the most attractive, but for £150,000 what could you expect; bloody hell she reasoned, it had potential in spades.

The keys were already on her key ring and grabbing her rucksack Kitty set off along the path. One hundred and sixty feet it had said on the details. She had intended to count the steps but gave up at eighteen because she could control herself no longer and broke into a jog. At five foot four inches and a squishy size fourteen, jogging was not something Kitty was accustomed to. Her natural inability and the after effects of all day behind the wheel resulted in what could only politely be described as a stumble. Undeterred she ploughed on, giggles escaping her as the small white – well greying - house grew closer.

Tide's Reach was approached from one gable end and being only one storey high it stood stocky and firmly rooted looking out over the bay. Obviously many years ago it had been painted white, but now sported a greyish green hue. Each large stone was clearly visible and defined despite the paint. Reaching the wall by treading down the dead wood of last years plants, Kitty laid her face on one of the vast bulbous stones. Arms outstretched she lay there for many seconds hugging her cold damp home.

Thoughts of neighbours seeing her run and now embarrassingly, cuddling her house pulled her together and Kitty pushed away from the wall. Renewed excitement moved her, and walking towards the water and enjoying the damp wind in her face, she turned at the low front wall to look back at the front elevation.

It was a traditional crofter's cottage, having the only door centrally at the front and small square windows on either side. The paint work had been blasted by the elements leaving hints of past care with peeling remnants. Kitty didn't like the red, her home would have something more cheerful, maybe it should match Pimples – greenish, navyish, turquoiseish – there, a plan.

The door opened with not a little difficulty, and on entering Kitty was confronted by three overwhelming things. The first was the musty smell of damage and neglect. The smell of wet stone and chill of years of no heat, the croft was more part of the land than a home. The second was the vile stained yellow and orange wallpaper swirls and lines a remnant to its last attentions in the sixties. But thirdly and most critically Kitty felt at home. It was the most monumental decision of her life and she had made it all on her own. Succeed or fail she had only herself to blame.

She was still the owner of the house in Kent, but having let it she knew one thing for sure, she would never live there again. It gave her security, especially when this plan did seem to all-intents and purposes, rife with folly. The rental income would cover her living expenses here, and Tide's Reach was paid for in full so the only expense would be renovating it. Thanks to the eventual sale of her parent's house and the ridiculous prices in Wimbledon Kitty still had £600,000 tucked away, this was her nest egg, and this was Tide's Reaches salvation.

There was a small oak barley twist table in the hall and Kitty rested her bag gently on it. On top of the orange lino was a small rug, edges curled and of indeterminate colour and pattern. Kitty wiped her feet and whispered, "It may be shabby but its home, Tee Heeee." Not for the first time Kitty was pleased no one was watching her, as the woman from Kent danced a very strange little jig and laughed out loud.

Two doors led off the hall and Kitty paused to stroke the large panels – four per door and the only adornment being the large round brass knob. These shone through the drab grime, testament to years of daily caressing, Kitty couldn't help herself and gently rubbed her hand over the golden orb whispering; "You're mine now," and in her mind; "My precious." The door to her right served one of the only two rooms, the kitchen. A cooker that Kitty guessed was much older than her, stood in front of the even older range. Thankfully it was electric and not gas or Kitty wouldn't have dared trying it out. Dusting the worse of the grime and dust off the wobbly round element with her fingers and standing as far back as she could, closing her eyes and screwing up her face Kitty turned one of the rings on.

"Ta dah" Kitty clapped her hands as the element changed colour from rusty black to red, but the smell of burning was very pungent so it was quickly turned off. Inspecting the inside of the oven she was delighted, obviously its previous owner had looked after it well and with a good clean it could work – and in the absence of any heating she knew this monstrous enamel beast and her could soon be friends.

The sink sat at a jaunty angle on the far wall, large rectangular beige stone, although quite shallow it was a good two-foot across. It was no surprise that the spindly wooden frame was struggling to support it. Two old round backed kitchen chairs sat either side of a grimy looking Formica table. The floor in here was slate or stone and added greatly to the feeling of standing in a fridge.

Stroking every sad, battered and filthy item of furniture Kitty made her way to the sink. It sat underneath a small window, two-foot square and set in eighteen-inch thick walls – great windowsills she thought. From here was the view of the back garden, extending some forty feet – (sayeth the details) and edged by a stonewall at waist height. The ground rose up behind the wall so no sky could be seen. A view of the bright rich emerald of the moss and the pale lacy grey of the lichen that covered the trunks of small stunted trees. Nestling amongst the rich copper of last years dead fern fronds shone clumps of primroses. Kitty was so delighted to have moved at the time when the daffodils were showing in the lumpy, grass choked garden, and bright cheerful faces of primroses were the perfect welcome.

Bracing herself and tearing her eyes from the view, Kitty attempted to turn on the tap. Gone were the days of combi boilers, immersion heaters and central heating - welcome one cold tap and an open fire – and thank god a working cooker, constituted warmth and hygiene. The build up of scum on the tap, and the need to hold it to the wall due to its lack of security were not filling her with optimism. Gently persevering and rewarded with first gurgling, then spluttering and finally an explosion of dark water. Soon it settled and Kitty felt safe to let go as the water poured out, cold, clear and most importantly here! Tentatively she turned it off and gently stroked the tap as she said "Thank you". Glancing around the room and happy she had taken it all in, she hurried back to the hall, allowing herself the merest glimpse out of the front kitchen window looking out over the sea.

Part of her grand plan was to write and paint and do all the creative things she had been too busy to pursue up until now. The second room was to become a bedroom / lounge / studio. She had plans to extend but realised she had no real idea how long this would take. Part of the planned purchases included a metal-framed day bed, she could visualise it in here now. All of her and Stephen's furniture except an old chair of her granny's and a collection of textiles and cushions she had been amassing had been left at the house for the renters. She would treat herself to the day bed and two lovely small soft leather winged armchairs she had seen. An old desk – which worryingly she had christened Desmond – another sign of her need to name every thing - was waiting in storage. Anything else she hoped she could get when the building work was finished. Pimples was to act as bedroom, kitchen and general haven until Tide's Reach was ready.

The second room did not disappoint. A mirror image, it had the square windows with one facing west to the water and a smaller one facing the back garden. The fireplace was the only feature of the room a cast iron insert stood in the middle of the end wall with a simple painted surround. This room although faded and drab seemed less neglected, and Kitty's fervent imagination could visualise immediately how it would look.

The window at the front was at waist height and she allowed herself a few minutes to rest her elbows on the sill and drink in the view, stretching out her aching back and legs. The water that lay out before her was calm, small peaks of waves grew and dissipated reaching the stoney shore. On the horizon sat the misted outline of mountains disappearing into the ever changing mass of clouds. The sun was low in the sky, her ferry avoidance had added to the already mammoth drive but she was here. Sore and aching all over, and more tired than she could ever remember, but she had made it.

With renewed urgency Kitty trotted to Pimples to unpack some supplies. There was little point emptying everything, the slug trails in the kitchen and the damp in the walls meant her meagre possessions would probably be best stored in the van. All of her planning and colour coding came into its own now. All red crossed boxes were taken to the kitchen, all blue crossed boxes to the bedroom. Kitty had doubted the extravagance of sturdy plastic boxes with lids but was now smug in the knowledge of their value and definitely their slug-proofness.

There was a sense of panic now to unload and get settled for the night, as it would surely soon be dark, as the sun seemed to bob near the horizon. One of the many things the ill-educated émigré didn't know was that up here dusk is not a brief affair. Despite the pains in her limbs Kitty jumped up and down when the final box was in, her bed in Pimples ready and inviting. She drew the water from her tap, plugged in her kettle, and it worked!

The red crossed box with the kettle contained a bucket, bowl, and numerous and varied cleaning cloths. Aware that the sewage and waste may be somewhat unconventional Kitty had thought it prudent to bring basic washing up liquid and vinegar. There wasn't a thing that wouldn't shine with that combo.

Suddenly her bladder reminded her that it had been many hours since the services. Placing her newly unpacked slippers by the door and slipping back on her trainers filled her with unexpected pleasure and contentment, and Kitty ventured out. Behind the house (the only entrance being at the front) she found the small stone built extension sitting between the two rear windows. The two red doors were protected from the worst of the weather and therefore mostly covered in paint. The first opened easily outwards and revealed a wood store,

"Oh thank you", were her heart felt sentiments at a wall piled high with split logs and a huge wooden block in the middle.

"Chopper – red box number four – am I good or what!"

Kitty smiled and closed the door on her precious hoard and tried the second. The door opened with a little difficulty and Kitty took a deep breath, but she was not horrified as it was actually ok. The high cistern and ancient toilet brush in a ceramic pot were obviously a bijou residence for a colony of spiders and thick webs hung in drapes from the textured walls. Kitty slowly advanced to peer down the toilet bowl, dirty and unused for a long time but definitely something she could work with. Flicking the chain and watching it sway for a few seconds to encourage any resident spiders to move, she then gave it a pull. With the gusto and power that modern flushes lacked the bowl filled and after a terrifying few seconds, sucked away. "Marvellous!"

The temperature had dropped and a gust of wind blew the blonde wavy hair around her neck and face, and added to by the presence of too many webs, Kitty shivered. Nipping back to the kitchen, red box number six was quickly grabbed along with the mop and bucket.

Within fifteen minutes the cobwebs were gone; everything shone and smelt of vinegar, a fresh toilet roll was on the holder and a new brush in place and Ahhhhh! Despite the wind whistling around her bare legs (reminding her that it must have been weeks since she had shaved them as she could feel the blonde hairs move in the wind), Kitty sat proudly, legs swinging on the high toilet, door wide, admiring her garden.

Not only driving the length of the country but her numerous trips up and down to Pimples suddenly caught up with her and the urge to sleep became painful.

"Night, night Tide's, see you in the morning."

Wrapping her coat tightly around her Kitty, looking back and beaming over her shoulder, walked very slowly and very wearily to her friend, Pimples.

Once inside it was quite a struggle to get out of her clothes, but she resisted the urge to tread them down into a heap and shed a huge sigh as she folded them neatly. For some reason it seemed appropriate to start her new life with new night attire. Opening the M & S bag she pulling out her satin pyjamas and matching dressing gown. She had already spent a small fortune, what was a few dozen knickers? Nothing is quite as nice as the feel as new knickers – and these were not just any knickers, these were Marks and Spencer's knickers.

Feeling ever so slightly absurd Kitty wafted around in Pimples. Hot chocolate in hand, she settled into her bed and reached for the box marked with a gold star. This was technology, as she knew it and the connection to her life she had left today. The smart phone obviously wasn't that smart as it had no Internet or signal – "Won't be posting anything on Facebook today then!"

Kitty wasn't quite as techno savvy as she would have liked. Work colleagues had tried to extol the virtues of streaming, UV and downloading but Kitty held a basic distrust of all this. Despite her limited understanding she happily patted her large wallet of DVDs.

The teenager in the electrical shop had been so condescending, "Madam, portable DVD players are really becoming obsolete." He said disinterestedly as he raised his eyes and mentally prepared to update another middle-aged woman. "They are so last decade!" was written all over his face and she found herself saying, "Young man," (oh my god – she had become her mother, she was thirty, just thirty!) Ignorant little shit! She thought.

"I know everything there is to know about new technology, I do all that anyway. But for the purpose I need, I would like, I want a portable DVD player! Do you sell them or not?"

Kitty could tell by the look on his face, mentally he was shouting back "WHATEVER" but still wanting his commission he forced a sort of grin, "This way." Kitty followed his stooping shuffle across the shop. Having found just what she wanted, with an air of dignified satisfaction, she took her bright blue DVD player – there seemed to be a blue theme going on here, and Kitty liked it.

Sitting in Pimples she knew this was to be her chief form of entertainment. Music was covered with her MP3 player and stand but she had thought about it, and could give up many things, but never films. Virtually every version of an Austen, because who can live without those? Complete works of Doris Day, for rainy, sad days. All the old musicals, to remind her of her mum. And a fair share of rom-coms and thrillers to keep it interesting.

Kitty didn't like shopping, *hated* clothes shopping and only went out of necessity. Her friend Carla's main objection to her grand plan was, "Where will your nearest shopping centre be? Have you googled the nearest White Stuff, Fatface or Boden – hell, even Marks and Spencer's! Where will you be able to go on a Saturday to have a good mooch?" Carla, bless her, didn't understand that for Kitty the prospect of not having to do this again was an immense relief. The pressure was gone now, would anyone expect her to be in anything other than wellies, walking boots and waterproofs? – She certainly hoped not, for they would be sorely disappointed.

Snuggled down in her nest she slept like the dead, probably with a good dose of snoring if her dry mouth was anything to go by in the morning. The light coming through her checked curtains played on her face and forced her out of the slumber. She doubted if she had moved all night and took a couple of minutes to struggle free of the quilt and sheet. Maybe tonight less would be more in the bedding department she pondered as she ran a finger down her damp cleavage.

"Oh shit" reality hitting home now – "NO Shower!"

Kitty showered every morning; bathing was a treat reserved as a ritualistic luxury, usually including candles, a book and a glass of wine. She knew she could go without a bath but a shower, "Oh bugger, a shower."

Sitting free from the quilt a very stiff Kitty looked about her. When she had bought Pimples the curtains were black with white skulls of varying sizes. There was very little time to change them but Brenda came to the rescue, a plump, dimpled woman who never failed to smile. She worked on reception at Kitty's firm, and though many of the stuck up people she worked with looked down on the unpretentious Brenda and her mummsy ways, Kitty had always taken the time to chat with her. She had for a long time considered her to be one of the few genuine people in her acquaintance there.

It was over tea and some of Brenda's notorious lemon drizzle cake that Kitty had bemoaned the horrid curtains and how she wished she had learnt to sew. With only ten days until she left for Scotland there was little or no hope of changing them. Brenda reached out and took Kitty's hand, drawing closer her eyes welling with tears, "Now listen here young lady… you will be sorely missed here. You are such a lovely girl and I would love to help you."

And so it came about, Kitty handed Brenda a carrier bag full of curtains the next day. Armed with a tape measure, pencil and scrap of paper Brenda made quick work of scribbling a plan.

"Now dear, if you get me five meters of fabric and some cotton I'll have them ready before you go."

Kitty had been quite overwhelmed by this unprecedented show of kindness, the like of which she had never known since living there. Racing into town in her lunch hour she headed straight to the material shop, confused by too much choice she settled on the fresh array of cotton checks. The blues were all the wrong shade but the orange she thought would complement his colouring perfectly.

True to her word Brenda had the pressed, perfectly made curtains ready in just two days. Handing them over to a very grateful Kitty, was probably the saddest moment at quitting her job. Brenda gave her a lingering maternal hug, patting her back and Kitty just couldn't prevent the tears from falling.

Loving the warmth of the orange, sitting now on her bed with the sun causing, if not a rosy hue, certainly an orangey one. Brenda had also made her a cushion cover, which sat in pride of place on the passenger seat. There were apparently no limits to Brenda's talents, nor that of her sewing machine. In the corner of the cushion in vivid blue and pretty italic script were the words, "Good luck on your grand adventure."

Pimples had been altered and reconfigured inside by one of its previous owners. The front seats were high backed, sporty bucket seats in navy blue leather with cream trim. A leather laced smaller wheel, chunkier, had replaced the steering wheel that the old one would have been, but Kitty found it very comfortable.

The back of the van had a central aisle lined with a strip of blue carpet. On the side of the sliding door grey units filled every available space. They cunningly contained a small sink, a two ring gas burner and under these a small fridge. The space had been well utilised and every available nook and cranny was packed. Kitty had treated herself to range of blue china and all the supplies to equip Pimples for the coming weeks or months. On the opposite side was the sofa cum bed, by day the supports slide easily under the bench seat and half of the mattress formed the back support under the window. Kitty could have slept on the thinner bed but knew the inside of this van constituted comfort for the foreseeable future and she intended to make it as cosy as possible.

She had no choice to sleep on the thin bed last night as the central aisle was still littered with possessions. After unpacking most of her belongings she could have slept on a line last night so didn't bother, but was looking forward to making the bed up properly tonight.

3

The Post

She had booked an appointment to see Donald McDonald, a local architect with whom she had corresponded via email over the past two months. The appointment wasn't for a week and Kitty worried it was too long – that was a whole extra week before she would have a bathroom.

After a successful talking to, her eager mind winning out over her weary body Kitty stepped out onto the gravel for a full on "Aaahhhh-Ohhh-Urghhhh!" stretch. A satisfying clunk sounded from between her shoulders on reaching her full height and then she slumped forward struggling to reach her feet. Climbing back into the van with difficulty she set about putting on the kettle.

Having a strip wash in the van wasn't so bad but did involve knocked elbows, a banged head and a little swearing. Chiding herself, she thought people had always washed like this and she decided she must perfect it. If you're lucky you can get a tin bath and sit in the front garden - "Add to the list Pimps, a tin bath."

Comfortable, practical walking trousers, two T-Shirts and good thick socks, and of course new knickers and she was ready to take on the day. Filling a bowl with cereal and milk and a large mug of tea in hand she stepped out to walk the path home. Standing long enough to take a deep breath and admire the view, placing her breakfast on the floor and hurrying back into Pimples where a fleece and waterproof coat where added. She emerged serene, took her supplies and this time counted her way to the front door.

One hundred and sixty feet equated to one hundred and eighteen of her steps. There would be no more guilt for not going to the gym in this life. She would calculate her daily mileage over the next weeks and tell her friend Michelle from work, (or little Miss Fit as Kitty called her.) She had always tried to motivate Kitty to join her, but usually with an edge of insult, "Not only would you feel better for it but you would lose some of that flab," Kitty recalled her hoity nasal voice - now there was one thing she wouldn't miss.

At the front door Kitty left her breakfast on the window sill and unable to suppress the urge any longer, braced herself and made her way round to the toilet. The seat was very cold and she thought she would have to perfect sitting down with the minimum of bare flesh on show. She was pleased with herself for cleaning it yesterday, as with the morning sun streaming in through the half-opened door the webs would have been magnified. There was still a lot to do but certainly not as terrifying. Layers safely gathered in, she hurried back to her now soggy cereal and unlocked the door. The front door key was so worn, any brand or makers name was just a distant faint line now, and the key was smoothed and rounded.

Once in the kitchen the small table and chair were lifted into the centre of the room to take advantage of the beam of sunlight coming through the back window and she hurriedly cleared the bowl. She soon shed most of her layers as she scrubbed years of grime from her new furniture. Running her hands over the yellow checked Formica, Kitty gave herself a figurative pat on the back for a job well done, all trace of dirt and stickiness gone.

After allowing herself fifteen minutes basking in the warmth of the morning sun, Kitty realised she had no idea what the time was. Bowl and mug in the sink she headed for the other room. It didn't feel appropriate referring to it as her bedroom because necessity dictated it had to be so much more. The same could be said for the kitchen so Kitty pondered and decreed the bedroom would be the North wing and the Kitchen the South wing – or was that too Tunbridge Wells? It added a bit of romance and Kitty fancied it was the same when a house was too big, "Oh it's in the East wing!" and thought her little house deserved a shot at grandeur. In the North wing Kitty found the boxes with purple crosses. (Precious and bureaucracy).

This was to be the contents of the yet to arrive "Desmond"; another rash move resulting in Kitty being the proud owner of a rather battered oak desk. Driving down the high street near her house on the way home from work Kitty's eye was caught by a stack of unloved office furniture on the curb. Amongst the torn, stained, swivel chairs and dented filing cabinets was a relic to offices past. Stopping to take a closer look it was love at first sight. At a slight angle, a poorly executed stencil read PAY OFFICE on one end of the drawers. Blotched memories of spilt ink splattered the top and pooled in two of the drawers. Kitty was sure the day she had seen him that great things could, and hopefully soon would be written at this desk.

Opening the first box, shining up in pride of place was a framed picture. Kitty's dearest friend from childhood had given her this as a going away present last week when they had said their very emotional farewells. Pushing back tears as she struggling to swallow at the raw memory of this now. Having been at nursery together, their mothers were friends and only living two streets away meant they were equally at home in each ones' house.

Amanda's father was a sombre, repressed man, short in both stature and hair. He commuted daily to the city and worked in "banking" whatever that meant. But underneath the stern exterior lay a calm, quiet, reliable albeit non-gushing man. As each loss hit Kitty's family Mr John P James would quietly be there. Helping with arrangements - dealing with paperwork and solicitors when both Kitty's parents were too devastated after the loss of Tommy, and when the widow Lillian couldn't bring herself to face it. After Leo's death Mr James (Kitty still didn't feel right calling him John even in her head) would take his wife Marie, daughter Amanda, Lillian and Kitty to every parents evening, school fete and day out.

Kitty recalled when she was quite little her mother had shared one of her special secret thoughts on John James, and as she grew older Kitty could see where his quiet devotion originated. "Amanda's dad always liked me at school, but told me once… too late, he had never had the nerve to ask me out."

Mr James stoic attentions and devotion served Kitty and her mother well. There had never been a declaration Kitty was sure, no accusation or inference of any impropriety. Marie being quite a flighty nervous sort was blissfully unaware. Like a well-balanced triangle; Mrs James encouraged and liked being a help to an unfortunate friend; Mr James mutely but faithfully could aid and have contact with Lillian; Lillian in return treasured and loved them both.

He had sobbed at Lillian's funeral and no one turned a hair. Kitty realised that day it hadn't just been one of her and her mum's secrets. Amanda had promised to bring her parents for a visit in May, and Kitty added another item on her burgeoning mental list – find a good B&B for them.

Bringing herself back to the present, Kitty held the frame before her and placed it ceremonially on the mantle piece. It was a simple black frame, plastic imitating wood and held a crumpled serviette from the lovely Lavender tearooms. Whenever Amanda visited they would book the same table by the window in the corner, it offered them the perfect vantage point for one of their shared passions of people watching. One of the shared phrases "Was It?" stayed with each woman, together or apart. "Was it – really such a good idea to get that tattoo?", "Was it – anyone's idea of a good look to wear those leggings with those legs?" When they were together they very often didn't need the elaboration, as theirs were minds very attuned.

Scrawled and barely legible was a list in Kitty's hand, written on their last meeting at that same table:

1 - Sell mum and dad's house
2 – Rent out Stephen's and my house
3 – Move to Isle of Skye
4 – Buy a house with the view of the sea
5 – Write a best seller
6 – Buy a private jet so Amanda doesn't have to drive ALL THAT BLOODY WAY!!!!

In a space at the bottom Amanda had added in beautiful italic,

Bon Voyage my darling friend, if anyone can do these things you can. Now write that bloody book!!
        Love always
            Mand xxx

How hard could it be? She'd accomplished four out of six already? Admittedly the last two may prove to be her biggest challenge but as she had made it this far she felt there was cause to hope.

She looked around her now, assessed the situation and decided she needed to really clean up in here. Putting the lid back on the bureaucracy box Kitty was very grateful for having bought a small house, less to do, but the prospect of cleaning it could be put off no longer.

The South wing was empty bar the table, two chairs, the cooker and the sink. Rolling up her sleeves she readied the bowl, filled the kettle and plugged it tentatively into the Bakelite plug socket by the cooker. Excitement tempered by fear of electrocution resulted in a quick couple of steps backwards, culminating in a small jig. There was no nasty wallpaper here but peeling tongue and groove to waist height and white washed wall above. Kitty gave up on the walls after an hour as her overzealous scrubbing had resulted in washing most of the paint off. It left a sort of distressed mottled effect, white and grey patches with traces of blue, three coats, and three colours the silent history of this room. Very on trend in Southborough, and a satisfied if slightly sweaty Kitty stood hands on hips grinning broadly.

On the windowsill under a blanket of dust and silk like white webs was a squat little milk bottle. A soak in vinegar and a wash had Kitty running around the croft into the back garden. Glad she had donned her boots the lush green moss was like sponge. As she stepped onto it the dark brown water threatened to breach the top of the laces. It was worth the effort and risk to her socks, as at the end of her brief scramble she was rewarded with a sprig of spring. White wood anemones, bright faces of primrose and three small early fern fronds, vivid with their light green coiled tips, feathered and fine. Filling the small bottle perfectly, Kitty knew this would always stay on this window ledge for just this service.

It was so rewarding, every clean surface such a transformation from the drab dirty start. Kitty was renowned for not liking, or more to the point, not doing housework – period. Chuckling to herself she began to sing;

"If they could see me now, te-te-te-te-tee-tum, that dee-dee-dee-dee-dee-dee-dee-dee-dee-dee-dee-dum." If her friends could see her now they surely wouldn't believe it.

Once the floor had been scrubbed on bended knees it was definitely coffee time, (add to list kneeling pad). The heaps of boxes could now be stacked along the right wall. In her haste and excitement she had missed a door on this wall yesterday and today felt the glow of treasure found. It was a fantastic cupboard; the hall obviously didn't run the full depth of the house leaving a larder the size of a third of the footprint of the hall. Kitty stooped within it, for although the ceiling was full height the webs in here were in a whole new scale. It called for the broom, the mop and a generous amount of vinegar, more of a deterrent to the spiders returning than a cleaning agent. Waterproof hood tied securely around her face and trousers tucked in socks, Kitty the Brave was ready for all-comers.

Once cleaned, her mind raced with the best options for storage. Floor to ceiling shelves on one wall and designated hanging space, would be the likely plan - what a boon! Stopping for a much needed coffee, the boxes were heaved in and arranged in a manner that would do for now. Wiping her hands on her trousers and then brushing her damp curls from her face, "Where is the nearest Ikea?" she thought out loud. But this was Southern Kitty, Islander Kitty corrected her, "Where is the nearest carpenter?" that's more like it, smiling she preferred that.

Stooping and realising how stiff she was from yesterday and really dreading tomorrow, after today's exertions, Kitty lifted purple box number four, recorded on the list of boxes as 'Pretty things'. The square tablecloth she shook from its confines could have been made for her little table. It was one of many of her mum's, and probably her Gran's before, things that were so beautiful they could never be thrown out. Stephen would have just looked and said "Really?" The hand-embroidered flowers were beautiful, yellows, oranges and blues sewn with thick yarn making the tablecloth extremely tactile. Admittedly there was a tear and a two inch hole in the middle, but this had been catered for and pulled next from the box a plate she had found at a car boot sale. It was round with two squared edges and was obviously hand-painted, in primrose yellow and warm orange. The paint was raised and the clusters of small dots within the centre of each flower, Kitty could never resist touching. What had been christened the 'Braille plate' had always been relegated to a cupboard but would now stand pride of place and serve as her fruit bowl. There was definitely a theme here no colour chart or mood board just all the precious things that she couldn't leave behind.

She pulled out an old teapot of her Granny's. Now smiling at remembered images of the short plump lady with white hair in a neat yet floppy bun. Walking as though her legs were made of wood, lurching around her kitchen, always it seemed, with this teapot in hand. It was deep red, almost burgundy with a worn gold leaf pattern around the rim. Granny treasured it because it had made it through the war and was very 'pricey'. Kitty was well aware that in another life, another grandchild, this chipped, sad old pot would have been scrapped years ago but to her it was a connection. This move and all her tribulations had made her realise that the only possessions that have any meaning are those with a connection. Those that make you smile each time you rekindle that connection, and see once more the faces of the people you held dear.

Teapot now proudly displayed on the window sill it was joined by two old cups and saucers, Wedgwood, her parents wedding present from fat Aida and family, now how could you part with these, I ask you? No longer had they the luxury of sitting on a shelf in a display cabinet, at long last, Kitty thought, they could fulfill their destiny and have tea drunk from them.

She must get another table or cupboard though, until then everything else must wait a little longer in its box. Still unaware of the time, with no phone or clocks to hand, Kitty felt sure it must be lunchtime, as the empty gnawing feeling inside could be ignored no longer. Briefly stopping to look around her kitchen she was satisfied, and with a renewed spring in her legs she set off to Pimples. With his visors facing onto the sun he glinted and looked like he was basking. The April light was wonderful, Kitty was so grateful for it, but the wind from the sea still had the steely memory of winter and reminded her it was still only spring - she was very thankful for the fleece.

Once inside Pimples the cold was forgotten as the sun had warmed her bed and she allowed herself to be enveloped within it. Reaching for her travel clock on the shelf above her, Kitty laughed aloud. It was a little after ten, considering the hours of work she had just done, she must have been up at the crack of dawn. Allowing herself to close her eyes she drifted into a very pleasant doze.

Distantly aware of knocking Kitty reached up, wiped the drool that had run down her cheek and stretched the stretch of a contented cat, arms and legs straight out, ending with an enormous yawn.

Knock, knock, knock!

"Oh shit." hissing and blinking against the sun coming through the window, eight inches away from her was the silhouette was someone? Scrabbling to her feet, trying to smile, she muttered again, quieter this time. "Oh shit, shit, shit." She opened the door and the gust of wind and her half awakened state made for an ungraceful stumble back into the van. The outline of the man now became clear as he leaned into the open door.

"Well, morning to you." He was a lean man in his fifties, with the whitest of hair and matching beard and moustache. "You'll be the new owner will ye?" Kitty, still trying to gather herself babbled.

"Oh, er, yes... yes definitely, I mean. I am." Glad that she was becoming more coherent towards the end. "I have been up for hours." He merely raised one eyebrow.

"Aye, we heard a southern lassie had bought the place. Holiday home will it be?" He said this with a look of resigned disapproval and Kitty was pleased to put him straight.

"Oh, no, no, not at all. I am to live here, you know, full time. Just me, on my own, for good." He looked a little puzzled. She suspected he thought her mad, and grinning at him she realised this hadn't helped as she probably looked like a bloody nutter now.

"Well, here's your post and welcome I suppose." Kitty took the outstretched envelopes and grabbed his empty hand, shaking it vigorously.

"I'm K, K…" and she hesitated, "Kitty Harris." She said finally. Really great Kitty, she thought, not doing anything to counteract this image as the new village idiot are you?

"You'll not be missus Kathleen V… Vr… Vrc…e…l…j" he struggle valiantly at the surname.

"No, that was my husband's name, V-r-c-e-l-j, pronounced 'Fritzle'. And I thought it would just be easier to start over with my maiden name, so it's Kitty Harris from now." The postman nodded slowly with one raised eyebrow pushed up even further.

"Aye, be easier all round, maybe. Harris is a good name; it'll do well for ye here."

"My granddad always said his family had come down from up here, so I'm sort of coming home."

"Aye." He was looking at Kitty now as if she was ever so slightly barking.

"So we'll keep the Vrcelj between us, sort of postman-client privilege." She laughed. But looking at his fixed expression, she realised she was just adding coals to the fire and decided to be very sensible. "Are you my regular postman?"

"Aye."

"And how often do you deliver?"

"Everyday bar Sundays."

"And your name is?"

"Jock, aye, Jock… Is the name."

"Well, nice to meet you Jock, I only arrived yesterday so I don't know anyone." Aware that she was still clutching his hand she let go and decided, he would be back. Better let him go and think of anything else to ask him tomorrow. Relief spread across his face as he wiped his hand across his jacket.

"Ok then, Mrs Harris."

Kitty hoped she saw a glint in his eye and the moustache curled at its edge as he turned to walk up her steep drive. He either liked her or pitied her mental illness, the jury was still out. Well, one down, now the rest of a community. Kitty hoped she could make a better impression there.

Maybe she needed to get a bit of good press out there. If Jock was a gossip the whole island may have her diagnosed 'Southern nutter' before lunch. She rethought her plans, the south room was done, and maybe she should venture out. Making herself a quick sandwich and trying in vain to make her curly blonde hair lay in one direction she hastened to the house. She allowed herself a smug look around; grabbed her rucksack and keys and headed for town.

She had researched from Kent and had already made contact with her nearest GP and decided that was somewhere to start. She unfolded the map of Skye she had purchased and already written notes on.

Pimples felt lighter and carefree now, which she was glad of as she apologised as he struggled up the drive – "Note to self, if fully loading Pimples, do it on the main road." Very appreciative of the continued sun, Kitty enjoyed the drive. The tension, worry and uncertainty of yesterday had lifted, she was here and here was wonderful.

Kitty timed her drive to the Doctors, on the map it looked like a ten-minute drive, in reality it was twenty-eight minutes – duly noted and annotated on the map. The surgery could easily have been missed. A single storey 1970's bungalow with a small brass plaque by the door being the only evidence this wasn't just another house. Dr Hamish Duncan and Dr Claire Duncan. Kitty parked in one of only two spaces and opened the front door. The waiting room consisted of a large hall with five wooden slatted 1930's dining chairs with red leatherette seats. Sat in the corner on the sixth chair behind a modern desk was a lady in her sixties. She looked very much in keeping with the dated furniture, in her sturdy pullover and neat curled grey hair – the desk and computer appeared quite alien.

"Good morning to ye." She was cheerful and smiling and Kitty was relieved.

"Oh, good morning." Trying now to sound sane and sensible.

"My name is Kathleen Vrcelj." Kitty smiled as the smile in front of her froze. "But I'm using my maiden name Kathleen Anne Harris."

"Oh aye, well, we'll be glad of that." The lady chuckled. "And I'm Gladys, Gladys Grant, can I be helping ye?"

"Yes, I've just moved up, yesterday, from Kent and I thought I'd pop in and register."

Kitty had come armed with National Insurance number, hospital number and a good pen, expecting questions and form filling.

"Oh aye, that's right. Ye brought the old cottage of Annie's. Well welcome to ye. Are you all on your own, an attractive lass like yourself, there'll be no Mr V…V.Vr…Vrc?"

"No, no." Kitty rushed in to prevent anymore attempts at the name. "Just me."

"And is it holiday place for yeself?"

"No, I'm here for good."

"Well, in that case." Gladys rose from her chair and walked around the desk. She took Kitty's hands in both of hers and shook firmly.

"Oh, thank you. It is a bit daunting I must admit but I love it."

"Old Annie loved that place. The stone wall around the back garden, Annie did that, took her many years mind, aye" pausing now to smile at a distant memory "She married a no good fella, Jim, aye that were his name. But he ran off and left her too" looking pityingly at Kitty and pausing in case the young lady wanted to add some information of her own – she did not.

"Well better for it she was, lived there on her own for years. I used to pop her prescription in on my way home, ninety six! She was a tough wee lady."

"I love it, it's so peaceful."

"Aye but bracing in the winter lass, I always say spring is the best time to be on Skye. You came at a good time; the weather won't always be so kind... or the midges so few."

"I know I'm lucky."

"I suppose you'll be tearing the old place down and building some glass modern house in its place?"

"Oh no" and Kitty now patted Gladys' rock hard forearm.

"No, no I've got plans to put a bathroom around the back and maybe a little room on the end and some bedrooms in the loft. But now I'm in it I think I'd like to leave it alone as much as possible."

"Aye Annie would be pleased, but don't get me wrong, and I'm sure Annie would have done what you're doing if she had been able – even tough old Annie would have loved some good heating and a proper bathroom." Smiling broadly, Kitty was the first to break the silence, "You wouldn't have a photo of Annie, would you Gladys? I'd love to see what she looked like."

"Aye I must do some where I'll look it out for ye. Now enough of this chit chat the doctors will be wanting to meet ye."

Gladys took Kitty firmly by the elbow and marched her down the short hall to one of the three closed doors.

"I'm quite well Gladys, I was just going to register" Kitty's weak protests fell on deaf ears as Gladys's twinkling smile remained fixed in place.

"No they'll be wanting to meet ya."

A quick rap on the door and Gladys pushed it wide open, not waiting for an invitation. The dowdy tweed clad image of the doctors in Kitty imagination could not be further from the truth. Lolling back in an old office chair sat a woman not much older than herself. Slim with short cropped dark hair, looking well suited to the casual fleece and jeans, she had the svelte frame of an active outdoorsy type. Across the desk from her, cupping a mug in both hands in what must have been the patients' chair was a blonde haired man, again in his early thirties.

On her entering – or more accurately being dragged in, the young couple both stood, lowering their mugs on the desk and walked towards her. Looking like a trendy young couple out for a walk on the common on a Sunday afternoon, Kitty couldn't quite believe these were her GPs.

Gladys made the introductions, "Kathleen V...Vr...Vr". The tall man smiled.

"Hi I'm Hamish and this is Claire, Gladys you know," smiling affectionately at Gladys. "You must be Kathleen Vrcelj" Extending a very befreckled hand Kitty returned a firm shake and smiled up at him.

"Yes, but I'm going by my maiden name now Harris. But well done that's the best effort I've heard for a long time but no one gets it that close, my husband's family were from Yugoslavia."

"I guessed it was Yugo, I worked with quite a few when I worked at Guys."

"You're not from around here then?" Kitty stated the obvious at his cultured accent.

"No" Claire joined in, "My parents were from the highlands but Hamish grew up in Edinburgh but has managed to lose his accent. Hamm and I trained together in London; we made the move like you five years ago when we had our first baby."

Shaking Claire's hand now and looking around at the smiling

faces, Kitty added,

"Oh it's great to meet you, everyone has been so nice but it's great to meet someone who knows what it's like to be a newbie."

Hamish perched on the desk and gestured for Kitty to sit in the chair he had vacated. Helped by a steaming mug of tea they sat and continued in easy conversation.

"Well this isn't how I envisaged my first trip to the doctors" Kitty giggled.

"Whole other world here Kathleen" Hamish smiled down again Kitty admired his impeccable teeth.

"Call me Kitty if you don't mind I'm only Kathleen when I've done something wrong."

All three laughed easily.

"Very well, Kitty then. There are none of your three minute appointments here and we have no clinic this afternoon as it's our admin day."

"Oh I'm sorry, am I holding you up?" Kitty made to stand but rested back at a barrage of,

"No, no no, stay, not at all. Please, please sit down."

In the end Kitty was there for nearly two hours, two cups of tea and countless biscuits. Leaving with the promise of a visit from Gladys on Wednesday - hopefully with a photo of Annie - and a much-unexpected invitation to the Duncan's for dinner Saturday evening. The reassurance that it would be nothing special as they had two children under five, and the promise that the house was a tip made the invite a touch less intimidating and more to be anticipated.

With added spring in her step, this afternoon had just added to and brightened her sense of arrival. Potential new friends, GPs who gave you biscuits – bloody marvellous. Placing her phone on the dashboard the journey home took forty-five minutes. Stopping at every crest of a hill leaving the shadow of mountains but to no avail, no Internet service available and zero on the signal bars. She had no desire to go on the net but had hoped to post an "I'm here, I've made it" and a picture of her and Pimples with the house in view.

Swinging not so scarily down her drive for the second time, she pulled on the hand brake and clambered into the back. In the purple box number two she found what she thought she may need to rely on. Ancient sets of writing paper with matching envelopes that were far too beautiful to throw away, but the necessity had never arisen for their use. Not since the days of writing to relatives thanking them for gifts, or exotic pen pals in far off lands had Kitty needed such things.

Who needed to know? Certainly Amanda, she could tell that circle of friends. A brief line to the office that would cover all there, and that would be chiefly for Brenda's benefit. Her cousin John who she hadn't seen in years but kept a loose contact with via social media. She would explain the technological desert and ask him to let the extended family – such as it was, small and scattered, know about her new location. Her mother being an only child meant no known relatives on that side. Her father's family she had last seen at his funeral and felt no compunction to see them since, and them her. So apart from John she wouldn't even know how to contact them.

She had kept in touch with a group from University, Sue and Dave were the king pin for that group and always arranged meet-ups. A letter to Sue would result in her news bouncing around the South of England in super speed.

Unaccustomed to writing so much, Kitty was glad that all four recipients did not know each other thus giving her leave to duplicate. Taking longer than expected and cursing herself for the length of the letter, she lent back and stretched her arms above her head. Her fingertips touched the roof and she rotated her hands enjoying the clunk from her right wrist. As always, smug in her preparations, she took four stamps and addressed the pale blue envelopes admiring the faint orchid design. Realising that she had not written a letter for a long time, let alone four, in as many years, it had been satisfying and Kitty hoped it was the start of habits yet to come.

As she slid the door of Pimples open the drop in temperature was marked, and looking up at the clock she was surprised to see it was a little after six. Zipping her fleece up under her chin she walked briskly up the drive to the road above. Thirty yards along the road was the post box, beside it a wonderful old red phone box. She had noted the post box when driving in today but laughed at herself for not seeing the large phone box. She could have called all these people but was very glad she hadn't. Placing the precious letters in the mouth of the box she skipped back down her drive.

Back inside her snug van she opted for the pre cooked chicken casserole from the small fridge. Suddenly ravenous, she dispensed with the idea of potatoes or pasta instead cutting a huge doorstop of bread and lashings of butter. A better meal she couldn't remember and it warmed her to the core. Wondering now, being somewhat of a van virgin, how long her gas bottle for cooking and gas fridge would last. But the thoughts didn't trouble her much and she rested into her pillows, sated and very content.

She had missed the house this afternoon and was sorry not to have completed the clean up, but as she kept having to remind herself there were no deadlines! No targets! No agenda! Kitty Harris was her own boss, answerable to no one and she was giving herself the night off.

Before settling for the night Kitty once again set off up the grassy path for the last visit to the toilet. It reminded Kitty of her trips to the New Forest camping with her family. "Come on squeeze one out," was her mother's favourite expression if ever they passed a toilet. "Go now or it's the bucket," Kitty had never needed the bucket and was appalled from a very young age at the prospect of it, and completely horrified if her parents did. A disgraced seven year old, afraid her family would be the laughing stock or worse still, thrown off the site because her dad had used the plastic facilities. These thoughts had made her laugh when she purchased the sturdy bucket, and she imagined if she could have seen her seven year old face there in B&Q weighing up the best bucket to perch over. She hadn't needed it yet but she certainly wasn't too proud for it now.

Again dusk lasted longer than anticipated. Placing a kitchen chair outside the front door Kitty was perfectly positioned to watch the sun fade mistily away. Replacing the chair when it finally sunk from view, standing with door handle in hand, its new owner took a long look at the hallway; "Brace yourself it's your turn tomorrow." The anticipation of her first proper visitor on Wednesday gave Kitty added drive, and drifting into sleep that night, her mind full of ideas and images of how the house was to look.

4

The Clean Up

Day two arrived and unlike yesterday, the sun didn't wake the slumbering van dweller but the patter of large drops of rain on the roof. Thoroughly toasty in her quilt, peering at the clock it was 9am. Lifting the bottom edge of the curtain the view was totally different today. The mountains that formed the backdrop of the view beyond the water that were hazy and muted yesterday, signifying the edge of her little bit of paradise, were today, missing. Instead the boundary was much closer. Rain fell vertically and the laden grey skies merged seamlessly with a grey sea. Gone were the bright blues and greens in the water. Today sky and sea, as wet as each other, had joined forces.

"Good, you needed a wash and I need to stay in and get on." Of course Pimples did not, could not, answer but Kitty found herself chatting over plans for the hall with him anyway. Washed and breakfasted quickly she reached into a large flowery bag, "Taadar!" With relish a pair of posh wellies and a golfing umbrella were hoisted aloft. "Can't catch me out."

This time taking the alarm clock and a mug of milk, for the plans she had were going to require a lot of coffee. The path had turned into a large stream, the option of treading around it was soon abandoned, as the moss-laden grass either side seemed wetter and more treacherous than the path itself. Brolly into the wind she splashed happily across to the house.

Once inside she put on the kettle, thanked god or who ever else chose to listen for the wonder of electricity and collected all the cleaning provisions. The small table in the hall was washed and the thirsty oak given a generous dose of wax, drinking it up through the open grain it shone and exceeded all her expectations. This was definitely a keeper!

First attempts at washing the walls failed, countless years of damp rendered it a futile exercise. One strip of paper was loose and Kitty tried to tear it off squarely. Instead the whole panel to the ceiling came away revealing a pale blue wash. Like the kitchen she had hoped, and was rewarded, as it was a vast improvement on the paper. Armed with a butter knife and steely determination the walls were stripped and washed by eleven, time for more caffeine for the sweating worker.

Gathering up the paper and sweeping the lino it no longer jarred quite as badly. Kneeling, Kitty tentatively peeled back a corner of the lino, through the accumulation of grime and webs she could see the camouflaged stone or slate beneath. Deciding that keeping the floor covered made it feel homely and warmer, it was given a reprieve and allowed to stay. So with a makeshift kneeling pad of old wallpaper in a carrier bag she set about cleaning it. This was the real McCoy, - Linoleum - and where it was most heavily worn the small grid of Hessian peeped through. It was a painstaking job, - what did that phrase actually mean Kitty wondered? As she shuffled her way further into the hall she didn't have the answer but the way her knees felt after an hour gave her some clue.

She would have to look out for a nice old bureau for here, but for now the table was reinstated and Kitty's reward was a pastry and yet another coffee. Rummaging again through red box number four, a lace table cloth with blue embroidery and three silver framed photos were taken and suited the table very well.

"Well here we are family."

Pink scrubbed hands lifted the largest of the frames, an exquisite Arts and Crafts design with blue and green enamel inlay – the colours of the sea, on a bright day. It wasn't old and she vividly remembered the day her mum had spent so long in a shop choosing it in Fort William. It seemed so apt to be bringing this with her. Her mum and dad laughing, rain coats on and hair whipping around their heads. Two smaller versions of them laughing at each other, blonde and ginger hair in all sorts of directions. They were on a sandy beach near Applecross, the figures, the horizon all at a slight angle. They had stood shivering waiting for her father to position the camera and set the timer. After many false attempts of capturing the back of his head he had finally found a rock on which to balance it and a second before the picture was due to be taken it listed off to the side. Kitty had contemplated cutting the photo to sit straight, but that was the whole point. That was why they were all laughing.

The second frame was half the size; pearl beads on each corner broke up the beaten silver. This was of Stephen and herself on their wedding day. She had not wanted a formal or fancy affair, Stephen, like every groom on the planet, wanting whatever he is told he is to have. Two primary reasons for Kitty were a). No money and b). No father to give her away, but she would not have changed it and for all its' simplicity she remembered it as a perfect day. The lace flapper styled dress ending below the knee was perfection. Looking at them now she could smell the lily-of-the-valley in her small bouquet and hairpin. Gently resting her index finger on Stephens's face this was still painful for Kitty but how she had loved him that day. It still tore at her wounded heart but she was determined to overcome this and not let anything spoil the memory of that special day. She would have the photo on view, she would endeavour to drown out the bad and sad memories of last year and hold onto the good.

Moving now to the third, an oval frame, art deco in design and guaranteed to make her smile, hence its selection. Stephen, Lillian and Kitty, all squeezed together on a swinging sofa in her mother's back garden. Stephen in the middle with a look of resignation, arms draped around the tipsy hysterical pair of her and her mum. The two women shared many traits, one of which was an outrageous laugh. Not just a chuckle, but as Lillian called it a proper belly laugh. So named because one is forced to clutch and hold your stomach as muscles there and in the face feel like they may, at any moment, snap. This was perfectly captured and Kitty cherished it.

Although they were all beautiful memories each one carried its' own shadow of sadness and she wanted to dwell no longer. Standing tall she smiled taking in her efforts and appreciating the transformation of her home. Although the hall had no natural light (Note to self – might have to put window or glass in the front door) It was bright and cheerful, the floor colours intense and the blue, white of the walls, light and clean. Guests could be invited in now with no embarrassment. If she had a vase she would have liked to pick some of the daffodils budding in the garden and place them here and determined to come up with a vessel by Wednesday.

Reluctantly she left the house with fond, long looks at the two rooms she had worked her magic on and smiled. Looking however at the third and final room, the North wing, Kitty's face fell. It looked dingier and dirtier than before, not helped by the persistent rain and dirty window blocking the light, "Your turn tomorrow!"

Realising on her splashing return to the van that she had yet to have a good look around her land – HER LAND! Tomorrow she hoped for better weather – now was not the time for exploring. Kitty had brought a cat litter tray with her for just such an eventuality and smugly stood her boots and the dripping end of the umbrella in it.

The macaroni cheese was designed to be warmed in an oven or microwave but seemed to fare ok on the small ring in Pimples. Treating herself to a glass of Rose from the box under her bed she set out her plans for tomorrow, Tuesday. It would be nice to at least get the other room clean and presentable, but she must without fail walk her boundary, hoping for some brighter weather. But for now, right now, even though it was only eight pm Kitty was snug in her bed, portable DVD on, Austen of course, and a crisp glass of wine. Not wanting to tempt fate but everything was going very well and she was most content. Very little of the film was seen and she was conveyed to sleep carried by eloquent language and clever wit. A dreamless sleep too soon turned to morning.

Much to her relief in the morning the sun was soaking through the curtains and despite the early hour Kitty's bladder had decided it was high time she was up and out. Kitty ran her hands through her hair, there was nothing for it she was going to have to wash it today.

Putting her clothes straight on and donning wellies she rushed along the slippery path, the sooner she was sleeping nearer a toilet the better. Kitty felt vaguely ridiculous, as she stood naked at the butler sink. Yes it was not as cramped, and certainly less restrictive than doing her ablutions in Pimples, but she felt very vulnerable with no curtains (add to the list!). Washing only the important parts quickly, Kitty's modesty was soon covered.

Armed with a bowl of warm water, a mug and some shampoo Kitty enjoyed washing her hair. The sink was huge and made the task easy, and delighted by the fact her shampoo bill would be quartered, the soft water meant three bowls of rinsing was required. Once the worst of the wet was rubbed out of her hair what she really needed now was a means to dry her towel (add washing line to list). The realisation dawned on Kitty that the time had come to transfer her mental list onto something more permanent. Sorting through boxes in the cupboard Kitty found the blackboard realising she would have to keep her writing small.

Tomorrow Gladys would be here. She had enough tea, coffee and biscuits so there were no urgency, but Thursday would need a trip to Portree for supplies. The mountains were once again visible beyond the water with the very specific colour palate that only Scotland claimed. Greens merged with mauves and browns of spent bracken, underpinning the dark foreboding of the almost black green of the pines. The sky overhead was blue, but as Kitty walked out of the front door dark clouds were advancing over the roof. Grabbing her boots and waterproof coat she decided there was no time like the present to explore.

A small wall at knee height marked the front boundary, running parallel to the jagged blackened rocks of the water's edge. A slight incline and twenty foot separated the two, the small wall protecting Tide's Reach - though not terribly well, Kitty thought as she toed the line of seaweed on the lawn not twelve inches from the front door step.

To the left as she faced the sea it was easy to trace the edge of her land, the lawn petered out into a tapering triangle culminating in the gravel round area – Pimples' new home. Turning now with her back to the sea, the drive down marked the farthest point by the water to her right. To the left a row of old wooden posts with a sagging wire between traced up the slope to its summit.

Shielding her gaze from the sun with both hands resting on her brows, Kitty followed the wire; dipping and raising it weaved between small trees and heaps of bracken disappearing off around the headland. So, the little wilderness behind the house as high as Kitty could see all belonged to her. There was a little ledge halfway up and making her way towards it she soon admitted defeat. The emerald moss was deceptively slippery and moist. The black peaty liquid rose up her boots and wouldn't have stopped her but the moss hid a tangle of roots and uneven terrain. Maybe a project for the summer, but if she could get a bench up there the view over the roof of her house would undoubtedly be fabulous.

She turned her attention to the garden at the back of the cottage. The wall she now knew was built by her predecessor Annie, stood at waist height and was as solidly set in the ground as the house itself. Looking like it had been there as long as the house, the northern side of it was patched with moss and a topcoat of icy green lichen.

Walking around the inner perimeter there was clear evidence of plants pushing through the thick mat of grass. It was going to be exciting watching what came up. Kitty had no desire for a highly manicured garden; it would be incongruous and quite frankly impractical in this location. However it evolved, Kitty knew she would enjoy tending to it and watching it grow.

On close inspection, the small wizened tree in the far right corner of the stonewall was not in fact dead as Kitty had supposed from the window. Albeit covered in lichen the ends of the branches showed tantalising buds soon to burst into blossom. Brushing the lichen with outstretched fingers, it felt like seaweed she thought - how apt.

A smiling owner left the back garden by the gate at the opposite corner, and let her fingertips of her right hand trace the undulating surface of the house walls. Passing the front door Kitty referred to the land registry map her architect had sent her. The red line on the basic line drawing showed the plot shaped like a long diamond, the tip of one end being Pimples spot, the house sitting in the widest middle section. Kitty was eager now to try and trace her land around the bend of the waters edge. Once at the edge of the front lawn where the small wall tapered out into the larger rocks of the beach, Kitty followed the line of wire above her in the wilderness of the bank. She assumed from the map that her land encompassed the beach almost to the water. A vague path of trodden grass was evident along the top of the rocks and the anticipation mounted as the destination remained concealed. The grass now all but gone, and using her hands to balance herself, Kitty climbed the large boulder feeling the smooth velvet of lichen in purples and greens and creams. Standing atop it, "Oh... Oh, wow, but…?"

Again consulting the map Kitty could relate the dotted lines of three sides of a square to the remnants of an old building. Set with its back to the rising bank stood the crumbling remains of a small croft. The door space was in the middle and the sills of windows were on either side, but none having tops as the roof had long gone and a jumble of stones filled the interior, along with a small tree growing determinedly amongst them.

Leaning in Kitty reached and ran her hands over the stone corner of the building. She had known these old buildings to be beautiful and strong but had never anticipated how tactile they would be. Large round stones, skillfully placed, not chiseled or formed but carefully chosen to form the rounded bend of the outer corner. At a rough guesstimate the building was twenty foot by twelve foot.

Now standing facing the front of it, Kitty was struck by how protected it was from the elements despite being very close to the water. She was able for the first time since leaving her own front door to release the blonde curls that had pestered and whipped across her face. Protected and sheltered by the large boulder, a quietness and peace washed over Kitty, and finding rest on a large fallen stone she looked about her. The bank behind wrapped its protective arm around this tiny dwelling, the large rocks that stood between it and the water like sentries. Hidden in the lea of the large boulder she had clambered over was a small inlet. It was impossible to know if man made or natural but a worn ancient path ran to the small gravel area, large enough for a small boat, closing her eyes and envisaged the croft with its grass roof and a small fishing boat moored for safety.

Did this really all belong to her! Leaving her daydreams she stretched and once again set off along the rocky terrain. About thirty foot beyond the derelict croft the wire and wooden posts of her back boundary made its way down the hill to a larger final post. Looking once more at the paper in her hand Kitty was happy she now knew exactly what her rash purchase entailed. Glad that this stretch of the waterfront was visible to no houses or roads, she completed her happy jig with gusto and returned to stroke the walls of the croft.

The emotions of many weeks and the self-belief to get her to this place overwhelmed and consumed Kitty. Returning to the stone she had vacated minutes before Kitty Harris cried. No control, no refinement she sat and sobbed, she didn't even bother to dry the tears or wipe her dripping nose. She sat, hands folded around her midriff, letting go with each sob the worries that had marred this move. The painful decisions she had made and all the things she had given up and walked away from.

All her hopes and dreams from this day forward revolved around this diamond shaped piece of land, and the relief of starting this new chapter of her life crashed over the small woman sitting by her derelict croft. After ten indulgent minutes the sobs subsided, and with an enormous sigh Kitty held back her head and smiled as the large drops of rain mingled with her tears and washed them away.

Normally this suburban girl would have been running for cover worried about the effects on her make up and hair – rain was the kiss of death to straightened naturally curly hair. But today, on her beach, Kitty rocked gently and let the large drops splash on her face and washed away her woes. It was only the remembrance of getting her last room finished that spurred her into action, and standing and looking around for the last time today at her little bit of Skye, "And of all this I am mistress," she said in a soft whisper.

Once indoors and tea brewed, Kitty, domestic goddess, rolled up her sleeves, twisted the damp ringlets of hair up with a clip and carried the vinegar wafting bowl of water to the bedroom. "Where to start?"

Flicking on the lights the dirty and threadbare shade hanging from the ceiling gave her the answer. What had once been embroidery anglaise now served to obscure most of the light from the solitary bulb. Skipping to the kitchen and shaking both the chairs to establish the least wobbly one she returned. The sturdier of the two was obviously destined for a multifunctional future. With storage so limited Kitty smiled smugly, balanced soundly atop it she knew that she wouldn't need steps after all, thankful to be able to remove something from the ever increasing list.

In the effort of taking the lampshade down it soon became apparent that the dust and webs were in fact holding it together, and the first attempt to wipe it clean saw the material rip and disintegrate like tissue paper. Letting it fall to the ground there was only one outcome for the tattered shade. "Sorry Annie, hope you weren't too attached to that," thinking of Annie as she cleaned the bulb, thus doubling its brightness. Kitty wondered about the history, the stories these walls could recount and eagerly hoped Gladys could share all she knew.

Climbing down now it was obvious the windows allowed little light into the room and the grey skies just a taster of the light a long harsh winter would begrudgingly give. (Something else for the list - good lamps). The front window boasted a thin dark metal curtain rail, hopefully that could be salvaged. The walls in here had been papered, obviously faded the blue pin stripe with tiny pink flowers looked as old as Annie had been. Kitty had always steered away from floral patterns but appreciated this room wanted it and suited it.

The fireplace was a bonus; kneeling in front of it tracing the relief with her index finger. The cast iron had borders of delicate flowers twining through trellis; on the hood larger flowers formed a bouquet. Although very dirty, Kitty had enough experience with fireplaces to know that with some Zee-bright and a little elbow grease it would polish up beautifully. The basket contained twigs, moss, and dirt and of course the obligatory spider's webs – only this time blackened with soot. Surrounding it all was a simple wooden frame, the mantle piece just big enough to accommodate a clock, some photos and of course a small vase of flowers.

Looking now at the carpet under her knees, which was especially dirty with a good dose of soot that had blown down from the chimney. The twig in the hearth snapped in two and was bone dry; there would be no fire here until it had been swept. She could only wonder with dread when that was last done. Peeling back the carpet from the fire, "Ohhh, lovely!" Kitty wiped her hand across the slate hearth that had been hidden there.

As if to beat a deadline or at the sounding of a gun, Kitty leapt to her feet taking the chair with her. Leaving her fleece on the back of it, sleeves pushed ever further up her arms she was a woman on a mission. Starting at the rear of the room, she knelt and prised the carpet up with her fingernails, "Eeeeek!" Shuddering, she ran to the hall cupboard and grabbed the broom and dustpan and brush. Raising her weapons she stood majestic in the doorway "Leave or be squashed" she growled in her best Arnie voice, looking every inch the spider exterminator, but her need to stop and secure her trousers in her socks did cost her some kudos.

The edge of the carpet was given a good sweep and taking a deep breath she slowly gripped the edge of the carpet, "Gird your loins woman". Hesitantly to start with but then, caution to the wind, Kitty rolled the carpet to the other wall. Expecting the stone flags as in the kitchen Kitty was not unpleasantly surprised to find more lino. A flecked pale blue with a wide border of brown geometric design, she opted to uncover it all and then decide its fate.

The carpet, though old and dirty was obviously wool – what to do with it, that was the question? Back in Kent she would have man handled it into the car and driven fifteen minutes up the road to the tip. Here there were two problems, a) Did Skye have a landfill and if so where? b) Pimples was her haven of clean and safe. She could not think of sullying him with this. Once rolled up Kitty attempted to drag it out of the room but her first attempt failed dismally. Clutching the end of the roll with her fingertips she pulled, and it stayed! Staying resolutely in place it was Kitty that moved on her second attempt, landing with a thud on her backside. After the initial "Houoof" that escaped the crumpled woman it was the burst of loud laughter that hindered her getting up. "Right you bastard" standing to her full height it took thirty minutes of cursing, pushing, pulling, kicking and a fair amount of perspiration to get the carpet half out of the front door.

Sitting astride it like a hunter on and her quarry and wiping her brow with a sleeve, "You know you won't beat me don't you!" Clueless but determined.

Enjoying the breeze from the sea which she knew would have struck cold an hour ago, but after her battle she lifted her head and enjoyed the sensation as it found the wet spots of sweat on her face, neck and scalp. She gazed besotted at the view, the new level of the water and yet another subtle change in hue. Pimples looked resplendent after his shower but her mood cooled as she looked then at the rock like floor covering below her. A deep sigh and chin resting in her hands she sat for many minutes waiting for inspiration to come. "What to do? What to do?"

She didn't want to dump it outside but struggled to see an alternative, she'd be lucky to get it out of the door let alone along the long path, Kitty stood wearily "This needs tea… and biscuits!" Always the go-to solution when facing a dilemma, soon outside with a steaming mug and as many ginger nuts as she could carry and circled the croft looking for the best solution.

Once at the back Kitty decided to examine the garden more closely. The small tree in the corner was fit to burst and a few small shrubs of unknown variety huddled under the sidewalls. The lawn here was very lumpy and uneven; the critical eye of even an amateur gardener could see these areas were once flowerbeds. Bulbs were pushing their way through, pale bright blades lifting moss and pushing aside the invading grass.

How was one to clear this grass? Then the seed of a memory flashed into her mind. Her mother always insisted on having the radio on Sunday afternoon, the Archers followed by Gardeners question time. Kitty hated it when young, and continued the derisory comments into teenage years and adulthood, though secretly it became a comforting backdrop to her favourite time of the week. Lillian could cook a damn good roast potato of which Kitty had never tasted the equal. Snatched sounds of those theme tunes ever since flooded her mind with vivid smell memories, Yorkshire puds full of rich gravy, stuffing, cabbage, and lamb with mint sauce.

Carpet! That was it, how to clear land ready for planting? Answer from the panel - carpet! Thinking of her mother now, Kitty promised herself there would be mint in this garden "You can't have lamb without fresh mint," her mother's voice joined her then.

Swigging the remainder of the tea she skipped back indoors over the carpet. In red box number two was found what she wanted - a frighteningly large glistening knife. With new determination and added zeal, the roll was dragged through the door onto the front lawn. Unrolling it and attacking it from the middle the new blade made for easy and satisfying work. Unrolling a strip at a time she cut each into three similar sized pieces, now much more manageable they were carried easily around to the back lawn.

Arranging them to form a large floral rectangle in the middle of the lawn. Darting back in the house she examined her work from both windows to check the position of her new to be flowerbed. Back on the lawn and a slight adjustment to the left. Kitty's horticultural knowledge extended to the understanding that by next spring the grass should be dead and gone. Any plants that had survived under the blanket of grass in the side beds could be assessed for a year and dug up next spring and relocated to their new home.

Glad that the tide was out, a still sweating carpet wrestler walked for ten minutes and gathered a line of large stones, sitting on her garden wall these would make perfect weights to keep the carpet in place. Very pleased with her efforts she returned to the carpet less room, it looked brighter already and now decided the wallpaper had to go.

Ably assisted by Michael Buble, Kitty sang as only you can when no one is listening. The damp was a huge help and the paper took little encouragement to fall away. Lying beneath was the blue, white patchy effect as in the rest of the house. It worked well with the lino which washed up beyond expectations.

The curtain rail was unscrewed and soaked in the large stone sink whilst the floor had all of Kitty's attention. The floor and the pole had polished up beautifully and the latter was carefully reinstated. Amazing how a couple of feet of curtain track can become such a valued and precious commodity when it was the only one you had. Drying her hands Kitty dug in purple box four and pulled out a white crocheted lace cloth. After draping it over the rail the light shone through the holes and offered a little protection against anyone walking past on the beach. "Oh I wish we had our furniture" She was talking to the house now as she polished the bright brass door handle. The sooner the builders came and she had some human company the better.

All her life, the clock had determined meals. Always breakfast as soon as she got up - woe betide the brave soul who came between Kathleen Harris and her brekkie. Without fail having to hold back the urge to eat her lunch before the allocated time. Always hungry early in the day she would not allow herself to eat a bite before twelve o'clock and dinner never after six.

The total lack of routine, clocks and any other human being to influence it, her dietary needs were now dictated purely by her stomach. After its first attempts of aching and moaning it now growled loudly. Like an ignored child it raised its tone and volume until someone listened.

Satisfied with a morning's work well done, she closed the door and whistled on the walk back to Pimples. Soup and bread sated her moaning monster and Kitty lay back on top of her quilt. Head propped up on cushions, eyes closed; she enjoyed the weak sunlight warming her lids. She mentally arranged all her possessions in storage and imagined the new rooms that were to come. The exertions of the past few days weighed her down and gently lulled her to sleep.

Knock... knock... and knock.

"Oh no, not again," mumbling as she reflexively checked her face for dribble. Trying to get up calmly and not look like the startled rabbit she felt.

"Oh shit" she mumbled in her best ventriloquist impersonation then smiling looked back at Jock's face pressed on the window nearest her. Close the curtains if you're going to nap she shouted internally at herself, but smiled sweetly as she slide open the door.

"Well you certainly have a knack Jock."

"Aye and what ma that be?"

"Catching me sleeping."

"Seems a waste when you have this view lass."

He looked at her now like a naughty but sweet child and she didn't mind at all.

"I've been really busy on the house", regretting it immediately she heard petulance in her voice.

"Not my business lass, here."

He handed in her post and recoiled quickly Kitty noticed - no grabbing him today then she thought.

"Thanks Jock."

"You alright, are you?"

"Yes thanks met the GPs yesterday and Gladys."

"Aye southerners like ye, Hamish and Claire but nice enough anyway" – when were the highlands and Edinburgh in the south? Kitty smiled.

"Yes Gladys was very nice, she's popping round for a cuppa tomorrow."

"Yes she'll do that," he answered knowingly. Kitty decided not to question that further as she didn't want to bias her first visitor.

"Friday night there's live music up at the hotel at the headland," and in answer to the quizzical look on her face, "Out of your drive turn right, keep going ten minutes walk so you can have a dram or two."

"Oh thanks Jock, will you be there?"

"Aye and ma wife Joan."

"Great, thank you Jock I'll be there," Kitty reached out and touched Jock's arm lightly but instantly regretted it, seeing his raised eyebrow and frozen expression.

In all the homes of her life she had never had a conversation with the postman. Maybe it was a sign of the close-knit community, but Kitty worried Jock suspected she was barking and was merely taking pity on her. Either way the newest Islander couldn't be happier. Pub on Friday, dinner at the doctors Saturday - she couldn't have expected or predicted such a welcome.

There was little left to do in the house until she saw the architect and the builders, both of whom were due to visit on Monday. Coming with glowing recommendations it left Kitty a little cold that two strange men were to transform her house. Before leaving Kent it hadn't been an issue, but after a couple of days she realised she now cared for this damp pile of stone. The house's guardian looked across now to the hunkered solid little building and made a promise to it and herself not to let anyone ruin it.

5

Post Office

Time now for a little explore. A strong coffee and a perusal of the map, Kitty settled on a trip to Broadford. Her research from the Internet prior to getting here, she had luckily printed off. As having no signal since she had arrived she was reliant on paper copies now. First priority, find the Co-op and replenish her supplies, and second find the post office with an Internet café.

Stowing everything away, there was a relieved sigh as Pimples started at the first attempt. Following the signs to Broadford was a pleasant twenty-minute drive and the rain, though always threatening had held off. Wanting to rid herself of the remnants of sleep she decided to walk the length of the town as she saw it. A restaurant with tables in the windows looked very inviting. Fresh flowers sat in squat vases on the white tablecloths. Kitty would pick up a menu another day it could definitely have potential when visitors arrived.

A castellated grey and white hotel stood set back from the road. Again that was useful intel to have as it looked clean. Kitty planned to do some research to see if the café did in fact have Internet. A garage, jewellers and gift shop, and only a few minutes walk and further out she found the butchers and supermarket. Another day she promised she would have a good wander and investigate them all but for now Kitty was on a mission - the post office – with Da, Da, DA!!! Internet.

Trumping grocery shopping, and taking in a deep breath Kitty pushed open the door. Walking into the shop the small bell tinkled above her head announcing her arrival. Eight eyes turned to examine her, unabashed they scanned the newcomer from head to foot. Squeezing down one of the congested aisles she narrowly avoided knocking over an over-stocked display of dog food. Pulling her bag closer, she sighed as the juddering ceased with no crash of fallen merchandise.

Making for her preferred corner seat, she set her bag on one of the aluminium bistro chairs, saving the least wobbly for herself. Relaxing down despite the chill of metal against her thighs, Kitty was pleased to be shielded from the inquisitive faces by the tall Lotto stand. A barrage of smells awoke Kitty's senses; paper and card reminded her of school. The undercurrent of over-ripe fruit and vegetables mingled confusingly with sweets. The overriding smell was that of coffee and Kitty took a deep breath and got out her laptop.

The two grey haired women in the queue continued their loud conversations, gorgeous local accents drifting easily from fortnightly bin collection to Margaret's husband's hernia, and their recent hairdressing expedition. Leaning back on the chair Kitty watched as the lady behind the counter smiled and chatted to the young boy on the other side of the well worn high oak divide. Drowned out by debates on setting lotion and hair spray brands, Kitty strained to hear the postmistress and was sure she was English. She had a nice round face and unnaturally straight hair, but Kitty quickly averted her eye as the boy left, pulling the head off a large blue sweet snake and chewing greedily.

"Well, there you are Mary, Margaret, hair is looking lovely!"

"And hello to you Angela, now we're in no rush lass if ye want to be serving the wee lassie over there."

Two immaculately coiffed heads backed down the aisle and peered, smiling around the lotto sign, Kitty smiling back.

"Hello."

"If you're sure?" nodding replies to the post mistress but still staring at Kitty, Angela opened the glass topped door at the end of the counter practically climbing over a huge blue post bag, "Back in a mo."

"Afternoon ladies," Kitty could feel a blush rise in her cheek as she spoke.

"Afternoon lass," they responded in unison and continued to watch her, Kitty suspected they were done with their own conversation and were waiting eagerly to hear hers. Swinging and weaving around the pet food a beaming post mistress advanced.

"Hi, what can I get you?" Angela had a bright clear voice, she certainly was not from around here.

"I wondered if I could get on the Internet?"

"Yes of course, hang on I'll get you the password."

The ladies were in no hurry to get on with their own business and smiled lightly, forcing Kitty to divulge more than she had intended. "I've just brought a place near Ord."

"Aye... aye." From the woman Kitty thought was most likely Margaret.

"Oh, that's nice" by process of elimination, Mary.

"Holiday home is it?" Angela called from behind the counter as she rummaged and found a scrap of paper.

"No, no for good."

"Aye well good for you, welcome," both ladies mirrored their welcomes. Angela's flushed face peered up "Really, why?"

"Well on a whim really." A full blush set in now at this admission.

"Well good for you lass," said Margaret, the purpler of the two greys, nodding. "Life's short," a hand ran gently over her super sprayed hair. "One day you wake up and realise you're old, and you never forget the things you've tried" a wicked smile now, "Even if you shouldn't have, but it's the things you didn't do you regret." Looking sagely at Mary they nodded in agreement, "Aye, aye... oh aye". Kitty had no idea how long these two had been friends, but the looks that they exchanged told the two younger women there were shared stories and secrets there.

"Are ya on your own or is there a Mr?" Margaret now rested her elbows on the bags of flour before her and painfully shifted her weight.

"Oh Margaret, you know what it's like these days." Mary added quickly at the perplexed expression on Kitty face, "Maybe a partner," Mary's intonation and elbowing wink to her friend had Kitty quick to reply, suppressing a laugh.

"Oh no, no… no nothing like that. I was married but I'm on my own now."

"Well never mind dear – that's not always such a bad thing." Angela joined in then introduced herself and the ladies.

"Always to be found here on a Wednesday."

"Aye, we come here, pension day. Our little treat, the hairdressers then a cup of Angela's tea and a wee piece of cake."

"Let me get you connected, and what do we call you?"

"Kitty Harris."

"Well welcome, welcome Kitty Harris."

"Aye we hope you'll be well settled with us."

"Everyone has been so friendly, even the postman is chatty."

"Aye, well, Jock will be like that – never in too great a rush," Mary stated with raised eyebrows and a knowing nod. All three women nodded in agreement, none more than Angela.

Shifting in the slippery seat, quite out of place Kitty thought a stark touch of bistro chic in the drab post office. Years of posters and signs left their blue tack and sticky tape footprints over walls and windows. The counter groaned under the variety and sheer mass of a local shop trying to meet the shopping demands of residents where big supermarkets had no place.

As Angela walked over her heels clicked sharply on the old battered parquet flooring. Flicking her highlighted hair over her shoulders she certainly didn't have the homespun look of a woman who had moved here for the tartan, heather and hill walking. Kitty reached for the small scrap of paper Angela's manicured red nails held out.

"Here's the code, slow as hell but I use it as a marketing tool... more tea and cake bought that way." A short silence followed and Kitty asked, as it seemed expected, "I'll have a tea then please, and what cakes do you have."

Margaret spoke now, reminding Kitty that they held their position and gazed over to her. "Can't beat her lemon drizzle lass if you want our advice."

"Thank you, well lemon drizzle then please, but please see to the ladies first I'm in no rush."

"Good job," Angela laughed as she shut the counter door behind her and called Mary and Margaret to attention.

Glad finally for a bit of peace the newcomer smiled as the ladies fading conversation now encompassed blind bulbs, the price of fish and Mary's bunions. With waves and good wishes the friends left the shop, arms linked and obviously fuelled with something new to discuss. The bell stilled and Angela was approaching with a large slab of cake and a pretty blue floral mug. In the time it had taken for the tea to brew Angela knew Kitty's address, state of dilapidation of the house, originating address, age, and by the way she had sized Kitty up and down, her dress and shoe size too.

"We'll get you logged on and I'll get my tea and we can have a good chat."

Not wanting to be churlish and risk alienating a key person in her new community, she put aside earlier ideas of quiet absorption in her emails and Facebook. The code was keyed in and Angela settled her self in the chair opposite. Keen not to be interrogated further Kitty was quick to jump in with questions herself.

"You're obviously not from here either are you Angela?"

"God no, oh no. Married a Skye man, I'm from Manchester and

decided to go to Glasgow University – many moons ago. Well, we had kids and all of a sudden the things that we loved about living in the city weren't conducive to babies." Looking into the middle distance, slumping slightly Angela sighed deeply.

"Don't... do you regret moving here?" Kitty voice faltered, would a negative answer have some reflection on her own decision.

"No" and after taking a moment to reflect, "No it was the right thing to do but I have to admit I miss the buzz of the city sometimes."

"So far I'm loving the quietness."

"Ummm" Angela looked like a lady who could live happily without quiet. "So you're on your own up here then?"

"Yes just Pimples and me", regretting it as soon as it was out of her mouth.

"Pimples?"

"Um," embarrassed now she lowered her face and added quickly "My campervan, he feels like company."

"Oh lovely, is he outside? I've always wanted one." Angela's excited reaction and the fact that she referred to the van as "he" decided Kitty that she could like this woman.

"Well see how you get on. When I came up here I had to get a dog, total pain in the arse mind, but wouldn't be without one. Every where is so much more dog friendly up here and if you're on your own it would definitely be company."

"Oh right, I hadn't thought of that, maybe when the house is ready it would be good, better than talking to the van I suppose." Both women lent back on the chairs and laughed.

"Well just let me know, most people put a sign on the notice board if they have a litter."

The laptop announced it was connected, and Angela drained the dregs of her mug and scraping the chair on the floor, she rose to return to the counter. Reaching over, Kitty assumed to take her mug, Angela instead rested a hand on her arm. "Well I'll let you get on, nice to meet you Kitty Harris."

"Thank you," not a throw away comment but said with a surprising soaring emotion. Alone now, finishing the last of the crumbs on her plate, watching the screen as reams of emails downloaded. Determined to wait until they all arrived, her tapping fingers failed her and she eagerly clicked on the message from Amanda.

Dear MacKitti,

Hope you and the pimp mobilè have arrived safely. It's taken a lot of control to not phone you, so as soon as you've landed and are in the land of technology let me know you're OK.

All same old, same old here, weather is really crap but I've been checking the weather map every day and it looks like the sun is shining on you.

Seen any lovely men in kilts yet?

Mum and dad send their love, mum's already packing the cases for our visit. You would think we were at least going to a pole! The provisions she packing – clear a shelf in the larder - if you have such a modern contraption. She's buying up Waitrose and can't get over the fact that you don't have a Marks and Sparks and Waiters or even a Sainsbury's. How are you bearing the deprivation?

I still can't believe you're on the other side of the world! I hope you are happy and safe and not smelling too bad by now. Remember do what the gypsies do and take up swimming, think of the lovely hot running water.

At this point Kitty stopped reading and jotted on her pad, swimming pool, location and opening times. Even optimistically it would be months before her bathroom would be built. Amanda signed off with threats of physical violence if she hadn't heard from Kitty in twenty-four hours. As this was sent thirty-nine hours ago and Kitty guessed the letter wouldn't yet have reached her good friend, she tapped a brief reply promising all other news in the letter en route. Finishing with reassurances that a bekilted hirsute man had not molested her, and the garden was not over run with Haggis.

There were lots of well wishing messages from friends she had left at work and distant family. Opening a new page and including everyone she thought required an update, she took the memory card from her camera and inserted it. She regretted not having put more thought into the pictures she was posting, and about the range of people who would see them. The windswept images of herself with Pimples and Tide's Reach were not the most flattering. Reminding herself that it was unlikely she would ever see many of them again and it mattered little, she attached a large announcement "Kitty

Harris at home."

Sat lost in her thoughts, she knew for the first time with clarity that she would never live in Kent again, and probably never set foot in it. If she had to make that journey again it would only to be to visit Wimbledon and the few people that still claimed threads of attachment to her heart.

Jumping as Angela disturbed her melancholy thoughts. It was not unwelcome and the warm hand on her shoulder, the quiet voice and a mug of steaming tea were ample apology. "On the house, are you ok?" but not waiting for an answer, "It's a huge thing you've done, very brave. Folks here are lovely and soon you'll feel like you never have, and never could live any where else."

Kitty reached up to wipe the tear that crept then tickled down her face before it could launch itself on the keyboard below.

"Oh bugger! I didn't mean to upset you." Angela, with concern in her tone and on her face, sat besides her and placed both hands on her forearm.

"Actually..." there was a pause as Kitty tried to collect herself and attempted to express what she felt. "It's... well it's, this was the rashest, biggest and well... stupidest thing I have ever done." Looking up through wet lashes into Angela's face. "I'm not that person, I'm not one of those people who like a challenge, have adventures but somehow I did and, and here I am."

Angela smiled and squeezed the arm and waited for her to continue. "I expected, I dreaded that I would get here and it would be hateful, that no one would talk to me and," at this Kitty laughed at her own stupidity "And the house would have fallen down and I had driven myself to oblivion in my little van."

"And?" Angela tilted her head forward and raised her eyebrows in the way only mothers and teachers can.

"Well it's been like a dream, not a nightmare at all, but a good, full, friendly dream."

The women smiled at each other, one patting the other's arm.

"I know it has only been two days – and that's the thing! In a couple of days I feel at home, as if… like it's been here all this time just waiting for me to arrive and find it." Kitty face shone now, smiling broadly and the tears rolled now in happy relief.

"Happy tears?"

"Yes."

Angela reached over and hugged Kitty. Not an awkward - I don't really know you but think you need a hug - but in a crushing - I know just how you feel - cliché. Kitty really didn't object to the sentiment of the contact. But as Angela had half stood to do it Kitty feared there was a real risk of her neck breaking or at least the chair toppling over backwards. Just when Kitty thought she would have to struggle free Angela released her.

"Now I've done the move, so I know. But I had Gavin and he was local, has family here... so not wanting to rain on your parade but if you get, you know, sad, homesick I'm here six days a week." And nodding over her shoulder, "The house is just over the back there." Adding with what sounded like genuine sentiment "Anytime Kitty I'm here if you need me."

"That's really lovely of you, thanks Angela."

"Call me Ange – all my friends do."

"Wonderful to meet you Ange," and Kitty thrust out her hand in mock formality and they both laughed easily and loudly as they shook vigorously.

The bell heralded a customer, and with a brief pat on the shoulder Angela was hurrying back to business. Letting the drone of their conversation wash over her Kitty finished her correspondence.

Angela was soon back and the two women of similar age chatted easily. Kitty drank in the tidbits of local gossip and equally enjoyed sharing her discoveries at Tide's.

"What, so no bathroom at all?"

Kitty thought then that she had never in adulthood gone this long without a shower or bath, and hoped it was her description of the house and not their recent embrace that informed her new friend of this.

"Nooo" Kitty added brightly, "The outside loo and the kitchen sink. But I figure if it was good enough for all the previous inhabitants it's good enough for me. Thinking of getting a tin bath!" Her cheerfulness belied the longing Kitty now had for a hot bath.

"Well... um..." Angela sat fiddling with her hair, absentmindedly flicking it between red taloned fingers.

"Well in the spirit of Island life, and the long tradition of bartering... I might just have the solution that might suit us both."

Kitty leant forward in her seat, "I'm all ears."

"Gavin and I have started Gaelic lessons on a Tuesday evening, tonight in fact. Gavin can speak a bit, but obviously being a Sassenach like yourself I know nothing. The schools here insist on all lessons being taught in Gaelic," the expression on Angela's face for the first time clouded. "Bloody ridiculous if you ask me, all their lessons! Who needs to learn maths in Gaelic for pity's sake!" Forcing in a whopping sigh Angela tried to calm herself. "Well I digress - what was I saying, oh yes, YES! Gav and I have to be up the school seven thirty till nine thirty, so we are out of the house from seven till ten. We only started last week and old Mrs Wilcox said she would sit with the kids. Lauren my eldest is seven, then there's Maggie who's five and John – the bonus baby is four. Well, Lauren said she called Mrs Wilcox as John was crying and had a bad dream, but Mrs Wilcox told her to shut up and go to sleep." Kitty made what she thought was an appropriate face.

"Oh dear."

"Now don't get me wrong I'm no mummsy type," (you don't say Kitty thought) Angela continued. "I tell my kids to shut up plenty, but I do worry if anything really bad were to happen Mrs Wilcox might just go home – little bit batty – but anyway the point is if you are free, would you like to baby-sit for Gav and me?"

Kitty felt a shiver of dread – oh, babies. She didn't do, babies. As if Angela had read her mind she quickly added "Don't worry they'll be bathed and in bed. Lauren might be awake but she's a book worm, and if you pretend not to notice the light she'll be as quiet as a mouse so she can have a sneaky read."

"Um, ok I suppose." Kitty still hesitant but warming to the idea.

"Well that gives you three hours doesn't it?" Angela nodded slowly and pointedly, eyes wide smiling waiting for the penny to drop.

"Oh... Ooooh, I think I understand now."

"Exactly we have a cooker, microwave, dishwasher and TV and more to the point a nice line in bathroom equipment."

"Ha-ha, win, win me thinks" Kitty blinked back at her.

"Now don't worry about a towel we get through tons. Bring what you want for dinner to stick in the oven and you can have a soak."

Resting a hand over her chest, "Wow, Ange I'm touched but you don't know me from Adam."

"Are you a murderer?"

"No."

"Arsonist?"

"No, definitely not."

"Dog beater or kiddy fiddler?"

"God No!" the look of disgust on Kitty face was enough of a recommendation for Angela.

"And besides we call Lauren WPC Macleod, so if you put so much as a toe out of line she'd snitch you up." They both laughed, the longer she spent in her company the more Kitty liked her new acquaintance, although technically if she trusted her with the care of her offspring should she being calling her a friend?

Closing the laptop and draining the cold dregs of tea she gathered her things and stood stiffly, muscles she had little used before complained at being disturbed now. The prospect of a bath excited her and she was keen to get her shopping over.

"I'd better get a move on, I'll go to the Co-op and get dinner." Something microwavable she thought giving her longer in the bath. They exchanged a brief hug and profuse thanks from Kitty and she was soon seated in Pimples. "Well then Pimples – to the Co-op and don't spare the horses." Smiling at a memory of one of her father's phrases, a very invigorated Kitty set off.

6

Babysitting Duties

By her reckoning she had just enough time for a quick shop, get back to Tide's then back to Angela's. Looking in her basket checking she had all she needed in the whirlwind tour of the shop, she was aware she had been tapping on her purse, drumming finger nails as she queued impatiently. Oh the anticipation of the bubble bath. She had never bought bubble bath herself, but had fond memories of visits to Amanda's as a child and forgetting to wash as she swirled, peaked and piled the foam around her. So bubbles - check, Microwavable curry – check, house magazine – check and finally most importantly a bottle of wine and a trashy gossip magazine. Let the pampering commence!

Life down south was a constant rush, squeezing in visits, hurried chores and juggling errands. Everyone was in equal haste and always at full tilt then, Kitty revisited that mind set, snatching up her bags and slammed Pimples' door closed. Starting the engine roughly Kitty sped from the car park, the few shops and houses passed by as Kitty drew a mental list of all those things that she must do and in which order, so as to be back in time for seven.

The sun had lost its intensity now the light had greyed. The road rose away from the town and Kitty changed down to third as Pimples struggled around the steep bend. The view that lay around the corner took Kitty's breath away, taking her foot from the accelerator the van coasted into a lay-by. Handbrake securely on, there was nothing to her left other than a dramatic rocky fall. She switched the engine off, and sat arms folded across the wheel with her chin on her forearm.

A large ball of warm rich orange hovered in the sky. Long thin streaks of cloud like white brush strokes crisscrossed the sky above, the underneath of each edged in bright silver. The sea was flat and the colour of green glass that had been tossed in the sea too long. The road ahead wound in and out of sight, and the distant mountains beyond stood peaceful in the brown, black, and mauve haze.

Kitty looked down at the clock on the dashboard, five thirty. There and back would take an hour, what was she thinking. All she needed wasn't at Tide's; it may be her home but still a shell essentially and lacked all the amenities of a normal house. All her supplies were right here in Pimples. Glancing around her and into the back of the van assessing the situation, Kitty looked up and down the road then restarted the engine. After a reckless five point turn the van was parked at the perfect angle. A large mug of tea and her daily ration of biscuits Kitty cut a very contented figure. "You'll be a fat Islander!" She scolded herself but plumped the cushions and tucked her feet up on the bed. There was nothing to do for an hour but sit and watch the sky change.

Not remembering ever doing this in her life, she promised herself this should be part of her new regime. It was better than looking at the greatest painting, every second it changed, subtly the clouds elongated and the sky turned from grey to pink. The sun bobbed ever closer to the water and the green morphed to slate grey with a silver coat. Birdsong in the nearby hedgerow was the only sounds coming through the open window.

The coldness of her tea jolted her to check the time; she had sat for over an hour. Setting off and at a new appropriate pace, a very relaxed Kitty returned to the post office. She sorted the shopping, added a few bathroom essentials and took a deep breath. Hesitating with her hand on the bottle of white wine she was struck by two thoughts; 1 – She didn't want to jeopardise what could be a weekly treat by Ange and Gav thinking she was a piss head and not fit to care for their children. 2 - It would be dark by eight thirty and she would need all her wits about her to find home. Putting the bottle back in the van's fridge, Kitty quickly checked Tide's Reach was still programmed into the Satnav and took a few more deep breaths.

Parking outside the now closed post office Kitty sat for a few minutes not wanting to be overly keen; her main purpose really to ensure the children would be safely tucked up in bed. The thought of small children terrified Kitty but it was worth a try for a bath. She thought then of Mr Postmaster, Gavin, oh dear! What would he think to his wife's impromptu childcare plans?

More than a little nervous Kitty stood on the doorstep, holding the carrier bag behind her back. She scolded herself for not using a real bag, she certainly looked the part of a desperate homeless woman, and thank god she'd left the alcohol behind. Suddenly the feeling of being a begging urchin overwhelmed her and she could have happily turned and driven home, "Man up!" she hissed to herself and knocked the door.

Minutes before in the chaos of feeding, bathing and bedding three small children, Gavin's response to being informed a stranger was coming to be with his children was testament to his trust in his wife.

"Do we think it's a good idea, leaving a strange woman with the bairns?"

"I don't know, it's this strange women or the one next door. At least the young one doesn't smell of wee. Anyway I like her."

"Whatever you say."

Gavin had learnt long ago, though he had never shared it with his wife, that she was nearly always right. She was a precise judge of character, if Angela Macleod trusted this person he saw no reason not to.

Gavin answered the door, he was tall and lean, brown haired with matching neatly trimmed beard. His broad smile was a great relief to Kitty.

"Hello, you must be Kitty, come in."

"Hi, you must be Gavin, thank you."

Both smiled at the formality of their meeting. Acutely aware of the blush in her cheeks Kitty was relieved as he turned his back and walked purposely down the hall. Closing the door quietly Kitty tentatively followed Gavin in to the kitchen, he turned and gave the stranger a very business like appraisal. Starting at her face he scanned down to her feet, stopping at the carrier bag that now hung by her side – she knew that was a bad idea.

"So you're from Kent, Ange tells me."

"Yes."

"On your own?"

"Yes."

"Why Skye?"

"Don't know really, bit of a whim."

"Oh."

There followed a short silence, Gavin continued to nod thoughtfully and looking her square on. Had Kitty considered this aspect of the deal she might not have thought it was such a good idea. Gavin turned to the sink he seemed to have resigned himself to the arrangement.

"Ange will be down in a minute, two down one to go."

Kitty hoped Angela was true to her word. She had thus far managed to get through thirty years with very little interaction with children. Stephen and Kitty had never got to the point in life to consider having them and the point was moot now. Although not quite over the hill, she had expected that door to never be open to her now.

Not being an Auntie, and all her nearest friends in the same boat as her, busy with careers, she only now realised how limited her contact with little people was. Standing here watching Gavin busy at the jumble of plastic cups and plates in the sink, this man was entrusting the care of his most precious possessions with someone who knew absolutely nothing about them. She reassured herself that they must be all old enough to talk and she was, after all, a child herself once – how hard could it be?

Angela raced down the stairs, clutching a load of dirty washing in one arm and a precarious stack of dirty mugs and glasses in the other, skillfully dropping a clean folded towel from under her arm on to the table. Gavin, in a show of well-oiled teamwork, relieved her of the washing up and stacked it efficiently in the dishwasher. Whilst kicking shut the door he leaned over, taking the heap of clothes and gathering a collection of escapee small socks from the floor and shoving them unceremoniously into the machine. On the shelf above he took a washing tablet (disguising itself as a tempting sweet) and flicked the drawer closed. Kitty marvelled at his efficiency, maybe this is what happens when you reproduce three times?

"No, no!" rather too sharply Angela reprimanded him.

"Kitty can put her towel in when she's done" The follow-up words of "Do I have to say everything twice" didn't need saying it was all there in her tone. No wonder her kids go to bed easily, I'd be scared not to thought Kitty. Gavin just smiled, like water off a ducks back. With theatrical relish he turned the dials and indicated to the start button with a flourish, Kitty suppressed the urge to laugh and returned Gavin's mischievous smile.

"Come on Ange we'll be late."

"Oh shit! Yes ok, ok."

Angela grabbed Kitty's hand; just in the way she would her children to ensure she had their undivided attention. "Now old Mrs Wilcox – batty but nice next door if you need her" pointing through the fridge. Microwave doesn't turn so well so stop it every fifteen seconds and move your plate". Taking Kitty's bag Angela removed the ready meal, "Oh lovely korma – Gavin!" Without further instruction the tall man opened cupboards and drawers and placed a plate, side plate and cutlery on the table.

"Be a love and put your stuff in the dishwasher and set it going and the same for the towel." Again as if rehearsed Gavin bowed slightly and pointed to the appropriate knobs and dials.

"All right, all right Gav don't show off just cause we have company." Kitty laughed louder than intended, or appropriate by the look on Angela's face, but was rewarded by a sly wink from the man of the house. She was going to like Gavin; she liked Angela but had to admit she did scare her a bit.

"Get the car started, I'll be out in a sec."

Gavin touched his forelock and Angela sighed, but dutifully Kitty watched as he took his and his wife's coat and waved goodbye to Kitty. Angela trailed Kitty around a whistle stop tour of the house.

"Lounge, sorry about the mess, remotes on top of the TV." Upstairs Angela's pace slowed and voice hushed as they crept across the landing. First one door than the next gently opened to show first John asleep amongst a mass of teddies. Kitty couldn't make him out but took assurance that if Angela was happy he was there she would investigate no further. The second tiny room was an assault on the senses, vibrant pink and lying under a garland of feathers and bunting was Maggie. A small brown mop of hair peeked over the top of the quilt; two asleep Kitty was feeling better by the minute. Lastly Angela strode into the room of a small elfin girl sitting up in bed, "This is the lady I told you about Lauren" Struggling to avert her gaze from the large book she held before her, the girl finally looked up suspiciously at the new babysitter.

"Hello," Kitty sounded pathetic even to herself.

"Hi," and Lauren's conversation was over for the evening and she resumed her reading. Angela bent and kissed the shiny brown head. "Remember, light off at seven thirty."

"Ummm" was the only reply. Leaving the room Angela winked at Kitty.

"Will me having a bath disturb them?" Kitty worried.

"Gosh no, sleep through a hurricane those three, the longer you stay in the bath the better friend of Lauren you'll make – means she can read for longer."

Feeling the burden of the responsibility now Kitty was anxious to get it right.

"Should I tell her to turn her light off?"

"No just leave her, you'll be her best friend."

Kitty was very happy with this and without further ado Angela was rushing out of the door. Before Kitty could turn to go to the kitchen the letter box opened, and Angela called "Oh I forgot, Eric the dog is in the back garden, let him in when you've finished your dinner, thanks, see you later." The brass rectangle snapped shut and Kitty was alone once more.

She stood for a few minutes taking in her surroundings. The house was probably built in the fifties, devoid of any period features and everything about it was practical. The furniture was all well worn and a little stained in places, similarly the carpet. A smattering of debris covered every surface, small toys, papers, letters, rogue odd socks, coins and a mass of "Stuff."

Standing on the threshold of the lounge a large canvas photograph of Ange and Gav's wedding dominated over the fireplace. Angela radiant in a huge white dress and Gavin cutting a dashing figure in a navy tartan kilt. Studio pictures of the three children showing them in varying stages of development, they looked happy, they looked like a normal family.

Moving now into the kitchen Kitty arranged her dinner. The local paper sat on the table and, feeling every bit the stranger in the house she tried to clear a space without disturbing the heaps in case there was in fact order in the chaos. Kitty was acutely aware she didn't want it to look like she had been rifling through their possessions.

As a child she had felt at home in other people's homes, notably Amanda's. There she could feel at peace, confident to move around the house, open cupboards even help herself to drinks and snacks – but never since.

Whilst timing herself to adjust the plate in the microwave every fifteen seconds Kitty worked her way through a list of her friends and acquaintances in Kent. Would anyone of them, without formal invitation, without thorough preparation to make the best impression let her in to cook in their kitchen, wash in their bathroom? The answer was a resounding no. Since living with her parents and sharing happy times with Amanda's she had never experienced this openness. There was no pretence, no airs or graces just a genuine offer of friendship.

Once the curry was ready, rice and Naan steaming, Kitty settled to read the paper. There were lots of announcements of events, a useful section of items for sale and, much to Kitty's delight a lonely-hearts section. Kitty chuckled at the image she conjured of, "Agnes – not in the first flush of youth, seeks companion for long walks, dining out and maybe more." Having absolutely no inclination herself to meet anyone for walking, eating out and certainly not more, Kitty could amuse herself with laughing at the pitiable individuals and enjoy her dinner.

Thinking now that it may be inadvisable to soak in a bath on a full stomach, and maybe that Lauren may be asleep if she left it a while, Kitty took a glass of water and headed for the lounge. The other bonus of tonight was a TV. Weaving her way though the smattering of plastic toys on the floor Kitty took the remote control and cleared a seat on the sofa. As with all modern sofas, so it seemed to Kitty, it was made for giants. Her legs cleared the floor by six inches and dangled uncomfortably. The local news was just finishing and she was pleased to see the weather forecast. Rain and high winds for the remainder of the week but clearing Monday for a spell of fine dry. Perfect, it would be good when the builder and architect visited.

A Gaelic programme started involving sheep and land rovers, prompting Kitty to investigate the bathroom. Reaching the top of the stairs the light was still on in Laurens room, "Just having a bath now," Kitty said in a hushed voice outside the room without looking in "K" was the disinterested reply. Kitty was more than happy with that, this babysitting malarkey was a piece of cake.

Like the rest of the house there was a layer of clutter. The house was in no way unclean just untidy. Laying her towel on the sinks edge she locked the door. The bath was still wet and the collection of ducks, a wind up snorkelling frog and a small flotilla of boats sat abandoned in the bottom. Kitty tried to be very quiet as she cleared the way, anxious not to disturb and jeopardise the silence. There being no obvious home for all she gathered it was placed in the sink. Rinsing the bath the efficient taps made quick work of filling the tub and soon huge mounds of bubbles awaited her.

Sitting naked on the toilet Kitty realised that in all her years she had never fully appreciated the wonder of modern bathing. Her mother had talked about tin baths in front of an open fire, shared by all. Kitty had nodded and listened attentively, but only now truly understood her mothers never diminishing pride and love for her bathroom. For Kitty and all her generation a bathroom had always meant hot water in the tap day or night, heated towel rails and radiators. But now after just two days denied these luxuries, Kitty felt sure she would never again take it for granted.

A little too hot, it took a few minutes for Kitty to gingerly lower herself in, "Ooh... Arhhh," not unpleasant groans and finally bubbles crackled and popped around her head as she found the bottom of the tub. She lay for many minutes; with no time constraints she smiled, closed her eyes and listened to the pounding pulse in her ears. She had forgotten about the softness of the water and laughed at the mass of bubbles, hoping she could get rid of them before the homeowners returned.

Head back, raising her knees, she lowered her head through the white cloud until she could run hands through the water, soaking her hair. The heat would play havoc with it so sitting up she filled a dinosaur beaker with tepid water from the taps. The chill as it ran down her back was not unwelcome on her flushed skin but still made her jump. Shampooed and conditioned Kitty scrapped the bubbles from behind her and rested back.

Calculating her next visit, (hoping, very much that there would be a repeat visit) she decided to try out the shower next time and spend longer in the kitchen. It had only been a few days but Kitty already mourned the loss of vegetables, woman cannot live on ready meals alone! And she would wash before dinner next time, the curry felt like a spicy stone inside her now.

By the time Angela and Gavin returned the bath was washed and all evidence of the mountain of bubbles drained away. The washing machine whirled for a spin and the dishwasher removed all evidence of the curry, bar the smell. Note to self – no smelly food next time, nothing must threaten the promise of next week.

After a few minutes of conversation and much declining of offers of tea, Kitty was anxious not to out stay her welcome. With a nod from Gavin and a hug from Angela and joint agreement for the same next week, a still glowing Kitty slowly found her way home.

7

First Guest

Kitty awoke after another uninterrupted nights sleep. The morning light was pink and beautiful. Drinking in the ever-changing view, peering out from her bed Kitty saw the distant mountains as never before. The details were clearer than she had ever seen. Gone was the misty blur, replaced by details of trees and waterfalls. The sky today boasted large fluffy clouds, the image of cotton wool, their softness and seeming lightness accentuated by the pink highlights. Kitty had memories of disappointing watercolour classes at school and unsatisfactory attempts at skies and clouds. Smiling Kitty knew if she had honestly replicated this sky she would have been unhappy, it looked too twee, too fluffy.

Not wanting to tear herself away from the view or her snug bed, the increasing urge to go to the toilet won out. Hurriedly wriggling into her boots and a fleece Kitty made the now familiar journey still watching the day unravel. A quick wash at the sink and she was soon hurrying back to Pimples to dress and simultaneously eat breakfast. Foolishly Kitty thought, she hadn't pinned Gladys down to a time. There was nothing she could do about it now, but was annoyed she hadn't gone to Portree and got more supplies.

Boiling the kettle and filling a bucket, adding a dash of washing up liquid and a generous glug of vinegar Kitty was set. Propping open the front door Kitty took several deep breaths of the fresh salty air. The only sound was the faint lapping of the approaching tide, harsh bird song from sea birds on the rocks and small sweet songs of unseen residents of the trees and shrubs of the garden and beyond.

Kitty quite liked cleaning windows, one of those jobs she would put off but once committed found very rewarding. The prospect of only having four and all within easy reach made it a much less daunting prospect. The conservatory at her last home was half a day's hard labour but Kitty knew today was going to be a breeze.

Each window had four panes of glass; the ripples were proof of its previous molten state. She would endeavour to keep this glass despite the renovations. What should have taken half an hour ended up taking over two hours. The robin that hopped from a small shrub onto the low garden wall and back was no less interested in Kitty than she was in him. Add to the list – bird feeder and food. Then there was of course the cove, the sea, the mountains and the sky all pulling her attention from the job at hand.

Once finished, Kitty brought one of the kitchen chairs out and sat in the open doorway, mug of tea in hand basking in the morning light soaking in all she could see. Within three days she had morphed into a Mediterranean crone sitting on her doorstep.

The tide nearly fully in, covered the array of green black rocks that made up the perimeter of the cove standing between the mossy bank and the seaweed covered beach. The sea was dark blue today with turquoise patches and crept stealthily towards her boundary wall. The mountains across the water and to the left never failed to fascinate. She would endeavour to get a detailed map of all she could see and have it framed in the house.

For the first time Kitty took the opportunity to take in the details of her neighbours. The road she turned from to descend into her plot continued round, high above the water level. The cove was in the shape of a long thin triangle, widening to the right as she looked at it now and opening to the sea. It was protected from the full force of the ocean by the headland around to the right and the mountains on the land opposite. She had been up as far as the post box and saw the front of a smart modern bungalow. She had noticed the garden, preened and edged to perfection with neat shrubs clipped into very unnatural globes. From her viewpoint now the back garden sloped down to the water and was just as controlled as the front.

Further down the bank sat a large modern detached house. It had the look of a newly finished project, with large triangular windows obviously designed to maximise the view of the cove. Although very new, the grey cladding and windows set into the shinny black slate roof were an obvious and successful nod to the architecture of Skye's traditional houses.

There were heaps of rubble and a lack of landscaping of any kind. As she peered at the back of the house it was obvious if anyone stepped out of the patio doors or back door they would face a good three foot drop. Sitting sipping her tea Kitty wondered if a sleek deck would soon be added, she was going to enjoy watching its progress.

Unnoticed until then, Kitty saw peeking from behind the house was the shadowy figure of a stone, single storey croft. Not dissimilar to her own, absentmindedly she rubbed her hand across the letterbox of Tide's Reach.

"Don't worry I won't hide you away."

It saddened her to see the forlorn little building dwarfed and shadowed by its replacement. Before the new house it must have been a mirror image of her own plot. Kitty felt very strongly with her hand resting on the remnants of paint of the front door, there was no necessity for grand modernity in this little cove.

To the farthest end of the land on the left a few small houses could be seen, but more intriguing were two spires of grey slate. Rounded, with the hint of white walls beneath them but other features obscured by dark green firs. After Gladys's visit Kitty promised herself a walk this afternoon to see what was hidden there, it was the direction Jock had gestured to for the pub; it was certainly time she found that.

The warmth that cleaning brings had now subsided and a brisk change in the winds' direction brought a flurry of ripples heading towards her, causing Kitty to shiver. Hurrying back indoors she replaced the chair in the kitchen, and the few objects she owned were positioned to their best advantage. Placing a selection of biscuits on her favourite plate and cutting fresh primroses from the garden Kitty was ready to receive visitors.

Gladys arrived by eleven o'clock. The fact that there were no windows to the side of the house she had to reluctantly admit was really a failure in its layout. It resulted in no way of watching for visitors, so Kitty resorted to the only option available to her, and kept popping her head out of the front door. This was rewarded on seeing a silver Micra swinging down the drive, a small cloud of dust drifting over Pimples.

Seeing her, Kitty waved and reached in for her fleece. Due to Gladys's ample size and advanced years, her assumption that she may need assistance over the lawn was ill founded. Kitty was only a third of the way across by the time Gladys bounded up to her.

"Morning lassie."

"Oh hello Gladys," Kitty turned and they walked back to the house.

"Well, well it's not changed much. Must be five years since I was here." Standing in the front garden looking over the front of the building Gladys picked up the gold cross around her neck and rubbed it gently between thumb and forefinger.

"Aye, Annie was a strong woman, nice to see someone here

again... aye, aye," turning to smile at Kitty "She'd be glad to see you here lassie."

Kitty liked this idea, and drank in all the tales Gladys had to tell and the photos shared and explained. Kitty's favourite was a seventies colour picture, the muted tones of the small square photo showing Annie in a wonderful paisley green and orange dress, standing next to a white hydrangea in the back garden. A proud hand was resting on the wall she had built.

"You'll be building on I suppose, adding mod cons?"

"No, well... here I'll show you."

Leading her through to the kitchen, Kitty took the folder from the table and showed her the architects drawing. She was excited now at her first opportunity to share these with someone. Gladys smiled and nodded, and although not that interested herself was attentive, as it was obvious how much it meant to this brave young woman.

Standing in each room and listening to the exuberant plans took little time. Once outside the footprint of the front extension was paced out and then Kitty stood where her new bathroom was to be sited.

Noticing Gladys's shivers Kitty apologised and they hurried back to the kitchen for biscuits and tea. Pushing her empty cup and saucer away Gladys rose and made her excuses, "Well it's been grand lass, thank you so much for the tea but I really must be off. My Hugh will want to know why his lunch is late."

Gladys gave Kitty a warm maternal hug and patted her firmly on the back.

"Thank you for coming Gladys, it's been lovely."

"Oh, you're welcome, and remember lass you are one of us now."

"Jock said there is a band playing at the pub Friday night, I... I think it's up there."

Kitty pointed up to the spire in the distance as they walked back to Gladys's car.

"Aye, aye, there's the hotel and the bar. I think its folk type bands, nothing fancy but a good way to meet your neighbours and some more of the locals."

"Will you and Hugh be there?"

"Me, heavens no," Gladys chuckled, "That's for you youngsters, but Jock will be there, a band won't stop him being in the bar for his pint on a Friday night. Jocks wife will be there and Joan's a wonderful woman, I've told her all about you."

Kitty smiled warmly, not used to neighbours being so friendly and involved. In her previous life Kitty may have thought herself offended at blatant gossiping amongst new acquaintances but it warmed her heart today.

Gradually she was growing accustomed to her new isolation in life. No parents, no siblings, no husband – now that he'd left her – and no children. Kitty knew she could make this long lonely journey - might as well be lonely here as well as in Kent - but the warmth of Gladys's embrace found the chink in her armour, there to protect her from the loneliness. Gladys reached into her handbag to fetch her keys, hesitating she held Kitty's gaze and half pulled the photo Kitty had so admired of Annie by her wall.

"I'm sure you don't want it, but it feels right that it should stay here."

"Oh Gladys I would love it!" Taking the photo a beaming Kitty continued, "I think she should be remembered here, thank you."

Kitty clutched the precious image to her chest as she watched until the silver car disappeared. At that brief moment a wave of great sorrow and a great happiness crept in.

The rest of the day Kitty tidied Pimples, unloading whatever she could to lighten his load. The last of the emergency food was at risk of making her ill so she walked it up the lane to the bins.

There was still plenty of light and Kitty walked past the post and telephone box. The lane passed the bungalow and Kitty could see now it dropping off the right to the new house. She looked down the drive and could see clearly the detail of the crofter's cottage at the back of the new house.

There were a dozen other houses along the single track of tarmac. As Kitty passed the last pair of white cottages she doubted she would find the owners of the slate towers as the lane dropped and narrowed. Pressing on she turned to the left and hesitated. A small group of buildings well maintained and all white with matching pale green paintwork, formed a small semicircle around a stone jetty. Kitty walked to the end picking her way over heaps of fishing nets and buckets and scrunched up her nose at the invading smell of fish. At the end of the jetty Kitty zipped her fleece high against the wind that seemed to come straight from the Atlantic Ocean, and knew it was much more by luck than judgement that her cottage had such a protected situation in the cove.

The largest of the buildings boasted three cones of black slate, rising from the roof. These must have been the ones she could see from her house. The thick walls were rendered and painted white with two entrances; one clearly marked *Garden of Skye Hotel*. The steps up to the door were flanked by black cast iron railings with large lead troughs either side, studded with bright green shoots - the promise of bulbs and flowers to come. Kitty peered through the glass panel of the door and could make out an ornate hallstand and guessed this wasn't the entrance for the Celtic band.

Walking around the building there was a much less imposing door to the rear. Marked Bar, with a notice board to its side. Kitty saw the flyer for Friday night. *Monros Boys* Celtic band. She was excited now and glad to be sure where she was headed, and now looked forward to Friday with new increased enthusiasm.

8

Over the Sea to Skye

Friday was a busy day; as for the first time Kitty had a packed agenda. The band started at eight, but Jock had told her there was good food to be had so she thought she'd get there before then, again on Jock's advice 'Or you'll no have a seat to rest in.'

Pimples was roused early and Kitty set her Satnav to Portree, supposedly the largest town. Kitty was armed with a list, a tape measure and detailed notebook with every dimension of her new home. The weather was the most inclement it had been since she had arrived but she drove on determined, wipers on full.

Portree seemed extremely busy after the deserted roads she had left. Parking up and grateful for the new wet weather coat, she set about finding her purchases. Tired after the hour and a half drive, and following four trips back to Pimples, Kitty collapsed in the driver's seat and rested her head on folded arms at the wheel.

"Well, all safely gathered in Pimps – home time."

Taking a better angle down the drive it felt a little less like a fairground ride. A brief reprieve in the rain meant Kitty could make three hurried journeys to the cottage to unload. A wheelbarrow or truck on wheels would have to be on the list, that would have saved quite some effort.

Placing a new acquisition on the kitchen windowsill. A retro cream alarm clock, set right by her phone, it ticked comfortingly now.

"Oh shit." Kitty sighed and scraped her hands through her mass of frizzy hair. Never before had she remembered going to the pub without showering, straightening her hair and applying makeup.

"Oh well, here goes." The kettle boiled again and she watched the rain pour and form rivulets down the clean panes. She was glad to now not own a mirror as she suspected her hair looked like it felt. In the bottom of her bag she found a crocodile clip and rolled her twisted hair up onto her head.

What does one wear to a Celtic pub night out? Kitty opted for clean jeans, a favourite jumper and walking boots. Keys and purse in her coat Kitty headed out. The walk seemed longer than yesterday, maybe trepidation weighed heavy and slowed Kitty's pace. And sinking her chin into her upturned collar she kept a securing hand on her hood. It wasn't what you would call rain, more like wet mist. It was still light as she walked up the steps to the pub taking a large deep breath and a quick check that none of her hair had escaped the clip.

The creak of the door as it swung open announced her arrival. A dark haired girl looked up from the bar and smiled easily. Stopping half way to look back at her chores, she looked anew at the stranger. Unabashed she examined the newcomer from head to toe and back again. Needing another deep breath Kitty gathered her resolve and closed the door, trying to look confident on the walk to the bar whilst snatching glances to see who else was there.

"Evening," the English accent was a surprise.

"Oh hello."

"Here for the band?"

"Well yes... and some food if that's possible?"

"Sure, yes, bar menu here," handing Kitty a well thumbed paper menu, "Or you can eat in the restaurant in the hotel if you'd rather?"

Looking every inch the efficient bar staff, tall and slim she was very smart in black fitted trousers and a tight white shirt. An asymmetric bob of dark brown hair revealed a band of bright red hair at the nape of her neck. She had a collection of silver rings, and the band of leaves tattooed around her wrist caught Kitty's eye – Kitty guessed her parents wouldn't have approved.

"No, no, here would be good, will the band be there?" Kitty pointed at the far end of the room where black boxes formed a low stage.

"Yes, are you on your own?" The bargirl didn't really need to ask.

"Um, yes, just me... on my own" Blushing slightly, Kitty thought she must perfect a better answer to that without seeming so pathetic.

"Good for you, well its up to you, you can have one of the tables or if you like you can sit up here at the corner of the bar. You'll have a good view of the band and keep me company until it gets busier."

Kitty was very glad of the invitation and felt very secure tucked at the end of the bar, leaning her back on the wall. The girl was right; she had a super vantage point to see all who arrived and the stage. Ordering a beef and ale pie and half a pint of local ale Kitty felt the nerves settle, and taking off her coat was pleased she had braved coming out tonight. Taking a large slug of the rich brown ale, wiping the back of her hand across her mouth.

"So you're not a local then?"

"God no! Parents moved here ten years ago now. I was only fourteen- talk about curb your social life."

"Where did you live, you haven't got an accent from here or there?"

"No we came from Harlow in Essex, just getting to the age when shopping with my friends and teen clubs with the promise of nightclubs, but no! *Let's move to Skye for a simpler life.*" My mother thought it was a great idea, they like it well enough but it's not really for me." Kitty looked into the far away stare of the girl opposite her at the bar and risked her admission.

"Oh well, I've done just that."

"Of course, are you the English woman who's brought Annie's croft?"

"Yes, that's me, mad I know… but like your parents I wanted to get away from it all. I'm Kitty" putting down her glass she reached across the bar, mirroring her they shook hands vigorously.

"Well I'm Lilly, welcome and good to meet you." Not releasing Kitty's hand she looked, brows furrowed, "Anyway you're nowhere near their age, what are you –twenty five? Twenty six?"

Kitty laughed "Thirty, but I like you already Lilly."

"Really? Well it looks lovely and all, and don't get me wrong it has its good points, but let me tell you it's a long cold winter up here. But don't you worry I can show you a few exciting things to do."

Kitty smiled warmly and guessed that anything Lilly thought was exciting she certainly would not, and as she nodded back to the enthusiastic barmaid hoped she would forget having offered. The bar was filling up, and a plate piled high with thick pastry topped pie and wonderful large crispy chips appeared. The gravy was thick and rich and went down very easily with the ale, She was on her second glass by the end of the meal. Leaning back on the high chair sipping her beer she watched as Lilly flirted, joked and pulled pints.

A group of men in their sixty's leant on the other end of the bar and sent her occasional disinterested glances. The round table by the door was overcrowded by a group of young lads and girls. Some were clearly too young to drink but it in no way dampened their enthusiasm as they chatted and laughed in good-humoured banter.

The hubbub rose as the door was opened, flung against one of the youth's chairs. Looks of indignation soon replaced by smiles as a throng of hairy men – not dissimilar in age to her she thought, jostled and forced their way through. Instruments in black cases were held aloft, others banging the backs of chairs. Scraping chairs and apologises and calls of welcome added to the rising noise.

"Evening Lilly!" a blonde heavy man with a ginger beard waved, and Lilly's bright reply followed them in.

"Hi Murdo! Davey, Angus, Jamie oh and Alistair. The usual for you all?"

A loud cheer and shouts to the affirmative was all that was needed, and Kitty watched in admiration as Lilly lined up their order. Sitting very comfortably, Kitty enjoyed watching unnoticed as they set about arranging music and instruments.

The door opened and the familiar face of Jock and, who Kitty assumed, must be his wife appeared. She rose from her slumped position and was pleased to catch the postman's eye.

"Arh, Aye here she is, well lassie glad to see you. Joan this is the poor wee Southerner I told you about."

Kitty coloured and Joan took her hand in both of hers. Kitty suspicions had obviously been founded; Jock had surely told his wife about the mad English woman whom was either sleeping, drooling or clinging to his arm.

"It's lovely to meet you," Kitty tried to pull her hand free but Joan tightened her grip. Looking intently at her and speaking slowly, so Kitty's simple mind could keep up.

"I t   i s   n i c e   t o   m e e t   y o u   t o o."

"Well come on woman, better we get a seat or there'll be nought but scraps" Jock held her arm gently trying to prise his wife away.

"W o u l d   y o u   l i k e   t o   j o i n   u s?" Joan squeezed her hands again and continued to gaze pityingly at her. Kitty had thought earlier that she would like nothing better, but now could think of nothing worse. She would stay and take her chances where she was.

"Thank you so much but you and Jock go and enjoy your dinner. I've had mine and can see the band from here."

"If you're sure lassie, come on over and join us if you've a mind to later" Jock smiled and Kitty could see the relief on his face, again trying to pry his wife away.

"A r e   y o u   s u r e   h e n?"

"Yes quite sure, thanks though, Lilly is keeping me company" Lilly raised a hand from the other side of the bar in acknowledgement.

"Aye well you know where we are, bless."

Kitty was relieved to see them disappear around a chimneybreast, only to see Joan lean back on her chair and smile and pity the simpleton at the bar. "Oh great", Kitty finished her beer and was going to get her jacket when the band started warming up.

"You're not leaving are you?" Lilly shouted from the other end of the bar. The older men all turned and stared at her, "Oh joy" Kitty hissed under her breath as the youngsters quieted and all looked at her too. Even two of the group with the band standing a few feet away along the bar lowered their drinks and turned her way.

"Um... well, um" – great she thought way to impress the locals.

"You should stay and hear the boys." It was the nearer of the band members who stood raising his pint in her direction. He had a mop of dark shaggy brown hair and pale blue eyes, which quite mesmerised Kitty. She suddenly felt small and stupid and all she could manage by way of reply was a muttered "Oh ok."

Gliding towards her as if on skates Lilly asked, "Have another Kitty? Another half?"

"Oh sod it! Make it a pint!"

Thankfully all parties looked away and continued their conversations, Kitty puffed out a huge sigh and slouched back into obscurity.

Three of the men now sat with instruments leaving the remaining two propping up the bar.

"That's Murdo, the blonde with the guitar; Davey the beard is on the fiddle; Alistair is the red head on Uilleann pipes" Lilly informed her whilst they exchanged beer for money.

"The what pipes?"

"Uilleann."

"Oh" a very puzzled look on her face.

"It's an old form of pipes, only has a two octave range but it's really haunting", this explanation coming from the blue eyed man in the richest broad accent.

"This is Angus, Angus this is Kitty, she's the southerner who brought Annie's old croft down the road" Lilly did the honours.

"Hi" Angus slid his pint towards her leaving a trail of beer in its wake, offering it to clank a toast with Kitty glass.

"Well to Kitty the southerner – welcome!"

"Cheers, thank you," Kitty slid her pint to meet his.

"Slaitemhath", Angus winked at Kitty "Hey Jamie, Jamie!" Angus elbowed his neighbour. "This is Kitty the southerner."

"Aye I heard ye", this Scotsman wasn't a patch on his friend. With no hint of hospitality this young man glanced across at Kitty but without a smile turned back to the band.

"Don't mind him" Angus's apologetic smiling eyes were some consolation as he flicked his head at the friend. "Doesn't like southerners much, coming up here and pushing our house prices up for rich holiday homes."

"Oh like I haven't heard that one before," Kitty snorted out and instantly regretted the effect the strong beer was having on her, enabling her to say what ever she thought – most unlike her. Angus smiled back at her and was obviously not offended, raising her voice so the other man might hear.

"It's not a holiday home, it's my home now... I moved here - I live here now, damn It!" She had expected some of this attitude, bigotry and was in no humour to listen to it.

"Well welcome Kitty! Three more pints Lilly if you would."

Aided by – (Oh dear she had forgotten how many pints of the rich velvety beer she had drunk) she lounged on the bar. Her left hand supporting the side of her head and her right hand tucked under her armpit between her and the bar. The music was lulling and the melancholic tones of the pipes could have easily made Kitty weep, but she was determined to enjoy them instead.

Angus chatted easily to her between songs and required little in the way of response. She was vaguely aware she was sliding happily into a cloud of intoxication carried by the beautiful haunting Celtic melodies. Murdo sang, eyes often closed, lost in words Kitty didn't understand. The blonde hair flicked and waved as he strummed, and although a very sweet voice the occasional catch of roughness conveyed the sorrow in the lyrics.

"Aye, I'd say you've enjoyed yourself lassie", it was Jock's voice now that stirred her. She was so absorbed in the current tune that she hadn't noticed Jock and his wife walk towards her. Kitty realised just how much she must have consumed as she struggled now to focus on the faces before her, beyond the outline of white hair and beard.

"Now will ye be able to get yon'sel back to that van? I think ye may have had a dram too many."

"Me, nar, I'm sober, sober as a... um... a... a... JUDGE!" Shouting out the final word in her excitement of remembrance.

"O dear, Jock should we see her home do you think?" It was Joan's face drifting in and out of focus now.

"Don't worry, we've already decided me and the boys will see her home safe."

Kitty felt giddy as she turned to smile inanely at Lilly and held the edge of the bar tightly in both hands. Lilly her new friend, Lilly her best friend, Lilly who she loved, "Hick!"

"Come on now southerner" Angus, Angus of the gorgeous eyes, Angus with the wonderful accent, Kitty thought she must love him too. Placing a steadying hand on her shoulder he pushed her gently onto the bar after Kitty had finished waving goodbye to Jock and his very worried wife. Once Lilly had finished behind the bar and the clatter of stacking chairs had subsided, Angus helped the wobbly newcomer on with her coat. Hiccoughing and smiling, a gruff voice now threatened to spoil Kitty's bleary-eyed contented haze.

"Well we would'na all fit in the car, unless we lay her in the boot" the second statement almost being considered.

"Oh, ohhhh, I might throw up." Kitty's dry mouth caused her lips to stick to her teeth; with her eyes closed she rested back on the cold wall and would happily have stayed just there if she could.

"Not in my car lass. Lilly you shoot off with the other lads, Jamie and I can handle her. My cars at the end of the lane anyway" Angus wrapped a strong arm around Kitty who slid obligingly to her feet.

"Are you sure Angus?"

"Aye she'll be sober time we get her down the drive."

Kitty's senses were awoken by the slap in the face of the wind straight from the sea as the door opened. Aware then that she was moving, her legs carried her forward but was guided and supported by one man on either side. Her arms draped around broad shoulders, and despite their stooped stature her toes barely grazed the ground. She hadn't remembered stepping out of the pub and cared little who carried her across the gravel. Letting her head hang back, the light from the pub faded and the blackness of the sky above gave up its glistening stars, more upon more twinkled into focus. Whether it was the alcohol or the unpolluted skies Kitty had never seen so many stars.

"Bloody hell! Look! Look!"

Angus turned a head and followed her gaze, "They are stars southerner, did ye not have them down there?" Husky laughs from both sides as her burly new friends navigated the dark lane.

"Where is it, which is her turning?" this wasn't Angus's voice and Kitty looked with effort – it was taking an enormous amount of effort to pull her head in the upright position.

"Is it you?"

"Aye it's me."

"The one who doesn't like me" Kitty's bottom lip pouted and both men laughed anew.

"I didn't say that, I dunna know ya."

"You don't sound like you like me," Kitty slumped heavier in their arms and the tears in her eyes glistened in the moonlight.

"Oh dunna cry, now, now, we like ya, Jamie tell her, tell her you like her."

"Really! Oh, aye right you are, I like you."

Truth be told, at that moment, in the cold with a snivelling, pissed girl hanging on him when he could have been in with Davey's warm car and nearly home, he didn't like her very much at all.

"Is this it? Kitty, Kitty wake up. Is this your drive?" Angus peered at the crooked shabby sign just visible in the moon light, "Tide's ree..."

"Yes, yes Tiiide'sreaaaach" Kitty finally got out.

"Come on then, bloody hell that's steep" the entangled trio built up quite a head of speed descending the slope and were all giggling at the bottom. They had set off across the grass before Kitty's mind caught up with her body.

"Oh no, no, no... It's not here; it's not Tide – no bed."

The men stopped, Jamie trying to straighten his aching back sighed loudly and added irritably "Bloody hell!" With a much softer tone Angus asked, "What do you mean, Kitty, Kathleen, isn't that your croft?" Kitty's head flopped from side to side trying to figure out which one was talking and which one of these faces didn't like her.

"No but... yes but... no bed."

"Oh god help us, is she staying somewhere else? Maybe Mrs Blackwell's B&B or somewhere," with a large groan and re-grasping around her waist and hitching her up. "Dunna say we're gotta get her back up that drive?" Jamie sighed heavily again.

"Pimples" weakly and muffled.

"What did she say?" Angus leant an ear to the drunkard

"Dimples?" Jamie hazards a guess.

Kitty chuckled and slumped back, "Pimples!"

"Oh, what is she saying?"

Kitty wriggled and took her arm from around Angus's neck and fumbled in her pocket. Jamie now had both arms around her to counterbalance the swaying and held firmly to her jean waist band due to her complete inability to lock her knees in the standing position.

"Ta dahhhhh!" Kitty jingled her keys and promptly dropped them on the grass. Narrowly missing Angus's head as he bent to retrieve the keys Kitty swung round to point at her van, "That's Pimples, he's Pimples!"

"Oh right ye are" Angus smiled.

"In your own time, dunna rush ya sel" Jamie muttered. Angus didn't rush and ambled back towards the van whistling as he unlocked it and slide back the side door.

"Let's get you in lass."

Turning her body but forgetting to take her legs with her Kitty was facing Jamie now and looked up "Oh I'm sorry," bottom lip pouting. "Sorry, sorry... you don't like me do you?"

"Well let's say you're not winning me over right now." Jamie started to walk and dragged her useless legs between his. Carrying the little English lush would have been a small ask for Jamie had she not been struggling and fighting against him.

"Come on Sassenach, help me out here."

"But I've got to get to the house" Kitty was winning now.

"Oh Angus, can we just get her in the bloody van already."

"Sorry, I'm sorry, I've got to go!" Kitty pushed against Jamie's chest and he released her in frustration only to grab both upper arms as she fell backwards. "I've got to gooooo!"

Angus laughed heartily, seeing now that Kitty was crossing and uncrossing her legs, "No toilet in the van?" speaking as if to a child.

"No I'm sorry," answering as if she were one.

"Come on Jamie, our work here is not yet done."

"Bloody hell," was his reply.

Angus relieved Jamie of one of the arms and they sang in unison as they marched a now desperate Kitty, legs gripped together from the knee up across the grass.

"Key?" Angus asked

"Outback its open," a weak smile up to the beautiful blue eyes. The path around the croft wouldn't accommodate three abreast and Angus relieved himself of the arm and walked ahead feeling his way around in the darkness now as the bank at the back obscured the moon. The light when found shone painfully bright and Jamie stood uncertainly at the threshold. "Can you manage?" for the first time since their meeting Jamie's voice was gentle and the change didn't go unnoticed even in her inebriated state. Kitty raised a hand and attempted a gentle stroke of his face but planted a not so gentle slap on it; biting her bottom lip he mercly raised his eyebrows. "Can you manage?" his new warm tone unaltered.

"I don't know."

"Angus, help me here."

"Rrrright" both men stood looking at the saggy stranger, ruffled hair across her face, nearly all clear of the clip now.

"Well what do we do now?" Jamie hissed at his friend.

"Oooh, I'm busting!"

"Oh bloody hell – hold her up Angus", Jamie knelt down lifting her coat out of the way, fighting with the tassels of her scarf. Fumbling with her belt - strangely difficult to undo from the wrong side, - Jamie cursed, but belt and zip finally came undone.

"Here goes!" Jamie looked up into Angus's grinning face to the side of the mass of flopping blonde hair, pulled and jerked her jeans and knickers down. His cold knuckles running down the outside of both thighs had Kitty squirming and giggling.

"Oooh thanks." Jamie and Angus simultaneously dropped her on the ice-cold seat and turned their backs on her, standing in the open door way in a strange act of chivalry.

"Just don't fall off."

Totally uninhibited Kitty rocked backwards and forward, humming Over the Sea to Skye, clutching the toilet seat as instructed to prevent falling off and peed for England! "Well I'm not wiping," Jamie announced, as the flow hesitated then stopped, "Is she done?"

"I'm done."

Angus pulled and folded a long strip of paper, "Here ye are". Turning away again as Kitty smiled up and took the offered paper. Wiping with difficulty but by ping ponging off the walls she succeeded and dropped the paper down the bowl.

"Oh I can't let go of the walls," came a small voice.

"Me again is it?" Jamie asked.

"Well you got them down."

Jamie didn't know if fumbling and not looking would be more inappropriate than just looking and doing the task quickly and efficiently. Kitty eyes were closed and Jamie guessed she would remember very little of this in the morning anyway. He reached for Kitty knickers; silky blue with lace edges and pink rosebuds. It surprised him that such a practically dressed woman would have such pretty underwear, he didn't expect this. What he really didn't expect was that he would even be thinking this! Mortified then that he was looking at and considering a strange women's knickers, he quickly hoisted up and fastened her jeans. Jamie reached over and pulled the chain and flicked off the light in case Angus could see the blush Jamie could now feel on his cheeks.

Kitty looked up as she walked back to Pimples and tried hard to make out Jamie's face. His dark ginger hair blew across it and when he looked down at her the breeze from the sea pulled it back.

"Do you like me?" she blinked up at him.

"Aye... I suppose I do."

Kitty hummed and let her head fall back, trusting implicitly as her Scots guard marched her back to the van. Once they had hauled her in the three circled, and Angus pulled back the quilt and Kitty was lowered into her bed.

"Well, should we take off her coat at least?" Jamie stood hunched in the doorway. Angus grinned up at him, "Suppose so – you do it you've already had her knickers off!"

"Shut your head!" Jamie swiped for his friend's dark head, Kitty snored gently.

9

The Hangover

Kitty was aware of three things simultaneously: a), her mouth was so dry her tongue appeared to be stuck to the roof of it. b), Something was making a noise – knock! c), Her head felt like it was going to explode –knock – KNOCK!

"Urr" was the only response her tongue would allow.

"Are you there? Lassie are you ok?" It was Jocks gruff voice. "Joan won't leave me rest unless I know ye made it home safe."

Kitty attempted to stand and grabbed her head in both hands to keep it in place. Pulling back the curtain Jocks face pressed against the window, nose askew made Kitty jump. Clutching tighter still as her brain rattled and bounced inside her skull.

Jock looked away quickly and only then did Kitty glance down to realise she was standing inches from the post man in nothing but a pretty matching set of pale blue bra and knickers ensemble.

"Shit!"

"Aye, aye well at least you're ok" Jock looked at his feet.

"Um, yes, yes, thank you Jock… did you and Joan get me home?" a new level of mortification crept up on Kathleen Harris – had the postman undressed her and put her to bed?

"No, NO!" with added emphasis "No lass that would be Angus and Jamie, glad to see they got ye home." Jock risked a glance up and was relieved to see Kitty had gathered the curtain around her showing only her face.

The thought of Jock and Joan settling her in bed had been bad enough but at least there was Joan! Joan a woman, Joan a mother, but no Joan… NO JOAN!

"Angus and Jamie?" her voice climbed and squeaked at the end.

"Aye they're good lads."

"Oh... oh," shakily now.

"Well I'll leave ye to, um, get dressed."

Mutual embarrassment made for a quick departure, and Kitty lay on her bed and covered her head with the quilt.

"Shit... shit… shit… SHIT!"

Running her hands over her body now, bra on, knickers on, rubbing her feet together – no socks. Rubbing her eyes with the heels of her hands Kitty tried desperately to remember the events of last night. Wrapped in the cocoon of her quilt Kitty started at the beginning. Walk to the pub – check, she remembered the nervousness she felt. Sat at the bar – check, Lilly the bar maid, nice girl, and the meal and Ale. "Oh the Ale" Kitty head pounded at the memory.

Jock and Joan – check, Joan thought she was a simpleton and Jock, well Jock had seen her in her underwear, "Shit and trice shit!"

But what then, she closed her eyes and worked her way around the bar. The youngsters, the older men, the band. "Blue eyes." Memories were returning, fuzzy and patchy. Yes, Lilly leaving the pub, chairs upturned on tables, Lilly with a black leather jacket on. Friendly voices whilst she slouched on the bar and, and... "Oh yes, Angus... Angus of the blue eyes."

And there was the music, upbeat, the stuff to dance a reel to but mostly haunting and beautiful. Out of any order the images returned to the shrivelled brain of hers, the man on the pipes – pipes called "U...Un..." no it was no good that was too much information, Alistair she wondered, was that his name? The one on the guitar with the sweet voice and the unruly blonde hair "Murr... Murdock – no – Murder – no!" Attempting to roll her R's she failed in the task too, due to her claggy tongue. On the fiddle with dark almost black hair, "Dave... Davey?" Giving up on remembering anything else she focused on the two men nearer her, one had chatted to her, the one with the blue eyes – so that was Angus. The other, the one that didn't like her – so that was Jamie. "Oh SHIT, they got me home!"

Trying to calm jangling nerves Kitty hummed a particular song from last night. Over the Sea to Skye, Kitty had sung at junior school and she had always loved it then, and loved it more so last night played on the pipes. It was haunting and sad but resonated and floated on the air of the land it was written for.

Calmed now, pulse slowed to a reasonable pace, Kitty regulated her breathing and soon became aware of other physical needs that urgently needed to be met, a drink and a wee. Peeking out from the quilt Kitty could see her clothes, jeans, sweat shirt, T-shirt and socks. Roughly folded but she had been very drunk. Sitting now she slowly leant forward to take the socks frowning as the pain in her temples amplified. Yesterday's socks were flat with just the top couple of inches folded back over them, Kitty had never done this to socks in her life, "Holy mother of god!" Kitty face paled and a wave of nausea started deep in her stomach and threatened to rage up her throat, swallowing "Oh my."

Kitty eyes darted around the van, everything seemed in place, iPod, phone, keys – KEYS – where were her keys. Kitty stumbled as she stood to hurriedly dress, "Why don't I remember?" Suddenly another thought occurred, if she didn't remember being undressed, what else did she not remember.

Her hands touched first her face, soft and smooth, lips dry but uninjured. Running her hands over her breasts and around her buttocks and resting on the front of her knickers. She was sure there would be some evidence if she had, if they had! "Oh bloody hell!" She trembled now as pulled on her jeans, reassured slightly to find the keys in her pocket.

Half falling, half jogging Kitty made her way to Tide's. Rounding the back corner she could see the toilet door ajar. Although there was no heating in the loo Kitty always kept the door shut and fastened in the futile hope that any heat that could possibly be in there stayed there. Also and equally important so no creatures could take up residence.

Again Kitty tried to explain it away, "You were REALLY pissed." Maybe she hadn't closed it, but then Kitty saw and knew for certain - the seat was up. "I wasn't that drunk." Sitting on the toilet Kitty bolted the door; it was a large rusty bolt of eight inches. She had never felt the need to use it before today. Kitty knew now with crushing certainty that someone – (cringing then at the image of it. Angus or Jamie or both, "Oh shit!") - Had marched her over the grass, helped her to the loo and put her to bed leaving her in her underwear. "Oh Kathleen what did you do?"

Head in hands Kitty sat, desperate to remember. In her minds eye she could recall now, yes, arms around her waist, her's high on big shoulders. The stars, she remembered stars, and seeing how they sparkled and multiplied, and on one side the buffeting dark hair of Angus and on the other the dark ginger of Jamie, Jamie the local who didn't like her. But there in her memory he was smiling, in fact it was all coming into focus and she was remembering. It wasn't in a threatening or abusive way and she stifled the urge to laugh, clearly recalling the gingery head dodging in and out of her scarf tassels and struggling and cursing with her belt. The cold of someone else's hands on her thighs, as she was relieved of her jeans and knickers, Kitty shivered now. The overriding feeling sitting on this toilet last night was one of gratitude and overwhelming relief. Yes, she could see them now, two square backed gentlemen blocking the door and whistling until she had finished.

Pulling the chain, there was only one thing to be done. Once inside her front door, again a first, she locked it. Wishing more than ever that she had sorted out proper curtains Kitty gathered all she needed drank her too hot coffee and left.

The sense of urgency to leave the scene of her humiliation was rising by the minute. Once again safely inside Pimples Kitty tidied away the bed and found her note pad, "Thank goodness." Patting the leather book to her chest she then looked up the notes she had made on the Islands public swimming pools. If Kitty had owned dark glasses she would have worn them now, not to shield her from the weak light but just in case anyone from the pub saw her.

The pool was a twenty five minute drive and Kitty couldn't be sure if she would pass a breathalyzer, one coffee was little reparation for all that beer. It was too late now and she parked up cautiously at the pool car park. Natural indecision saw Kitty dial Amanda's phone number, so pleased to have a signal, only to hang up but try again a few minutes later. There was no answer and Kitty was relieved, she hoped she could order the flashes of memories that were making her blush into a more coherent confession.

Once in the water a very hung-over Kitty floated for many minutes. Remote from the squeals and splashes of the families in the shallows she laid, ears under the water gazing through the high wide windows to bare trees dancing outside. It was all coming back with embarrassing clarity and breaststroke was the answer. Making herself take long slow pulls and a deep breath with each stroke, she could at least avoid hyperventilating. Her instinct was to thrash into front crawl and plough through the families, but she was determined to have some semblance of order and organise the jumble of images bombarding her sobering mind.

Angus had seemed nice, Jamie, although he obviously didn't much like southerners or her for that matter, hadn't seemed like the raping and pillaging type. She should be grateful, two perfect strangers looked after her, helped her to the toilet and undressed her. "Good grief" forgetting the fundamentals of swimming her words were lost as her open mouth disappeared under the water.

Would the gossip of the drunken Sassenach's night have spread this far across the island? The lifeguard in his high chair eyed her suspiciously, "Bloody hell Kitty does he know?" Taking on water again she spluttered and coughed. Of course he doesn't, Kitty reasoned, it was just her erratic swimming that caused attention. "Get a grip" hissing at herself she trod water for a few minutes before regaining her rhythm and swam eight lengths.

Suddenly legs leaden and the dehydration and lack of sleep caught up with her, hauling herself from the water she walked heavily to the showers. Kitty was at least pleased with her new temporary wash facilities. Unlike most public pools these changing rooms had individual cubicles with curtains so Kitty could take off her costume and shower properly. She had never been one of those rare breed of women who strip naked in communal showers – all power to them but not for Kitty.

Soaping her armpits and legs anew horror struck her. Since being single and having a non-existent love life the necessity to shave was no longer there. Glorious abandon resulted in probably six weeks of growth, soft and until today unnoticed. More thankful than she could ever remember she blessed her fair genes at least.

"Note to self – shave you lazy bitch, you know, just in case random Scotsmen undress you," she muttered to herself. She stayed under the hot water until she could get a grip on her erratic breathing again and get the blush to leave her checks.

The shower was most welcome as too was the hair dryer. Feeling exhausted Kitty climbed into Pimples and enjoyed the anonymity of sitting at the back of the council car park. A large growl from deep within reminded her she hadn't eaten, so making a doorstep of a sandwich and a mug of tea Kitty nestled on her bed and redialled Amanda's number.

"Oh great, hi babe, great to hear from you. I've missed your voice, how's it going? How's the house? What have you been up to? Why am I only hearing from you now?"

Kitty didn't interrupt but let her have the vent, it was wonderful to hear her familiar cadence, - eyes closed and she was home, she was safe. As Amanda took breath Kitty replied.

"It's ok, the cottage is lovely, and, well..." Kitty voice was flat despite her best effort to sound cheery and Amanda could hear the sadness loud and clear.

"Right what's happened?" no reply was forthcoming, "Oh Kit, what's happened? What's the matter?" taking a deep breath, "Tell me all about it, start at the beginning"

"Oh Amanda," Kitty weak voice was almost a sob.

"You're scaring me a smidge here babe," trying to keep her voice calm and steady.

"No nothing terrible – well, it's a bit awful."

"From the top, take your time."

Kitty could visualise Amanda sitting straight, hands slapped on thighs ready for a serious conversation, serious listening pose.

"Well everything up until yesterday evening had been good, really good – well lovely really."

"And last night?"

Kitty shook her head, wiped away the traitor tears, swore and cobbled together all the coherent and vague memories of last night. Amanda didn't interrupt and her friend was pleased for it. Kitty finally told her about exposing herself to the postman and there was silence.

"So let me get this straight" Amanda took a long breath, "Two handsome?"

"Yes I suppose."

"Our age?"

"Ish, maybe a bit younger."

"Good, good, spent the evening talking to you at the bar?"

"Uh huh."

"You get rat-faced on too much local ale?"

"Um."

"They see you safely home?"

"Yeees…but – didn't you hear?" desperation evident now in Kitty shaking voice. "They walked me to the toilet and, and…" whispering now though there was no one to hear. "Took down me knickers and jeans and …" sob "And pulled them back up."

"I see, so the other alternative could be, lets think; a), they left you by the van to piss your pants or bed, or b), you walked your self home and fell and cracked your daft head open and O, lets say died!"

Silence followed, Amanda waited for logic to prevail.

"Weeell, if you put it like that." Kitty sniffed.

"Exactly, and did they molest you in the toilet or the van?"

"No they turned their backs, I think" cringing now "I think I was… singing." Despite herself Kitty joined Amanda in a long uncontrolled laugh.

"So to the undressing in the van?"

"Yes" Kitty mumbled in renewed mortification.

"What underwear did you have on?"

"What, ON EARTH, does that have to do with anything?"

"Well if it's your favourite holey grey ones and mismatched bra then you have a right to be embarrassed. Hell I wouldn't ever go back to the pub again!"

"You're not taking this seriously and, and I had some of my new Marks and Spencer's stuff on."

"Well that's good, are we talking M&S dull, pretty and practical or lacy 'hello boy' undies?"

"Blue silky and lace with rose buds if you must know!"

"Well, what the hell are you worried about? I think you should be proud of yourself, HELL I am!" Amanda sounding every inch the teacher she was, continued.

"Like my mum always says – always wear underwear you are proud of, you never know when you might be hit by a bus - or come to that get undressed by strange kilted men!"

"She says no such thing – you lying bitch!"

Amanda was relieved now as she could visualise the smile on her friends face.

"Now I grant you if they were stone cold sober and took pictures for Facebook there could be some residual humiliation."

"Thanks, really helpful."

"But it sounds like they'd had a few."

"I think so but one of them was driving so not so much, the only truly sober one was Lilly the barmaid."

"Well there you are, get yourself back to the pub when it opens and see what her take on it is."

"I think I might just drive back to Kent and have done with it."

"No you don't lady! Not till you've written that best seller."

Talking to Amanda had been just the tonic she required, and Kitty drove home feeling better about her prospects. Singing along to the CD she swung down her drive and skidded, applying the brakes too hard on the gravel slope. A green Landrover sat where Pimples usually resided. Letting the engine idle in a moment of indecision, she finally pulled on the hand brake and cut the engine.

The instinct to turn and run was forced away, this was her drive and she had to face whomsoever the visitor was. Desperately trying to rationalise – it could be Jock – it could be the doctors – even the builder or architect come early. With this happy prospect Kitty hopped out onto the gravel.

No one was in the green car, and looking along to Tide's Reach no one was on the path or at the front door. Kitty was happier by the second; maybe people were so used to the house being empty that they parked here to access the beach. That was it, she was confident now, problem solved, no worries.

As the house neared Kitty was enjoying deep breaths and looking forward to shutting her self away in the kitchen. Flashes of black caught her attention above the low wall between the beach and the front lawn, and unsure what she was seeing, Kitty slowed her pace. Making her jump, the cause was soon evident as a pretty spotted spaniel leap the wall. Shaking vigorously Kitty took a few quick steps back. Coming forward head down, Kitty bent and stroked the damp neck and laughed as the whole back half wagged enthusiastically.

"Pip! Pip!" A sharp male voice followed by a whistle saw Pip fly back over the wall onto the shingle below and was gone as quickly as she had arrived. The lowered head of the owner could be seen coming over the headland past her derelict croft. Kitty didn't stay to look closely and turned and was safely in her hall, door locked behind her.

Kitty had just put the kettle on when there were two loud raps on the front door nearly making her drop the milk. Cautiously Kitty looked out of the front kitchen window but even on tiptoes she could only make out Pip. Sitting, with tail still wagging the dog was looking adoringly at who ever had knocked her door.

Taking a huge breath and running her fingers through her hair, (which, by the way she thought, loved this water), Kitty was annoyed with herself for being intimidated by a visitor but the horror of last night was seeping back. Really wishing she had a peephole or window at the front door, it took a lot of courage and two more deep breaths to open it. As she did the man removed his hat and the windswept vision of Angus was before her.

"Oh... hi, hello," the blush shot up Kitty face.

"Morning ta ye – or should that be afternoon?" in response to the vacant expression on her face, "Kitty isn't it, from the pub last night... do you remember me?"

Kitty stepped back, more in shock but to Angus it was tantamount to an invitation. "Stay Pip, good girl" and with that he was in and closing the door behind himself.

Kitty struggled to think for what seemed like minutes and Angus smiled at her.

"Ur, um, did you, would you like some tea? The kettle's just boiled."

"Eye that would be grand."

"What the hell are you doing?" Kitty screamed to herself, but led Angus into the kitchen. She tried to calm herself whilst making the drinks.

"You're alright then, not too much of a hangover?" Kitty knew there was nothing for it; she would have to answer, to speak to this man. Asked him to sit, placed his tea down and stood straight.

"Just tell me. Did you have to take me to the loo, undress me and put me to bed?" she was hoping to go for calm and self assured but quite certain that he heard panicked and embarrassed. When she had plucked up the courage to look at him he was smiling and resting his mug down.

"Well that would be yes... and yes."

"Bloody hell." Kitty turned and lent on the windowsill.

"It's ok," Angus sounded worried, "Are you offended, or something? We, we didn't do anything – you know - inappropriate." He cleared his throat and was now feeling as uncomfortable as Kitty.

"No, well, thank you I suppose," quietly now, "I'm just a bit, well, mortified." Kitty could feel the sting of tears and cursed them for betraying her.

"Look, Jamie and I, well, it was'ne anything we'd not do for each other."

"Yes, but…you are friends and…you're blokes."

"Oh that doesn't matter, we didn't see anything." Angus renewed his blush as he remembered her creamy skin and that pretty underwear. "I've done it for me girlfriend afore now." Kitty was comforted – Angus had a girlfriend, he was just being chivalrous. "Look now, we'll say na more about it. Only Jamie and I know and we're not about to gossip and sully your reputation. If you make a habit of it mind, we'll not be responsible."

Kitty forced herself to turn now and look at him and they shared an equally red-faced smile and giggle.

"Biscuit?"

"Aye, that'll be grand."

Glad to have that over with she felt she could now face the locals without fear of recrimination, only the other witness to her shame to face.

"Jamie's ok is he? I remember he didn't like me, I don't suppose I have done much to help English girls rise in his estimation?"

"Ock he's brilliant, don't you worry about Jamie, he's a rare one and no tattletale."

With the worst of the awkwardness gone, Kitty sat, and to both their relief, they discussed the plans for the house and sipped their tea with no further reference to last night. Angus bid farewell with a promise, "A solemn promise now, mind!" that she would join them all Friday night for a game of darts and a few drinks.

"Remember Kitty Harris, if ye think about not coming we know where ya live and we will come and get ye." Said in jest but with an edge of menace, Kitty knew she would be playing darts willingly or not.

Kitty was due at the doctor's house this evening in a little over four hours and the emotions of the day and the swim had taken their toll. Locking the door behind her a weary, slumping Kitty retreated to Pimples, found an old favourite and snuggled under a blanket and watched the gorgeous Cary Grant in "Mr Blanding's Builds His Dream House." This film had been a rainy Sunday tradition for her family and was probably, being so deeply ingrained in her psyche, one of the reasons that in her darkest days Kitty decided to buy a wreck. Drifting delightfully, Kitty too dreamed of a completed project, exuberant flowerbeds, even a Great Dane but thankfully drew the line at the pipe.

10

The Builders Cometh

The prospect of having supper with your GP, if Kitty thought about it, was quite a bizarre concept. Doctors had friends – of course but Kitty assumed they too were doctors. Thinking about it now Kitty worked back through her previous GP's and would never imagine socialising with them. But Claire and Hamish seemed very unaffected and, well, normal.

Deciding casual would be acceptable, it took a few minutes of preparation and she was on the road. The instructions were simple, pass the surgery, five minutes further along the road and turn at the white painted boulders. The surgery passed, Kitty began to doubt she had gone the wrong way, and was contemplating turning, when the small bright landmarks came into view.

She turned into the drive, which swept back on itself and down hill, thankfully more gently than Tide's. A large gravel parking area sat to the side of an imposing white house facing the sea. Unlike her croft there were neat lawns, perfectly positioned tables and chairs and even a weather beaten rowing boat staging the scene beautifully. The back was the original house but there was a large glass and slate extension wrapping around the front and both ends, and from a door here Hamish waved a welcome.

"Come in, come in." Hamish took her coat and guided her through a very well equipped boot room into the impressive family room. Forming part of the new extension a wall of glass maximised the view that could be enjoyed from the lounge area and the very large old refectory table. The back of the room was lined in muted green kitchen units and the cream Aga that Kitty guessed was responsible for the wonderful smells.

"Claire is just getting the little ones settled, please, please have a seat. Glass of wine?" Hamish was all easy smiles and as suspected no pretence, gliding silently in well-loved sheepskin slippers splitting at the seams. Directing her to an equally well-loved leather sofa, perching on the edge Kitty felt like a small child – her feet swinging. "Oh no, no, no."

"The lady doth protest too much" - Hamish thought and maybe they had got themselves a teetotaler?

"Just a soft one please, with no street lights and those bends I'll need my wits about me later."

"Oh ok – tea or coffee then?"

"Just some water please... I was – well I was at the pub last night and... Well enjoyed a drop too much local beer."

Sheepishly Kitty looked away and renewed her attention to the view, "Ahh!" Hamish exclaimed, "Say no more, we've all done that," and whistling quietly he soon returned with a large glass of water.

"That's a fabulous log burner," the black cube was quivering with the intensity of the red remnants, a shadow of a log and a covering of white ash.

"Yes its Scandinavian, we've been very pleased with it. I'm sure Claire can give you details, she could write a book with all the research she did on this house."

Claire soon joined them and they moved up to the table. Like Angela's home there was a littering of children's paraphernalia but wealth and plentiful space meant it was much less overwhelming.

The meal consisted of a chicken stew, garlic and white wine giving it a definite French flavour. The conversation was dominated by talk of architects and builders. Kitty was delighted to discover the architect she had been corresponding with was a good friend of the Duncans and had worked on their house.

Hamish gave Kitty a tour of the ground floor, and not wanting to risk disturbing the children Hamish and Claire explained the upstairs over coffee. Drawing a rough image of Tide's Reach in the back of a child's colouring book she shared the plans for the build. Hamish apologised as he drew over them with red crayon, and there was much lively discussion between the couple about what essentials Kitty should include. Having no opportunity to test her new GP's medical know how but was sure they would prove invaluable as house restoring buddies.

With plates tidied and drawings of the house put away, the trio adjourned to the sofa and watched as the light faded and was replaced by a pink streaked sunset, while the burner quietly ate its way through a small Silver Birch.

"So are you married?" Claire interrupted the silence without taking her gaze from the window.

"Claire really!" Hamish admonished his wife.

"What? It's a reasonable question, you don't mind Kathleen do you?" looking sideways then at Kitty. Obviously to the doctors she was Kathleen, and after twice trying to get them to call her Kitty she admitted defeat.

"No… no I'm on my own."

Claire had wanted to probe further but saw the look her husband had thrown at her. She would like a better explanation, after all Kathleen wore a wedding ring but it could wait – she had time. Hamish could imagine just what Claire was thinking. Since they had met at medical school she had made it her mission to match make many of their mutual friends. Pickings were slim on the Island and Hamish saw that gleam in her eyes as she was telling the new comer about their friend – her architect Donald. He'd have words with his wife when their visitor had left.

It was a very civilised evening and Kitty felt eminently relaxed. She almost told them about her humiliations of yesterday evening but thought they may think less of her for it.

"I enjoyed the Celtic group last night," safe enough Kitty thought.

"Oh yes, they are good aren't they, and all local boys. We'd have come to see them but its tricky getting sitters" Claire sighed.

"I looked after Angela and Gavin's children Tuesday night."

"Oh yes we know them, the post office." Hamish nodded blandly but Claire sat up "Yes, goodness! They didn't waste any time did they. You had only been here a couple of days hadn't you?" not waiting for a reply "Just shows you how desperate we all are to get out."

"Claire!" Hamish reprimanded his wife for the second time.

"Oh! God, sorry Kathleen, yes that did sound terrible, I am sorry – not that they must be desperate to ask you – sorry!"

"There are no flies on Angela," Kitty smiled, "They said they needed a baby sitter and there was an offer of…. well, a bath." Kitty was embarrassed just saying it but soon relieved when husband and wife roared with laughter.

"Oh good god, Hamish do you remember this place before we got the bathroom?"

"Yes, yes oh the swimming pool! I don't think we've been back there since the plumbing was sorted. We really should take the children but we were so pleased not to have to go again."

"Kathleen, use the end shower cubicle it's larger and if it hasn't been altered the pressure is better in that one."

Relieved at the shared experience the evening rounded off nicely with Kitty excusing herself at just before ten not wanting to outstay her welcome. "Thank you so much Claire, Hamish it's been lovely. Every one has been so friendly and welcoming."

"Our pleasure, drive safe Kathleen." Hamish bent and kissed her on the cheek.

"It's been a lovely evening... I don't work Mondays, would it be too cheeky if I pop over and have a look at the croft? I know you have Donald and the Stewarts going so don't worry if not." Claire glanced at her husband, had she been too pushy?

"Oh no I'd love it, and you know Donald so it would be really nice if you could be there. I'd appreciate your input."

"Careful what you wish for Kathleen." Claire jabbed her husband in the ribs for that comment.

Kitty waved over her shoulder, striding with envy over the slate gravel path – add that to the list she thought. Hamish rested his hands on his wife's shoulders as they saw Kitty get in her van. It was lovely to welcome a new patient who undoubtedly was to become a good friend, whispering in her ear, "Let the girl move in before you have Donald and her married."

Claire just smiled.

As she hugged her hot chocolate in bed she thought back over the week, was it really only six days since she left Kent? It felt like a lifetime ago and she could safely put one worry to bed. Any fears she may have had at missing her life in Kent had come to naught. She felt at home here and she wished for nothing she had left behind. Humming a tune from last night that had drifted into her mind she decided she must get a CD – if they had made one of course!

Tomorrow's plan was predominantly finding more provisions and as "Over the Sea to Skye" swam around her head her thoughts drifted to her derelict croft. She decided she would endeavour to find the heritage centre to buy Celtic music and books full of history.

Kitty was relishing a day with no commitments and enjoyed a leisurely breakfast. Donning her walking boots and today estimating that the tide was on the retreat, she would walk again to her boundary and hopefully further. The air was colder and she was glad of the scarf she had thought to wear, fastening her coat over it. Walking into the wind, and leaving her home she rounded the waters edge, again struck by the shelter the derelict croft enjoyed. Sitting once more on the fallen stone in its doorway Kitty was determined to restore this building sympathetically and with respect, it didn't need water, it didn't even need electricity. A roof, a floor, windows and a door, here she could write she was sure of that.

It's position further round the headland, tucked behind the large rocks meant the road and houses visible from Tide's were hidden here. Sitting huddled on the stone the view must have remained unchanged since the first stone was laid, and this little house intrigued her more every time she visited.

Standing and thrusting her hands in her fleecy pockets a shiver ran up Kitty's spine. Heading further around the beach she hoped she would warm up now she was on the move. Venturing along the waters edge her boots coped well with the gravel and shells and stayed dry despite the odd puddle. The bank continued steeply up to the right, thick with bronze ferns and struggling trees looking impenetrable.

Straight ahead the undulations levelled and Kitty could now see far into the distance. Smiling broadly her eyes danced between a bright stretch of white sand, and beyond this an outcrop of rocks topped by a small white and red striped light house. With renewed vigour Kitty pushed on, the white beach grew as she neared and Kitty skipped onto its edge. Anticipating the soft slide of sand she pulled up as the ground beneath was firm and crisp. Bending to inspect it the sand it was in fact crushed bleached shells and maybe coral, infinitely more interesting than sand and Kitty was anything but disappointed.

Looking now to the lighthouse and the open water beyond, it was markedly rougher and darker. Small peeks of white against the brown grey, it was hard to believe it was the same sea as her tranquil inlet. Arms stretched back, Kitty took a few deep breaths, it really was the ideal place for a dog. Kitty had never considering owning a dog before in her life, but whether it was the scenery or the seed of an idea set by Angela she would now give the option serious thought.

On her way back Kitty stopped again at the croft – this time examining the slipway. She could still not determine if it was man-made or natural, but the gentle gradient of the slope protected by high rocks on both sides was a wonderful mooring for a small boat. Knowing as much about sailing as she did about dog ownership it seemed unlikely she would ever test this theory.

Once the builders had finished the house Kitty promised herself, and this forgotten shell to make it once again a serviceable building, a studio, yes that was it, a studio to paint and write. Like Annie's wall, it would be her legacy, without time scale or any great plans she looked forward to working on it. Cold now seemed to eat through her layers and she skipped quickly back to Tide's.

Indoors she watched the now returning tide cover the seaweed, and again raise the listing small sailboat to bob. Not for the first time she thanked her luck at buying blind and being blessed with this sheltered haven when she could have been facing the North Sea.

Tomorrow she must ensure Donald understands the necessity for maximum windows to enjoy this vista. The sills as they stood meant only by resting her elbows on them when standing could she drink in all the view. Kitty looked forward to the day when she could sit, feet tucked up in her soft leather chair and see the entire picture. She was very glad to have visited the Duncan's yesterday, not only did it give her a glimpse of what could be, but also the reassurance that her house was in good hands with their shared architect.

For the first time since her arrival she sorted through the boxes and found her favourite fountain pen and the new book Stephen had given her their last Christmas together. "It's as good a time as any!"

Dragging the small table and one of the chairs to the window Kitty stroked a flat hand over the cover of the A4 black leather bound book resting for many seconds on the inscription *Kathleen's book – a work of genius.*

Stephen had a knack of finding quirky, personalised presents and Kitty loved it. But well aware of the pressure, not until today had she had the courage to start. Having cooled after the exertion of the walk, Kitty fastened her fleece and thought hopefully that the builder could give her the go ahead to have a fire tomorrow.

 She wrote easily as it turned out. It had been a good couple of hours and her fingers were numb around the pen, rubbing them on her thighs and tapping her icy feet despite still being encased in her walking boots. "Ahhhh!" leaning back with a gratifying clunk from her upper back she stretched and yawned. Closing the book and tracing the words that meant so much, Kitty had reached one milestone and buried one ghost. She could write, and she would write, here.

Enjoying a swift lunch and a much-needed mug of tea, Kitty hoped the heritage centre would be open as she was hungry now for some history of her little plot of Skye. Opening the brochure on the passenger seat it looked a reasonably straightforward drive, and without further ado Kitty and her trusty transporter were on the road once more.

Last nights pleasantries and the fresh air of her walk had forced memories of Friday night to the back recesses of her mind. A carefree Kitty turned off the engine and alighted in a virtually empty car park. The heritage centre was situated high on a bleak road with far reaching views of mountains and the distant sea. Two large crofter's cottages with turf roofs held in the traditional way with round boulders acted as anchors. Hunkered to the ground the walls splayed and low, they had been built to withstand the worst that the weather could throw. Kitty didn't doubt they had been well tested over the years at such an exposed site. Standing resilient they were rooted to the ground – immovable objects.

There were two other cars in the car park, a very dirty Volvo estate, which she presumed belonged to the squabbling family of five stood outside one of the crofts. The other a battered VW Golf sitting in Pimples shadow allowed Kitty the hope that someone may be inside and may be able to help her. Inside the low door the smell of damp paper caught in her throat and Kitty coughed.

"Can I help ye?" A gruff voice came from behind a tall glass cabinet full of pictures and facts about the clearings.

"Oh, yes please" Kitty replied enthusiastically. Looking around the display Kitty caught sight of the mop of red hair, just as its owner looked up and stammered.

"Oh… it's you... the southerner."

Jamie shot back behind the cabinet aware the colour was rising in his neck and would soon cover his face. Neither party wanted to face the other and a very awkward silence followed.

Jamie was the first to act and without looking directly at her he sought refuge behind the small counter – Why? Why was it that the sight of her had affected him so much and why, oh why could he only now think of her laying on her quilt with the rose buds on her lacy blue knickers?

Kitty on the other hand, picked over the booklets on the counter unable to look in the face of the young man who had taken down her knickers! One of them had to speak and in the end it was Kitty. "Angus came to my house yesterday," coughing nervously now risking a glance at his hands. Hands that clenched, she looked at the skin tensed over large flexing knuckles. Kitty liked the fluff of red hair over the mottled mass of freckles and was trying to imagine those large fingers undressing her. But this wasn't helping and she returned her attention to the leaflets.

"Aye," Jamie attempted a glance but quickly was examining the counter edge again. Kitty was worried now, had they discussed her, he didn't seem surprised at Angus's visit.

"And, well… it seems I owe you… a thank you?" Kitty herself didn't sound too convincing.

"It was nothing" still completely unable to look at the pretty blonde before him.

"Well thank you... but I must say... I don't usually behave like that. I mean, I don't usually get drunk, let alone require strangers to put me to bed. Yep, yes that's a first! Never EVER have done that!" Gripping the edge of the counter Kitty now looked at her feet. Her face burned and every fibre screamed for her to run, but she had gone this far she would have to wait for a reply.

"Aye... Well. If it's any consolation it was a first for me too."

Smirking now Kitty risked a look to see the corner of his mouth lift, and they both laughed quietly as their eyes met. Seeing the colour in her checks Jamie added, "At least you've met everyone." Dropping his voice with a conspiratorial look around "Angus and I really wouldn't say a word to anyone – our secret."

The worse was over now Kitty told herself and was eager to leave it behind her, changing the subject to both their obvious relief.

"Well I came here to find out more about my house, I didn't know you worked here or I never would have come."

"Oh" Jamie sounded hurt; looking square onto his face Kitty was quick to add.

"No I didn't mean that! I mean, oh I just meant I would have been too embarrassed."

"It's a small island Kathleen, it would have happened eventually. It's done now and we needn't avoid each other."

"Yes, yes you're quite right. You can call me Kitty."

"Really? Kathleen is such a nice name. I am Jamie, James Stewart."

Kitty was unable to respond to this as the receding blush had returned. His voice was intoxicating, and the way he said her name raised the hairs on the back of her neck. With a voice like that he could call her anything.

"Well, um, as I was saying Jamie, it's about my house." Jamie smiled and unleashed a row of white teeth and hiding in the rust coloured stubble a large dimple in his right cheek. Throwing her off again Kitty coughed and looked once more at the counter.

"Um... yes well, I was wondering if you had any information on the property?" In her swing now she could look back into his face. "And, and there is a derelict little cottage - croft on the land and I wanted to know the history of it."

Thankfully free from the worst of the embarrassment Jamie led her around the museum. Walking behind him Kitty found she was looking at the woollen, dusty green jumper and as she started imagining the broad shoulders underneath she looked quickly away. Catching her eye was the swirl of tartan above his knees causing her mouth to gape. Hanging heavily to the knee, Kitty was glad he walked away from her enabling her to peer closely at the red hairs above the long socks and sturdy walking boots.

Her eyes travelled up – having never seen a man in a skirt, or Kilt come to that - Kitty again could feel the flush upon her as she realised she could see each buttock moving under the thick wool. Did they really not wear underwear? She stopped herself looking for visible panty lines with a silent, "Get a grip!"

Throughout his explanations of a brief history of Skye Kitty struggled to get her mind from those shoulders, those legs and what did or didn't lurk beneath that kilt. Trying to suppress a giggle Kitty reprimanded herself for the thought, (Fair's, fair, he's seen my undies, surely just a peek.) and tried very hard to concentrate on all things historic. The clearings obviously disturbed him and Kitty noticed the clench of his jaw and furrowed brow as he told her the horrific facts. Moving to lighter territory she learnt about the clans of the island and Lairds and how the island was divided.

Arms laden with books and maps Kitty paid for her purchases. She was relieved to have dispensed with the awkwardness and now very happy to have met this young man today. He was right of course, it would have happened one day, better now than later. Now she was here, with this man, she was in no rush to leave.

"I have the architect coming tomorrow to go over the plans for the place."

Jamie asked about her plans for the house, "Tearing the old croft down are ye? All modern stainless steel and glass."

"God no!" horror plain in her voice, "More white wash and slate" Jamie smiled at her response. "Although call me old fashioned I would like a bathroom, a bed and maybe an inside loo!"

"AYE, aye that toilet is a mite breezy" immediately their mirrored blushes returned along with a strained silence. Jamie cleared his throat and made the first move.

"What... who have you got doing the work?"

"Donald McDonald is the architect and Stewart and Sons are the builders."

After an initial frown Jamie laughed, a very relaxed deep, rich laugh. It had quite an effect on her, and Kitty became acutely aware of her hot palms and the thought required to swallow and breathe. Kitty was confused and a little concerned. "Oh dear is there something I should know?"

"Aye, aye," folding his large arms across his chest "Malcolm Stewart is my uncle and Jeff and John would be my cousins."

"Well, small world." Kitty had to force herself to stop looking at the large arms, the muscles defined clearly through the jumper.

"Aye, even smaller island," Jamie raised an eyebrow and flaunted his dimple, "Well you may see me again, I help out sometimes especially if it's a sympathetic build."

Kitty once again found herself imagining the thick arms and broad shoulders making light work of manual labour, shared too by the memory of those arms holding her up and half carrying her across her lawn. Dear God! When would it stop? Kitty shook her head, trying to rid the images now crystal clear in her mind. Unaware of Kitty's remembrances, Jamie's mind too flashed to the night and the smell of the knot of blonde hair resting against his chest – roses, he thought.

"Oh, well I might see you then."

"Aye."

And yet again, was there to be no escape from this uncomfortable cringe-making silence for both of them. Jamie stepped up yet again, "Aye and Angus said you were up for darts Friday." He hoped maybe on their next meeting with others there it could put an end to what ever this palpable atmosphere was between them. Jamie couldn't understand or explain it.

"Yes, but I might stick to tea or coffee."

They both laughed, and thanking Jamie for the books and his knowledge, Kitty put away her purse and smiled until outside the museum door. Closing the heavy latch Kitty leant back on the ancient door, and wrapping her arms around her waist she waited until deep breaths had eased the pounding in her chest. "Good grief!" she hissed, and a little shakily clambered up into Pimples.

"Wow" was all Jamie had to say as he stood holding the counter and shaking his head, trying to rid the image of blue lace and rose buds yet again. Making himself a coffee, Jamie spent many minutes thinking about this newcomer with such a strange effect on him. What was the history of Kathleen Harris? She wore a wedding ring with no mention of a husband. What work did she do or was she independently wealthy? Was there a rich husband waiting for her in London or wherever it was she hailed from. There was nothing for it but try and forget about her, (who was she? – No one to him), till Friday anyway. Jamie suspected forgetting her was going to be easier said than done.

Taking a blanket from Pimples, Kitty carried a tin of soup, half a loaf of crusty bread and her museum purchases along with a bottle of wine to her house. Trying to save energy in Pimples she was going to spend the evening in her kitchen. Once the soup was warmed Kitty left the glowing ring turned on and opened the oven door and turned it to its maximum, "Sod the expense." Having the desired effect, aided by a belly full of hot soup the chill was gone. It was however replaced by an acrid smell of burning ancient food that lined the oven. Closing the door, the cooker was turned off and Kitty wrapped the blanket snugly around her.

The woollen blanket in tones of pale blue and fawn looked very at home here with the distressed walls, and Kitty decided this would be the colour pallet for the interior. Sated with far too much bread and the warm spicy red wine as company, Kitty began the exploration of the books she had bought.

There were photographs of early Highlanders standing hard and resolute outside their crofts, layer upon layer of wool and tartan. The men were in kilts with large beards and furrowed brows. The women in long dresses exposing lace up boots and the shadow of ingrained mud on their hems. Suffering and cold etched on the lined faces with not a hint of a smile. Did they smile? Could they laugh? What toll did real hardship and deprivation take? Kitty's saddened heart hoped there had, in its history, been laughter in this house. Love, laughter and joy were essential and free commodities to everyone, but looking back into these long forgotten faces Kitty feared there had been precious little of any of them.

Reading on she got a sense of the deprivation in terms of cold, living conditions and hard work to eke out an existence here. Add to this the tyrannical landowners and invading English. If the elements and famine didn't get you the English would! No wonder deep ingrained distrust and hatred still called these proud people to pull away, fuelling the fight for independence even in the 21st Century. In such barren places little had changed since the clearings and memories were long and self-perpetuating.

A small booklet on the specific history of her lower corner of Skye informed her that the current Laird was a Stewart – like Jamie! Not for the first time Kitty had to try to push thoughts of this particular rugged young man from her mind.

The warmth of the pink light coming through the front window was rising up the wall and a suddenly weary Kitty rubbed hers eyes. Stretching tall and letting the blanket fall to the chair, she turned off the light and locking the door behind her, Kitty Harris, proud land owner, bid her home good night.

The reality of having a tiny house with no carpets and only the barest of furniture wasn't lost on Kitty. Her usual habit of fluffing cushions and tidying in anticipation of visitors was now redundant. Planning for tomorrow, the only thing to be done would be refreshing the primroses on the table and windowsill. Smiling on the walk back to Pimples she was well aware the builder and Donald wouldn't notice – but Claire might.

Before turning off the battery operated lamp by her bed Kitty pulled out the annotated picture Hamish and herself had created and added a list of things she wanted to discuss tomorrow.

That night Kitty's dreams were vivid and drawn out. A strange mix of modern day building site with Jamie, and occasionally Angus, sporting huge beards and period kilts. Shirtless and glistening from exertion, blustery winds caused tantalising glimpses of thigh. Frustratingly there was no answer to the age-old question of what a Scotsman wears under his kilt.

In her dream she was desperate to use the toilet, opening the toilet door a frowning formidable Jamie glared back at her. She even, in desperation scurried around the headline and thought she would squat in the little croft but they had erected scaffolding and looked down on her. Like the ancient men in the photo's they did not speak but frowned and looked ferocious.

When she awoke her hair was damp at the roots and she wiped the line of sweat from her cleavage with her pyjama top. Kicking free from the tangle of bedding, embarrassed by her own dreams Kitty had never felt the need for a shower more. It was only seven thirty so ensuring the curtains were drawn tight she washed away the dreams of last night and ate a hearty breakfast.

Once inside Tide's Kitty collected her buildings folder from the purple box. All the correspondence with Donald, including the beautiful first draft drawings Kitty had spent many hours recently dreaming of. Laid out in orderly fashion on the kitchen table Kitty was ready – bring it on.

For the second time this week the necessity for a window with a view of the drive was apparent and a high priority. Trying to wait patiently inside lasted nearly ten minutes. Increasingly frustrated at the lack of view, Kitty fastened her fleece and opted to pace in the garden and wait for arrivals.

The first to arrive was a large flatbed truck, bouncing down the drive and settling in a cloud of dust. Two heavy men slid from the cab. Kitty had waited for this moment, so much hung in the balance. Smiles returned, they loomed even larger as they approached. Thinking then of Annie, would she approve? Would she even have been envious? She found herself, she knew not why, retreating, stopping, braced as near the gable wall of the house as the bracken and grass would allow Kitty's finger tips felt for the cold wall.

Had her days getting to know Tide's been a mistake, albeit squatting more than living. She would not have believed she could have formed such an attachment in such a short time. Kitty wondered if her emotions would have been better served by staying away until the work was done. The older of the men, greying blonde hair and beard, strode ever nearer, hand outstretched. The Calvary? Or the enemy? Kitty rested her back on the cold damp stone. If she was to be its' saviour she must let this man in, and watch helplessly as he would inevitably begin dismantling Tide's Reach before it could begin to be renovated.

She minutely stroked the wall before stepping forward and shaking the plate-like hand. Malcolm introduced his son John and spoke with a deep soft voice. Kitty wondered if she would ever tire of hearing this wonderful accent. Whilst waiting for Donald they moved to the front wall overlooking the bay. Nervous excitement was making Kitty chatty, "I met your nephew at the heritage centre yesterday, he said you were related"

"Aye he's my nephew, and this here his cousin" nodding at John.

"Yes, he helps us out some time so you might see him here; he's a softie for a renovation project."

"Now are you sure lassie? Before the pen pusher gets here. Look at that new one over there, we could knock this down and start again." John winked at her as he pointed across the bay.

"Oh NO!" she realised she had almost shouted the answer. "No, no I love it, its charm and simplicity" Kitty felt a little panicked.

"Ye have been talking to Jamie right enough. He'd have ye living with stone floors an open fire and hair shirts." Jamie's cousin laughed at his father's description. All eyes turned then as a silver Mercedes glinted in the sun. Kitty was surprised but pleased to see Claire sitting next to the man Kitty assumed must be Donald.

"Well the gang's all here" Kitty skipped across the lawn to welcome them. Claire introduced her to Donald who lowered his head and smiled warmly. Once inside Tide's Kitty put the kettle on, and was very pleased she had unpacked six mugs. Drinks in hand the five walked from room to room, outside each aspect was examined. Malcolm and John were armed with a mighty tape measure and notebook, measuring, re-measuring and muttering. The Stewarts excused themselves, "Aye we're happy, good, yes. Donald ye ken where we are, can start pretty much right away, that is if you've a mind to lass?"

"Oh yes, yes sooner the better... that is if you think so Donald?" Looking up at the tall architect, he must have been a good couple of inches over six feet. A very smart yet casual man. Another man could wear that outfit and look scruffy but he possessed the talent of catalogue models to look polished even in the most casual get up. He hadn't said much since his arrival, and when he had it was in slow quiet words with no discernable accent. The silver propelling pencil always in his left hand idly rolled between his fingers. In thought he would tap the end on his chin – he'd make a terrible poker player Kitty guessed, with such an obvious tell.

"Yes, no need to delay," Donald smiled back at his client and gave a curt nod to the builders. Claire loved every thing, had countless ideas – mostly good but some down right ostentatious. Kitty was glad of the input and female companionship and realised as the three discussed windows, finishes, kitchens and bathrooms that Claire would be an invaluable and über-enthusiastic local guide. Claire's chatter was the perfect counterbalance to Donald's brooding silence.

Re-entering the kitchen now, Kitty insisted on her guests having the only two chairs. Willing Claire to hush for a minute, Kitty was pleased when after examining the plans again Donald cleared his throat.

"So… a few areas to consider" waiting as the pencil tap, tap, tapped on his smooth chin. Kitty suspected he used moisturiser to maintain the glistening smoothness. Taking a small leather bound book from his inside pocket he flamboyantly propelled enough lead to write a long list:

1. *Front window – amend height lower sill to 45cms*
2. *Window in Kitchen side elevation to view drive*
3. *Side access to boot room*
4. *Stair case – one return*
5. *Two bedrooms – No en suite??*
6. *Under floor heating throughout*
7. *Log burner make and model?*

"There's little alteration on the originals, I will have these amended in a day or so and then we can get the Stewarts started ASAP."

"Great, is there anything I can do in the mean time?" Kitty minutely clapped her hands.

"Yes you could be looking at these details" pulling a previous email from Kitty's folder "and let me know what finish you want for the windows. They will need to be ordered this week. Also it would be helpful if you decide on bathroom tiles and door furniture and specify flooring throughout." Kitty gulped "Also these flags look good. I wasn't sure until I'd seen them but you could reuse these for the utility, kitchen and hall." Kitty liked the idea of that and at least relieved her of one decision so she nodded keenly.

Claire patted her arm, "I know, it's seems like a lot of things to consider."

"I've listed all the web sites you should need and Claire will be a great help if she's happy to assist." Kitty looked fearfully at Claire who smiled and nodded reassuringly back.

"This isn't Kent I'm afraid, you'll have to go to Inverness if you want show rooms."

"Oh no, no need for that I'm sure."

"No, no need, I can help and you can see what we've used and

John and Irene – retired School teachers from Surrey - well Donald transformed their house and they're only twenty minutes away. Irene would love to meet you and is always happy to show off her home. Oh Kathleen I'm very pleased for you!"

Claire was obviously very excited and Kitty smiled affectionately back at her, she was certain her friendship was to prove more valuable than her medical knowledge.

"Well with some fair weather on our side we should get you in before the worst of the winter", Donald laid down his pencil and drained his mug. Looking at Kitty standing in front of the window with the light shining through the bright shades of blonde of her soft curls. Obviously happy and excited, Donald had not known what to expect from their correspondence but he was pleasantly surprised. He didn't know her story or how old this young woman was but she had a freshness and exuberance that was most captivating.

"Yes as much as I love P – my van I wouldn't want to spend Christmas in h –it."

"Aye not much room for a tree." Donald laughed gently whilst looking at Kitty. Claire looked at them both, her architect friend and her new very promising patient cum friend and could feel the spark of an idea.

"Would it be possible to have one of the rooms ready first? Not completely finished necessarily but so I could use it for storage?"

"Aye seems fair, I will talk to Malcolm. There shouldn't be much to do in the study so we'll endeavour to have that ready first. But remember Kathleen, the outside shed will be the first thing done and that will give you quite a lot of dry storage."

If Claire wouldn't call her Kitty she thought it a safe assumption that neither would Donald, so let it go.

"Thank you so much Donald," Kitty reached out to shake his hand, a moment's delay and he took it in both his and held gently, even his hands were smooth and soft Kitty noticed. There was a short silence, and looking and holding in earnest he replied, "It will be my pleasure Kathleen."

She was going to have to get used to being called Kathleen, until now it implied she had done something wrong but with the accents she realised she wouldn't mind. Gone were the harsh Kathleens of her youth, Ok, bring it on she thought! Claire grinned and rubbed her hands together.

After ordering all the papers, and making the client clear on her allotted homework, Claire and Donald bid her farewell. They left with the promise of a meeting at Donald's office on Thursday, and a grateful acceptance from Kitty for coffee at Claire's the next day to go over samples, and use her computer to search options. Walking with them to the car, the sun was fast being chased down by grey clouds. The weather seemed to fall over the distant mountains and race across the water, turn your back and a completely different day could sneak up behind you.

She had sat too long in the coldness of the kitchen and washing up the mugs she looked around her house. Kitty hoped not to lose the simplicity but had to admit under-floor heating couldn't come soon enough.

With all her papers around her, warm now in Pimples, ideas and plans were clattering around her mind. She had thought to write, but her head was too jumbled with the conversations of the day. Sitting in a cocoon of pillows and quilt, Kitty looked out at her ever changing picture, doing she suspected, what she would spend much of her future doing – watching the scenery. The myriad of colour, the sea, the sky, and the mountains – no two minutes the same. Hugging her knees the newest islander wondered if she would ever tire of it.

That evening Kitty enjoyed a couple of glasses of rosé and her favourite version of Persuasion. It still felt like a holiday and the reality of having no job, no deadlines or list of chores. It was tough – but a grinning Kitty thought someone had to do it and it might as well be her. However tomorrow she would have errands so settled down with the sun and slept dreams full of decorating and tiles – rows upon rows of endless piles of tiles!

11

Meeting the Locals

Waking at eight she decided the time had come to wash out some clothes. Kitty had contemplated slipping back into University habits, wearing jeans and jumpers until the smell necessitated washing such cumbersome and difficult to dry items. But she was older, a grown up now, standards were standards and pyjamas, underwear and T-shirts were easily washed in the large stone sink. Wringing them out until her knuckles ached, she lay a large towel across the table and positioned the wet clothes across it. Rolling the towel long ways, a veritable Swiss roll of towel and laundry, she squeezed them dry.

Her mother had taught her this trick on holidays, then Kitty and her father or brother would each take an end and turn. If it was her dad, he would laugh and twist fast and hard, the trick at the other end was just to hang on and not be forced over, twisted off your feet. With no one but memories to help her now, Kitty trod on one end and turned with both hands – nowhere near as much fun but just as effective. Past dripping point Kitty shook the handful of garments and hung them on the clothes airer she was glad to have packed. Placing it on the part of the kitchen floor she hoped the sun would eventually find.

What she wouldn't have given for a full English breakfast this morning, but made do with cereal. Kitty had always had a hearty appetite and could easily eat a roast dinner straight from her bed. Stephen had always felt the need to graze in the evenings, chocolate, biscuits and crisps – it had always amazed her that he managed to keep such a trim figure. Now she was on her own she realised, chewing on the horrid bit of fruit the manufacturers insisted on hiding in the otherwise nutty breakfast, that she really didn't enjoy this. She promised herself that once she had a serviceable kitchen she would fight it no more and have the breakfast of kings every morning.

Heading off to the Duncans', Kitty arrived in time to see Claire standing on the lawn with a long line of washing falling and soaring. Propped high it caught the sea winds, inflating the shirts, trousers and jumpers as though so many invisible people still wore them. Now that would be useful, making it the second time she thought to add to the list.

Replacing the fresh briny air with the warm smells of home, porridge and fabric softener cheered Kitty's soul. The Aga in the kitchen was most welcome and Kitty warmed her hands and backside while Claire cleared the breakfast bowls and heaped the children's pictures and letters from school and nursery. "Here, here we can work here. Pull that chair up and you'll be near the Aga – you are having an Aga aren't you?"

"Yes, I thought of power cuts - and it still warms your water if you use wood... it does doesn't it?"

"Yes, oh yes, well you've done your research. There will be plenty of power cuts in the winter, have you stocked up on candles? A good wind-up lamp is always useful."

"I have some but I will get more." An earnest nod.

Using the Internet and surrounded by samples and lists, Kitty had decided on tiles for the kitchen and bathroom, and the kitchen units, sink and even door handles and taps. Claire produced a piping bowl of leek and potato soup, "I know it's early but I have to get back to the nursery by twelve thirty. Eating quickly not to waste valuable time, they both wiped the bowls clean with crusty white bread and butter.

With obvious pride Claire showed Kitty around the entire house. In socked feet the merits of the different floor coverings were discussed. Claire could not say enough good things about the wet room, or elaborate showerheads. Trying to convince her that she must have an en suite, Kitty "Ooohed" and "Ahhhed" in the right places but knew simplicity was the way forward for Tide's, she would be more than happy with one bathroom with one bath and one shower head.

The utility room, or boot room as everyone seemed to call it this side of the border, had reused the original stone floor of the school it once was. Cleaned up it looked and felt wonderful under foot, and she rubbed her toes over the contours, smoothed by countless feet.

Claire was keen to point out it was the best floor for not showing the dirt, and Kitty tried to calculate just how many rooms she could stretch her slabs to.

"I'm so excited for you Kathleen, and I do admire you, taking on all this, and on your own." Claire's hand rested on Kitty's where she had reached out to stroke the granite worktop – yet another decision.

"Well you're a long time dead – that's something my dad used to say and he was right. The older you get and the more people you lose the more it rings true... and I tend to think now, sod it!"

"Yes I quite agree, in my job you realise how tenuous life is. But it's not like you're from here. What made you? No... What decided, persuaded you that you could be happy here?" Claire looked directly into Kitty's eyes now and for the first time today Kitty remembered this was her GP talking.

"Well, all I did know once I was on my own, was that I couldn't bear the idea of staying in Kent. The thought of growing old there, the thought of stagnating in that cold place – terrified me." The last words little more than a whisper.

"Cold place? Oh dear Kathleen you'll know what cold is here believe me. They say you have to endure two winters on Skye before you can call yourself an Islander." Claire chuckled.

"No, not physically cold" Kitty wondered how best to express herself, running her hands over the smooth cold granite.

"You can adapt for that, with triple glazing, and lashings of insulation, so Donald tells me. Good boots and socks and a wide range of thermals I've already discovered. No... no, I mean the coldness of being surrounded by people with no warmth of companionship. Being in a crowded room and feeling completely alone." Kitty fought back traitorous tears and swallowed deeply, "Since I've been here, what is it a week?" Claire smiled and squeezed her arm. "I've felt more genuine friendship and community than I had in five years at Royal Tunbridge Wells" Using her best snooty accent she smiled back at Claire.

"Well I'm glad, truly glad. People are welcoming – bordering on downright nosey to tell the truth." Shaking her head side to side, "But, if you're happy to let them in you will be part of a truly wonderful community."

Both women smiled in the short silence and Kitty added "And... I thought of the place I'd been happiest in, and in all my life... well, it was here. Only holidays but last week it felt like coming home." Claire sat quietly wanting to know more without risk of upsetting her guest further.

Sitting back by the Aga, the array of paperwork was gathered and ordered, and Kitty put away her lap top and enjoyed another cup of tea, spirits much brighter now.

"So, I don't want to be too nosey – but is there no Mr Vrcelj?" Claire couldn't help herself.

"No" louder than she ought, "No" quieter this time. Sorrow flooded Kitty's face now pale and drawn, and Claire was acutely aware she had touched on a very raw nerve, added brightly,

"Oh ok. I won't pry; you don't have to tell me anything. I just wondered if that was just now or, um permanent?"

"Oh! Very, very permanent Claire". For the first time since meeting this young woman Claire peeked behind the smile to see the pain. She was sure Kathleen would share the details with her in her own good time. As soon as her last GP forwarded her records, Claire knew she may find out more than Kitty would like.

"Oh well, that's twice as exciting. At least you won't have to fight over every decision of the build." Lightly now "Goodness, Hamish and I bickered over every tile, appliance and paint colour."

Harmony restored, Kitty asked after Claire's children, knowing full well how animated a mother can be about her progeny with little input from the other person. Resting back in her seat Kitty was happy to have escaped the spotlight without having to disclose anything. Getting up to leave, Kitty hugged Claire longer than their social standing warranted. She realised how much she missed physical contact, and an astute Claire, all too aware of Kitty's sadness, hugged back waiting for Kitty to pull away.

"Are you busy Sunday?" Catching Kitty on the hop she had no alternative but to be totally honest.

"Urm – no – no plans, none at all."

"Good well, if you can bear the noise come over for Sunday lunch, the kids will be home so you can meet them," and then as if an after thought, "Oh yes, and Donald will be here."

"Oh" Kitty for some inexplicable reason, felt suspicious. Reading the quizzical frown Claire added matter-of-factly, "Nothing special, Donald often has Sunday lunch with us. Like you he's on his own, and who wants to cook a roast for one?"

"Who indeed."

"Anyway you can talk over all your decisions, think of it as a free business meeting only with benefits – and – if I do say so myself, some of the best Yorkshire puddings North of the border."

Kitty laughed, even if this was a set up who cares if there's Yorkies! Claire waved as Kitty drove off, heading straight to the supermarket - where was the time going? So much for no agenda – life was becoming a whirlwind of engagements. A pizza and a bag of prepared salad was tonight's meal of choice. Picking up a trashy magazine full of wannabes and caught out celebrities, Kitty was looking forward to babysitting duties tonight.

Angela and Gavin welcomed her like a long lost friend,

"We're so grateful Kitty, sorry" Angela moved Kitty to the other side of the sink as she rushed around the kitchen.

"How did you get on with your builders? All sorted?"

"Yes, yes I think so." Kitty struggled to concentrate with Angela skipping around her.

"Oh, carry on, carry on I am listening," passing a fleeting smile at Kitty.

"Yes and I've been to the heritage Centre and got some books of local history."

"Oh Aye, you meet Jamie Stewart did ye?" It was Gavin that had entered the room, arms full of dirty washing.

"Umm, yes I had met him up the pub Friday." Kitty looked down and began intently removing fluff from her trouser leg.

"Aye bit of a local historian is our Jamie, that's who teaches us tonight."

"If you weren't as valuable to us as a baby sitter I'd recommend you came with us Kitty." Angela grinned and winked at her.

"Maybe next year when I have a bathroom and you're fluent."

"Take more than a year!" Gavin winked at Kitty as he spoke, Angela swiped, but missed the target with a well-practiced duck from her husband.

"Come on Gav, come on!" Gavin smiled ignoring his wife's urgency, "Same as last week Kitty, two down, and one reading." Angela called over her shoulder.

Closing the door quietly behind their rushed departure and heading straight for the cooker she turned it on to warm up while she was in the bathroom. Opting for a quick shower she quickly carried out her duties. Peeking into the half opened door, "You alright?" Small eyes peered over the top of a large book and nodded. Kitty liked this girl; she wouldn't need to check on her again. Locking the bathroom door and removing the new razor from its packaging, she had no intention of being undressed again in a hurry, but just in case.

Eyes closed, and appreciating again just how wonderful it was to have hot water run through her hair, and for the first time allowed herself to think again of the kilt wearing, red-headed new acquaintance. After the shower Kitty enjoyed her dinner, under the watchful eye of Eric who shared her crusts, boxing up half of the pizza for lunch tomorrow. Timed to perfection, the Macleod's came home as Kitty lost interest in her magazine, there were only so many poor women in bikinis unknowingly flashing their cellulite and belly folds that Kitty could bear.

Debating the finer points of Gaelic tenses they continued to talk over each other as they entered the lounge.

"Well evening Kitty, you must learn Gaelic it's fascinating. I learnt some at school but it wasn't compulsory then like it is now," Angela rolled her eyes and raised her brows.

"Well I'm learning it because they make the kids, and I'm fed up with them talking it, and me not knowing what they are saying – need to know basis."

"Yes I'd give it a go one day but I'm not great at languages. My poor French teacher blamed me for her grey hair!" Smiling at the memory.

"Jamie asked after you," Gavin added conversationally.

"Oh... did he?"

"Mmmm" Angela looked at Kitty noticing the flush before Kitty shifted her gaze, just as she had seen Jamie do earlier this evening.

"Yes, yes he seemed nice and Angus and the Celtic band."

"Ummmm!"

"Good man Jamie." Gavin added devoid of the innuendo in his wife's voice.

"Yes well I'd best be off – let you get on." Kitty gathered her things and wanted to be free of Angela's prying eyes.

Emotions raced, and Kitty had the first bad nights sleep since she had arrived. She had been with Stephen for nearly ten years and now considered herself just a single person. She hadn't chosen to be alone, it was definitely not her choice. She had never given any thought to being with someone else. The plan was to move here, renovate her house and live quietly alone and write. Nowhere in her plans had there been even the faintest wish or desire to meet someone. Odd though it may be, the notion of being with anyone else had never entered her mind and now, well, now it terrified her.

Dreams merged with bleary-eyed thoughts. Had she planned to stay alone forever? Never to date, to love, or be loved? The realisation that at thirty there could again be someone else in her life had come as a real shock to Kitty. The embers of attraction she had assumed were extinguished she knew now could be reignited. The nearest feeling she could relate it to was the painful, fruitless crush she had harboured for Brian Johnson the last two years of senior school. She had wasted too much daytime dreaming on that boy.

Tossing and turning, a mass of creased sheet and quilt forced an irritable Kitty to abandon her bed at 3am. Huffing and swearing Kitty straightened the bed, donned her coat and wellies and stomped across the moonlit grass to Tide's Reach.

The moon was nearly full, was it waxing or waning? She never knew the difference, and questioned her sanity at even asking the question at such an ungodly hour. Giving ample light to see, Kitty paused and took refreshing lung fulls of the cold moist air, chilling her from the inside and wiping away any vestige of sleep that might have remained. The white light reflected on the calm water, which now looked silver, an undulating expanse of mercury. Hugging her coat around herself, Kitty cleared her confusion of thoughts with every deep breath.

After braving the clammy cold of the toilet, Kitty walked to the boundary of the lawn. Hitching up the very impractical long satin nightdress she tucked it up into her knickers at the top of her thighs, keeping it well above the top of her boots. Walking around to her derelict croft, the water to her left produced the only sound, all other life safely asleep. Drawn to the boulder at the door, Kitty pulled her coat low and drew her knees up balancing on the icy stone. With no artificial light visible, she marvelled at the shimmering sea before her and the magnitude of the sky above.

Now a sober Kitty again marvelled at the myriad of stars twinkling into view. Layer upon layer, for the first time in her life the sky no longer looked like a flat backdrop but an infinite expanse. Rather than question the universe and the meaning of it all, but the blast from her childhood past; "To infinity and beyond!" The laughter spread across the sea before her.

A rising band of ripples made their way up the slipway and the accompanying wind flapped the satin around Kitty bare legs, causing a shiver that ran from her scalp to her toes. All the thoughts of new acquaintances, relationships and her future now settled and filed away, she walked calmly back to her bed.

Sitting propped up with cushions and with the help of a hot chocolate Kitty wrote. She wrote until her hand ached at the end of a heavy arm. Her eyes burnt and were the cause of her having to finally replace the ribbon in the page and put the lid on her pen. Kitty had two days with nothing planned, two whole days until chaos would descend on her little patch of paradise. The sleep that followed was still, deep and without dreams.

12

Baring All

"Oh dear god, not again!"
Bang! Bang!
The van shook slightly with each blow. Rubbing sticky eyes and unable to open them before sliding back the door.
"Oh erm... erm."
"Morning Jock, caught me again." looking up she was about to share the fact that she had been up most of the night writing but her mouth gaped open. The wind blew into the muggy van and caught the fine pink satin, Kitty glanced down at herself as she lent to hold the door open and could see straight down the front of the lace trim to her knickers. She quickly raised an arm to cover her breasts.
"Oh shit!" was all she could muster.
Looking gallantly at his feet as he scratched at the gravel with booted foot, Jamie held out a small book. Without looking at her, as much to hide his own blushes as to spare her hers, he said quietly, "I, erm... well... I was talking to Gavin and Angela last night and remembered this wee book and thought ya would like a loan of it."
"Oh... thank you," Kitty forced out. Jamie looked up just as Kitty released the door and reached to take the offered book. Transferring the book to her other hand, Kitty, on reflex, had to stop the sliding door as it began to close, thereby releasing the little clothing she had and exposing herself once more.
Jamie let out an involuntary snort of laughter and covered his eyes with a large hand. The silence was palpable, broken only by Kitty cursing yet again,
"Oh shit!"
"Dunny worry ye'sel lass" Jamie's hand still clamped in place.
"Ohhh SHIT!" Kitty voice trembled.
"It seems I'm destined to be seeing ye naked" He tried to joke in an effort to lighten the atmosphere.
"Hang on," Kitty slammed the door shut, grabbing her trousers she stumbled and knocked her head on the overhead cupboards.
"SHIT!"
Jamie released his eyes and laid a hand on the door handle but thought twice about opening it, "You alright?"

Shoving her nightie into the jeans she gave up on the fly. Swinging her coat around her shoulders she just managed to catch the mug that the sleeve knocked from its shelf.

"Bloody hell!"

Jamie opened the door an inch, "Ok?"

"Ok" a little defeated voice replied.

Jamie opened the door fully and clicked it to its limit. Sheepishly peering in he smiled at the young woman rubbing the back of her head, seated on the unmade bed with a waterproof coat fastened tightly under her chin. "Too little, too late" Jamie thought to himself. Not content with the images plaguing him night and day of her in her underwear, and the feel of her skin when he undressed her, but now the vivid sight of her breasts as her silky nightdress fell from her front.

"I'm sorry... I'm so embarrassed," Kitty said quietly, all saliva had evaporated and it was a struggle.

"I'm not," It had come out before Jamie realised what he was saying, and wished he could take it back as a squirming Kitty brushed her hair back in blushing mortification. "No now I'm sorry... I just mean, well I mean you don't have to be embarrassed. Probably better me than the post man, Jock might have had a heart attack." Kitty couldn't help a small laugh.

"And I've seen it all before."

"Oh... not helping," Kitty shook her head and buried it in her hands.

"Did... um... are you unwell?" Looking at his watch Jamie asked, seeking an explanation for her state of undress at one in the afternoon. With much effort they finally looked at each other, exchanged weak smiles and with mutual relief saw their reflected blushes.

"No... not at all. I couldn't sleep last night so I was up writing till dawn." Her voice was weak and Jamie wished with every fibre of his being to ease her discomfort.

"I didn'a know you wrote, is it your job or just a hobby?" hoping to at least glean one answer to the many mysteries surrounding this woman. Kitty sighed, feeling the tension finally relaxing across her hunched shoulders, aided greatly by the soft green eyes and dimpled smile before her.

"Well it was a hobby, but now I've moved here I want to dedicate some real time to it."

"Oh right" None the wiser he raised his eyebrows and nodded.

Wishing him gone, and he wishing to be gone but seemingly unable to leave, they just smiled at each other.

"Well I'm really sorry to have disturbed you… and causing you any embarrassment Kathleen," now that was how to say her name. Remembering her manners and keen to end this meeting on a better note, as Jamie went to turn Kitty stammered "And I am sorry – you've not seen me at my best, AGAIN!"

"Not at all." He regretted the overly positive response, as now having seen even more of her than before he was finding this intriguing creature increasingly fascinating. His thoughts of satin and roses were interrupted once more.

He was looking troubled, brows furrowed and Kitty suspected that, like Jock, Jamie probably thought she was stark raving mad. Not knowing what else to do she resorted to the English solution,

"Do you want a cup of tea?" Kitty shook her head, what on earth had possessed her to say that. Jamie bowed and made to climb into the van. Making him jump, Kitty leapt to her feet and he had to side step as she alighted on the gravel next to him. The thought of being in such a confined space with this man, not to mention that it was the scene of the two crimes, and to sit on her unmade bed! No this was not to be.

"Sorry, sorry again. I meant in the house."

"Oh right, yes, that would be lovely. I mean it would be good to see the croft."

Kitty darted sidelong looks as they crossed the lawn, and allowed herself a small smile. Once inside the kitchen Jamie imparted what he knew of its previous occupant. Kitty busied herself making tea and plating up biscuits, suddenly ravenous.

"I've been thinking about your croft and found this book" tapping the book on the table.

"Yes thank you."

"It has pictures of old maps and your derelict croft and some others that are no longer there."

"Oh brilliant!" Momentarily forgetting her shame, she stood to the side of a seated Jamie and looked down at the pages he had marked with scraps of paper. For his part Jamie was glad he had marked the pages as his hands oddly trembled. Leaning nearer him to look more closely, Jamie took the opportunity of looking at the clear skin of her flawless cream cheek. He then became acutely aware that only inches from his shoulder, through the thin fabric of the waterproof he could make out every detail of her left breast. Taking up his mug he took a large gulp and scalded his tongue on the too hot tea.

"Ow, ouch."

"Are you alright?" Kitty turned a concerned face down to his and only then realised how close they were.

"Yes fine, tea was hot."

"Usually is," Kitty smiled sympathetically at the man who was obviously as uncomfortable as herself. Taking the book Kitty walked away on the pretext of getting a spoon to stir her tea, and returned taking the other chair, giving them much needed space. Jamie reached over to the book once she was seated,

"So this is your crofter's cottage, and this is the one around the headland, but look there were five dotted along here," pointing at square outlines on the faded map. "The others were nearer the water, I think that's your derelict one. Look it's more sheltered and protected by the rocks on either side."

Kitty nodded "and this must be the one over the water, hiding behind that big new house." Kitty pointed through the wall.

"Yes, monstrosity!" Jamie's voice suddenly with a rough dark edge.

"I know, I'm sure it's a lovely house but I feel sorry for the little cottage peeking out around it." Kitty wondered if she sounded pathetic but Jamie's broad smile across the table reassured her. He had such lovely teeth – she hadn't noticed that before. Stop looking, she told herself, and then remembered she hadn't yet brushed hers and was horribly aware of her own furry teeth.

"So you're really not going to wreck all this" Jamie's hand gestured around the room. From anyone else the comment could have been taken as sarcasm, but looking at his face Kitty knew he was genuine.

"I know, I love the walls as they are – I am a little afraid Donald, the architect – do you know him?" Jamie rolled his eyes; Kitty thought she would ask about that later. "Well Claire – the GP" at this Jamie nodded and smiled, "We went over the plans and I'm just a bit afraid they envisage it – how did you say? – all stainless steel and glass." They exchanged their first easy smile. "Would you?" Kitty hesitated.

"Anything" Jamie offered too quickly and too eagerly he thought.

"Would you look at the plans – I mean I know you like things traditional, and you know this place and I'm afraid I'll lose the soul of it."

"Aye, aye I'd be glad to."

Kitty pushed her chair back to go and collect the plans but was hit by the sudden realisation that she still had her nightdress on, hadn't washed and was short of half her underwear.

"I'd, well I'd better get dressed," she mumbled.

"What are you doing for dinner?" His retort was swift.

"Um, urr... I don't know, I hadn't thought about it." Taking on board her flustered response Jamie interjected, "It's just that, as lovely as all this is" sweeping his hand around the room "There's basic, and there's basic," smiling up at her "I haven't got plans and we could take ya drawings, it will be quiet at the hotel and we can have a good look at all the plans and get someone else to cook dinner for us." Pausing and when no response came, "The venison is delicious."

Unable to come up with any rational reason not to and the growing growling moans of hunger Kitty found herself nodding in acceptance.

"Grand, I'll come for ye at six," a very pleased Jamie stood.

"Yeh, that will be lovely" a slightly shell shocked Kitty stood frozen to the spot.

Jamie whistled as he walked across the grass, and Kitty watched his strong steps and broad shoulders topped by the chestnut hair that shone now in the spring sunlight. Although he didn't look back he was sure she watched.

13

When is a Date, Not a Date?

Kitty washed at the small bowl in Pimples. Was this a date? – Surely this wasn't a date? Then why did it feel like a date? Kitty hadn't had this dilemma since University and wondered if life and relationships had changed in the last decade. What would Jamie be thinking? He had seemed casual, more like a working lunch "You think that my girl if it makes you feel better!" Oh, if only her mum was here and not just talking in her head. Kitty thought she might have to talk to Amanda to put all these confusing thoughts in any sort of order.

There was no denying this Scotsman was having a very strange effect on her. She hugged herself now and closed her eyes, oh those legs! He had undressed her, and now she was pretty sure she had flashed her breasts at him, and then he was taking her for dinner. Kitty struggled to remember the finer points of courtship etiquette but was sure something was awry here. What to wear? What to do with her hair? Makeup – no makeup? "Aghhhh!"

Kitty put on her jeans, a jumper, twisted her hair up with a clip and compromised with a light coat of mascara and a good brush of the teeth. "It is NOT a date!"

Jamie mirrored the preparation, sans mascara. At twenty-five he had managed to spend three years at University without a serious relationship. His last real girlfriend was Rosie, a sweet plump girl he dated from thirteen through to highers. She guarded her virginity with thighs of steel, and honestly it was such a relief after it ended, when he left for University.

There had been enough dalliances, (though usually drunken) to understand the mechanics of a sexual relationship and vent the long-standing frustrations of his youth. The knowledge that he had never felt the bizarre array of emotions that he now felt for this shy, beautiful woman terrified him. He thought of her constantly, every waking hour since half carrying her across the lawn in the moonlight. A subtle nausea haunted him, kept him awake at night and distracted him from every task he attempted. Jamie had paced the heritage museum since eight am, picking up the annotated book and putting it back down countless times, arguing with himself until he finally decided to take it to Kathleen. In none of his imaginations had it resulted in what he saw this afternoon, and he had taken a colder shower than usual in preparation for seeing her again..

Parking along side the van, "Damn" In his eagerness he had arrived fifteen minutes early. He had left as late as he could bear to, but had obviously driven too fast.

Kitty paced the kitchen and had been ready for a quarter of an hour before he arrived. Pimples had been too confining and the house too viewless for her state of agitation. She decided to wait on the beach, letting the breeze, damp with spray cool her flushed face. Watching him pull up, she enjoyed watching him unseen. His hair was damp and lay close to his head in large even waves. Wearing a different shirt, pale blue, Kitty could see he had shaved. Enjoying the sight she let him start for the grass before calling out.

"Jamie!" waving as he smiled over to her. Returning the smile Kitty walked confidently to him. After the slight awkwardness of not knowing quite how to greet each other, Kitty opened Pimples and took the rucksack containing the plans – that was the purpose of this after all.

Together they climbed the drive and headed for the hotel. Kitty struggled to keep pace with the burly man beside her, she estimated she came up to his armpit. Skipping occasionally and hoping not to have much in the way of conversation, Kitty concentrated on breathing. Her companion must have noticed and slowed his pace and without asking permission, lightly lifted the strap of the rucksack from her shoulder and effortlessly swung it over his. They walked the remainder in silence and Jamie held open the hotel door for Kitty to go in.

"Well, evening Kitty – back for round two," Lilly winked and laughed and then raised her eyebrows, "Oh and evening to you Jamie." Smirking now, Lilly watched closely as Jamie gestured through the public bar to the lounge bar.

"Here, will this do?"

Jamie held a chair out and Kitty obediently sat.

"What do you want to drink? The Ale you were on Friday night?"

"Oh I don't think that's a good idea" Kitty snorted a laugh.

"Don't worry we won't have much, I wouldn'a let ye have too much" not that Jamie would mind in the least tucking her up in bed again, "I'll get the drinks" he left abruptly.

Bringing back two pints and menus tucked under his arms. Kitty busied herself setting out the paperwork, neutral territory they could both get lost in.

"I'm most worried about the front elevation, the extension," she took a settling mouthful of the velvety beer.

"I know what ye mean, it will define the whole look of the place," picking up the drawings of the front of the house Jamie considered it for many minutes. "I think a lot will depend on the finish, will ye have plastic? Obviously hard wood would be best but ye are so exposed there." Rubbing his hand around his chin and then through the drying hair Kitty struggled to concentrate on windows. "Being right on the sea and it being ya lounge I ken it will need to be triple glazed, I wonder what colours are available?"

"There's a heritage green – dark sort of muted racing green I was considering, or a paler grey green."

"Yes that could look good" Sipping his ale he turned his attentions to the second floor and nodded his approval, "The windows are good, very in keeping."

"Donald seems to know what I want."

Jamie put down his pint too sharply and a little splashed onto the beer mat, "Ummm."

Kitty noticed the frown forming "I noticed before, do you not think he is a good architect?"

"It's not his professionalism I have issue wi" he looked down into his pint.

"It's?" Kitty waited.

"It's not something… it's personal… and" but he was quiet. Jamie reached out and laid a hand on her arm, a haze of dark red hair disguised freckles on his hand and fingers and Kitty was amazed at the gentleness of his touch.

"I'm sure he'll design ye a super house, and my uncle will build ye a grand home" his voice was low and intent.

Lilly walked over prompting Jamie to whip his hand away and tuck it under the table, Lilly's smile told them not fast enough. Meals ordered, the heavy silence that seemed to perpetually fall over them was back. Jamie cleared his throat and taking more Dutch courage asked, "Why did you come here Kathleen?"

"What to the pub? You invited me" Kitty was a little confused. Jamie lowered a shaking head and leant further across the table to her inclined head.

"Why did you move here?" his eyes rested on the wedding ring Kitty unconsciously twisted around her finger.

Quietly "I was alone."

"Aha" waiting and wanting her to elaborate.

"I was all alone, my family had gone… and well I had no one to stay for."

"A husband?"

Kitty turned away slightly shifting in her seat "I…" but faltered and wiped away the swift tears that betrayed her.

"Now, now then, I'm sorry. Hush," then no more than a whisper "Hush lass, hush." Placing two hands across her fidgeting fingers. "Dunna fret lass, say no more."

Kitty concentrated hard to squash the tidal wave of grief that threatened to breach her defenses. Since planning this move Kitty, much to Amanda's worried concern, had managed to pack away all the emotion of Stephen's going. For the first time in months, here in a pub at the far end of the country with a relative stranger, it threatened to escape.

Taking a couple of large gulps of beer followed by several deep breaths, Kitty rushed to the toilet not daring to look at Jamie. Hands gripping the cold rim of the sink Kitty looked for many minutes at the reflection before her. She knew it was a mistake to come out tonight, everyone wanted to know her story. Claire, Angela and now Jamie, why couldn't they just accept her for what was in front of them. She hadn't the strength to explain. Saying the truth of her life would unleash the sorrow that she could not face. The thought of letting that out would be like letting a lion in your house. How would it ever be contained without mauling every one around it?

Berating the pale face in the mirror "Were you going to hide under a rock forever?" She washed her hands and let the hot water run over them until they were dark pink. It was many minutes before she gathered enough courage and composure to face Jamie again.

Jamie rose from his chair as she approached, concern etched on his face.

"Sorry, are you alright?"

"Sorry" was all Kitty could come up with and was just glad her emotions didn't let her down again.

"No I'm the one who should be sorry, sorry for upsetting you."

"It wasn't you, it is my life Jamie – life in general has a habit of upsetting me… and I suppose in answer to your earlier question, that's why I came here. I think I was trying to run away from it… but I guess today proves that didn't work."

"Well lass ye could'na run much farther north."

Jamie smiled warmly at her and they were both relieved when Lilly arrived with their dinners. The rich dark meat in the venison pie was as Jamie had said, delicious in its red wine gravy.

"Umm, Jamie you were right this is beautiful."

"Aye" he smiled back and was relieved to see the sorrow gone for now from her face. They finished the meal in silence, not strained but companionable. Kitty insisted on going to the bar and buying a second round much to Jamie disapproval. Had Kitty not been upset earlier he wouldn't have let her but was acutely aware of not pushing the point now. Lilly skipped along the bar to serve her, "Well Kitty you didn't waste any time did you love?"

"What… no, no, nothing like that. Jamie just offering me some advice on the house"

"Yeahhh, right! – Well – whatever. You know he's super hot don't you, Skye's most eligible bachelor."

"Oh no pressure, thanks Lilly, anyway it's not like that, he's just being friendly," Kitty tried very hard to sound convincing but the twinkle in Lilly's eyes told her it was futile.

She had only been away from him for minutes but looking at his profile Kitty's heart raced as she walked back toward him. She could not explain, had no experience to draw from but she had a real and pressing need to be near to him. Avoiding the heavy topics they talked quietly, Jamie told of his small Island school and the reality of growing up on Skye. Kitty in turn shared her memories of childhood in Wimbledon. Not sure what prompted her, but pleased with his animated response, Kitty shared her mother's secret notes on everyone in their acquaintance. Jamie tossed his head back laughing loud and free as Kitty shared the butcher's dark secret.

"I ken I would have liked ya mother."

"Oh I know she would have liked you, she was a sucker for a Scotsman, not to mention a red headed one in a kilt!"

"Aye is that right?" Jamie raised an eyebrow and showed his dimple, "And might that be a trait you've inherited?"

"Might be" Kitty turned a vivid shade of puce and hurriedly took a swig of beer. Trying not to dwell on her embarrassment Kitty looked around as Lilly clattered and hummed tunelessly as she cleared tables. The few other customers had left without Kitty noticing, the hours had passed far too fast.

"I think we've outstayed our welcome."

"Reckon you're right."

Kitty stood and was surprised at Jamie's speed, behind her now moving the chair and helping her on with her coat. The level of chivalry was all-new to Kitty but she liked it.

"Night you two, sleep tight!" Lilly sang out and winked as they left. Dripping in innuendo, Lilly's laugh was cut short as Jamie slammed the door behind them. Kitty was very glad of the dark, and looking up at the sky took some much-needed jagged deep breaths. The three pints placed her just on the edge of sober and she would have to concentrate if she wasn't going to disgrace herself again. Jamie's hand barely touched the small of her back causing Kitty to shudder. Stepping forward Kitty's foot landed awkwardly on a stone.

"Umph, ouch!"

Reaching out Jamie took her right arm and threaded in through his, placing her fingers out over his upper arm. The closeness rendered Kitty quite speechless but was glad of the support. Was it the ale or just this mans' effect on her, but basic functions such as walking in a straight line seemed again impaired? Through the coarse woollen jumper he now wore Kitty could feel the warmth and firmness of the muscle beneath, she really did need to get a grip she told herself.

They walked in silence along the road and down her drive, neither wanting to reach their destination. It would certainly mean the end of this contact and leave the uncertainty of what would follow.

They stood for several minutes in silence next to Jamie's car, the quiet belying the cacophony of thoughts screaming in both their minds. Both gazed out at the water, arms still linked, under the twinkling sky, both aware of the pounding of their hearts and the now burning touch.

Turning slowly, forcing a reluctant Kitty to drop his arm Jamie held lightly on both her shoulders. Patiently he waited until Kitty met his pale green eyes, all blood drained from her face and her body morphed into the substance of a rag doll. If she had wanted to move, at this moment it would have been impossible.

"Kathleen," his voice was husky and deep.

"Ummm" was all she could manage.

"You're bewitching me Kathleen, I can'ne think of anything else" Jamie lent forward and tenderly and hesitantly rested his check on her forehead. The warmth of his skin in the cool night air, and the response of his touch had her heart racing and suddenly breathing became a conscious and laboured effort. Releasing her right arm he held her chin between thumb and fingertip and tilted her head back. A feeble attempt to prevent his control was soon abandoned, and there on the drive they stared into each other's eyes. In the clouded moonlight Jamie watched as the sparkle of tears rolled down her checks.

"I will'na hurt you Kathleen," his voice a mere whisper. Bending lower he kissed her cheeks, brushing so gently one then the other along the tracks of her tears. Frozen in place, she concentrated hard on forcing herself to inhale and exhale. His breath was warm and smelt of ale, hesitating millimetres from her lips. His hold was gentle and it seemed to Kitty he was giving her every opportunity to pull away. Rooted to the spot she wanted so badly to kiss him but in equal measure to turn and flee.

Jamie closed his eyes and rested his lips on hers, Kitty gasped and caught her breath. he pulled away only to have Kitty reach up and clinging to his neck to draw him back to her. They kissed for many minutes, gently initially but with growing intensity, exploring each other. It was Jamie who pulled away first.

"What?" Kitty gasping for breath stared up at him.

"Don't get me wrong... I don't want to stop" Kitty could hear the concern in his voice. "But you were... upset earlier, I dunna want to, to take advantage of ye... if... if you're not ready."

"You're too much of a gentleman James Stewart" Kitty dragged in crisp salty air. Placing her hands in either side of his face Kitty drew him back to her. Wrapping his arms around the small waist he held her close as they resumed, there in the moonlight, for countless minutes. But this time it was Kitty who prised herself free, panic replacing passion.

"I think you might be right... I don't know if I can do this... at least..." looking away she hung her head resting her forehead on his chest, "I mean... I think I could do this all night... but..."

"Hush lass."

Jamie squeezed her closer to him, turning her head she rested her ear on the centre of his chest focusing on the pounding heart, "I just can't do... anything... more" her voice small and fearful.

"Dunna fret lass, hush... hush."

In this tight embrace it was plain to Kitty he would happily do a lot more and the thought of that had her wanting to run to the hills. Again he kissed her cheeks but pulled away. Neither knew what to say or do.

"Shall we say goodnight for now? Whatever ya want Kathleen… we dunna need to rush this."

They parted, equally caught off balance by the experience, with a simple goodbye. A shiver awoke Kitty's senses many minutes after his car had disappeared, and she walked hunched to Tide's for her nightly loo visit. Numb with cold and raw emotion, having made it on to the toilet just as a torrent of pent up tears overflowed and clutching her head in her hands she gently rocked and sobbed, and sobbed. It was a long time until she had composure enough to walk back to Pimples. The lack of sleep the night before and now the ferocity of her crying left her wrung out and wretched.

Pouring herself a mug of Baileys Kitty attempted to reseal her Pandora's box of grief - it fought hard. Like a holiday suitcase, neatly packed at first, now dirty and crumpled, try as she might Kitty could not close the lid. Held down but unlocked Kitty knew it was only a matter of time before it spilt out again.

When finally it came, her sleep was fretful and haunted by dreams. The final and most vivid forced her awake, heart pounding and oily sweat oozing from her hairline. Lying on the beach, on the little slipway as small waves played with her feet. Jamie on top of her, his kilt covering their modesty, and Stephen leaning over the large boulder, rock in hand ready to stove in Jamie's head. Jock and Lilly sitting outside the derelict croft, watching.

Jamie fared no better; despite his best efforts to drown his feelings with much whiskey he too had fitful sleep, tossing and turning. This was all new to him; he had never felt this before. He had heard the expression but now knew for himself the desperate truth of needing someone.

Having remained dressed, too distracted to change he raked his quilt into a twisted mess. Several times he sat on the bed holding his keys desperate to drive back to her. Wanting nothing else but to knock on the van and not leave until she let him in. Even if they did nothing but hold each other, if that was all she was ready for? Three questions bounced around his mind, firstly what was the truth? Second, what was her story, was she not free? And thirdly why had she such an immense pull on him?

Remembering the vision of her this morning and what lay beneath the pink satin was going to drive him mad. Jamie was revisited by the frustration of his youth with Rosie but magnified ten fold. Hard as he might try, the images of the first night they had met, and every minute he had spent in her company since played over and over in his mind. Awake or in fitful sleep, every minute detail was played over in a relentless loop.

14

A Girl's Best Friend

There was a knock, it was light outside, and a stirring Kitty didn't move from under the quilt. No one called out and after another louder knock there was silence. Finally the crunch of gravel and a car leaving was the cue for a weary Kitty to peek out from under her covers. She would see no one today of that she was certain, and by the feel of her swollen eyes, she was not fit to be seen.

Amanda had said this would happen "You wait my girl, you'll bottle it up but one day the cork will pop." Kitty decided another phone call was in order, but not now, now she would try to find oblivion again and sleep. Drifting in and out of sleep for hours it was the incessant grumbling of her stomach and the nagging awareness that she needed the toilet that forced her from her bed. Grabbing a tin of soup and the nearest clothes Kitty rushed to the safety of the cottage.

Again cursing at herself for not having curtains, it would have been far better to be able to totally block out the world today. Eating her soup slowly she flicked from daydreaming about the incredible kiss, his strong arms around her to the last memory of her and Stephen in a similar situation. Not wanting to make a comparison, and hating herself for it, she repeatedly tried to clear these thoughts from her head – but in vain.

"Oh why? Why now? Why ruin your new life?" Kitty screamed, why could she not rationalise the facts against the level of despair she felt. A seriously hot young man obviously fancied her and kissed her like she had never experienced. Why then did she feel so dishonest, so disloyal, and so bad?

As soon as the bowl was empty the need to get away was paramount. Within minutes Pimples was crawling up the drive and they were safely en route to the swimming pool. The anonymity here was fabulous. Hanging on to the edge of the deep end with her fingertips Kitty let her legs rise out behind her as she gently kicked up and down. Soon chilled she swam again, but too preoccupied with thoughts of yesterday and forgetting how to breathe a gasping, soaked Kitty waited again in the deep end to regain what little composure she could. The high window framed the patch of sky crisscrossed with branches moving faster with the rising wind.

Kitty took longer in the shower than she had in the pool, letting the hot water wash away the chlorine and hopefully some of her worries. Not for the first time, Kitty wondered if maybe it was the fact that she was a Piscean that explained why she had always found water so inviting and soothing. Hurried out from the shower only by a mother and three children who threatened to ruin her peace Kitty dressed slowly. In no rush to return home she let the adapted hand drier dry her hair.

Stopping at the post office on the way home for a large slab of cake and some Internet numbness was just what she needed. What she hadn't reckoned on was Angela! Thinking she could use a friendly face Kitty had not allowed for the island gossip machine.

"Afternoon Ange." Kitty forced some cheer into her voice as she sat on the chilled aluminium and unpacked her laptop.

"Oh hello you." excitedly from behind the counter, "Tea Kitty?"

"Yes please, and some cake, Victoria sponge if you have it?"

"Coming right up... you alright?" Angela hurriedly dished up the cake and making two mugs of tea Kitty could tell there was going to be an interrogation. "Bugger!" Kitty muttered to herself, she knew she wore her feeling on her face.

"I'm fine," trying to smile convincingly.

"What's wrong?" Angela's tone proving Kitty had failed.

"Nothing" hearing how pathetic she sounded she tried again, "Nothing."

"Tell me everything" sitting opposite her and sliding the cake and tea towards a nearly defeated Kitty.

"There's nothing wrong," cutting and eating a large piece of cake.

"Don't give me that," lowering her head to make eye contact with Kitty's down turned face "Is it that Jamie, he didn't disgrace himself did he?" Angela half laughed.

"What, WHAT! How... why would you say that?"

"You might as well tell me anyway, I'll find out sooner or later" using her best, well tested motherly tone, Angela sat back, folded her arms over her bosoms. "And well Lilly was in earlier." Waiting for a response and getting none, she continued.

"Well she did happen to mention you had a date last night with our very own Gaelic teacher – the lovely James Stewart."

"It wasn't a date" head in hands now.

"You did go to the hotel with him didn't you, last night?"

Quietly and through gritted teeth, "He was helping me with my plans for the house!"

"Oh" making no attempt to hide her disappointment, "Oh, shame, we've been waiting for him to meet someone, he's lovely." Angela shared. Kitty looked up sheepishly through her lashes aware her cheeks would yet again betray her.

"Oooh, but you do like him…don't you?"

"Well he does seem very nice."

"AND?"

"Annnd, I don't know what else to say."

"Does he like you?" leaning towards her once more.

"Well" immediately regretting giving Angela any ammunition, "Ange I've only just got here. I came for a new start."

"Well I'd say you're doing a bloody good job so far."

"But all my plans… never did I think it would include meeting someone."

"Why?" Kitty thought the question was reasonable; for an outsider it made no sense.

"Well I don't know really, actually." Kitty tried hard to understand it herself, how could she possibly explain it to someone else.

"If you don't like him, tell him. If you do like him, and you're single go for it, what have you got to lose?" Kitty couldn't help herself and laughed into her tea, "I know him, not really well, and not in a biblical sense – more's the pity. But Kitty, if I was single I would jump at the chance… are you single?"

Kitty's stony face looked back at her and was unable, or unwilling to answer. The bell on the door jingled and the first of half a dozen customers arrived and over the next twenty minutes Kitty tried to concentrate on the Internet, avoiding winking smiles from Angela but it proved to be a fruitless business. As the eager post mistress escorted the last of the queue out, keen to resume discussions with Kitty she was clearly disappointed as Kitty stood, "I'll be off now Ange, what do I owe you?"

"Ok, but Kitty you know you can tell me anything." Kitty knew she could but also strongly suspected that everyone on that side of the island would be privy to the litany of embarrassing moments betwixt Jamie and herself.

"What happened last night? You do look upset." Real concern in her voice, "Nothing bad I hope, I mean, I'm sure he wouldn't…

but... he didn't, misbehave did he?"

"No" sadly Kitty now thought.

"Well you'd tell me wouldn't you, if you were in trouble I mean. I know you're on your own, and I know what it's like to move to a strange place, away from family and friends, and well, you are the best baby sitter we've ever had, I need to look out for you."

Kitty couldn't help herself and smiled warmly at Angela.

"No, I'm worrying about nothing, he did nothing wrong. He was the perfect gent – it's me."

"Ok if you are sure, but look I should have given you these before. Here is my home number, the post office and my mobile number. I know you haven't got a land line but you can always use the pay phone if you have no signal."

"Signal? What's a signal?" They both laughed.

"Welcome to Skye, Kitty Harris!" touched and now very glad to have seen Angela today, she smiled back at her new friend.

"Thank you Ange. I'm not good with, well emotions at the mo, doesn't take much to upset me."

"You've been through a huge upheaval, but remember people here will always help, Gav and I, would always help."

"Thanks, really."

Exchanging a fleeting peck on the cheek Kitty left, feeling better for the tea and cake, and even better for the chat.

Parking up in a lay by with a signal and much to Kitty's delight a fantastic view, the time had come for a much needed Amanda debrief.

"Hi" sighing in relief that she was home.

"Helllloooo" in her very best Mrs Doubtfire impersonation. "Oh Kit how lovely, how are you? Any drunken dalliances with kilted strangers this week?" Oh if only she knew, but of course she would know for there was nothing Kitty had ever kept from Amanda.

"Well"

"Bloody hell! Hang on, hang on, and let me get comfortable. This isn't going to be a short tale, I can tell!"

"Sorry no, right are you sitting comfortably? I'll begin."

"Yes, yes but start from the very beginning," Kitty smiled at her excited friend.

"So you're sure he could see right down your nightie?"

"Yep! But on the up side I did have knickers on."

Amanda roared and despite herself so did Kitty and relaxed back into her seat.

"Well, thank heavens for small mercies! What the hell did you say to him?"

"I ... sort of panicked, slammed the door in his face, shoved some clothes on and then... invited him in for tea – I told you I panicked." Kitty tried to justify her irrational behaviour.

"Well that's the least you could do after flashing your baps at him!" Waiting for the raucous laughter to subside Kitty continued.

"Oh I knew I could count on a rational, sympathetic response from you – best friend!"

"So, not too awkward then, did you offer him biscuits?"

"Yes actually!"

"Not Jammy Dodgers I hope?"

"Stop it! Anyway he had brought over a great book about the history of this region of Skye and my house and the croft. And anyway, I thought the sooner I faced the embarrassing face off the better."

"Face? How long did he stay? Did he return the favour and let you peek up his kilt?"

"STOP IT!"

When Amanda had once again gathered herself and dried her eyes her friend continued.

"It was nice actually, once we got talking about the history of the place – he is so knowledgeable."

"I bet he is!" Full of innuendo.

"No stop it, stop it. Well he invited me to the pub that evening to check over the drawings" rushing so as not to be interrupted, "Not a date, just to eat and look at the building plans."

"Yeah, right! Nothing to do with the fact within one week he'd undressed you and put you to bed and then," (in her best Scottish accent) "flashing ya tuts at him!"

"Why, WHY! Amanda? The two most embarrassing things, by far, in my entire life, and both with him."

Both laughing now it was Amanda that cut it short this time, "Come on, come on, getting older here! Cut to the chase what else happened, details, details?"

Kitty told all, his gentlemanly way of always walking on the roadside. "I didn't understand Mand, he kept nipping around me, we'd cross over and he'd be on the other side. It was only after he held out my chair and every door for me I realised he was such a gent." Kitty voice was gentle now as she warmed in the memories of that evening.

"What, keeping himself between you and the road, bloody hell is he real? It's not Briga-bloody-doon up there is it?"

"I know; how lovely is that?" Running her fingers through her newly conditioned hair, recalling the details of last night shame and embarrassment now faded to insignificance - it had been a very good non-date.

"Dinner was lovely but the young barmaid was all winks and nudges."

"I bet she was!"

"We went over the plans and he had a few good suggestions for the renovation, and then... well, then he walked me home."

"And, AND? Get to the good bits; I know that voice – how good a bit are we talking?" Amanda was on the edge of her seat now.

"Um"

"Kit you're killing me here!"

"We did… kiss," her voice was weak, but she had done it, she had admitted her treacherous truth.

"And! Details?"

"He said I'd bewitched him."

"Shit!"

"I know!"

"Details?"

Tears welling now "Am I a terrible person?" Kitty struggled to speak.

"Oh Kit, love – you are the best of people. Why on earth shouldn't you be happy?" Straining at the earpiece at the quiet sniffling Amanda asked, "Was it terrible?"

"No!" Kitty couldn't stop the sobs that followed.

"Hey, hey, you know I love you and I'm sorry you're sad but for god's sake Kathleen, DETAILS!"

This had the desired effect and Kitty's sobs were replaced by choked laughter.

"Waiting!"

"Mand he is so big and strong but… but so tender and gentle."

"What do you mean more like a brotherly kiss?"

"Oh my no! More like bone melting, dizzy, rip your clothes off sort of kiss."

"SHIT!"
"I know!"
"And?"
"Well I don't know how long we were there."
"Where? Where were you? In the van or in the cottage? Oh have you got a bed up there apart from the van?"
"Stop, wait a minute Mand, for the love of Pete!"
"Well?"
"We stood on the drive… in the moonlight," Kitty let out a loud long sigh.
"And then what?"
"I know, I know, details. I've never experienced anything like in Mand, like I melted. Oh Mand I wanted to sleep with him so badly." With a sob the tears returned cascading unchecked down her cheeks.
"Oh Kit, lovely, I'm sorry. So what happened did you?"
"NO!"
"And now you wish you had?"
"Yes… no… maybe."
"Oh Kit!"
There was a silence but for some sniffing and the rustle of tissues.
"God I enjoyed it but I was terrified. I haven't kissed anyone except Stephen for years, and then only a couple of people. And… well… I liked to too much."
"But Stephen is not there and he's not going to be! Babe you need to move on. Kit you're only young, and you haven't secretly joined a nunnery up there have you?"
"No but I'm supposed to be playing darts with him and his friends Friday night, what do I say?"
"Nothing, just let it evolve, I know it's a long time since you were courting. Trust me it's still the same, it's the same as it was when we were seventeen."
"Um"
"You did only kiss a man, and a very nice man by the sound of it and it's not a crime – unless it is up there on your back water island?"
Kitty had always loved and relied upon Amanda's ability to make her laugh at herself, especially when she started, as she usually did, to over-think everything. Feeling so much better for a bit of best friend therapy Kitty said her goodbyes.
"Ring me afterwards?" Amanda asked.

"Yes, I promise definitely Saturday morning."

"Good I'll stay in till lunch time, but remember you can do what ever you like. If any thing happens before then I need to know about, call!"

"Yes mum."

"Love you Kit."

"Love you more."

15

The Old Man and The Architect

Once parked up at home Kitty ensured any gap in the curtains were tightly closed. There was only one thing for tonight – Jane Austen's Pride and Prejudice - the long version. No one disturbed her tonight and she was very grateful for it. Sleeping much better, lost in her dreams before even Darcy proposed. Keen to be on the road the alarm woke her at seven, and a speedy wash left her ready to investigate the island.

Heading north and keeping as close to the coast as possible Kitty headed for Uige at the north of the Island. The roads were now mostly single track, passing places often on precarious edges looking down over increasingly rugged and undulating landscape. Dark clouds and rain that had followed her now lifted, and shards of sunshine burnt away the water from the black ribbons of road. Fine wisps of steam curled and billowed in Pimples' wake as the bright light changed the dark foreboding view before her into the most romantic vision.

Wondering if she was on the right road it was a relief when a left hand turn finally revealed signs of habitation. Isolated houses began to gather and the first of Kitty's destinations was in sight. Set on high ground, Kitty silenced Pimples and fastened her fleece. The wind literally took her breath away as she stood and stretched, and an icy gust blew into her yawning mouth.

Flora MacDonald's grave rose high above the other stones in Kilmuir cemetery. Flora was part of a vivid memory for Kitty. Mrs Currie had been her year six teacher with a soft, R-rolling Scottish accent. Not only did she teach Scottish dancing in the lunchtime, but would share her passion for her native country in singing lessons. This was where Kitty fell in love with *"Over the Sea to Skye"* and would daydream of rolling heather and highland cows, the ink drawing on the cover of the songbook enough inspiration to let her imagination fly.

Standing, leaning into the wind that raced off the sea up and over the ancient head stones, Kitty battled to keep her hair from her face. She resorted to holding tight to her head with both hands, resenting its persistence. The tall cross was framed by racing clouds and a strip of eau-de-nil sky. The stone looked too well preserved for Flora's 1790 interment, as she remembered the obscure fact that 300 mourners attended her funeral and drank 300 gallons of whiskey. Mrs Currie had passed on her fascination for this woman and this place, and Kitty surprised herself at remembering these snippets of information.

Running a hand over the plaque Kitty silently thanked Mrs Currie for planting these seeds in her. Walking around now, she toed the ancient cross lying broken and unmarked on the ground. The pitting and erosion looked over two hundred years old, and Kitty surmised by the size of this cross it may well have been the original.

Struggling to decipher the inscriptions Kitty repeated in whispers the names she could make out, conjuring images of strong brave Islanders. One stone stood like an arrowhead, no inscription visible but the wounds from the man that had shaped it. How she would have liked to know the history of this grave. Did any living person, a descendant maybe, remember and keep the knowledge alive?

The squeal of the metal gate broke Kitty's silent appreciation and a family made their way noisily towards her. Camera in hand they were obviously tourists, ticking another sightseeing box. The laughter of the children for some reason offended Kitty and she hastened to the farther edges of the enclosed graveyard. Seeking shelter behind the old chapel she almost trod on the most unusual stone. Laying flat on the sward with tufts of long grass waving around its edges was the stone form of a man. The finer details were lost to the harsh environment, but the domed hat and kilt were still obvious along with a huge broad sword. Kitty promised this lost soldier with his cloth of white and green moss and lichen that she would discover his name and his story. Jamie could help her, and for the first time that day her thoughts were transported back to that kilted man. As cold and desolate as this Scotsman was, Kitty felt a tangible pull back to the warm and very alive James Stewart.

Walking now to the edge of the area giving her the optimal views over the sea Kitty stood inhaling the fresh air and attempted to clear her mind. Once again she delighted in the knowledge that the view from here had probably not changed since Flora last stood here. The cleansing air had the desired effect and she enjoyed many minutes thinking only of the subtly changing view.

So far she had managed to idle away five hours of the day, it now took thirty minutes finding somewhere serving hot food. A small café cum craft shop offered respite from the wind, and a hearty bowl of macaroni cheese with warm bread and butter that melted down her fingers.

Resting back in the well-worn chair, Kitty enjoyed watching the coming and going of fellow diners. All had the look of visitors, passing through this small village, maybe to the ferry to further islands, or like herself to visit the graveyard and small museum. She smiled as she too looked every inch the traveller, boots too clean and raincoat too new. Little did they know she was one of the Islands newest recruits, given a little time she would have the weatherworn look of a local.

Feeling she had outstayed her welcome and with others loitering for her table Kitty enjoyed one last look around the shop, taking a mental note to come back when the house was finished. Her early start and the long drive, and now heavy and warm from her lunch Kitty opted for a rest before driving further. It was still taking some getting used to the fact that parking was free. Having left a county where it was impossible to park anywhere for a few minutes without shelling out, or risk a parking ticket, or worst still, a clamp. Kitty would giggle when the frequent waves of panic would strike, she hadn't paid! But no, you didn't have to – how very bizarre, and yet, how wonderful.

Laying on the bed, coat and shoes discarded, the afternoon sun warmed her. She enjoyed the delight of drifting in and out sleep, a true catnap. Alert enough to be aware of voices in the car park and the distant rumble of the arriving ferry, but totally relaxed. The patter of heavy rain on her window finally stirred her. The sun was now gone and she woke with a small shiver. Yawning and rubbing her upper arms briskly, she clambered into the front seats, and savouring a humbug checked the map for the drive home. She hadn't used a map since her childhood and hadn't realised how dependent she had become on her Satnav. Signal appeared a rare and precious commodity on the island and knowledge of her whereabouts on a map was crucial.

Pushing further north the aim was to get to the most northerly Duntulm and come back down the East coast to take in the views of the old man at Storr. Signs of habitation were few, and her corner of Skye seemed like a thriving metropolis compared with the comparative wilderness here.

She had seen pictures of the rocky outcrop in guidebooks, and with the low cloud draped on its shoulders and grey light of an overcast day it was an imposing sight. "A pot bellied pinnacle of crumbling basalt" was one description Kitty randomly recalled. She could hear her mother's voice now, "That old man of Storr... got a right pot belly and they say he's made up of basalt – not the good stuff mind, crumbling he is."

Having her mum's voice to keep her company Kitty shook off the drab day and smiled as she discovered new roads and new beautiful horizons.

Turning into the now familiar drive "Home" she said quietly only to herself, and patting Pimples she left him and walked stiffly to the house. Closing the gate, she could make out white paper flapping in the early evening breeze at the foot of the front door. Stooping Kitty picked up the neat bunch of pink roses, a note pirouetted in the air *"To Kitty from Jamie x"*. Carrying them in Kitty arranged them in the small jug and placed them in the window. The front window just in-case a certain Scotsman might walk along the foreshore and see them.

Friday arrived and Kitty struggled to concentrate, Friday was darts night! Angus had already threatened to come to the house and get her if she didn't show. Darts she liked but the prospect of seeing Jamie was all she could think of. The intensity of her, and she was sure, his feelings would be obvious to all – could they possibly act like the relative strangers they were? Distraction was the order of the day and she decided to visit Donald and try, at least for a few hours to focus on the house and put Jamie out of her mind.

She drove slowly to Donald's office with her final decisions. Any hopes of a quick visit were soon dashed. Donald walked out into the reception as she approached the desk.

"Good afternoon Kathleen, wonderful to see you." If Kitty had to describe his voice, one word sprang to mind - "oily," - each word flowed faultlessly into the next. It was a rich deep voice, and there in his office it reminded her very much of Shere Khan. Donald gestured for Kitty to follow him back into his office. A young dark haired receptionist eyed Kitty suspiciously, looking her up and down and only then returning Kitty's genuine smile with a forced flash of teeth.

"Do come in Kathleen, this is very pleasant, sit, sit." Pointing Kitty to a large angular orange leather sofa, before sitting himself,

Donald called back to the reception, "Sophie, some coffee if you would?"

Kitty thought about declining but liked the idea of the surly Sophie having to make her a beverage.

"And what have you been up to Kathleen?"

An innocent enough question, Kitty struggled to give an innocent answer when all that popped into her mind was satin nighties and snogging!

"Oh not much really... I've been to the swimming pool a couple of times," lame answer she knew.

"Are you a keen swimmer? I myself swam at University – Edinburgh – but don't do it as often as I should these days."

"No ... no not keen as such, but I have discovered their wonderful showers," colouring slightly at the admission.

"Aye, aye of course" he grinned down at her.

Expecting Donald to sit at the other end of the long sofa Kitty had to turn on the spot to face him uncomfortably when he sat inches from her. Removing the arm he had placed on the low back of the sofa he thumbed through the folder Kitty eagerly produced. Jotting notes in the leather note pad Kitty remembered, and the silver pencil she found quite mesmerising as he turned it slowly in his long thin fingers.

"Well good, I do like a decisive woman" his arm was back behind her and Kitty cleared her throat as she realised it was his aftershave or body spray that now clawed at her throat. She would be glad of the offered coffee now. Trying to inch away Kitty found the immovable arm of the sofa and was very glad to see Sophie enter stony faced, with a tray of coffee. Placing it heavily on the table on the furthest corner to Donald, it had the desired effect for both women. As he stood to pull it towards them Kitty put her bag and folder on the seat besides her so he was forced to sit at least arms length away. Sophie grinned as she turned to close the door, for their own reasons neither wanted Donald to sit too close to his client.

"Here, sugar? Cream?" Donald took his time and was obviously in no rush for her to leave.

"I didn't want to hold you up, if you're busy Donald?"

"Oh no, no I've been looking forward to seeing you."

After a little silence Kitty sipped her coffee self consciously, she could feel the blush high on her cheeks.

"I drove to Uige yesterday."

"Why?" Donald frowned down at her.

"Oh just to see some of the island, its wild up there isn't it, I liked it though, I like the lack of people," aware she was rambling a little she retuned to the coffee, he made no attempt to talk but eyed her, unnerving Kitty.

"I went to the cemetery at Kilmuir, to Flora MacDonald's grave, it was bleak there but I thought it was a very peaceful place."

"It's not huge but it will take you a life time to explore. Are you here for the long term Kathleen?" It was a very pointed question and took Kitty aback slightly.

"Um... well, yes I am."

"Grand."

"I have nothing to go back to in Kent, and my home, where I grew up is in Wimbledon and apart from some old friends no ties."

"No one special hankering for you back south?"

Kitty looked into his eyes, there was something there she didn't trust. There was no reason, he had given her no reason, but there was definitely something she couldn't quite put her finger on. You're over thinking it again, and channelling Amanda now, she chided herself, "Get a grip Kit, man up."

"No, free as a bird!" she finally replied.

Donald smiled broadly and continued to sip his coffee in the ensuing silence.

"Are you free this evening?" the words washed over her and the sense of someone walking now over her grave rattled the small cup and saucer.

"Oh, no... sorry, I'm off to the hotel, the one at the headland. Apparently its dart night and Joan the postman's wife is always on the look out for new talent – or victims in my case."

"Oh" Donald looked displeased as he digested this information.

"Who else do you know there? Have the locals been friendly?"

"Yes very" coughing and leaning forward to place the empty cup on the table and hide the rising glow of her cheeks.

"The lads from the Celtic band will be there." The less she said about them the better. "Lilly the bar maid is on the ladies team."

Donald was looking singularly unimpressed with the idea of darts in a pub.

"It's only a couple of minutes walk from home and should be fun" Kitty was annoyed at herself then for trying to justify her actions.

"Well I know an exceptional pub with a stunning choice of whiskey and an a-la-carte menu, are you sure I can not tempt you?" He had a very persuasive manner and his accent though obviously Scottish, was more Anglicised and polished than Jamie's. Making this comparison Kitty realised there was no way she would forgo an evening of darts with Jamie for all the fine whiskey in the Highlands.

As Donald leaned towards her, Kitty took the opportunity to duck around him and stand.

"Oh thank you for the kind offer, I'm really not dressed for fine dining, rain check?" Wincing Kitty embarrassed herself, not only did she despise this expression she didn't actually want to go to a fine dinner with her architect. Trying to back peddle, "Maybe when my clothes make it out of storage." Knowing that would be months away she tried to redeem herself.

"It's a date Kathleen!" Donald said too assuredly for her liking. Taking her by the hand she returned the handshake, and tried to smile as he held her hand in both of his for more seconds than Kitty found comfortable. Once released Kitty resisted the urge to wipe it on her jeans but gathered her paper work and bag.

Walking out past the reception Donald maintained a constant pressure on the small of her back. Kitty could well imagine Sophie's expression and enjoyed turning to thank her for the coffee and seeing she was right.

"Well, till Sunday Kathleen."

And purely for Sophie's benefit, smiling up at Donald Kitty replied, "I look forward to it Donald, twelve o'clock was it? I'll see you there." Regretting her enthusiasm slightly as he eagerly replied.

"Oh, do let me pick you up, it's on my way."

Again knowing it was wickedly indulgent to behave like this for effect, Kitty couldn't help herself, "Oh would you Donald, thank you I'll see you at mine."

Kitty could barely contain herself as Donald leant and kissed her slowly on both cheeks. Stifling a giggle as she glanced around him and saw Sophie, "Oh and Sophie is it? Thank you for the coffee."

Once in Pimples and safely out of sight Kitty threw her head back and laughed until her face and belly ached. Sophie was an attractive, and judging by her accent, a local lass. Early twenties Kitty estimated and obviously madly in love with Donald. Her eyes on him were like large brown doe's and would fire flames if she could when looking at Kitty. Well good luck there lovey, not a chance.

16

The Truth

Smiling all the way home, Kitty was in just the right frame of mind for a night up the local. A quick wash in Tide's sink and some fresh undies and she was all but ready. Standing folding the washing that had dried well on the airer, something caught her eye at the front window. Heart in her mouth she waited and then the knock came, three gentle taps on the front door.

Afraid but excited all at the same time Kitty brushed back her hair and straightened her clothes, buttons and fly fastened – no bare inappropriate parts on show – she walked nervously to the door. Her heart leapt at the sight of the down turned mess of conker red hair, and she felt it could possibly stop beating altogether as the large pool like eyes met hers.

"Come in."

"Thanks."

Turning to walk into the kitchen Jamie closed the door quietly and followed. Kitty, aware of him close behind threw a tea towel over the pile of clean knickers on the table.

"You and ye penchant for showing off ye underwear," Jamie smiled trying to lighten the mood.

"Well at least it's only you that seems to... keep seeing it." Kitty forced a smile although she was fast feeling quite nauseous.

"Dunna get me wrong I'll not be complaining," the corner of his mouth curled, god she wanted to kiss him.

"Jamie?"

"Yes Kathleen."

"Jamie about the other night?"

"Yes."

"Well... I don't know what to say... I'm new to all this." Unable to further explain she pointed to herself and him.

"Ye did'na seen all that new to it, to me."

"I've been with my husband since we were eighteen, there's only ever been, him..."

"Oh... I see."

"And, well at thirty."

"Bloody hell are ya thirty – that old?" with fake shock.

"Oh don't tell me how old you are?"

"Twenty five."

"Ohh... that only makes it worse."

"Kathleen" his voice was low and Kitty swallowed with effort. Jamie stepped towards her now but she backed away, she needed space if she was going to get through this conversation – hands raised to deter his advance.

"I'll not hurt ye," his forehead furrowed.

"Oh I know that… I'm just afraid… afraid you might kiss me again," her voice sounded weak even to herself.

"Ye dunna like it?" he visibly sagged, dejected, rejected! "Do ye not like it, ye… dunna like… me?" barely audible now, half statement, half question.

"God no, NO! The trouble is I liked it far too much" it was Kitty's turn to whisper. "More than I have liked kissing anyone."

Stepping back was futile and Jamie soon had firm hold of her upper arms, Kitty struggled to turn and hide the tears that began to pool and blur her vision.

"Come here lass, at least let me touch ye," Pulling her closer he wrapped strong arms around Kitty who finally relaxed onto his chest and slowly slid her hands around to his back. Jamie's sigh was huge and juddering, and Kitty could hear and feel the pounding of his heart through the rough wool that tickled her face.

After several minutes their breathing settled, and hearts regained a more sustainable beat. Jamie leant down and lifted her chin with thumb and forefinger, to seek her mouth with his. Turning away Kitty now pushed against his chest.

"Why?" Jamie's desperation was clear to hear, "Why not? Kathleen talk to me."

Kitty turned to the window that she had backed up to; maybe it would be easier to talk if not looking into his gorgeous eyes.

"I don't know, this is... it's so unexpected… too soon… not right - I feel so disloyal" A sob escaped and she clutched the cool sill for support.

"Is there someone else? Kathleen are ye… still married?" Jamie stammered over the last word as if it could have choked him. "You wear a ring, is that it? Are you not free… free to be with me?" Jamie had been floored by the intensity of feelings he had for this woman that bore no relation to the short time he had known her. The thought that whatever this was, and wherever it was going, could end here completely winded him. Clutching the back of the chair he too needed support.

They stood under the weight of the silence, Kitty picked at the roses, finally breaking the quiet.

"Thank you for these they are beautiful."

"You are beautiful." Kitty could feel his breath on her bent neck. "You must tell me Kathleen... I've never felt like this, never been like this. I can'na sleep, I can'na concentrate and I certainly can'na eat. All I think of is you and I fear it's driving me mad."

Gently then, afraid of her recoiling he placed his hands softly on her shoulders and planted the briefest of kisses on her neck. Kitty let out an involuntary "Oh!"

"That's it... isn't it, you're married?"

Kitty couldn't find the words, couldn't begin to sound them. Her throat stung as she struggled to not cry. They both leapt as a loud bang shook them and the front door.

"Oh shit, now, really!" Kitty made to make for the hall as the second bang resounded but Jamie held her back roughly by one tethered wrist.

"Tell me?" pleading now.

"I can't Jamie… not now."

Releasing her Jamie felt he would explode and only because he reasoned he would break it, he didn't thump the back of the chair.

"Angus... oh hello... come in."

"Thank you," Angus tucked his head under the doorframe.

"Jamie's in the kitchen." Kitty suddenly feeling an explanation was needed for being caught together.

"Aye I saw his car from the road, I guessed he'd come to convince ye to come."

"Angus," Jamie's welcome was anything but friendly.

Angus was cheerful and seemingly ignored Jamie's gruff response, and if he was aware of the atmosphere he ignored it or at least valiantly tried to lift it.

"Well we'd best not take ta long about it, Lilly is counting on ye lass, evening Jamie."

"Angus, we'll meet you up there." Jamie gruffly nodding and sending a loaded wink his way, but oblivious Angus chatted on.

"No away wi ya, come on, come on now wi ya we daresn't be late."

Kitty, keen to take advantage of the reprieve grabbed her coat and followed Angus as he headed for the door.

"Come on Jamie."

The glare he returned was ill disguised and as she stooped to lock the front door after them, Jamie took firm hold of her arm and whispered into her hair.

"Will ye tell me or no Kathleen?"

"I will Jamie, but not now, not here!"

Angus's buoyancy carried the quiet pair along to the hotel and once inside the bar Joan came, and taking Kitty by the arm swept them to the huddle of women in the corner. Jamie stood silently at the bar, eyes fixed, unblinkingly on Kitty as his friends laughed and chatted around him. Kitty listened to the tactics and game plan of the darts team but strained her ears to catch Jamie's voice. She had hoped despite his obvious agitation at her house once he was with his friends he would relax, and they could both get through this evening without trauma. But not a sound and every furtive glance was answered by a silent steely stare and the fact that he was knocking back a lot of liqueur.

The darts match started, if she wasn't involved she would have borne it no longer and taken Jamie outside and told him everything. Lilly, Kitty, Joan and Morag took on the Sleat team of Pat, Irene, Maggie and Annie. After a very flushed and rusty start Kitty soon found her swing and it was a close run match. Joan was up last and had a fabulous 140 finish and double top sealed the deal and gave them an overall win.

There followed much good-humoured banter and jeering between all the women. Kitty was well aware ordinarily she would have thoroughly enjoyed the evening's entertainment and counted it as a success, but today, with those jade eyes fixed upon her it had been quite an ordeal.

Making her excuses Kitty left the bar to find the toilets, aware all the time of Jamie's stare upon her. She was feeling worse with every minute that passed and wished she had just told him in the kitchen and saved them both an agonising few hours. Walking behind Jamie surrounded by his friends, but not feeling able to speak, Kitty let her fingers brush over his where they rested on a bar stool between them. Fleeting, as the touch was it caused them both to jolt and Kitty forced a smile as she walked on to the ladies.

Kitty really did need to use the toilet, and locking the enclosure door she felt for the first time she could relax since Jamie had walked into her kitchen today. Head in hands she sat longer than she needed and stirred only when the outer door creaked. Expecting it was one of the darts party Kitty left the only cubicle whilst still looking down to fasten her belt.

Stopping dead, the doorway was blocked by the not insubstantial Jamie. Arms outstretched he gripped the frame; there was no way around him.

"Oh, god Jamie, you made me jump." Kitty's smile was not returned but Jamie's face remained unaltered, like thunder.

"Out of the way, Jamie... Jamie please?" Kitty voice trembled and Jamie's voice cracked in reply.

"Not until you tell me" his jaw clenched as he spoke. Tears welling in his sad green eyes. "Please, I need to know. Its torture watching ya this evening – I need to KNOW!"

Reaching up for his face she stroked the bristles gently, "Not in the toilets," her voice soft, trying to make Jamie smile, but he stared resolutely back at her. Jamie moved fast and catching her off balance pushed her back into the stall. Swinging her around he had her pinned against the now closed door. Lifting her head, her attempts to keep looking down at her feet futile. Jamie kissed her, the tenderness of previous kisses gone and in its place anger and frustration drove him on. At first Kitty kissed him back, she had thought of little else all evening, all day come to that. This kiss was pure passion, unrequited need, and Jamie for the first time was strong and persistent.

Gone was any hesitation, and when Kitty, desperate to breathe, tried to push him away he only held her tighter. Panicking slightly now, Kitty tried to push on his chest with the flats of both hands. Jamie was lost in the moment and the fog of too much whiskey and no food that day. Taking both her hands in his and holding them to her sides he continued to kiss her oblivious of her struggles. Stopping only to pin her arms above her head, both slim wrists in one huge hand, gave Kitty only enough time to gasp in desperate breaths.

About to protest his lips crushed back on hers, probing and bruising. His free hand held around her neck and she was pinned to the door. After what seemed like minutes but was only seconds Jamie's hand travelled from her neck to her chest, fumbling, untucking her top and he began pawing at her breast. Passion and lust had crossed over to attack and hurt. Kitty's stifled scream and now frantic attempts to free herself jolted a drunken Jamie back to sanity. He didn't let go of the hold on her arms but took his arm quickly from her chest. Looking shocked into her wide eyes he lowered her now red wrists and gathered her gently to him and wept in her hair.

"Oh god, forgive me, Kathleen, Kathleen, I'm sorry, sorry," his voice trailed away as his body shook. Kitty was unable to speak and could feel herself begin to shake, rubbing her wrists she stayed frozen to the spot. Jamie lifted his head and Kitty waited until the tear lined eyelashes lifted and they stood inches apart, eyes locked. Backing away he slowly she tentatively rested two fingers on her red lips.

"Oh god, what have I done? I'm sorry, so sorry!"

As he pulled further back Kitty managed to raise a trembling hand and land a flat handed slap across his cheek. Kitty hoped it hurt him more than her smarting hand.

"I deserve it Kathleen, I told you, ye have bewitched me... and I have never, would never treat a lass like that. I dunna ken... you make me wild. I, I want ye so badly."

Kitty's face looked unblinkingly back at him.

"And... and y, you think this will win me over?" her voice growing stronger and louder with every word. "I'd like to, I want to go now" assertively she stood to her full height.

"Aye, aye... but let me explain, I'm so, so sorry."

"My coat and bag are in the bar, I can't go back in there, not now."

"Aye, aye I'll fetch them."

"Ok."

Jamie reached again and touched her face, the merest of contact and she flinched. It was all he could do to contain himself long enough to collect her things. Drying his face on his sleeve he muttered to Angus, head down and was glad of the subdued lighting. His explanation that Kitty felt a little worse for wear and that he would see her home resulted in jibes and laughter. It had not gone unnoticed that James Stewart had followed the pretty southerner out of the bar. Their absence for the past ten minutes had already been discussed at length in the bar, and the likely outcome decided upon – no one was surprised Jamie was "seeing" her home.

Jamie heard the laughter and banter fade away as he rushed out. With a much greater problem at hand he rushed to the ladies.

"Kathleen!"

Calling timidly but with no response he pushed open the doors, she was gone. She was gone! Jamie sobered by the minute, the fresh air much appreciated. Feeling her coat he sighed with relief as he found the keys to her van. Stumbling now over the cobbles, tripping and falling towards her drive, straining to see in the black night where had she gone? He must apologise, must make her believe before she could lock herself away or worse still go away.

Running down the drive after her Jamie slowed as he neared, seeing the look of fear on her face. Teeth chattering and pale as a star she jumped back as he reached for her.

"Kathleen, please... please" pleading and with slow movements he handed over her coat. "Here please you're so cold."

Hesitating for a moment Kitty took the coat hurriedly put it on and fastened it and drove her hands deep into the pockets.

"I need to apologise I need to make you understand."

"Understand what? Exactly!" Kitty hissed back at him, fear turned to anger now. "Understand you're a bully? Understand you want to hurt me?" She shouted up at him, taking deep breaths she wanted to be angry at him. Why did he have such beautiful eyes? Even in this dim light the tears had darkened his lashes and they were truly beautiful. Both struggled to control their ragged breathing until Kitty broke the silence.

"I... I've, never... never been treated like that, touched, frightened like that before."

"And I've never done that before. I ken I've had a dram too many, but never this, Kathleen please. I've never been rough with a lassie... I dunna ken what happened. I, I have never."

"So you thought I'd be the one to try it on, did you, the lonely Londoner – bit of sport for you was it?" She spat out these words.

"No... no, no!" Jamie staggered, the force of his denial knocking him off balance. Retching now he lunged towards a small tree and vomited. Waves of nausea, not from the whiskey or his lack of food but from the sombre realisation of what he had done. He had attacked the one, the only woman who had entered his heart and mind but refused him the truth and refused him herself.

Kitty ran, she was scared and in shock. Terrified he would catch her she glanced repeatedly over her shoulder, and when the darkness and distance rendered him invisible she craned her head to listen for his footfall. Rounding his car she shook and fumbled with the keys until she was safely in Pimples and locked the door. Checking the curtains were closed she buried herself under the quilt fully dressed.

Surely she could not be cold? But coated and booted she shivered under her covers. She hadn't expected to sleep and with surprise the dawn chorus awoke her. Lying quite still for many minutes Kitty listened. With no other noise than the birds and the gentle lap of the tide Kitty decided there was nothing for it and she must venture out.

Despite being still fully clothed Kitty was cold. Hesitating with hand on the curtain it took a moment to pluck up the courage to peek out to where Jamie's car had been.

"Oh SHIT!" The blue polo was there, not ten feet from Kitty and there in the drivers seat, hunched and asleep lay Jamie. Her first thought was to be afraid but the soothing, sensible voice of Amanda was in her head now.

Did you enjoy the kiss? – Yes at first.
Did you kiss him back? – Yes again.
And when you got really into it and he touched you up? – I told him to stop.
And did he? – Yes.
And was he sorry? – Yes.

Kitty mouthing what she knew would be her friend's final word – *and your problem is?*

As quietly as she could manage she slid Pimples door open, hesitating at each noise to be sure the sleeping form didn't move she closed it after herself. Tiptoeing over the gravel she took the shortest distance to the grass. Once safely on the boggy lawn she hurried to the house.

Using the bolt for only the second time since she had been here she sighed in relief at making it to the outside loo. Soon outside again and with no sign of Jamie, she rushed around to the front door and bolted that behind her.

"Buy some bloody curtains!" she shouted to no one but herself. A mug of tea helped, which of course it always does, and she could feel the ice inside her thaw. Nibbling absent-mindedly on a biscuit all she could think was, what she wouldn't give for a hot bath right now! There was nothing she had to do today so a visit to the swimming pool was in order, after she had put things straight with Jamie.

Making him a cup of tea she felt sure they could talk reasonably today. Splashing her face with the crisp tap water Kitty went to him, he was gone. No car, no Jamie.

"Shit!"

Kitty was going to tell him everything, but what now? She sat on the low garden wall facing the rising tide and drank his tea. Amanda (blissfully as yet unaware) had put it all straight in Kitty's mind. He had seemed truly sorry, repentant even. The more she thought about his words the more she understood, she knew what he meant.

The passion, the immense longing to be touched by him, the like she had never known. Remembering and replaying his words.

"All I think of is you and I fear it's driving me mad."

"I deserve it Kathleen, I told you, you have bewitched me."

Comparing her feeling for Stephen now, as unpalatable as it was, with her feelings for Jamie, she could not deny that they were worlds apart. Never had it been so desperate, so urgent and Kitty remembered their easy comfortable love. Love and sex had grown from friendship and laughter, and even in their early years had there ever been the intensity she had experienced in these past days?

Surprising herself and feeling the blush on her cheeks Kitty wondered if that was what making out was like, what on earth would sex be like? But this thought truly terrified her and she tried to push that far from her mind. She had to find him, but realised she had no idea where he lived.

Washed, dressed and a hurried bowl of porridge later, Kitty Harris was on a mission. First stop, the Heritage centre. Pulling up, hopes plummeted, as there was no sign of his car. Pressing her nose to the locked door there were clearly no lights on and no sign of life. A roughly written note was taped crookedly in the window, *Closed due to ill health.*

Kitty had no idea if anyone else worked there, or, if it was a full time job for Jamie. Heading now to the post office Kitty would have to risk causing more gossip and adding more wood to her own pyre and ask Angela.

The next frustration was a long queue at the counter. Kitty mooched around the shop waiting for Angela to be free, but soon realised she would have to take her place in the line. Maybe it was pension day, but just for the purpose of her frazzled nerves a trickle of customers kept jingling the bell over the door. Picking up items she didn't need and even a large bar of chocolate, which perhaps she did need, Kitty waited, and waited… and waited! Then waited just a little bit more. Finally with a roll of the eyes from Angela she was ahead of the line of four, strangely self-conscious.

"Hiya Kitty what can I do for you?"

Kitty leaned as close to the counter as she could.

"Is it just these?" Glad of Angela's prompt she had forgotten the cake, rolls and loaf of bread that were squashed under her arm.

"Ange" leaning closer still and whispering, "Do you know where Jamie Stewart lives?"

"What? Speak up love."

"Do you know where Jamie Stewart lives?" a little louder and mouthing to Angela as if she had suddenly been struck deaf.

"Jamie... he lives in one of the estate cottages on the road to the ferry, I think so, hang on."

"David, DAVID! Do you know where Jamie Stewart lives?" Yelled Angela, rising on tiptoe, much to Kitty's mortification. The bearded man at the far end of the queue looked up,

"Who's that? I dunna keen lass, what's she saying?" He turned to the woman in front of him bewildered. Cupping a withered hand to his ear he looked back at Angela. The woman in front of him shouted back at him.

"Ya ken, the Stewarts eldest laddie, Jamie, fine young lad, big like his da and fine red hair."

"Oh Jamie, aye, aye right enough, I know Jamie."

A mortified Kitty held her head in her hands and drooped onto the counter.

"Aye, on the estate, after the ferry turning, after the loch." There was general agreement from all in the now stifling room that this was where Jamie lived. Kitty left with a red face of shame, some patchy directions and a chorus of giggles and calls referring to her corrupting the wee laddie!

She followed the instructions as patchy as they were. There was a turning signposted for the ferry and a large strip of black water, which she reasoned, could be a loch. Still new to the area she decided she would have to learn what constitutes a loch and not just a large pond. The land here was barren, no flat ground but undulating boggy grass stained with patches of dead bracken. Kitty was becoming accustomed to the speed with which the weather turned, and the black cloud occupying half the sky would drop at any moment.

Having not seen a house since before the loch Kitty slowed as she approached a row of small stone cottages. Well, good old David said you couldn't miss them so Kitty turned off the engine. "Come on!" Kitty slapped her thighs in a weak attempt at a pep talk and to motivate herself into movement. All the cottages were in a similar state of repair and nothing distinguished one from its neighbours. There was nothing for it, she would have to start at one end and work her way along.

Heart pounding, Kitty tapped gently on the first door, and waited. Nothing, harder this time, swallowing the bile rising in her chest, but still nothing. Risking a peek in the front windows framed by heavy cabbage rose curtains Kitty could see matching wing armchairs and the small table by the window sat a pile of knitting atop a lace cloth – surely not!

The next door received a firmer knock but again no reply. Not bothering to knock again Kitty stepped between the shoots of bulbs covered her eye brows with one hand pressed against the glass – I hope not! A chaos of plastic toys and a bright plastic highchair sat in the window complete with toast crusts. Lilly had said he was a bachelor, surely someone would have mentioned a small child.

Nerves were fast being replaced by frustration and Kitty hurt her knuckles on the third door, again no reply. "Really!"

Peeping into this window Kitty's heart skipped. Tartan cushions squashed down on a large well-worn brown leather chair in front of a small wood burner. Next to the chair a small dark oak table housed a decanter and glass, whiskey Kitty guessed and a very heavily worn leather rucksack. This was Jamie's, she had seen the bag before and everything screamed him. Banging loudly now Kitty strained to look through to the back of the cottage; she could see the kitchen window but no sign of life.

Rushing back to the van Kitty ransacked the shelves in desperation, finally pen and paper in hand she began to write;

Dear – should she call him dear, but he was, is dear to her so sod it – it's dear!
Dear Jamie,
I felt terrible this morning, the things I said yesterday. You have bewitched me too. Please come and see me and I can tell you everything.
Love – Oh was this too soon? But it was written now.
Kathleen

Folding it carefully and adding a Jamie to the outside she returned to the front door, a final large rap for good measure but when no reply was forth coming she posted the note, turned reluctantly to Pimples.

Wanting now to be back at Tide's Reach incase he should come looking for her, Kitty didn't look back but sped past the loch. Safely back on the drive Kitty spent an hour tidying the van. Trying not to look at the drive and the road above - she failed. Every car that passed was noticed and even the couple walking their dog along the top road were scrutinised.

For the first time Kitty keenly felt the lack of signal, the inconvenience of the isolation. If she were back home – no this was her home now without doubt - but if she had been down south they would have exchanged mobile numbers and have been texting already.

The day dragged, unable to concentrate on anything. Writing was abandoned after staring at the empty stark page for over an hour. Reading was impossible, his words replaying in place of the text and she threw her book at the kitchen wall. She knew the best thing would have been a long walk on the beach but she couldn't risk not being there if he came.

"I can'na sleep, I can'na concentrate and I certainly can'na eat."
And Kitty could not eat.

The sense of unease haunted her all day and disturbed her even in sleep. Running across bleak hills chasing an ever-distancing figure of billowing red hair and tartan. Kitty's feet, bare and bleeding, were sinking into the claggy moss, hampering her every step as if thousands of minute hands pulled her down.

17

Snap and Yorkshire Puddings

On waking Kitty still felt tired, there was nothing for it she would have to go swimming today. Waiting for the pool to open she tried to focus on the positives of the day. She was pleased to have the distraction of the offer of dinner at the Duncan's and she was determined to conquer this. She had moved to Skye for a new life, to renovate a cottage, to paint, to write a book. Not, within days, to become obsessed with a man, a younger man, a man who occupied the majority of her thoughts. Kitty knew the sooner the builders started and she could busy herself with the house the better.

She ploughed countless lengths and again was very grateful to the long hot shower. After the disappointment of seeing the empty drive and checking for any sign of a certain visitor Kitty decided on a walk. Once again feeling the claustrophobia of waiting with little hope of Jamie coming, she set off to the derelict croft. Passing the croft she was too keyed up to sit as usual but slipped down onto the blackish green of the high tide mark. She reminded herself to investigate when high tide was, as the walk around the headland was much more enjoyable when the tide was out. She seemed to think it varied an hour a day but didn't know how she knew this or if in fact it was true.

Frustrated at the difficulty of walking high on the beach Kitty ventured inland, and attempted cutting through the undergrowth and up the bank. With broken flashes of her dream now, every attempt failed. What looked like soft lush ground teasing her with violets and primroses was in fact a tangle of roots and gullies. With a blanket of saturated moss obscured what lay beneath, threatening to overflow her boots with its sinister black ooze.

Kitty pushed on further than she had before and sat to rest on a high crop of rocks jutting out over the water. The sea outside Tide's Reach could at times be mistaken for a millpond but for the gradual ebb and flow of the tide. From the time she had arrived she had seen only the smallest of waves, white capped, gently rolling in to embrace the rocks and boats outside her garden.

Not so here, outside the protection of her cove and facing the open expanse of the sea. Waves had strength and menace; the white horses rolled and tumbled onto the lower rocks where she sat. It was she thought, a little insight into what winter could bring to her peaceful cove. The sky today was clear and bright and covered three tones of blues, a pale forget-me-not overhead blending into a bright sapphire and merging with the sea on the horizon a dark steely sinister threat of rain to come.

The ancient coldness beneath her had seeped through her layers and Kitty could feel it searching out her bones. Standing now she knew the diversion had been a success, and by the time she had made it back to Tide's helped by the receding water it was nearing the time for Donald to collect her.

She had in fact been out longer than intended and rushed to change and was mid tooth brush at the kitchen sink when a knock on the window made her jump. Disappointed that it wasn't a different Scotsman Kitty forced a smile, it wasn't Donald's fault after all. Welcoming him in Kitty gathered her coat and keys.

"Well that bathroom can't come soon enough."

"No, but as I don't have to go to work its no great hardship going to the pool, and you never know it might get me fit." Kitty chuckled but her mood soon soured.

"Oh you look fit enough to me." Donald had a way of saying one thing and implying something quite different. There was an tone in his voice, a veneer of smugness or was it arrogance which Kitty suspected hid something or some thoughts that weren't necessarily very pleasant.

"Well it will all start tomorrow, I'm excited!" Kitty shrugged off negative thoughts.

"As well you should be, and dunna worry I will keep a ready eye on old Stewart and keep him in check."

Again rather than being comforted or reassured she felt indignation on Malcolm Stewart's behalf and was sure he deserved no such monitoring or censure.

"Well he seems nice enough to me, and Claire said he was very good."

"Aye, yes, but these old highlanders move at their own sweet pace. Not what you'll be used to in London."

"Kent." She corrected him and continued, "Well that will suit me fine, I'm very pleased to be out of the rat race now."

Aware, whether because of the angst over Jamie or a genuine dislike of Donald the sooner they were in lighter company the better.

"Come on Donald, we don't want to let Claire's Yorkshires get cold."

Donald opened the front door and strode through it and marched to his Land rover. Kitty locked the door and attempted to match his pace, breathing deeply as she opened the car door and struggled to clamber in.

She had been spoilt by her brief acquaintance with Jamie and this marked Donald as singularly un-chivalrous – but she realised in this respect so was Stephen. She could grow to like doors being opened, chairs pulled out and even walking on the safe side of the path.

In an effort to impress, she felt sure, Donald raced around the roads. Flaunting his prowess as a driver and the superiority of his car resulting in a slightly green Kitty, very relieved to step out on the Duncans' drive and take deep steadying breaths. Donald, oblivious to her plight, for which she was very glad, marched off to the house without waiting for her. Enjoying a few more deep breaths Kitty was in no humour to catch him up.

Once in the open plan kitchen living room Donald melted in as only old friends can. He and Hamish chatted easily whilst Hamish made tea. There was no sign of Claire and Kitty was drawn to the squeals of laughter from the mat in front of the humming log burner. Two blonde children sat cross legged on the rug playing snap, bending forward effortlessly, elbows near to the ground poised to slap outstretched hands on the battered cards.

Kitty hadn't noticed Claire's arrival until calls of introductions came through the steam from the Aga.

"Heather, Jonty say hello to Kathleen."

"Hello," they chorused with the briefest of looks and smiles, neither trusting the other to take their eyes or concentration off what was obviously a fiercely fought competition.

"Can I help?" Kitty started towards the kitchen but was soon stopped in her tracks by Claire's insistence that she was fine.

"Donald, Hamish stop talking about golf, we have a guest."

"Am I not a guest also?" Donald's wounded expression had Hamish chuckling.

"You, old fellow are more in the category of furniture I'm afraid" Hamish slapped Donald across the back then, assisted by a raised eyebrow look from his wife, he stood and walked over to Kitty.

"Oh Kathleen how rude, come, come have a seat, what can I get you to drink?" Gesturing for her to sit on the opposite sofa than

Donald, Kitty felt sure she saw a look of disappointment on his face. She would endeavour to get at least a sofa's length distance from him today. Hamish soon returned with a very large glass of red wine and Kitty settled back into the large feather cushions and sighed a very contented sigh, breathing in the smells of a roast dinner.

Nothing took Kitty back to her childhood more than the smells wafting over her now, those carefree Sundays. Old movies, playing cards with Tommy on the threadbare red and blue rug. Always a fire on a Sunday, even if it wasn't really cold enough, Kitty loved lying on the rug, the smell of dirty old carpet strangely comforting as she watched the logs crack, grow pale and crumble. Siblings taking it in turns to sneak in to the kitchen and steal the juicy, rich small off cuts from the meat from the edges of the platter. Both convinced of their stealth but never knowing the truth. Their mother always turned to the sink with a wide smile at the telltale sound of the hall floor boards creaking. Kitty had always thought these the prized part of any roast, and she retained the guilty pleasure to this day of eating them surreptitiously when dishing up.

Kitty was brought back to the present by her host, "So, Kathleen I've not seen you since that first meeting, what have you been up to?" She chatted easily with Hamish, watching Donald whom she knew listened to every word whilst prodding Jonty's back side with his toe in an effort to put him off his game – mean of him Kitty thought. Hamish on the other hand was all easy manners and gentleness of speech, once a doctor always a doctor Kitty thought. Questions were worded thoughtfully, ample time given for response. The nodding smile of reassurance crafted and honed over years making you feel you could easily tell him anything.

The squeals of delight at winning the pack made the entire party smile. Sitting floppy blonde hair almost touching they were alike in looks and manners as any brother and sister could be. Kitty waited for the floor shuffling that marked the end of a game to engage with them.

"How old are you Heather?" the large brown eyes blinked up at her, and the small girl straightened her legs to the side wriggling her feet. After no inconsiderable thought proclaimed.

"Six!"

Hamish laughed and lent forward to ruffle the now indignant looking head.

"Four Heath, you're four! I'm five, I'm nearly six. Aren't I dad, tell her!"

"Yes Jonty you're right, but Heather, four is a wonderful age to be" Holding out his arms, and embarrassed by the newcomer Heather launched herself with complete trust into his arms as he gathered her in for a bear of a hug.

As lovely a sight as it was, Kitty couldn't help but feel the fragility and sadness that one-day this relationship would inevitably be taken from them. Happy, strong and solid the bonds that tie father and child. A child's hero, someone who would always provide and protect, have the answers to all things. Yet Kitty knew only too well all this could vanish – be snatched away and never be replaced. Maybe it was the wine, or the brief window back to thoughts of her own childhood. When she was that little girl buried in the expanse of warm chest, life was less terrifying when you have your father.

Sitting here it seemed a strange place and time to have an epiphany, but for the first time realisation dawned uncomfortably that maybe that was the reason Kitty had never wanted children of her own. The inner fear, now very aware of its existence - that to have all this, only to lose it, was a risk too high. Would it be wiser, more prudent perhaps, to isolate oneself – you cannot lose what you have never had. First Tommy's death, then her dad dying so suddenly had left huge holes. Kitty would not, could not, let herself imagine losing her mother, she dare not! Blaming that denial for the long held anger that she still carried at losing her, and then Stephen. Stephen had left her and she had no idea the depths of that sorrow, or the void it had left as she was well aware she had not faced up to it as of yet. Thinking now of Amanda's analogy that the sticking plaster she so carefully covered over his leaving merely disguised it, and the longer it remained in place the more it would fester.

Claire's cry of, "Up the table" shook and brought Kitty back to the now. She followed the children as they sprang to their feet and raced each other to the table, barging and poking at each other until Hamish's large hands guided them to their seats.

"Here Kathleen," Hamish pulled out the chair next to his at the head of the large oak table. Donald was next to her and Claire opposite her husband, the two wide-eyed children now looked across the table at the new visitor. For the first time since her arrival they could look at the stranger, for there were no more games to be had at the table. Kitty didn't mind their blatant stares, and smiled back at them as a large blue and white willow patterned plate heaped high with sliced lamb was placed between them. Tureens containing swede, cabbage, carrots and green beans arrived, and with a small cheer from the children a bowl heaped with crispy golden brown roasted potatoes and parsnips.

"Mummy, mummy, mummy, mummy" Heather was tapping her mothers arm with her fork in great excitement.

"Yes darling, what is it?" Kitty admired her calmness as Claire smiled down at her daughter whilst stilling the fork.

"Mummy, what is missing?" in a tone too old for her years and obviously an imitation of one of her parents, Heather comically raised her eyebrows. In unison father and children shouted "Yorkshires!"

Claire started to get up but Hamish beat her to it and left to fetch a matching bowl to the potatoes piled high with mug-sized Yorkshire puddings. The table was a clatter of knives and forks, little in the way of conversation, but a murmuring of shared enjoyment of a delicious meal. After being tempted by yet another Yorkshire Kitty wiped the remnants of her gravy and rested back in her chair with a huge sigh of repletion.

If she had been back in Kent she would have been undoing her trousers now, but the walking and swimming must be paying off and although stuffed she was very comfortable.

"Oh Claire that was really wonderful, thank you. When I have a kitchen I will try to repay the favour, although I don't think I will ever be able to compete with those Yorkshires."

"Well let's hope it won't be too long, and if you would be kind enough to invite me too I will make it a priority." Donald raised his wine glass.

"To Kathleen's kitchen" everyone raised their glass, crystal and red wine chinked with milk in plastic beakers.

"When does the ground work start?" Hamish aiming his question to Kitty and Donald.

"Tomorrow" they answered together and smiled.

"Malcolm's other job finished a little ahead of time." Donald added matter-of-factly but was music to Kitty ears; maybe her Kitchen would be a reality sooner than she thought.

"That's an exciting day," Claire shared a knowing smile with Kitty.

"I must pop down to the old croft before you do too much. I did go in a couple of times when old Annie was ill, we had not long moved here. She was a rare breed that one, do you remember Claire, how stubborn she was, do you remember her in the end?"

Flashing a cautious look at her husband Claire replied.

"I don't think Kathleen needs to know the details of our old patient darling." Emphasis loaded on the patient, obviously reminding him despite the wine of his professional responsibilities.

"Well, no... no obviously, I just mean... as a home owner she was devoted to that croft – I'm sure she would be delighted to know it is in such safe hands. She used to say she wouldn't leave because someone would destroy it."

"I have a photo of her now, Gladys gave it to me," Kitty smiled at the memory.

"I am sure she would approve of its new custodian and her plans for it." Claire reinforced patting his shoulder as she leant over him to clear the table.

"Tide's Reach, and its lovely lady owners" Donald again raised a toast and drained his glass; Kitty was having misgivings at his ability to drive her home safely.

Kitty was happy to help Claire tidy the table and dry up as Claire very efficiently loaded the dishwasher, cleaned surfaces and washed the chipped but treasured dinner service. Feeling she had been a little use, Kitty didn't mind sitting back on the sofa as the children resumed their game.

"Play with us, play with us?"

"Oh good god no, can't abide cards," was Donald's immediate and impolite response and Kitty was glad of it, as she said she would happily play.

Sliding to the floor, resting her back against the sofa's arm Kitty enjoyed the feel of the thick pile of the rug beneath her socked feet and the warmth from the fire all down one side of her. Once again Kathleen Harris was transported and she was five again.

After a couple of games of snap Kitty wondered how far their repertoire stretched.

"Can you play fish?"

Both little pale faces shook back at her.

"Would you like me to teach you?"

Both turned to each other, exchanging quizzical looks then lips tight and brows furrowed they nodded eagerly. Kitty explained the rules and looked to their mother for reinforcement and Kitty was delighted when Claire slid to the floor between her children to assist.

"How exciting, Heather, Jonty mummy will help you until you get the hang of it."

Kitty worried she had set the bar to high as she watched the slender tiny fingers grapple with holding seven cards. Jonty would insist on fanning them so no number or suit was visible, and it was only after the second game and with his fathers help he conquered it.

After a faltering start Kitty was amazed by their aptitude to learn, and was soon in danger of being well and truly trounced at her own game. The afternoon drifted as only a Sunday can, aided by more wine and Hamish's attentions to the log burner. By five thirty Claire was warming homemade cheese scones.

Kitty, exhausted from too much wine and her relentless game mates, rested her head back on the seat cushion, the children now absorbed in a movie fidgeted quietly in the far corner of the room. Hamish busied himself in the kitchen with Claire and the shift of the sofa as Kitty rested her eyes prompted her to sit back up. It was not Hamish however returning to his seat but Donald who sat inches from her. Getting wearily to her feet and slapping her backside that was numb from too long on the floor. Donald had sat in the centre of the sofa forcing her to sit close to an arm to give her any distance from him.

She had been aware the entire afternoon of his gaze being often on her. He had said very little in general conversation and Kitty was ignorant as to whether this was usual for him. But looking at him now he looked like he had been planning what he wanted to say, smiled at him in anticipation.

"You are very good with children Kathleen, have you nieces or nephews?" It was Hamish who asked though; Donald didn't take his eyes off her. Kitty didn't fail to be thankful that the obvious question was side stepped – that of not having children of her own. Kitty guessed as her GP he already knew some of her story, or certainly soon would.

"Well its easy isn't it if they are nice kids, and yours certainly are." Kitty's smile was returned with genuine warmth, her face fell as she continued. "No I only had one brother and he died when he when we were children."

"Oh I'm terribly sorry for that!" Hamish was quick to respond.

"Awful shame, what happened?" Donald asked reaching his hand out on the gap of the sofa between them.

"A tragic accident on a school trip, he always was a bit of a clot."

A silence followed only interrupted by Claire's entreaties that it was bed and bath time for the children. Caught quite off guard Heather launched herself into Kitty arms and hugged her tight around the neck. Kitty had never had such an abandoned cuddle from a child, let alone one she had just met. Jonty, not to be outdone clung to Kitty's shoulders, squashing his little sister to Kitty, a huddle of laughter and warmth.

"Night, night!" Kitty waved as they hurried out of the room, competition even to be first up the stairs. Once again she was reminded of Tommy, what friends they would have been now she was sure.

Kitty sat now, sufficiently relaxed, with her legs tucked underneath her. The men discussed in detail the plans for the build and she was very happy to listen through her wine fuelled haze – the contented bystander. When Claire returned Kitty was privy to the warring opinions between the husband and wife. Butting heads as both argued their corner on wind generators versus ground source heat. Kitty was relieved she had no one but herself to consult on her build.

Tired now and at risk of nodding in front of the throbbing fire, Kitty stirred herself and stood and stretched.

"Well it's been truly wonderful, thank you." Looking at both her doctors "Great food and I can't remember having such a good game of cards in years."

"No, don't thank us. Truth be told, snap was beginning to play on my nerves a little so thank you." Hamish stretched back in his chair.

"You might retract that when all you hear is *go fish!*" They all laughed lazily. Quite forgetting whom she was with, Kitty was anxious to ask before she left. "Do you know James Stewart?"

Aware of the awkward silence Kitty looked between her three companions and saw the furtive glances dart between them. Claire was the first to speak.

"He is the eldest son of the Stewart family, I believe he works at the heritage centre." She was matter of fact.

"Oh so you know the family?"

"Yes, well they do have a very large estate. The clan Stewart were from the highlands but James's forebears settled here generations ago." Hamish added a little warmth in his voice and frowned at his wife.

"Aye, land rich but penny poor if ya ask me." If Claire had

sounded cool, Donald sounded arctic. There was unmistakable venom in his voice and Kitty looked, blinking down on him.

"Well, that's as may be, but he seems a genuine enough fellow. Do you know him Kathleen?" Hamish asked.

Donald's "Umphh" was unconcealed and the ladies jumped as he brought his glass down heavily on the table in front of him. Bemused by the reaction to a simple question and aware all eyes were trained on her, Kitty opted for caution.

"Oh it's only because he was at the pub with the band" and trying to steer the conversation away from him entirely, "I've joined the ladies dart team."

Jamie was mentioned no more, but Kitty's interest was piqued by the fact that Jamie's animosity for Donald was reciprocated. Kitty planned to pursue the subject when she was next alone with Claire.

Offers for more coffee were declined, and as they walked out into the crisp night air Kitty reprimanded herself for accepting the lift. It didn't seem worth getting one over on the young preening receptionist she thought, as she heaved herself back into black leather interior. Probably due to his blood alcohol levels Donald drove sedately back to her house, she was thankful for that.

"Just drop me at the top of the drive." Kitty tried to hide the desperation in her voice. But without a word Donald descended the steep slope and stopped next to Pimples. Hurriedly releasing herself from the seat belt she slid from the car onto the crunching gravel. By the time she had turned to say good night to Donald he had already alighted himself.

"Shit" Kitty mouthed to herself, "Well I'd invite you in for a coffee" (Not for the first time this evening his smile reminded her of a shark.) "But the house is far too cold and it would spoil such a lovely day."

"You could always invite me into your van, I bet it's cosy in there." Donald nodded his head to the side.

"Not on your life!" was what she wanted to say but instead, "Not tonight."

Crestfallen Donald stepped towards her and Kitty fought to stay rooted to the spot as her instincts were all for flight. He reached slowly up and held her by the shoulders with his slender fingers, she was fast regretting not running when she had had the opportunity. Bending to kiss her and aiming straight for her mouth Kitty turned at the last minute and kissed him on the cheek.

"Thank you Donald, thanks for the lift. Will I see you tomorrow or will Malcolm just crack on?"

"Well… Uumm" Thrown off guard now he struggled for an answer, "Well I needn't come, but of course…" his voice silky now, serpent like, "I'll happily come, if you want me to" Immediately Kitty read all the connotations, intended or otherwise and shivered.

"NO! No… no need. I will probably be out and about a bit anyway," lying through her chattering teeth. Determined not to open Pimples until he had gone Kitty stood arms folded willing him to leave.

With ill-tempered resignation Donald returned to his car and sped too fast off over the hill.

18

Breaking Ground

"Phew," Kitty sighed and walked slowly towards Tide's, but it was too cold to enjoy a coffee inside and after visiting the loo she instead made herself a hot chocolate and spent ten minutes walking slowly around her three rooms. Sipping the hot loveliness, she wandered examining and brushing fingers over walls, surfaces and details of the house which tomorrow would begin its transformation.

Lying in bed safely locked in her van, Kitty tried hard to fend off thoughts of Jamie. He had been absent from her mind for the majority of the day but now in the dark silence it was a battle to keep the idea of him at bay. Forcing herself to work over and over the plans for the house she finally found sleep.

Awoken by the dawn chorus, everything precious was boxed in the house before seven. Not wanting any damage to her beloved tablecloths, all but tea making provisions were put carefully back in the lidded plastic boxes. Warmed by her activities and excitement she stood outside and took countless photographs. Every elevation, zooming in on details, the rats tail window furniture, the slate floors, the front door, desperate to capture every inch, every angle before chaos ensued and changes were made.

The truck arrived before eight, ploughing heavily and noisily through the gravel. Kitty stepped back and rested her hand out protectively on the honed stone corner of her home. The chill of exposed stone, green over white, ate into her hand. "Well this is it Tide's, brace yourself," forcing a smile, all confidence fast draining away - Was this the enemy or was it the cavalry? It was too late now, for good or bad the day had come.

"Well it's a bonny day to break ground lassie" bellowed Malcolm who smiled paternally and Kitty skipped excitedly to greet him hand outstretched. And that was the last doubts she would have about the builders and the build.

"We'll get everything set up now, lots of deliveries today lass. I think you'll best be moving your van up on the road today. Wouldn't want a lorry denting him."

Kitty knew she would like Malcolm, after all he knew Pimples was a "he!" Keen to have him out of harms way she left the van in the lay-by on the way to the Hotel. Putting away her bed for the first time she slid the wooden supports back under the bench seat. Taking one of the rectangular cushions and placing it up the side of the van, the table was reinstated. She enjoyed a few minutes to look down from this vantage place as Malcolm and Jeff paced around her cottage.

Mid morning had seen a large lorry arrive with grab bags full of sand, ballast, and cement. Pallets of breezeblocks and bricks wrapped in plastic made it all now very real. Kitty was torn, wanting to stay safely out of the way in Pimples but drawn to the bleeping reversing efforts of the lorry. After a few minutes she was pulling on her coat to investigate the shouting and snapping of branches. She smiled apologetically at the cursing driving who was now scratching underneath his woollen hat, debating with Malcolm how best to manoeuvre the steep drive.

"Go on wi ya man, dunna mind them trees turn it in hard."

The driver didn't appear to appreciate Malcolm's input and stomped back to the cab and slammed the door behind his large black boot. Kitty raced past and followed Malcolm down the drive as the heavy load bounced the lorry, straining its brakes. The combination of squeaking branches clawing in protest and the beast of a lorry pushed to its limit was very unnerving, and Kitty only stopped to turn around and look when she was well on to the lawn. Arms folded tightly around her she cringed away. Being half hidden by Jeff helped, his broad frame being well over six foot offered some protection from the precarious load that bore down on them. Jeff turned and winked at her.

Jeff was to be Malcolm's chief helper on the build, his brother John was apparently working on a project of his own. Jeff was the younger, less creased version of his father. They shared the build and stature of Jamie she thought, looking at the back of the two men. Both blonde, their defined brows and long straight noses gave them a very Viking-like look. When not smiling they looked more than capable of raping and pillaging, but as soon as they did, their bright blue eyes sparkled and they were converted to boyish friendliness.

"I don't think he's very happy," her voice felt weak.

"Na Mac is never bloody happy, don't ya worry ya wee head. He likes to make a fuss and bother." she smiled back at him. Looking at Jeff she was reminded of his cousin, although not particularly alike in looks they shared the same soft, strong voice. With Jamie in her thoughts now she wanted desperately to ask Jeff about him, but sensed the tension in the air and held her tongue.

After yet another attempt the lorry levelled out, juddering to a halt. As if in complaint the cab chugged and shook after the engine was cut off, and a small cloud of dust billowed around it.

"Ye best not be wanting more loads like this Malcolm Stewart, I dunna want to be doing that again."

"Quiet down man, hush ya noise" Malcolm and Mac glared at each other and Kitty was surprised when Malcolm walked over and slapped Mac on the back. Frowns replaced by smiles.

"How's ya wee grand kiddy?"

"Oh aye, bonnie, bonnie."

Kitty watched, drinking in their accents as the two old friends caught up on news.

"This won't get anything built," Jeff interrupted.

"Aye, Aye."

And without further ado the bags and pallets were unloaded on the drive nearest the house. Mac waved his hat out of the window of his cab and crept out onto the road above. Kitty's offer of tea was eagerly received by Malcolm but, "Jeff off ye go and get the digger, careful now down that track."

"Aye, but what about ma tea?"

"It'll be here when ye get back, the sooner ya do, the warmer it wi be."

"Ta dad."

Winking once more at Kitty Jeff climbed into the van and sped off. Malcolm followed Kitty into the kitchen and looked in no hurry to start work without Jeff so Kitty grabbed the opportunity to question Malcolm about his nephew. Plying him with tea and biscuits seemed to have the desired effect, and Kitty was keen not to waste this window.

"I played darts with Jamie on Friday" (very true but a small part of all that went on) – she tried to keep her voice light and cheerful.

"Oh... aye."

"Yes up at the hotel, Joan roped me in – do you know her, Jock the postman's wife?"

"Oh aye."

This was not going to be easy.

"Jamie and the others in the band seem like nice lads."

"Aye, happen they are."

Pulling teeth came to mind.

"And I had dinner with Claire and Hamish Duncan yesterday."

"Oh aye, nice people, like you, southern, real nice. Well I'm glad the locals are making ye welcome lass."

Blood from a stone! Kitty decided to play her ace, if this didn't make him open up she would concede defeat.

"Yes Donald the architect was there too."

"Was he?" the tone was subtly different and his putting his mug down and facing the window and starring out told Kitty she had been right.

"He seems very nice" (light the touch paper and retire).

"Aye..." there followed a long pause "Happen he might to folks that dunna ken... the real man."

So there was something, something between Jamie and Donald? Or was it Donald and the whole Stewart clan?

"I got the feeling, a sense from Jamie that he didn't think much of Donald." Waiting and receiving no response Kitty watched Malcolm as his ran his hand firmly over his beard, smoothing and pulling, repeating all the while looking far out to the water.

"He said it wasn't professionally, but personally" Still he stroked. "Should I trust him? As an architect that is?" Kitty hoped he would respond now as she approached it as a client/builder stance – she was right.

"Aye... aye lassie. Nought wrong with him designing ya house." Kitty started as he turned and reached for her arm. A large hairy battered hand, not dissimilar to Jamie's she noted, held her forearm firmly but gently.

"I'll tell ye this lass," leaning in and looking seriously into her unblinking eyes, "Other lassies, close to my heart... and closer to Jamie have been meddled with, heart broken by that man. Dunna trust him! With ye house yes, with ye heart no!"

Kitty's mouth was dry and she forced a swallow whilst considering a response, not sure how much he would share.

"What happened?"

"Not my secret to share lassie, but ken this... men like Donald are attracted to one thing. Now I'm not saying ya not attractive, and he would'ne be interested in you for you. But I fear its status and money in the bank that stirs his heart. I don't mind telling ya, he told me ye were wealthy and had *"cash to burn"* his words lass, not mine."

Kitty attempted to speak but her mouth gaped open in disbelief.

"Now, that's as may be lass, I dunna know and I dunna care. I would'na have told ye but I like ye and would hate for ya to come all this way and fall for any of his nonsense."

She nodded but still failed to say anything.

"Now maybe he's changed, maybe I do him a disservice. And well lass, if you want to be friends with him forget I said anything." Finally Kitty found her voice.

"But I'm not wealthy" indignant now.

"Aye well, dunna matter to me, nought for me to know."

"Was that what it was about with Jamie then?"

"Aye."

"But I'm confused."

Malcolm faced her now, indecision obvious and he looked down at the pale face and wide eyes. Stroking his beard he considered his answer.

"You're not much older than my lass, I would want someone to look out for her if she was so far from home. I've said too much already... It was Jamie's sister lass."

"Oh."

"I shouldn't be tattling but I wouldn't forgive myself if my silence brought grief to your door."

"What happened?"

"Florence, my niece, Jamie's little sister was only sixteen. Donald came here and set up after University, setting his cap at wee Flo. Jamie was away on Harris at the time working on some heritage project. I think that's half the reason he holds such a grudge, blames himself for not being there. Donald, a good deal older than Flo convinced her to run off wi him. He was all set for them to wed, to get his hands on a slice of the Stewart estate. Jamie's mother called Jamie back and he tracked them down and brought Flo home."

"Oh how awful!"

"Aye there was a right sabaid – a real punch-up. Jamie was a sight for sore eyes when he came back, but nowhere near the pasting Donald got. Donald said things he oughtn't in the fight and Flo heard the worst of it."

"What happened to Flo?"

"Oh right as rain now, quiet couple of years but went off to Glasgow and works in a gallery now."

"I'm glad... it makes sense now. The animosity, the way neither likes to hear the name of the other."

"Aye our Jamie will never forgive him." There was a pause.
"Malcolm?"
"Yes lass."
"Do you know where Jamie is?"

Malcolm leant back on the windowsill releasing her arm now and stroked his beard and looked at her again, Kitty feeling like he could see into her soul and see all that had passed between her and his nephew.

"Why?"

Blatantly lying now, fearing him seeing through facade.

"He loaned me a scarf and I wanted to get it back to him." Not comfortable fibbing Kitty turned and walked to the sink, but not before seeing Malcolm's eyebrows lift and the corners of his mouth rise.

"Oh... is that it? Have you tried the heritage Centre?"
"Yes, and no it's closed."
"His cottage is on the estate."

"No one there." Desperation edging her voice now she leaned on the sink glad of her back facing Malcolm. She was saved the grin on the builders face as he offered a suggestion.

"Well I ken ya should ask Jeff when he's back, he might know… must be an important scarf."

Feeling she had said too much Kitty was keen to leave it there, Jeff was soon back and Kitty was pleased for the distraction. The first job was to construct the outbuilding. The logic as Donald had explained it would act as a shield for the oil tank, wood store and be valuable storage during and after the build.

Jeff bounced across the lawn on the well-sprung digger seat, looking huge and slightly comical on the small machine. Tearing two black strips in the lawn from the drive to the house, Kitty was aware she was holding her breath as the beautiful green was so easily torn open. Climbing off and silencing the engine Jeff whistled through his teeth and beamed at the worried looking Kitty.

"Dunne fret lass, that will be a grand path by the time we're finished."

Kitty knew eggs had to be broken to make an omelette and she could hear her mother saying just those words but "Oh sorry Annie" she whispered. Watching now from the back kitchen window Kitty stretched to see Jeff demolish the right hand corner of the back boundary wall. "Oh Annie!"

Racing from the house she tapped Malcolm on the shoulder. "I thought we were leaving the wall?"

"Ahh so we are, but the outbuilding will go there so the door opens in the garden. Dunna fret we will reuse the stone to edge the new building it will look like it's always been there."

"Oh, oh... good I'm relieved."

Shoulders hunched Kitty struggled to envisage it so returned inside to consult the drawings. The light was fading, as was her energy. Strange she thought how tiring it was to watch other people work, feeling like she had not relaxed since their arrival she was relieved when a ruddy faced Malcolm nodded to her through the window.

Jeff lay sheets over the wet cement of the outbuilding foundations, and Malcolm waved.

"See ye in the morning lass."

"Yes, lovely, thank you."

And so begun the ritual, pacing the site she photographed the changes of the day, particularly delighted with the sunset behind the digger. Standing in the centre of what would soon be a large store room Kitty referred to the plans. There was to be a window looking out over the water and a door to the front, also a door into the back garden. What excited Kitty most was the thought that this would soon be a dry heated base. She would move the table and chair in, microwave, kettle, cooker and who knows maybe a bed of sorts.

Sitting in the main kitchen she ate hungrily. Microwave sweet and sour pork was washed down with a large glass of Rose The up side of icy cold slate floors was that the box of wine kept perfectly chilled under her chair.

Contented sighs between sips of wine, Kitty put her feet on the other chair and lounged back. Breathing deeply for what felt like the first time that day she allowed her mind to wander back to thoughts of Jamie. Closing her eyes she remembered that first kiss, his large hands – like Malcolm's today - tainted now by the less tender memories of their last touch, the strength, the roughness. But she had felt it, the desperation, she thought she understood. She also was convinced of his remorse. But why then, why had he not come to her? Was he embarrassed – but surely her note was clear, was she not inviting him back to her?

Her plan for tomorrow was set, she would ask Jeff, maybe get a mobile number and be brave and phone him. For now she would finish her wine and watch the square of orange and pink sink under a blanket of navy blue.

Retiring to Pimples Kitty wrote by the soft light of a wind up lantern. Amanda had given her a large book covered in light blue silk with embroidered flowers in pastel ribbons. The pages were thick and fibrous, the tactile softness of hand made paper.

The front page was inscribed by her friend *"For Kit, and her bestseller."* At the time Kitty had doubted she would have the courage to start writing in such a beautiful journal but today came the inspiration. Underneath Amanda's neat inscription Kitty wrote, *"Tide's Reach, The Journey, by Kathleen Harris."*

After three pages under the heading of day one Kitty recorded her first meeting with Jock and all she could remember of what seemed like so long ago. Hoping to recount every day to the present, itchy eyes and incessant yawning forced her to put this off until tomorrow. Dreading the Stewarts finding her asleep Kitty set the travel alarm and slept easily. When the beeping forced its way into her consciousness Kitty awoke wrapped in her quilt covered in a light sweat – she had dreamt of Jamie. Not at all pleasant, it was Fifty shades of grey on a building site. Wiping the wet from her neck she was very pleased it was baby-sitting night, or bath night as she thought of it.

Day two of the build, pulling back the van curtains Kitty was pleased to see the weather had held. Malcolm and Jeff were prompt and welcomed with a mug of tea. Kitty pottered happily with them as Jeff started building the breezeblock walls. Kitty absent mindedly started stacking the demolished wall.

"Here lassie" Malcolm throw a pair of leather gloves onto the grass next to her. "It'll cut you hands to shreds."

Wearing them Kitty felt a touch ridiculous as the fingers folded over where she only half filled them, but nonetheless wore them with gratitude.

"Old Annie hand built this wall, or so Gladys the doctor's receptionist told me."

"Aye she was a bonnie wee lady. If you've a mind to, as soon as the walls are rendered ye could build the wall back up, Jeff could teach ye."

"Oh I'd love that," Kitty beamed up to Malcolm as he smiled

back; hand on beard.

"And would you like me to fix a pulley up here and on the far corner of the croft? You'd get you washing dry in a trice here."

"That would be great, I thought I could do with a line."

Kitty hummed along to the radio the men worked to and she enjoyed the companionship. Stopping at eleven for offered tea, all three made their way to the low front wall. Sitting facing the rippled water they enjoyed the hot drinks and stack of biscuits.

"Do ya not get lonely lass?" Malcolm asked.

"Well to be honest I haven't had time to yet" Kitty blew on her tea and kept her gaze on the view.

"Well if'n ya were my bairn I'd be a bit worried, do you not think you should at least have a dog to keep ya company?"

"I know," looking around Jeff to Malcolm she added "Angela has said that to me, but I've never had a dog."

"It's not hard, all you'd have to do is feed it. It could have all the exercise it needed here on the beach" laughing now, "and it would hardly damage ya carpets as ye have'n any."

She helped for the rest of the morning, or maybe it was hindered, she wasn't sure? Stopping for lunch, father and son insisted on taking their tea to their van where Kitty watched them eat sandwiches absorbed in their newspapers. Eating her own lunch she was drawn to the window once again as she looked at the rising walls. The spaces for the doors and window were not topped yet but as little as Kitty knew about building she was certain it was going well.

By the end of the afternoon all the walls were up, minutely clapping her hands there was little doubt how pleased she was with progress today. Standing in the stock room of 10 foot by 12 foot she waved the men off from its doorway, a very happy islander. Making her way wearily to Pimples she appreciated the comfort as she lay back on the bed and closed her eyes. For as nice as these men were to have around and she thrilled at watching the daily developments as they happened it was very tiring. Kitty realised she would have to pace herself as this was going to be her life for months to come.

Rallying herself she set off for the supermarket for tonight's meal. Chicken pie with a bag of prepared carrots and Swede soon in her basket. Kitty had scoffed at people buying prepared vegetables in shops in her past. Unashamedly judging them, did they lack prehensile thumbs? Could they not hold a knife? Yet here she was, and very glad of them, she had a long bath planned for tonight and didn't intend wasting time grappling with a swede.

For the first time Kitty found Angela obviously relaxing in the lounge on her arrival. Gavin opened the door and pointed her in.

"Hi Kitty, come on in."

"Evening Gavin."

"Building started?"

"Yes second day today, building the shed first. Well I say shed, but it's the size of half my house and is going to act as temporary home while they knock the house about."

Angela joined the conversation now as she pushed herself from the sofa.

"You are brave Kitty, I get completely stressed even if we are only decorating one room."

"To clarify Kitty, "we" don't decorate, I do and she doesn't only get stressed my wife here verges on psychotic."

Angela swiped for him with a tea towel she had draped on her shoulder, but after years of practice Gavin ducked in the nick of time.

"Shut your head Gavin McLeod! Anyway I pick the paint and paper."

"Oh yes, sorry," fake sincerity "Of course that is as hard as rubbing down paintwork, papering and painting – how silly of me!" As Gavin smirked at Kitty Angela's second attempt found touch.

"Ooouch" Gavin rubbed his thigh that obviously stung. Glares exchanged, Kitty was keen to defuse a domestic and turned the conversation back to her day.

"Malcolm said today I should have a dog."

"Aye and so you should, out there on your own." Gavin snatched the tea towel from his wife and walked to the kitchen. Angela watched him leave and Kitty was sure Ange was checking him out. As fiery as their relationship seemed it was clear they loved each other despite the squabbles. Turning her attention back to Kitty Angela added.

"You could have a cat I suppose, less responsibility."

"No cats are dull; it would spend all it's time killing things and leaving them under your bed!" Gavin called from the kitchen – obviously a dog person then.

"Take no notice of him, anyway I will keep my ears open and if I hear of any I'll let you know. Any preference on type?"

"I think its breed, dearest" again Gavin could be heard over the clatter of washing up.

"Do you WANT another slap man?"

"Promises, promises!"

Kitty laughed, she liked their banter, especially now she could see through it to the genuine affection it obviously masked.

"The smaller the better I think."

Nudges and complaints accompanied the couple to the car, leaving Kitty to put on the oven and run her much-anticipated bath.

"Evening," Kitty looked in as a small hand waved above a large colourful Dr Seuss book. If this is what constitutes baby sitting Kitty would have taken it up years ago. She still hoped each new day would bring a visit from Jamie so a quick shave was in order. The water worked its magic and after 15 minutes Kitty was suddenly hungry so dried quickly, "Night" probably her last communication with her charges she tiptoed down the stairs and prepared her dinner. Sitting at the table she flicked through the channels of the small kitchen TV, pleased to see the weather looked settled for the remainder of the week, so she hoped the roof could be on by then.

When they returned Kitty took up Angela's offer of tea. Gavin sat heavily on the sofa in the lounge and turned on the TV, settling on snooker.

"There, he's happy" having taken him in a cup of tea Angela sat opposite Kitty at the kitchen table. "Were the kids ok?"

"I hope so, I got a wave from your first born but not a peep out of the other two. You know it's the third time I've baby sat for you and I don't even know what two thirds of your children look like!"

Angela threw her head back and laughed loudly – culminating in a snort. Gavin leant his head around the archway and raised his eyebrows.

"I'll keep them all up next week if you like?"

"No, no, no… not on my account. I'm sure they are lovely but I do cherish my bath, meal and TV fix."

"Of course you do, only joking."

Kitty took a large swig of tea and asked the question she had been burning to ask since the front door opened.

"Was Jamie there?"

"No he wasn't, old Dougal stood in and said Jamie was indisposed – whatever that means?"

"Oh" Kitty's juddering sigh confirmed what Angela had thought.

"You don't seem yourself Kitty, is it the building work?"

"God no... no!" defiant now.

"Is it to do with Jamie?" Kitty stayed silent "You seemed agitated in the post office the other day."

Kitty rested her head in her hands, the weight of it through her elbows on the table, quietly she asked.

"Ange... if I tell you something, could you? Would you keep it between us?"

"Oh Kitty of course," Angela reached over and rubbed Kitty forearms with slender hands.

"Start at the beginning" Angela whispered and moved to the chair next to Kitty who, lifted her head long enough to offer a weak smile then buried her head back in it's rest.

"The first night I went to the pub I got... well pissed and Angus and Jamie walked me home..."

"Well?"

"Weeeell, they had to help me to the loo, undress me and put me to bed." Kitty rushed out the information before she could change her mind.

"Oh... Oooooh! Little embarrassing?"

"Very!"

"And then there was the little matter of the gaping nightdress and boob flash." Kitty shook her head now.

"Ooooh, both of them? Men I mean not boobs."

"No just the one, just Jamie."

"Well that's something I suppose."

"And then there was kissing," and in answer to Angela's "And?" - "Quite a lot of kissing."

"Uh ha!"

"Well then I told him I couldn't, couldn't be disloyal to my husband and ... well... I didn't handle it well and, and, well he was really upset and got a bit..." frightened eyes now looked entreatingly at Angela, Kitty whispered. "He got a bit overexcited and... well, well he... hurt me." Saying the words that almost choked her, Kitty fought back tears.

"Get out!" Angela's voice raised in disbelief causing Gavin to peer round once again. "Back to your snooker you." Gavin smiled and settled back into the sofa. Angela rubbed Kitty's arm and waited until she was sure her husband's attention was back on the match.

With great seriousness and concern "I knew it, what did he do, what exactly did, he do? He didn't ra" Kitty stopped her before she could finish.

"God, no, NO! It was just kissing and a bit of... of a grope."

"Phew, ok."

"I know I haven't known him anytime, but he was always had been such a gentleman, so… so tender. But in the toilets."

"Toilets?"

"Yes we were at the pub, he followed me out and had me pinned to the cubicle door."

"That's not good."

"No, he'd had a drink and I think he was really upset."

"I don't know if you should be defending him?" Angela tutted and Kitty wondered if she had been mistaken confiding in Angela.

"How did you leave it with him?"

"When I cried he let me go, like he'd been in a daze. He had had a lot of whiskey but he was so apologetic."

"Well that's good; I mean I've only ever heard good things of him. He is the heir to the Stewart estate."

"What does that mean?"

"You mean he didn't tell you?"

"What?"

"Well the Stewarts own this corner of Skye, and young Jamie is set to inherit the lot, castle included!"

"Castle?" Kitty face paled, could this situation get any stranger.

"When did all this happen?"

"Friday."

"And you haven't seen him since?"

"No." Kitty sniffed, she was determined to not get upset.

"Right, did you find his cottage the other day?"

"Yes, but there was no sign of him, I left a note saying I wanted to see him again... but nothing."

Angela looked into Kitty's face and wished away the tears in her new friend's eyes.

"It's just I want to know he's ok, he was so distraught. He was so upset he threw up."

"You don't think he did anything stupid?"

"I don't know, and even if he didn't want to see me again I really need to know he is alright."

"Quite, quite!" Angela took a hair band from her wrist and passed false nails through her hair, scratching it back into a tight pony tail.

Running the hair through her hand as she thought, Kitty was reminded again of Malcolm and his beard stroking.

"Don't worry I will do some discreet snooping. The housekeeper will be in tomorrow. I can ask after all the children."

"Oh thanks, you're a star. I just don't understand why I've heard nothing."

"It will be alright Kitty."

"Well it's good to have told someone."

"I'm your friend Kitty, I'm here for you."

Covering Ange's hand that rested on her own she gently squeezed. Such friendship she had never experienced. Amanda's friendship had evolved and grown over many years but never in her adult life had she connected to someone so quickly and honestly. Women she had known for years in Kent would have been incapable of this genuine kindness – without agenda or motive.

Saying her goodbyes she felt a sense of relief at having shared her woes, and promised herself a trip to the post office tomorrow for an update.

19

Every Girl Loves a Shed

Throwing her energies into the build there was a general sense of urgency to press on and get the storeroom watertight. Malcolm and Jeff worked hard. No news was forthcoming from Angela and the weeks passed in a blur of building and shattered sleep.

With the waste and services connected, it was left to Kitty to clean the old kitchen sink in preparation of reinstating it in the store. Kitty spent a whole afternoon scrubbing and picking unknown substances off it. She could tell Malcolm had thought her mad wanting to keep this sink, but she was not to be swayed. Jeff was more understanding and built a sturdy wooden framework for it to be properly supported.

Kitty enjoyed the three hour round trip to purchase the taps, yet another distraction from thinking about Jamie. Much to her disappointment time did little to alter her thoughts about him. No one thus far could tell her were he was.

Once plastered there followed the most frustrating of times for Kitty. So near and yet so far, she longed to unpack her boxes that still resided in the hall cupboard. As soon as she was given the go ahead by a laughing Malcolm, donning her decorating clothes she set to work. By late afternoon Kitty walked triumphantly into the back garden waving a white roller thick with paint and covered in a fine speckling of emulsion all over herself.

When finally dry and declining offers of help Kitty ferried her few possessions into it. The table and chairs sat by the window, larger and lower than the cottages windows, and sitting at the table gave a very pleasing view of the water. A countertop and shelf by the sink housed the mini fridge, microwave and kettle.

All the lidded boxes were here, transferred and piled neatly in the far corner. There was nothing else left in the cottage and without her sparse possessions it seemed colder and bleaker than ever. Kitty found it too sad and decided for a last minute trip to the post office. This had become a regular occurrence, often to collect supplies but primarily to glean any news Angela may have obtained about a certain elusive Scotsman.

"Hiya Kitty I'll bring it over."

Kitty was waiting for the Internet to connect - she had an important errand today, checking delivery of her day bed. The store was insulated, dry, had running water – albeit cold, and with the help of a small electric heater promised to be a very cosy home for the coming months. Pimples had performed valiantly but for over the weeks she had slept on the foam mattress and her thoughts, when not on Jamie, were focused increasingly on the prospect of sleeping in a real bed. Kitty's daydream of stretching in clean sheets was shattered by three words.

"I've heard something!" Angela knew she would be excited by today's news so pouring two teas she was quickly scraping her chair conspiratorially close.

"Quickly though the bus from town will be in soon and it's pension day – you've lived here long enough to know what that means." Kitty just nodded not wanting to waste time talking. She'd been behind that crowd before.

"Well Agnes, the housekeeper came in first thing this morning, saying she was in a hurry as she had to plan for a big family party tonight." Angela grinned as if Kitty should have deduced some interesting facts from this information.

"For?"

"Jamie's little brother's twenty first."

"And?"

"Well I asked, you see, if all the children would be there?"

"Yes?"

"Well that's it, yes, yes! They are all expected, she said master James was back, came back today."

"Where has he been?" Kitty could hardly contain herself.

"I asked all casual where he'd been."

"AND!"

"Agnes said she didn't know what happened", and in her best local accent Angela continued "Aye and him such a gentle wee bairn. I've known him since he came into the world and never a crossed word or bad action. Twas right terrible seeing him in that state. And we still dunna ken what happened but he'd packed a case and had been gone for weeks."

"Oh Angela do you think it was that Saturday, has he been gone since then?"

"I guess so, but it turns out he has been staying with a friend on Harris. On his small holding apparently."

Kitty clasped her hands over her chest and puffed out a long sigh, sitting back in her chair relief washing over her.

"Oh I am so relieved Ange."

"Yes and the party is tonight, Kitty you must get a land line, if I hadn't been on my own I would have popped over to tell you. What are you going to do?"

"I'll go this evening and leave another note, I think that's all I can do. He probably thinks I don't care, what a relief he's ok."

"Well go, go!"

"Argh, I've got to finish this, it's for my bed delivery."

Fingers stumbled, pressing the backspace more than any other keys, she found out that frustratingly the delivery wouldn't be for another five days, but at least it was on its way.

"Right, wish me luck," Kitty ran to the door only to rush back for the bag she had forgotten.

"Here, here!" Angela held out a pad of paper and a biro offered in exchange for the best smile she had seen on Kitty's face for a long time.

"Let me know for goodness sake, even if it's to let me know you're alright and he hasn't come back to finish you off and dump you in the foundations."

"Gee thanks, you know you remind me of my friend Amanda."

"Is that a good thing?"

"Yes," was a distant reply as Kitty skipped to Pimples. Angela's heart pounded nearly as fast as Kitty's. Who knew the quiet looking girl from Kent could bring such excitement to their little patch of Skye?

Kitty's pounding heart wasn't helped by the ragged breathing, which equally did nothing to suppress the nausea that was bubbling deep in her stomach. She knew the way to his cottage; she had driven to it on bored evenings since he vanished in the vain hope of a light in the window or a sight of his car. Hope welled within her as she spotted the battered VW outside the cottage.

Jumping from the van Kitty ran up to the front door. Forcing her lungs to drag in three deep breathes Kitty banged with a tight fist. Impatient she knocked again, rubbing her knuckles she was sure she had bruised them. The door opened leaving Kitty quite literally speechless. The tall blonde girl tilted her head and leant into the doorframe examining the stunned woman on the doorstep.

"Can I help ye?"

"Oh… umm…oh."

"Yes?"

"Um, I was looking… does Jamie live here?" doubting suddenly she had the right cottage.

"Aye."

"Is he in?"

"No."

"Oh."

So confused and disoriented by this turn of events Kitty had no words, after an awkward silence the girl asked.

"Do ya know Jamie?" the girl's annoyance now shifting to concern. This young woman was obviously not local and looked pale, drawn and upset.

"A bit… a little," Kitty stammered.

"Well he's not here, shall I give him a message when he gets home?"

"No, no, thanks... sorry to bother you."

Kitty could barely get Pimples started and pulled to the edge of the road around the corner before a torrent of tears escaped. She was unable to drive for many minutes. Once composed enough she drove slowly home, tears continued to roll down her checks and collected in the cleft of her neck. She tried hard to disguise the blotchy skin and red eyes but Kitty knew Malcolm had seen immediately.

"Lassie are you alright?"

"Fine, yes fine, nothing's wrong."

"Ummm" not sounding in the least convinced, "Well we will be off a little earlier tonight, a partaidh - family party lass."

Of course, Kitty, annoyed at her own stupidity. This man stood before her, looking sorry for her, was Jamie's uncle and the whistling was coming from his cousin. Of course they would be attending the party.

"Wwwhat's that in aid of?" Kitty could feel her voice tremble.

"Alistair's twenty first, Jamie you know – his younger brother."

"Will Jamie be there?" Kitty managed to get out despite all the saliva vanishing in her mouth.

"Oh aye, all the clan together. It'll be a bonny night. Un we might be worst for the whiskey in the morning lass. May well not be in till after lunch. Would that be ok with ye?"

"Yes, yes of course... say hello to Jamie for me. Jeff did you never know where Jamie has been?" Kitty was annoyed, she had given up asking his cousin where he was, as his usual response involved a vague suggestion that he had, "Buggered off ta restore some crumbling relic."

Wanting them gone now – just to be left alone. As soon as their van disappeared from the road Kitty climbed limply into her pyjamas, and with mug of rose in hand she settled into the embrace of her quilt and watched Love Actually. When Kitty wanted company for a good cry it never let her down. The film was half way through, and she had wrung out the last of the box of wine when it dawned on Kitty that if Jamie was back this was no way to greet him. To her relief she then reasoned that the party would be in full swing now and he wouldn't leave it to seek her out.

Putting her coat on Kitty went over the churned lawn and splashed cold water on her face in the old stone sink. A cup of tea and she headed back to Pimples to try and sleep.

Kitty realised just how much she had enjoyed her cheerful company in the mornings and was aware how quiet it was here on her own. The store was finished and under Jeff's tutelage Kitty was slowly rebuilding Annie's wall. She now knew her foundation stones; Jeff was a strict teacher and Kitty had worked for an entire day getting the bottom stones to his exacting standards. He would walk along the eight-foot length and only when none of the stones moved was she allowed to construct her batter and coursing strings. Having to ask for help with the huge through stones and some of the larger building stones, her favourite part by far was the hearting stones, small stones that filled the voids and packed between the others.

In the crisp hazy light of the morning Kitty walked around the outside of Tide's Reach. The slate slabs that once formed her floors from the two rooms now sat in neat rows on the lawn. Looking in through the front door Kitty decided not to step down into the eighteen-inch drop which now replaced the floor. Looking in the empty shell would just be sad.

Standing where the front lawn used to be and surrounded by the foundation trench. Kitty tried to visualise where furniture would go and how best to use this room. At the far end of the existing house another grey concrete square marked out what would be her bathroom. Sitting on an upturned bucket Kitty lifted her head, closed her eyes and imagined laying back in her bath. The skylights would allow her to see the sky with no risk of anyone seeing in. She looked forward to seeing her patch of sky and was sure after so long without a bathroom she would never again take it for granted but would cherish it always.

Frozen in fear but desperate to see, Kitty forced herself round the front of the house at the sound of tyres on her gravel drive.

"Oh shit! Really, now!"

Not the blue VW she had hoped for, but big, black and very unwelcome it was the Land rover. If Kitty hadn't been sure Donald had seen her she would have ducked back around the wall and escaped up the beach. She had no desire to see her architect now, and Kitty gritted her teeth and waved back as the tall man waved as he slammed the door closed.

Arms folded she realised she probably looked like a petulant child, she certainly felt like one, but taking a deep breath she manufactured a smile.

"Good morning to ya Kathleen."

"Hi Donald."

"Just thought I'd come and see the progress." Donald reached her and laying a spidery finger on her upper arm ducked down to kiss her cheek. Kitty showed him around with as much enthusiasm as she could muster. At least as far as the house was concerned she was equally delighted and excited. Jamie's return had come just as that part of her life had started to settle. Although left so up in the air she was just getting used to it, and focusing on the build and her new routine.

Walking now into the back garden Kitty smiled her first genuine smile of the day looking at the, - her! - Store room.

"Yes I love the shed, store room and I must admit I doubted the logic of building it first but I love it. Once the bed arrives in the week it will be so snug."

"Yes at least it has the amenities and will be warm and dry; you'll need it when the roof comes off."

"When will they start do you think?"

"Soon I would think, they will build the outer walls up but once that's done the roof will be taken down. Once the new roof is on you will get a true feel for how it will be"

"Jeff and Malcolm work very well."

"Well I'm surprised not to see them, are they usually this tardy?"

"No, no not at all," Kitty indignant on their behalf. "They are always here well before eight but had a late night so said they may not be in till lunch." Watching for his reaction. "It was Malcolm's nephew's twenty first, do you know the other Stewarts?"

"Um" Donald sneered, he wasn't being drawn. "The amount of whiskey they will have consumed I think you can safely say you will have no work done here today." He sneered. "Now young lady, you've avoided the question too long - when are you coming out to dinner with me?"

Kitty wasn't expecting this and was temporarily dumbfounded, unable to come up with any excuses she looked blankly at him.

"Well you look quite decent enough for me to take you for a spot of lunch at the Stag's head."

"Um... well no, but."

But Donald would brook no excuses and Kitty, behaving like the proverbial rabbit in the headlights found herself being led to the open door of the store.

"Come on now jacket and keys that's all you need."

"Is it even time for lunch?" Kitty had wondered aimlessly and was surprised when Donald pointed to his watch Eleven twenty. What had she done all morning?

Having neither the energy nor a reason not to, and reasoning he wouldn't rest until he taken her out she relented. As it looked like there was going to be no builders today after all there seemed little reason to stay.

Sitting next to Donald's smug expression Kitty regretted her decision as soon as they were out of her drive. The radio played and Kitty's mind flipped between two trains of thought while she pretended to be engrossed in the view. What on earth was she thinking going out with Donald, Donald of all people! She now was privy to what had passed between him and Jamie. Why on earth, if Jamie mattered to her in the slightest, would she risk his displeasure in being in the company of this man? A man Kitty had to admit she herself was not truly comfortable with – and that was before she knew about Jamie's little sister.

The devil on her shoulder told her if Jamie had any interest in her he would have been in touch days, weeks ago. He had ignored her messages and brought some young blonde back from Harris. For all she knew he was wining and dining the hoity girl that very minute. Kitty was angry with herself. Digging fingernails into her clenched palms she was, as her mother would have said, disappointed in herself. That always cut the deepest, you could return angry with anger. But disappointment just left a cold hole. Why had she wasted so much time and energy on a man she barely knew when it was clear she meant nothing to him.

The pub was a forty-minute drive, Kitty gradually calmed and unclenched. Donald pointed out the landmarks and shared his knowledge of the island. Whether bragging about his achievements on different projects or just sharing his knowledge of this beautiful place Kitty didn't mind as it required little in the way of conversation on her part.

Once at the destination Kitty mouthed silently, "No that's fine don't mind me," dripping in sarcasm at Donald who having slammed his door walked off towards the pub. Inside Donald took a menu from the bar and guided Kitty to a table by the window. If nothing else she thought she would order the most expensive thing on the menu, least he deserved for the exorbitant fees she paid him.

The food was very good, venison pate to start with beetroot and rocket. She hadn't realised how hungry she was, her appetite very muted these last weeks. The duck with red wine was washed down with a smooth Shiraz. Clearing the vegetables Kitty really appreciated anywhere that could cook Cabbage properly, bright green and enough crunch. The food and wine worked their magic and the mellowing that the drive had started was now complete. Sod Jamie if he could be with that blonde she could be treated to lunch by her architect.

The conversation covered both their experiences at University, life in Kent and life on Skye. Kitty avoided any thing of a personal nature, glad to not have to explain any of her losses and why she was here. Odd she thought that he didn't enquire, but Kitty strongly suspected Donald had asked Claire about her and she had warned him off sensitive subjects. Kitty quite forgot herself and enjoyed the lunch. Donald did have charm, and with more wine she had to admit - for a few hours she had enjoyed his company.

The drive home was much easier, the lady quite relaxed and Donald triumphant. She had half expected him to take up her offer of splitting the bill but as he had paid for it all she felt obliged to offer him a coffee on their return. True to his theory there were no vans on the drive and the site was quiet.

Sitting on the rickety chairs in the store seemed a bit of a come down after the plush pub with black and white flock paper and ornate crystal drop chandeliers, but Donald didn't seem to mind.

Asking more questions of Donald on technical aspects of the build worked to her advantage. As Donald droned on about the minutiae of the correct way to build, Kitty found she could allow herself to think of Jamie. All that Donald required was an occasional nod and smile. Kitty had to know either way, was that girl living there? Would Jamie ever come here again so she could finally explain, and more to the point make him explain!

"Well I suppose I should be on my way?" Hoping for encouragement to stay Kitty failed him. Standing, weary now as only midday drinking can do, Kitty opened the door with a reluctant Donald in her wake. Blinking at the afternoon spring sun they walked together to the drive. Once there Kitty stood by the glistening bonnet, expecting Donald to get in so she was surprised when he came and stood in front of her. Slowly placing his long hands either side of her on the blackness of the cars paintwork. Kitty smiled up at him, with effort, edging back, the bumper hard against the back of her legs.

"I really enjoyed lunch Kathleen."

"Yes... yes so did I, thank you Donald it was lovely," Kitty tried to take the surprise from her reply.

"Don't mention it, it was my pleasure."

Kitty was growing more uncomfortable with every second that passed, leaning forward slightly to relieve the pressure where the number plate dug into the back of her leg. Whether this was seen as an invitation, or if he indeed needed one, Donald leant down and planted a kiss on her lips. Kitty could not move. Not only did his frame prevent it but the shock rendered her motionless. Her non-response in no way dampened Donald's ardour, pulling away a few inches to smile down on her he returned for a second.

By the time his lips left hers for the second time Kitty had regained her senses and reached up to put both hands on Donald's firm chest and thus literally, keeping him at arms length.

"Well thank you again Donald."

Donald's smile was broad and showed a set of expensively whitened teeth – one of Kitty pet hates. Managing a small smile she thanked all that was holy as he responded to her hint and stood tall.

"I will arrange a date with the Duncan's. We must do supper at mine soon."

"Yes that would be ... lovely," All the better for having chaperones Kitty thought. Smiling as she waved him off "Yes go, and don't come back on my account."

Kitty swore at her own weakness, why had she not slapped him? Why could she not tell him what she thought of him? Another first, kissed by a second man, but this time not of her choosing. Was there something in the water here? Kitty's best guess was there must be a severe lack of available young women on this island.

Could she tell him to keep his lecherous advances to himself? - But where would that leave Tide's Reach? She would have to keep him sweet, at least until the build was finished. That would be her aim, to ensure they were always in company, and smile and be pleasant. She certainly didn't want to make enemies in such an isolated community and jeopardise her happiness here.

20

House call

The Stewarts did not come, and as the afternoon drew to a close Kitty resigned herself to seeing none of that family today. She paced the stretch of beach in front of her home, aimlessly kicking pebbles and collecting the mussel shells that littered the beach. She had never before seen them this large or in such vast numbers.

Indecision was Kitty's only companion for that dragging afternoon. Torn between staying put and trying to do something constructive, or rush to Jamie's house and confront that girl or him. Laying the shells on the low garden wall, being about a foot deep it not only acted as a useful seat, but enabled her to place the shells in large circles creating purple black petals.

Absorbed in her work the noise of the car now stopping on her drive was the first she knew of these visitors. For the second time that day Kitty's heart sank at not seeing the car she longed to see. Squinting Kitty could make out four heads in the Volvo. The back doors opened and two blonde heads raced around the car and down to the beach. Kitty walked across the lawn to meet Claire and Hamish who were waving enthusiastically at her.

"Is this ok Kathleen? We were passing and Hamish and the children were keen to see you and the croft."

"Oh of course it is, I'm delighted to see you, come in I'll put the kettle on."

"Kids! Stay up this end by the croft, Heather stay with your brother" Claire shouted at the squealing children throwing stones in the water,

"Welcome, come and see what we've done."

"Wow, look at the out building, that's completely new isn't it?" Claire was very excited to see the changes since her last visit.

"Yes, yes this is the store, home from home! And when the bed is delivered I am all sorted until the house is finished. Come on in."

Claire stood at the open door, keeping a wary eye on the children while Hamish pored over the drawings on the table.

"I'm liking it a lot Kitty, very in keeping. But you weren't tempted to extend the footprint even more – you could have got four bedrooms" Hamish asked, gratefully taking his tea.

"Oh I'd rattle around in it as it is. There is only me, remember I'm used to living in a camper van."

"Awh you won't know yourself Kathleen. Hot and cold running water, heating and not to mention a bed. Are you really going to put a bed in the store?"

"Yes I've ordered a day bed which hopefully will be with me in a few days. It will go over on that wall where the boxes are. It should be warmer and more comfy than the van."

"You really are a hardy little camper Kathleen," Claire smiled over her shoulder.

"Well people lived here for hundreds of years with much less than I have now so I consider myself lucky."

"Yes, yes very true."

Mugs in hands they walked around the plot, now joined by Jonty and Heather.

"Hello Kathleen, can we play fish?"

"Oh Heather I'm sorry my cards are all packed but I promise when I find them you are the first person I will play fish with."

"Promise?"

"Promise."

"Pinky promise?"

Kitty looked from the moon like face to her parents for explanation but they were both leaning in through the open front door of the house. Heather reached up extending her little finger. Kitty looked at it and Heather giggled, then offered her own hand, little finger mirroring the child's. Heather wrapped her tiny finger around Kitty and shook firmly.

"Pinky promise."

"Pinky promise," Kitty mimicked and the girl was gone, giggling as she caught her brother on the garden wall.

Hamish jumped down into the void that once had been her hall. Bending he examined the foundations and looked at each room from its threshold.

"What are you doing with the fireplaces?"

"Well there will be an Aga in the kitchen, the room on the left will be a study cum snug so I want to retain the old fireplace in there. The extension that will be the lounge will have a log burner."

"And this whole wall will be glass - even when it's triple glazed you'll want a heavy duty burner here."

"So Donald said, there will be under-floor heating in the

bathroom and radiators in the bedrooms from the Aga."

"With the new building regs it will be a very toasty home." Heaving himself out, the five walked across the front garden and around the bend. Kitty was keen to share with them her little derelict croft. She was not disappointed; the whole family shared her enthusiasm. Heather particularly liked it.

"It's a baby house – for your babies" Claire and Hamish exchanged a glance but Kitty was not put out, but rather charmed.

"Actually Heather I had hoped to put a roof on it and use it myself"

"Why?"

"To write."

"What... what like books?" Jonty had come to join the debate.

"Exactly like books!"

"I didn't know you were an author Kathleen," Claire asked.

"No, not published, it's something I've always done and ... well, now it seems the perfect time to try it properly."

"Good for you. What did you do Kathleen, before you came here?" Hamish asked casually, then darting a look to his wife, "That is if you don't mind me asking."

"When I was married, that is since I left Uni I have worked as a concept artist – for film mainly."

"Woah- but you're not planning on doing that here?" Claire looked astonished.

"I loved painting, always have, but when you have to paint what is in someone else's head it's quite wearing. I'm looking forward to painting something that I want to. But for now I am enjoying not picking up a brush."

"Oh I'm sure you will one day. I think painting is one of those things if you do it, you will always do it. This little croft would make a brilliant studio. I like that there are no distractions of habitation. You could have a glass roof."

Hamish clambered over the fallen stones; standing in the middle he stretched his arms to measure the span of its walls.

"You said *when you were married* ... are you not now?"

Claire asked knowing full well she may have overstepped the mark. Kitty looked out over the water and simply said, "No."

As no further elaboration was forth coming Claire changed the subject.

"Malcolm not here today?"

"No apparently a big clan party last night so tools down."

"Oh Alistair's twenty first, yes of course we were there, but left at a respectable hour to get back for the babysitter."

"You're not related as well are you?"

"No" Hamish laughed "But we are their GPs and know the family well."

"You... you know Jamie well then?" Kitty felt the rise of colour in her cheeks that mirrored the pitch of her voice, and faced the light breeze hoping it would help. She remembered they hadn't been forthcoming about this in Donald's presence.

"Yes, actually he was quite chatty. He told me he had met you a couple of times."

"Really... did he? W-what did he say?" The breeze wasn't working.

A smiling Claire replied, "That he had met you at the heritage centre. He seemed quite interested in you Kathleen, he was asking about you."

"Asking, asking what exactly?"

Kitty's voice raised and Claire stepped around to look at her.

"What we knew about you."

"What did you tell him?"

Claire put her hand on Kitty's arm, holding her back as Hamish and the children headed off to the water.

"Only what we know, that you moved here from Kent – he knew that. That you seem lovely – and I think he knew that already!" Claire raised her eyebrows. "You are a mystery to us all Mrs Harris, and that is fine, I am looking forward to getting to know you. I think Jamie likes you... but I think I should say something." Leaning closer and passing her arm through Kitty's, Claire continued. "Donald has confided in me and I think you should know he is quite smitten with you too."

Kitty sighed and for the first time looked Claire straight in the eyes. "Oh really... the thing is Claire I didn't come here looking for a man. I came here to be on my own, to find peace. I would appreciate it if you could let Donald know I'm not looking for a relationship."

"I could try but what are you afraid of? He is an attractive, successful man Kathleen. You could find happiness as well as peace."

"Peace is just fine."

"He's quite a catch Kathleen, maybe you should just let it play out and see."

"Ummmm" Sighing deeply and gazing out across the water, Claire waited and was rewarded with; "So did Jamie say anything else?"

"Oh, I see how it is" She squeezed Kitty arm and smiled. "Well he didn't seem his usual cheerful self, a little on edge now I think of it. Is there something I'm missing?"

"No… well, not really… I do find him… intriguing."

"Well he's really got the brooding highlander thing going for him."

"Did he say if he was hanging around? I think he's been on Harris," Kitty couldn't hide the emotion in her voice now.

"And you haven't seen him since he's been back?"

"No."

"Why don't you just go and see him?"

"Well."

"What Kathleen?"

"I did, and well… I'm embarrassed."

"Oh Kathleen, trust me… I'm a doctor."

The women laughed, and Kitty took some much-needed deep breaths.

"Well there was a girl there."

"Oh."

"I felt such a fool, I can't risk that again."

"What did she look like?"

"Slim, tall, blonde. Bit of a bitch really."

Claire roared and patted Kitty's hand, picking up their pace to catch the others.

"Well if it's any help, Jamie's sister is tall, blonde and slim but definitely not a bitch."

"Oh I do feel stupid now. Do you think it was her?"

"Well the only blonde on Jamie's arm last night was Flo."

"What a fool, why didn't I think of that?"

"Well we will be off now, why don't you go and see him if that's what you want?"

Waiting for the car to disappear out of view, Kitty rushed back to grab Pimple's keys. Knowing she probably shouldn't drive with the wine she had consumed lunchtime, but she felt cold stone sober and really there was no choice in the matter. Spirits higher that they had been in a long time Kitty drove with the windows down and the music up.

"Not again! Bloody hell!"

Kitty yanked on the hand brake and thumped the steering wheel. No car in sight but she knew she had to try anyway. Knocking the door Kitty stood fiddling with her keys and tapping her feet. The door opened and the beautiful blonde Kitty prayed was Flo folded her arms. Determined to make a better impression today, Kitty cleared her throat.

"Hello again, my name is Kathleen, I wondered if Jamie was in?"

"Did you?" Surprised at the coldness in her response Kitty tried again.

"Are you Flo? I was just talking to Claire and Hamish Duncan."

Using the doctor's name Kitty hoped to soften this steely looking girl.

"Aye I know them."

"Well they said Jamie was back from Harris."

"Aye."

"Is he here?"

"No," bloody Stewart's they were all the same.

"Where is he?" Kitty annoyance was rising and this girl wasn't about to lighten up. Randomly Kitty thought this must be the lot of the poor Jehovah's Witness.

"Not here."

"Oh now, Flo is it. I just want to talk to him."

"Kathleen, I dunna ken what happened twixt the two of ya, but I have never seen my brother like this. And then today... after lunch. Well he was in a right state."

"What? Why?"

"Wouldn't say but he scared me he was so upset," glaring at Kitty with gritted teeth.

"W, we had a bit of a misunderstanding... and, well I really need to talk to him."

"Well ye might be too late he was heading back to Harris, he did'na seem keen to stay here."

"Oh Shit!" Kitty felt winded and grasped her thighs above her knees, leaning forward trying to force air to the bottom of her lungs. Flo unfolded her arms and tentatively placed a hand on Kitty shoulder.

"Are ye alright?"

"Just, just... give me a minute" raising her hand to Flo.

"Oh for goodness sake come in, come on." Flo took Kitty's hand and pulled her over the threshold. Once inside Flo pointed to the leather armchair. Easing back into the buttoned back Kitty stretched out her hands to the log burner in front of her, suddenly cold.

"Do you want a tea or coffee? But by the look of you, you could use something stronger."

"I'd love that but tea would be more sensible, yes please."

Tea making gave Kitty time to regain her breathing. It had taken a lot of effort to confront Flo and she felt wrung out. Handing Kitty her drink Flo smiled and for the first time Kitty could see a slight familial resemblance.

"How is Jamie?"

"Well, as I said, not great. All he would say was he had done something terrible." Flo looked over the pale fragile looking young women and tried to image how she was involved.

"Kathleen, I know ye don't know me and I certainly don't know you but can ya please tell me what this is all about?"

"Well – no, not the particulars... it's not for me to say, certainly if Jamie hasn't."

"Because you don't know or because you don't want to?"

"The latter" Kitty sighed and sipped her tea she clutched in both hands.

"It's... just we have all been so worried, our parents... and well they don't know what to think. My mother fears he's done something awful," Flo looked genuinely upset now. "He's carrying a huge black cloud around with him. It's like he has forgotten how to be happy, that is so not Jamie. He is the most placid happy person I know."

There was silence as both women concentrated on their own tangle of thoughts and conjectures.

"But if he had done something," slow and calculating now, Flo continued, "Like, let's say a hit and run... hurt someone could you tell me? I'm really afraid for him."

"No Flo... no, no, nothing like that." Not knowing how much she could share to put this girl and her poor parents out of their misery. "All I can say without betraying your brothers confidence is that the incident - the misunderstanding involved only him and me."

Flo sat on the edge of her seat and looked into Kitty's eyes. Kitty felt the colour rise in hers cheeks and she had gone from frozen to the core to very hot under the collar in a matter of minutes.

"Flo... I really... I like your brother. We parted on, well, not on good terms. But I'm sure if I could just see him and talk to him we could work it out."

"Well I hope so Kathleen, it's most out of character and I want my big brother back." Flo tapped her fingernails on the mug she held whilst she plotted. "Jamie is out but will be coming back for his bag before he returns to Harris early tomorrow."

"Oh" at least he hadn't gone yet. "What shall I do Flo?"

Flo smiled, she liked this woman but wished she knew what on earth had gone on. If Jamie had done something "terrible" with/to this girl she seemed ready to forgive him.

"Do you think he would come and see me if I asked?"

"Don't know, with his state of mind at the moment I don't know what he will do." Flo continued to tap, "Why don't you stay here with me? I'm reliant on his car at the moment, and he is round a friend's at the moment. When he comes in I could pop out and let you two sort this mess out." Picking up her mobile phone and texting as only young people can and just as swiftly swiping the screen to blackness again.

The buzzing vibrations of the reply that caused the edges of Flo's thin mouth to rise broke seconds of silence. Recognising an artful sister's smile Kitty daren't asked, and Flo was as disinclined to share, so the silence continued.

"You wouldn't mind?"

"Not at all, if it gets Jamie back on track I'd do anything."

The silence could have been uncomfortable for both strangers but reruns of "Friends" on the TV were common ground, and their shared laughter disguised the elephant in the room.

The light was fading and the flickering yellow from the fire was comforting. White rays moved across the wall heralding a car. Without hesitation Flo turned off the TV, scooped up her bag and jacket. Waving from the window at her brother she said over her shoulder, "He's had a good look in your van," turning to face Kitty she added, "Good luck, and please sort it out." Smiling fondly Flo turned then and opened the door before Jamie could put the key in the lock. Half falling through the opening he looked at Flo as she pushed past, planting a loud kiss on the side of his face and patting the other cheek she took his keys and called from the front path.

"Now sort this out James Stewart. I'll stay at Mum and Dad's tonight. Bye Kathleen, lovely to have met you," her voice trailed off and then there was quiet. Kitty could barely speak but managed a croaky "Hi."

Jamie rested his head on the door frame, coldly and calmly "Why are you here?"

"I need, we need to talk Jamie... please."

"Why... why would you want to be here, with me?"

"Oh Jamie, is it not obvious. Did you not read my notes, what did you think?" Each word was an effort.

"No, frankly! I am just as confused, I know what you should think." With that he slammed the door and marched over to her. His sudden movement startled Kitty and she flinched back into the chair.

"Sorry, Kathleen sorry. I... I, I was just getting a drink." smiling apologetically down on her Jamie moved slowly past her and reached for the decanter and a glass. Filling the glass to the top he drained it in a few large gulps. Holding the back of his hand over his mouth and closed his eyes.

"Sorry did ye want one, where are my manners, oh no, that's right, I have none!" Hostile sarcasm did not suit him.

"Don't Jamie... please don't." Kitty pleaded.

Jamie sat heavily on the front edge of the small sofa and flopped back into the feather cushions. Right arm across his face, hiding his eyes in the crook of his elbow. Kitty eased out of her seat and moved cautiously to the sofa. Sitting next to him moving as slowly as she could, he didn't respond to her weight as she sat. Kitty was desperate to touch him and slowly, hesitantly lowered a hand onto his knee. He shivered at her touch.

"Why are you here Kathleen?" His voice was weak.

"I have felt so terrible since-" but Jamie cut her off,

"Of course you have, don't you think I know. If it's an apology you came for it's yours" taking his arm away from his face to reveal the red wet rims of his eyes.

"Oh Jamie no, no, that's not what I meant." But Jamie wasn't listening.

"I can't tell you how sorry I am. I wish, I have wished over and over again to take it back, but I can't!" Looking at her properly for the first time, but for the shortest of time before he buried his head in his hands, slowly shaking his head.

"Jamie, you didn't hurt me, not really."

"Huh, not really!" he scoffed.

"I mean it, I was shocked, but not, not hurt." Jamie looked at her now shaking his head. "It shocked me... scared me – but you did not hurt me! Jamie, please!" Kitty knelt now in front of him and took his wrists in her hands. "Jamie, please."

Pulling his hands towards her but he, not wanting her to look at his face any longer, freed his hands and pulled her into a tight embrace. Talking into her hair now.

"I've thought about you every day. I thought going to Harris and being busy would help, but it didn't. I think it's just got worse the longer it's gone on."

"I know me too. I brought you out a cup of tea that Saturday morning and I was going to tell you everything – but you'd gone." His bristles scratched her face as she spoke.

"I felt so terrible, I stayed because I was in no fit state to drive. I thought seeing me would be the last thing you would have wanted."

"Jamie I know, I knew by morning. You didn't mean to hurt me... I felt it too, the intensity." Breathing quickly she clenched her hands and said what needed saying. "I loved my husband... but I never felt with him what I have felt in the few hours with you."

Holding her upper arms Jamie pushed her back and their eyes locked, following them when she tried to look away.

"The husband, your husband. I need to know Kathleen."

"There is... no husband."

"What does that mean?" pleading now.

"He... he left me… he's…"

"Please" so quietly Kitty barely heard "Tell me."

"He died." The simple words she had caged and hidden now flowed, free at last. Jamie held her face tenderly, cupping it in his palms and rested his forehead on hers. Kitty had never said the words out loud. She had embraced the denial phase of grieving and not let go. Despite Stephen being dead for sixteen months Kitty had managed to avoid the subject wherever possible. In her mind he had left her – so maybe not just the denial phase but a generous helping of anger rolled up in it as well.

"When?"

"December 2010."

"Kathleen why couldn't you tell me before?"

"It's not just you. I don't tell people, I don't know why. In my mind he deserted me, it's still not real, he left... but he's dead."

"I'm sorry, you poor thing. That makes me feel even more of a heel. I was so frustrated and scared. I was afraid that I would lose you – even before I ever really had you... that someone was going to come and take you away, steal you away, have a claim over you."

Placing her hands over his and lowering them to his lap she reached up and stroked the dark red stubble, long enough to be soft. She had struggled to remember every detail in these weeks and her eyes greedily took in the contours and colours of his beautiful face. His eyes were remarkable, like warm jade glistening under glass. He was slimmer she thought than when they last met.

"I'm not going anywhere" leaning in Kitty kissed him lightly.

"I don't want to hurt ya."

"You won't, we'll take it slow."

"Ok."

Jamie suppressed all urges to explore with his hands and held them still on her back. There was none of the violence or passion of that last dark memory but only gentleness and tenderness.

Kitty pulled away and drank in his glorious face once more.

"There, wasn't too bad." she smirked.

"Cheeky wee bitch!" They hugged now, much of the iciness thawed and Kitty drew in long deep breaths of the musky scent of the man.

"What now?" Jamie was serious now.

"Meaning?" Kitty looked bemused.

"Meaning, I'm supposed to be going to Harris on the early ferry tomorrow." Jamie led out a huge sigh.

"Oh shit, no, no not now, so soon! How long for?"

"A month," he said sadly.

"Oh Jamie, I don't think I can cope with you being gone – not when we have only just straightened things out, not now."

"I know... I'll put it off" Kitty's smile was all the convincing he needed.

"Can you do that?"

"Yes, for you Kathleen, hell yes!"

They kissed again for many minutes now with heightened urgency and Jamie yearned to move his hands but kept them fixed to her back.

"Kathleen would you stop with me tonight?" His chest heaved.

"Oh Jamie I can't think of anything I would rather do... but" Burying her head into his neck it took a few minutes and patience and gentle rubbing of her back to get the words out.

"Well I don't know why, it's not like I'm being disloyal to Stephen – although actually it does feel like it. But also I haven't... I've not slept with anyone but Stephen. I just don't know if I'm ready for... for sex." She whispered.

"Hush" Jamie stroked her hair.

"Do you mind?"

"No how can ye think that, we don't have to rush... I just want you here with me. I can loan ye some pyjamas" he lifted her head now and kissed her cheeks, her eyebrows and finally her forehead.

"I have a nightie in the van."

"Aye... I ken I've seen you in that, and I can'na promise to protect ya virtue if you'll be wearing that!"

She laughed "Point taken."

"Are you hungry? Let's eat."

"Starving."

Holding her hand Jamie led her to the kitchen.

"What would ye like? Although choice may be very limited, I haven't really been here."

Cheese and bread were the choices and Kitty couldn't think of a better combo. She tried sitting at the small table but was pulled to be with him. Jamie prepared some of the tastiest cheese on toast she had ever had whilst Kitty held her arms around his waist and rested her head on his back. The pounding of his heart was comforting and Kitty was sorry to have to let go.

Settling on either end of the sofa, her legs lying on top of his with the high stack of thick toast balanced on her lap, they each held a glass of crisp white wine. Kitty updated him on the build and he in turn told of his antics on Harris. Leaning around her Jamie reached for the phone that disturbed them, stealing a kiss before he spoke.

"Aye... aye... uh huh... aye" Grinning now he winked at Kitty, seeing clearly the colour that rose in her face. Reaching out he stroked her face with the back of his hand whilst hissing in Gaelic down the phone. "Oh aye... if ya dunni mind, uh huh, be gone ya cheeky wee bitch" laughing as he replaced the phone he stopped again for another kiss.

"Everything alright?"

"Aye just Flo and the folks checking up on me."

Kitty blushed brighter, "Do they know I'm stopping over?"

"Oh aye" Jamie winked again, it had a very intense effect on Kitty and she drained her wine glass. Worried she would soon be past the point of walking straight she prised herself from the sofa and stepped out into the crisp evening to get supplies from Pimples. Taking a few minutes to process the events of the evening Kitty sat in the van. This was all she had hoped for and she loved every minute of it, but nonetheless it was new and terrifying. *"Buck up girl"* Amanda's words empowering her she returned to the cottage.

Jamie took her hand and kissed her lightly.

"Now I hope ya no mind but I've run you a bath I thought you'd like it."

"Oh Jamie, yes please that would be perfect." Squeezing his hand she followed him up the steep stairs.

"Come on then lass" putting down the toilet seat and folding a towel neatly on it he bowed theatrically and gestured for her to sit.

"Bubbles madam?"

"Please," she giggled.

"You are lucky Flo has been stopping." After a thought he added, "Ridiculous but she insists on staying here rather than our parents' – I think they have been worried about me. I'm not great at hiding my feelings."

"Yes I didn't have you down as a bubbles kind of guy. Is Flo coming back this evening?"

"No" the simple answer made Kitty's heart skip.

With a flourish Jamie poured a thick column of velvety pink under the running water and they both watched as a tower of bubbles rose to meet the taps.

"I promise to behave, but if you leave the door ajar I will sit outside and we can talk... if that's alright?"

"Of course, I'd like that." Bending he kissed her hand,

"Well shout when you're ready I will top up the glasses."

Undressing quickly, adding more cold and clipping her hair on top of her head, she lowered slowly into the embrace of heat. Arranging the bubbles to perfectly retain her modesty. When Jamie returned she told him to come in assuring him she was decent.

"Aye well" he looked down at the arms and head visible above the undulating bubbles. "You'll be right I ken I've seen much more indecent views of ya." Kitty flicked some bubbles in his direction and he handed her a glass of chilled wine.

"Would you mind if I sit here?" Jamie pointed to the toilet seat, coyly Kitty nodded and he moved the towel and sat sipping his wine looking at the girl in his bath. They talked, Kitty bombarding him with questions about his family. Staying on the toilet for a few minutes but almost unconsciously he slipped to the floor and rested his back against the bath. Kitty sipped her wine with one hand and ran her free fingers through the thick chestnut hair.

"I did come to see you," he said quietly.

"What, when?" Kitty sat forward, sloshing a wave of bubbles towards the tap and splashing back over her now exposed breasts.

"This afternoon," Jamie drained the half a glass of wine and reached for the bottle to top it up, downing that too.

"When? Why didn't I see you?" Wracking her brains, "Was I there?" She knew she shouldn't have gone out with Donald.

"Three thirty" His voice had taken on the sad edge of earlier and Kitty tried to piece together the timings of the day.

"Was I out?"

"No."

"Then why didn't you knock, come in, we could have sorted this all out then." Jamie lent forward hugging his bent knees, out of her reach, and there was a silence Kitty distrusted.

"You... you had company."

"Oh the Duncan's?" relieved she tried to reach out for him.

"No!" as cold as the wine.

"Jamie wh... oh... shit, Donald!"

"Yes," Kitty could see the muscles in his face tense as he gritted his teeth.

"What, did you see?" she didn't want to ask but judging by his tone she could guess and this needed clearing up.

"What do you think I saw?" turning quickly Jamie was on his knees, a flash of the rage and hurt she had seen before. Forgetting the cover of the bubbles Kitty knelt up and reached out to the flushed tense face.

"Please it isn't what you think," He backed away out of reach. "Jamie hear me out," Jamie after a brief glimpse of her naked breasts turned and sat once more with his back against the bath. He was determined to get the truth without distraction and there was plenty of that on show. Kitty was relieved when he let her return to stroking his hair. Taking a long drink she settled back into the bath and endeavoured to best explain what passed between her and Donald. Retelling the events as best as she could remember, Kitty got to the part of the story involving the kiss.

"I walked him to the car, and he put his hands on either side of the bonnet. I would have moved if I could, but he kissed me. I was so shocked and before I knew it he did it again. But that was it Jamie. I didn't want it and I pushed him away. That was it, honestly. Is that what you saw?" Kitty tugged gently on his hair when no answer was forth coming.

"Yes, just as you've explained" Kitty stroked the back of his neck and the tension dissipated, resting his head back on the edge of the bath Kitty could see the thick lashes close over his eyes. Taking a deep sigh he continued, voice thick with emotion. "I thought I had really blown it, that I had left it too late and you moved on. With Donald of all people."

"God no, I find him a bit creepy."

Jamie bent his head right back to expose a wide upside down grin. Kitty knelt up again and kissed him enthusiastically.

"Now if we do not have ye dressed soon I really will not be responsible for my actions." Jamie stood slowly pushing up from the bath, this time looking for many seconds at the half naked form of Kitty kneeling before him with a shining covering of tiny bubbles.

"Good god Kathleen Harris ye are beautiful, but I am going to find ya something very unattractive to put on." Leaving the bathroom Kitty slid back into the water and laughed quietly. A large muscular arm held out a heap of navy blue.

"I'll be downstairs, I think I need a coffee. Can I get you one?"

"No I'm fine with wine if that's ok?"

"Fine by me."

Kitty lay listening to Jamie tidy and rearrange the bedroom. Once she heard his soft footsteps on the stairs she reluctantly pulled the plug and dried. This was a tiny cottage and Kitty thought there was only one bedroom – Arhhh the thought of a proper bed. But Kitty was faced with a dilemma, she couldn't put him out of his bed, but was it appropriate to share his bed and not lead to sex? After all he was just a man, and come to think of it she was just a woman and maybe sleeping with Jamie – in every sense of the word wouldn't be a bad thing.

Kitty thought it would be safer to keep her underwear on. Trying on the jogging bottoms Kitty could have fastened the cord above her bust, but settled for empire line and rolled up the legs. The T-shirt was from the highland games and came nearly to her knees. Well it would have to do.

Venturing out onto the landing Kitty looked into the bedroom, yep definitely only the one. The double bed looked freshly made, even the corner of the quilt folded invitingly down.

"Jamie?"

"Down here lass."

She walked into the lounge to see Jamie kneeling, stoking the fire, feeding it a couple of logs and then fastening the door. He turned to look at her as Kitty gave a little twirl to show case her new look. Expecting him to laugh he merely smiled, and a sad smile at that.

"Oh my goodness ya even look ravishing in that" A small defeated smile, "I'd hoped you'd look plainer. I am struggling Kathleen. To be completely honest I am finding it hard, I want to make love to ya so badly."

Kitty didn't know what to say but sat in the chair next to him.

"If it's too much" sigh "I could go and sleep in Pimps."

"NO! No way, no."

"So that's a no then?"

Reaching out she turned his shoulders so he leant against the chair. Tucking her legs up she rubbed the defined muscles of his shoulders. Grateful groans dropped his shoulders as he sipped his coffee.

"As much as I'm loving that... my brain knows we're not having sex – and I'm fine with that, but certain parts of my anatomy are getting the wrong idea."

"Oh sorry Jamie." Her hand froze and she sank back into the chair.

"Don't apologise, please. It's wonderful to have you here. Tell me about you, about your life before Skye."

"Well after Stephen... died" sighing deeply.

"Well done, I'm sure it will get easier lass" Jamie half turned and hugged her legs and she touched his hair. Conscious now to just rest her hand on him.

"We met, going back to the beginning, at Wimbledon Art College. I did a degree in fine art and Stephen was a graphic artist. We were just friends until a night at the end of year exams, second year, not planned but not unwelcome."

Jamie rubbed the back of her free hand with his thumb.

"We graduated and Stephen got a job in Kent, Royal Tunbridge Wells to be precise. It was too good an offer not to take; we needed a mortgage so it seemed sensible to get married."

"If you don't mind me saying it dunna sound very romantic."

"No... I suppose it wasn't. But at the time it was all I knew. Do you mind me talking about him?"

"Of course not lass, I want to know."

"Stephen and I were very practical people, I don't think it ever occurred to me to be romantic or spontaneous. It certainly didn't to Stephen. I struggled to get a job for a year, ended up working in the local café. But then I got a break and started working in Soho on concept art for films." Jamie topped up her glass and sat back down taking her hand again.

"Carry on lass."

"Well we lived there for five years. I never liked it really – too snooty for me but Stephen loved it. He was from Kent and he liked it... but I always regretted moving away from my mum."

"Where does she live?"

"Lived, Wimbledon, she passed away four years ago."

"Ock, I'm sorry lass. Your father?"

"Died when I was fourteen."

"Ock, I... I can'ne imagine."

"You see Jamie, I literally have no one. My brother was first to go, when I was twelve, then dad, then mum and... well Stephen. You see I have no ties. My best friend is the closest thing to family I have and she is in Wimbledon."

Turning onto his knees he reached out and stroked the large waves of golden hair.

"Jesus Kathleen, so much loss, no wonder you don't want to talk about it." Taking Kitty in his arms he pulled her close and kissed the top of her head. Sitting back on his heels he raised her down turned chin.

"Why here? Not that I'm complaining of course."

"It was the one place that reminded me of ... peace. We had our last holiday as a family here – well Applecross on the mainland." Kitty smiled at the memory and Jamie nodded.

"There was the most beautiful beach, golden sand. I remember being amazed that there were no footprints but our own. Like no one had ever trodden there before us. Mum, dad, Tommy and a pink football. We ran, we played and oh how we laughed... we even tried to swim."

"Tad cold for ye?"

"God yes we couldn't even get up to our ankles, who knew you could get brain freeze from paddling." Kitty was lost in her thoughts and Jamie sipped his coffee not wanting to interrupt. Wiping away a tear Kitty continued.

"Stephen... died! – There I'm saying it. And nothing in my life had any meaning. I was desperate to leave Kent and never look back. I was money rich but family poor. I sold my parents house for a ridiculous amount of money and with Stephens's insurance I had money to spend."

"Have you sold you house in Kent?"

"No... but I will never live there, but the rent is great and gives me an income to live off, - my new salary."

"You may change your mind."

"No absolutely not," Jamie didn't doubt it. "I would never have thought it possible but I can restore Tide's, have an income, still have plenty in the bank and never have to do a day's work again. I wake up sometimes and think it must be a dream but then I remind myself it's a nightmare. It's only possible because of the trail of death."

They both sat in silence watching the blue flame dance and caress the crazed, blackened log.

"More wine?"

"No I'm afraid I've awoken too many ghosts, I will get too sad if I have any more."

"How about the Stewart tradition of hot chocolate?"

"That sounds very intriguing." Looking up as Jamie stood he looked back into the saddest of hazel green eyes, rimmed with red and glistening with tears, Bending to kiss her forehead.

Walking back in, Kitty had no idea how long he had been gone and stirred only when he gently touched her shoulder. Handing her the mug of steaming hot chocolate he sat once again in front of her. With his back to the fire Jamie laid his head in her lap as she absent-mindedly ran her fingers through his hair.

"That was gorgeous, thanks. Is it a secret family recipe?"

"Aye and I'd have to kill ya if I told." Jamie took her hands and relieved her of the mug. "Time for bed."

"Oh" Jamie felt her stiffen.

"Dunna fret lass you're quite safe with me, ye can trust me Kathleen."

"I do Jamie."

She trailed after him, her hand feeling small encircled by his. They stood on the landing and Jamie held her.

"Well I'd better use the bathroom," Kitty spoke quietly into his chest. Jamie opened the door and followed her in, realising his mistake he laughed.

"Oh I suppose ye dunna need my help."

"Not tonight," they both laughed.

Seeing her reflection in the mirror the bizarre nature of her current situation seemed suddenly clear. Her cheeks were flushed and her hair, which had seen no attention since the bath was curling in a very haphazard way. Brushing her teeth for a long time Kitty was lost in a whirl of thoughts. She felt sure she shouldn't sleep, (in the biblical sense) with him, but she wanted to. She was single, well past the age of consent so why not? The reason she knew was not physical; if she listened only to her body she would have dragged him into the bath. Jamie had made it clear that he would have no objection. The problem was her mind, a mind that had layer upon layer of defences. A mind and heart so mercilessly torn by the losses she'd had. Not only could she not risk further loss she was afraid that by opening her heart and mind to another person would weaken her defences. She held a tenuous grip on normal. Shut away and unresolved feelings couldn't be released without consequence, and there was no telling the devastation.

There was nothing for it, to bed. Just for tonight the thought of those arms wrapped about her was very appealing. Finally shaking herself into action she walked into the bedroom. A small bedside lamp was on but the dark green shade allowed little or no light to penetrate it but cast a gentle light on the ceiling and the table next to the bed. Jamie sat uneasily at the foot of the bed. He had changed Kitty noted into similar trousers and T-shirt combo as her.

The dark red shirt suited him and fit snugly over his flat stomach, accentuating his shoulders and heavy chest. The V-neck exposed a mat of thick dark red chest hair. Jamie watched her as she scanned over him. Kitty felt the disadvantage, Jamie had seen an awful lot more of her, than she him. Both were glad of the dim light to hide their blushes.

Standing Jamie pulled the quilt back.

"You should be comfortable here Kathleen."

"Are you joining me?"

He looked quizzically back at her, attempting to decipher the question.

"To sleep?" he asked quietly.

"Yes" She felt like a silly schoolgirl and looked down.

"I thought I would take the sofa."

"If ... you don't mind," Kitty gulped and took a deep breath. "I'd like it if you stayed with me tonight."

"If you're sure lass?"

"I'm sure."

Kitty climbed in and pulled the covers over herself. Jamie joined her and they lay in the dim light on their backs. Each at the height of self-consciousness, hearing breath and heart beat above all else.

After many minutes Jamie turned his head to look at her, here in his bed. Kitty had not the courage to reciprocate but searched atop the covers for his hand. Finding only his hip Kitty exclaimed and jumped.

"Now you'll not be about to sully my good name lassie?"

"Oh sorry" the pent up tension gone they both laughed.

"But if it's not too teasing I would like a kiss before I go to sleep," Kitty was happy to oblige and they rolled to face each other. Both aware they where tempting fate they shared a soft gentle kiss. Jamie's arms around her and he hugged her to his chest.

"Best if we stop there if ye dunna want to go farther lass."

He stroked her hair. It was blindingly obvious in this tight clinch that Jamie would readily have gone further and Kitty was glad of feminine ability to hide desire. Her rapid pulse and catching breath left them both in no doubt she wanted it just as much.

They lay like this for hours. Jamie was unsure if and when she slept but ignored the ache in his shoulder that supported her head and the tingling in his hand. Afraid to move and disturb her only his eyes roved over her form in his bed. Her hips a small round mound under the quilt, the lamp light caught flecks of honey and cream in her hair where it fanned over the pillow. His body pressed close to hers, the warmth of this beautiful creature besides him.

Jamie realised then he had never done this. Any previous conquests usually involved copious amounts of alcohol on both sides. Desperate fumbling love making – no just sex actually, and usually she would be gone in the morning. Never had Jamie Stewart at the ripe age of twenty-five ever shared his bed like this.

It had taken a long time for him to relax; this woman had a very potent effect on him. Kitty surely must have felt it and been aware and he hoped she didn't think less of him for it. Finally Jamie succumbed to sleep and snored gently into the top of her hair.

Kitty slept initially but woke by one o'clock, unaccustomed to being cuddled she could feel the sweat on her chest. Carefully so as not to wake Jamie she rolled away and as gently as she could fold his arm across his chest. Lying on her back, Kitty now did what she never had allowed herself to do before. If memories or ghastly images tried to resurface she would refuse them. Buried deep, so deep she thought they no longer existed and for some strange reason, in a strange man's bed she allowed them their freedom.

21

Where Did Stephen Go?

Christmas would see two years since Stephens's death. The funeral was delayed a day short of three weeks because of the Christmas holidays. It was a strange kind of limbo that Kitty allowed herself to remember now. The rhythmic rise and fall of Jamie's large chest and gentle snore was calming, and Kitty tried to remember those twenty days. It was a blur of visitors and tears. Kitty woke, she dressed, she accepted flowers and cards and an endless stream of pitying stares. But she could not recall the details as each day played like the worst of dreams.

Although Kitty had known sudden death with her brother and father, she still held the anger deep within her that Stephen's demise was too quick. She had been completely unprepared and Amanda had always blamed this for her poor processing of her grief.

The visit to the Oncologist, sitting arm in arm in a huge waiting room. Who knew so many people had cancer? Kitty passed her time in the macabre game of guessing what cancer each of the patients had. Who was patient and who was relative? Mainly blindingly obvious but some, Stephen included she thought, looked well. The women in an array of wigs and headscarves, complexions of shades of white, grey and yellow indicated many more.

Stephen flicked through a car magazine. Of course Kitty knew he wasn't reading it or even looking at the pictures. He had told Kitty not to worry when he booked up with his GP. He had laughed off her concern when he winced when standing. Fervently denied he had lost weight and that his bones were more prominent, his trousers still fitting.

But Kitty knew, Kitty could see his cheekbones and ribs becoming ever more prominent. Kitty noticed every time he winced and took a deep breath on standing. Every time he stopped when walking to rub the top of his thighs or the small of his back. Lying night after night awake and eyes closed, knowing her husband lay next to her unable to sleep as well. Neither brave enough to share their fears incase it made them true.

The GP had taken blood, examined him and ordered an urgent Ultrasound. That was Monday and by Friday the tests were done.

The phone rang Friday evening and Kitty answered in her usual chirpy style.

"Hello" shortly followed, in a much bleaker tone, "Oh yes... hello Dr Jones. Sure, hang on, I'll hand him over."

Husband and wife stared hard at each other as Stephen took the phone. Kitty stood next to him and pushed her ear to the outside of the receiver. Reaching round his middle Kitty hooked her fingers in the belt hoops of his trousers to hold him near. Stephen flinched and caught his breath and she loosened her hold and any pressure from his trousers.

"Ahha... Oh... I see... yes" Kitty couldn't make out everything the doctor was saying but the shaking that had now started to jolt her husband sent shards of ice down her spine.

"Ok... yes ok... nine forty five, yes I..." glancing now down at Kitty the threat of tears in his eyes "We can make that."

Did they tell everyone else that was the question? Next Wednesday they were to see a Specialist Oncologist. Dr Jones hadn't beaten around the bush – blood and Ultrasound results pointed to there being an abdominal tumour.

"I'm terribly sorry to explain this over the phone Mr Vrcelj, but in these circumstances, with this sort of tumour..."

Stephen interrupted then, "Tumour you said... is it... could it be C, c... cancer" Struggling to get the dreaded word out.

"Yes I'm sorry, Stephen. I'm afraid that could well be what it is. You must prepare yourself, and your family for that diagnosis. Although not definitive it is indicated that there is a tumour and it may be cancer."

Nothing else to do, nothing else to say Stephen hung up. Kitty hurriedly asked him about snippets that she had heard, but too shocked, Stephen stood shaking. For a long time they stood there in the dining room hugging in silence. Only when Stephens' shaking changed to shivering was Kitty aware of the failing light and her own coldness.

There is a limit to the amount of sobbing a person can take and a little after an hour later husband and wife let go of each other. Both desperate for a drink to sooth their ripped throats. Kitty filled two glasses of water and Stephen two of Sherry. Raising his glass in a morose toast, "In sickness and in health."

For the next five days they told no one. Both leaving for work the secret left at home. The trivia of mundanity was infuriating, the complaints and the whines from colleagues intolerable. The overriding need for both of them was to get home, shut the door and ignore the phone. They waited, and waited, and waited the unbearable wait.

Lying in bed night after night, unable to sleep, unable to switch off the worries and fears. Lying next to Jamie, arms folded across her chest, fearful of moving and disturbing him. That was how she spent her nights then.

The oncologist was a very smart middle-aged blonde, calling them in to the consulting room herself. Following her in Kitty admired the tailored dress and my, those shoes! Kitty wondered where she had bought her shoes, high and shiny, not what she had expected – but then what should women who work with Cancer and death wear?

An air of the surreal had clouded everything that day – dream like –as if watching the whole scene on stage. Brutally, but not unwelcome this woman told them the diagnosis so far. Wasting no time she explained the most likely scenario was a lymphoma. A fast growing, aggressive tumour that needed urgent attention.

Stephen nodded and the only hint that he was being given a potential – and short, life sentence was the tensing of the muscles in his cheeks as he ground his teeth. Kitty bit the inside of her mouth, and thumbnails dug painfully into her forefingers. The tears edged rebelliously and tumbled down white cheeks, converging under her chin, silently and without hindrance dripping into her cleavage.

The prognosis potentially could be good. Kitty held onto the 50; 50. After chemotherapy and radiotherapy, if it worked, which it didn't always.

They were introduced to the specialist nurse and given copious leaflets.

"Cancer and you."

"Cancer and your finances."

"Living with Lymphoma."

"Macmillan."

"Chemotherapy, common questions."

As if that wasn't enough to drown you, photocopied pages on the specific Chemo he would receive. The specialist nurse, who smiled and kept a weary eye on Stephen and herself, the Oncologist, serious and intent were merely doing their days work. But Stephen, her Stephen was shell-shocked and she for the first time in her life knew what that meant.

Voices, words, statistics babbled and distant, as if her fingers were in her ears or trying to listen under water. The ticking of the clock however was magnified and the thick second hand bounced and tapped with every passing second, comforting and hypnotic. Kitty battled to focus on the Doctor and the nurse but time and time again the clock stole her attention.

The consultant rose and reached to shake Stephen's hand. She could hear his voice distant and faint thanking the Consultant. "What are you thanking her for – she just ruined our life!" Kitty's addled mind screamed, but she merely looked into the warm friendly face and the guiding arm of the nurse ushered them out of the room. It was someone else's turn to have their life shattered, Kitty thought as she passed the bleak line of fellow waiting patients.

Jackie was the Associate Lymphoma Clinical Nurse Specialist, or so her card said. But to Kitty she was just Jackie, her most cherished contact whose phone number Kitty could still recount nearly seventeen months later.

The hardest part was telling people. Of course it was so hard to comprehend; Stephen had always been so fit and was only twenty-eight. Everyone they told was shocked, and all without exception pestered for all the details, of course they did, they cared. But Stephen and Kitty had limited energy and hurt themselves a tiny bit every time they had to explain it, over, and over again.

His parents were told at their house. Kitty would never forget the silent scream behind his mother's blank expression. The trembling lip of his father and seeing the large brown eyes fill to overflowing. Kitty had never seen her father-in-law cry before, or show any great emotion and it had a profound effect on Stephen. As they left the house and waved as cheerfully as they could muster, Kitty was impressed with Stephen's positive attitude. Stephen's self control lasted until they rounded the corner, jolting to a halt, head dropping to his hands on the wheel, Stephen wept like never before. She rubbed his juddering back but no words were exchanged – there were no words.

Kitty tried to recount the days now, twenty-one in total from Dr James's phone call to leaving his bloated cold body in intensive care. In the beginning there had been hope, there was a light. But the darkness descended and she tried now to remember exactly when.

Speed was everything with Lymphoma so they were told.

Chemotherapy was to start ten days after seeing the doctor, she did remember that. Pauline was the ever so smiley Filipino nurse and Kitty remembered that was the best day Stephen had in the whole sorry affair. Efficiency aided confidence and for the first time in ten long days there was a shared feeling of optimism. Kitty could see his drawn face now as she squeezed his hand. They could beat this, they would, must beat it.

But this was a brief window in a chapter of hell. The Chemo made Stephen feel rotten and the next week drained and sapped any glimmer of joy or hope from them both.

Day nineteen she remembered. For the first time she worked through the events as she could remember them, not pushing them back but allowing them to surface. Yes, day nineteen was a Wednesday, the rain had battered the bedroom window and the true nightmare began. Stephen screamed in pain and Kitty was terrified, the chemo had worked too well apparently – who would have thought – how bloody perverse. The tumour had shrunk and Stephen's bowel had perforated.

A phone call to Pauline, a hurried call from Jackie and sirens and lights soon resulted in Kitty sitting beside an unconscious Stephen in intensive care. The waiting room echoed to constant sounds of weeping. Day turned into night and day once more as Kitty kept stunned vigil. Two days later Kitty held one hand whilst Stephen's mother held the other and the ventilator was turned off.

Twenty-one days from normality to nothing.

Twenty-one days from life, plans, future, family and a marriage to widowhood.

The irony of the fact was that it took as long to get Stephen buried as it did diagnosed to dead. All that the future promised was shattered, all that made her life whole gone.

The three weeks without Stephen merged into a blur of visitors, cards, flowers and crying. Kitty actually cried very little and found herself comforting everyone else who seemed to let loose a tide of grief. Kitty thought back now, and waiting for the funeral her main recollection was the flowers. Never before had she seen so many flowers, and had to borrow vases and utilise jugs to cope with the amount. Watering and rearranging every morning, Kitty found peace. Taking deep breaths she would inhale the perfume, something beautiful and pure in a bleak life.

One memory that was clear was the nights. Well-wishing visitors gone, the door locked and curtains drawn Kitty would make her way to bed. There was only one bed, their bed. The second room was a study. Each attempt to lie on that bed was futile, the air would chill and waves of emotion so intense -a grief too enormous to face, and capable of overwhelming and drowning her, Kitty would sit gasping for breath.

The sofa and Stephen's pillow were her bed now. The smell of him so real, if she closed her eyes and buried her face in the pillow she was hugging him. Safe in his embrace once more.

But always they came, the nightmares. His face distorted and waxen, bloated like a drowned man, his eyes were glazed and unresponsive. For the first time Kitty allowed the image of his corpse into her waking mind. Edging nearer to Jamie for warmth, remembering the chorus of bleeps from the wall of machines and then the eerie silence as they were switched off one by one. Stroking his lank hair, looking for the last time at his hands Kitty remembered trying to capture the memory of everything – even though everything was so hideous.

Some ghosts were laid to rest that night. For the first time since it happened Kitty let the memories out. She was sure she still could not say them out loud but felt the relief of finally facing them. With an enormous sigh Kitty turned and rested her head near to Jamie's chest and breathing in his scent and let the pounding heart lull her into a deep grateful sleep.

22

Facing the Music

Jamie had woken at Dawn, lying on his side the chink of pink light shining through the curtains. It took his brain a few seconds to compute, listening now he could hear the soft sounds of Kitty's breath. Turning incredibly slowly so as not to disturb her Jamie rolled over - he had to see for himself that she was really here. Kathleen Harris, asleep in his bed!

She looked so peaceful and he took the opportunity to scrutinize her. Her lashes being fair were never very obvious when her eyes were open. Closed Jamie could now see how long and thick they were as they rested against the ivory cheeks. Her nose was small and neat with a slight upturn at the end, which he suppressed the urge to touch.

Her hand lay between them, flat on the pillow. Inches from his face he scanned every detail, the nails, and the creases. The fingers were long and tapering with elegance and delicacy and the back of the hand the finest blonde down. Jamie lay contented to just watch as she slept beside him. The pink of the morning light was replaced by bright white light that crept its way across the walls.

Finally he could wait no longer to wake her, desperate to waste no more time. Taking the upturned hand resting by her face Jamie kissed the warm palm and then the ends of each fingertip. Eyes squinting open Kitty stretched and smiled back at him.

"Sorry lass but I couldn'a bear to lose any more of the day."

"Hmm" Kitty reached up and ruffled his hair.

"Morning."

"Morning Jamie."

"Stay here," he leant over, kissing her and then was gone.

Kitty could hear him singing, a deep soft voice and a tune Kitty didn't know, and words she knew to be in Gaelic. Taking the opportunity to nip to the bathroom Kitty beamed at her reflection. The hair was wavy and willful, and even though she had dark shadows under her eyes they were bright and shone from the rosy complexion. Suddenly aware of her morning breath she hastily brushed her teeth and was eager for the day.

Hearing Jamie's dulcet tones approach, Kitty just managed to get back in bed before he returned to the bedroom. Placing a tray on her lap he lifted the two mugs of tea and putting them on the bedside table. Climbed in next to her he took a bite from one of the pile of buttered crumpets.

"Is tea ok? Sorry I should have asked."

"Perfect, thank you it's lovely."

Exchanging furtive glances and smiles they devoured the breakfast.

"When do you have to leave for Harris?" Kitty tried hard to hide the concern in her voice.

"I'll call my friend, he'll understand. He's the one person I confided in, what I did, how I felt." Kitty reached out and held his hand, how long would he beat himself up over that one incident. Turning to face him she tucked her legs up to one side.

"I dunna wish to be presumptive... but I would like to spend at least the next week with ye. No pressure though lass, just ta get ta know ye."

"Oh Jamie I couldn't bear it if you left now. Just when we have found each other."

"Aye, I'll phone him now."

Jamie skipped from the room, leaving Kitty to lie down and stretch under the quilt. The soft springy mattress she had been too busy last night to appreciate. With the sun shining through the cracks of the heavy curtains Kitty felt light, as if a weight had literally been lifted.

With a stretch that pulled the tips of her toes to her fingertips, Kitty rolled over in the bed and giggled face down into the pillow. Whatever was going to come of this, Jamie and her? She had no idea but the difference from yesterday and today was that she was excited. And what was more; today she had shed the guilt that she should not be here – in fact now she felt she should be nowhere else.

Jamie walked in to find her face down and playfully jumped onto the bed straddling her and wrapping his arms under and around her. After a weak attempt to throw him off Kitty murmured and moaned as Jamie bent his head and kissed her neck. Wriggling free she turned and was soon facing his earnest face. Keeping his weight off her they started to kiss. All hesitation and trepidation from last night gone. Neither held back and Kitty soon was kicking to free herself from the quilt that lay between them.

Sudden realisation of what he was doing halted Jamie in his

tracks. One hand still on the small of her back, the other had reached around and cupped her breast. A memory of the dark moment when he had last done this sprang into his mind and all the angst it had caused. Pulling his hand quickly from under her T-shirt it was Kitty who reached down and put it back.

"Don't stop" Kitty was breathless and held his hand in place. Although they continued to kiss Jamie slowly moved his hand and once again wrapped it around her back. Shifting his weight he moved so as to lie next to her, and all too soon he pulled away.

"We don't have to stop," she whispered.

"Aye... we do. Kathleen I want to court ye. I need ye to be truly ready." Jamie stroked the hair from her forehead and kissed it. "I will'na risk ye making a hasty decision and regretting it, we have time lass."

"Oh."

"Patience lassie, it'll be all the better for the waiting, when are ye needed at the croft for my uncle, will he be there? It being Sunday."

"Oh shit, shit SHIT! Yes he said he would as he missed Saturday!" Kitty sat up and Jamie laid a hand on her stomach smoothing his T-shirt.

"Does he no have a key?"

"Yes to the store, but, shit! What's the time?"

"Ten thirty."

"Oh double shit!"

"Have a quick shower and I'll drive you home."

"I, I don't know if that's a good idea," Jamie looked rebuffed.

"Why?"

"Do we want your uncle and cousin... to know I spent the night with you?" She smiled at him and stroked his face.

"Well I dunna mind lass, but if you'd rather. At least it would stop them teasing ya – which by the way they will do mercilessly when they find out."

"You think its inevitable then?"

"Ock aye!"

Kitty leapt from the bed and headed for the bathroom. Not bothering to lock or even close the door Kitty undressed and got under the shower. Jamie sat against the headboard, arms behind his head smiling broadly.

"You know," shouting towards the dark shape washing behind the curtain, "You know I need to see ye, I'll not be able to stay away from ye today – ya know that right?"

Her wet head peeked around the curtain and smiled provocatively, "I think you're seeing me just fine now."

"Ya know what I mean, I will have to come with ya, and remember Flo took my car last night."

"What if I drop you at the top of the road, maybe you could come and advise me on the derelict croft?"

"Whatever you want but I'm coming with ya."

Turning off the water Kitty looked out, standing before her hand outstretched a naked Jamie offered her a towel.

"Aye well, I thought about what ye said... about ya disadvantage. I figured it was time to settle the score and let ya see more of me." A crooked smile and a flash of a wink. "Choice is before ye lass" teasing now "Get in the shower with me or go and see Uncle Malcolm?"

Eyes fixed on his she had been too shocked and embarrassed to look further but pulling back the wet curtain she slowly reached for the towel taking the opportunity to slowly rove from head to toe.

"Oh my!"

"Well, might I be tempting ya?"

"You are, but if I don't go home now... well I'm afraid I won't ever go."

Wrapping the towel around herself she slapped a naked buttock as she ran back to the bedroom.

Driving too fast around the bends Kitty dared not look at the man sitting very real and large in her van, struggled to clear the image of his beautiful body. He was bigger than Stephen in every way. Where Stephen had been slim, Jamie was burly. Stephen was tall but narrow across his shoulders and hips; Jamie's large muscles were round, covered in soft flesh and his thighs, arms and chest wide and heavy.

Although Stephen had almost black hair, he had the palest of skin and the merest smattering of body hair. Again she could see Jamie and the fine covering of red hair all over his body. Freckles were abundant and where the sun had caught they threatened to join forces and completely cover him. Far from having pale skin Jamie had a warm gold hue.

As she dropped Jamie on the road above her house a sudden wave of nausea threatened to drive her off the road, she was being unfaithful to Stephen, was she cheating on him. How could she compare them, what was she thinking? The small fact that he was dead did nothing to lessen the guilt she now keenly felt.

Glad of the end of her journey and the necessity to sweep this particular time bomb under the rug, she must now face the builders. Taking the top of the drive at speed Kitty careered down nearly tipping poor Pimples over. Settling on a cloud of dust she parked next to Jeff's van. No sign of the men she did her best to gather herself, taming her hair and straightening her clothes she set off for the building site.

The radio was blaring, Kitty guessed they turned it down when she was there on her behalf. The burly outline of Jeff could be seen in the store, singing tunelessly as he made a drink, uncannily like his cousin.

"Morning Jeff."

"Oh, morning to you Kitty, you're up and out early today."

"Yes… I had some, er, errands to do."

Jeff raised his eyebrows and looked properly at her now.

"Are you alright lass you're looking, a little frazzled?" Feeling as enormous blush creeping up her neck she struggled to answer.

"Ur, um... yes, no, I'm Ok."

"If you're sure?" Sarcasm and laughter clear in his tone.

She jumped as Jeff shouted to his father.

"Kitty is here da" Jeff kept his eyes on the flushed face before him in fascination. What could this woman have been up to, to make her look so flustered? Malcolm walked around the back of the house.

"Morning to ya lass. Sorry we did'ne get here yesterday- you'd have had no straight brickwork if we had." Laughing now the sore throat evident, too much alcohol and singing Kitty suspected.

"But, are you quite well lassie you look…?" but Malcolm didn't continue but looked first from the girl's blushes to the smirk on his son's face. He had missed something but decided to leave it be.

"Jeff?" in a tone only a father can use. Demanding information and offering a threat to behave, and of course woe betide you if you lie to me.

"What, WHAT! I did'na do anything, she looked like that when I said good morning."

"Oh" Malcolm looked appeased.

"Well lass, are ye sure? You're not ailing?"

"Honestly no, no... no I just had been rushing, here Jeff I'll make the drinks." Taking the kettle from Jeff she was very glad to turn away from them and busy herself in normal chores.

"If she were my bairn I'd think she'd been up to no good." Malcolm whispered more to himself than to his son as they left the store and a relieved client.

Glad of the cold solidity Kitty gripped the old stone sink with both hands. Concentrating on deep breaths, why could she not outgrow these two infuriating traits? The inability to conceal her emotions and control the blushes that frequently betrayed her. She knew she could gather herself, were it not for the fact that Jamie could arrive at any moment.

Crunching on a cereal bar hoping to quell the gnarling in the pit of her stomach, and tea brewed, she carried them out to the Stewarts. She was eager to see what advances had been made, and at least enjoy the normality until chaos and confusion reappeared.

"How was your party?" Kitty asked as she handed them their mugs.

"Aye, grand, grand. A dram too much of whiskey and maybe a dannsa and song too many."

"But very little in the way of sleep." Jeff added.

"Our Jamie was asking after you lass." Malcolm watched and grinned at the anticipated blush.

"I ken you'd been asking a fair bit about him yaself, those errands ye were about may have just followed ye home." Malcolm tilted his head towards the drive where Jamie now came into view. She couldn't bear the grins, and all thought of keeping their relationship, as new as it was, secret, were futile.

Kitty marched across the grass meeting a quizzical looking Jamie half way. She reached up and held his face firmly in both hands and pulled him down to her and kissed him. Being shocked at first, having seen his uncle and cousin raise their mugs in acknowledgement of his arrival. But a few seconds were enough to rid any question of doubt and he wrapped his arms about Kitty and pulled her tight and they were lost, oblivious in the kiss.

"Well, I see you two have met, good morning to ya James" Malcolm called.

"Sorry, but he knew, I don't know how but he knew anyway" Her breathless voice in his ear.

"Are ye mad, dunna apologise I'm delighted. I ken ya can greet me like every time! Let's go and face the music and let them have their fun." Releasing her, Jamie took her small hand and led her over to a waiting Jeff.

"Well, James Stewart! Ye dunna hang around," nudging Jamie with a forceful elbow and a wink to his cousin.

"Thoir do chasan leat - sod off" Jamie's retort was harsh and Kitty could guess its meaning.

"Well I'm happy for ya both; you'll no find a better man on Skye lass, present company excluded."

Malcolm gave a low bow and Kitty froze as Malcolm approached, slapped James's arm and placed a gnarled hand on Kitty's shoulder and lent and kissed her forehead.

"Well I ken we'll have this place finished all the sooner if we have Jamie here hanging around like a love sick pup." Malcolm's smile of sincere warmth for his nephew was plain to see.

"Well if you'll excuse us, Kathleen was going to show me her derelict croft."

"Oh aye is that what they call it down south" A laughing Jeff ducked out of the way of Jamie's swipe. Jamie took hold of the stunned woman's hand and led her across the front garden and around the headland. Leaving behind the fading laughter and Gaelic jeering, not for the first time Kitty was glad she didn't understand the local language.

Both giggling and a little out of breath they stopped by the ruin. Standing down by the inlet to the water they rested their backs against the damp blackness of stone and were obscured form the world.

"Sorry lass but it's out now, they'll get over themselves soon enough, then we can relax."

"I can't imagine ever relaxing with you," Kitty looked out at the sea.

This statement worried Jamie and he moved to stand in front of her and gently force her chin round to look at him. Seeing the worry on his face Kitty quickly added, "I have never felt like this Jamie… not like, this. Every time you touch me, even if you're close you spark something in me. Like…"

"What?" his voice rough.

"Like there is a current, an energy… that threatens to stop my breath, my heart." Barely a whisper, Kitty tried again to look out at the water but Jamie held her fast. Hardly making contact he ran his fingers around her face, marvelling at its velvety smoothness, brushing then her lips.

"Aye I feel it to. I have never felt like this before. But surely didn't ye..." but he didn't finish the sentence and looked down. "No"

Their breathing mirrored each other's, laboured and ragged they stood for many minutes as Jamie traced every detail of her face and neck. Not feeling he could ask but desperate for answers to understand this novel and powerful emotion.

Kitty hugged him now and glad to hide her face that betrayed too much she buried it in his chest.

"I... I never felt this with my husband" Peering up at him, "Do you mind if I talk about him?"

"God no... Kitty he was your husband, ya loved him and I, I worry ye are not ready for this" Kitty smiled up at him but retreated to the security of his jumper. It was so much easier to talk to him whilst not looking into the beautiful pools of his eyes.

"Well we were mates, friends for a long time, and, well as I said it was a drunken end to a party when we first slept together. I'd never been with anyone else so had nothing to compare it to." Kitty took a few deep breaths, not believing she was going to share the most personal and intimate of details with a relative stranger. Again the bile of betrayal threatened to choke her.

Aware of her obvious struggle Jamie kissed the top of her head and shushed her.

"Ye dunna need to do this," Jamie whispered in her hair.

"I think I need to... because I feel unfaithful, is that silly?"

"No lass, no." Hugging her closer. Kitty took a deep sustaining lung full of the sea air.

"Sex was, well always... pleasant – OH god that sounds terrible – sorry Stephen. I just mean I enjoyed it but it was never desperate. With you, just touching your hand does something to me that I have never experienced. Just holding your hand ignites something in me I don't know, or understand... to be honest it frightens me."

Jamie pulled back so as to look upon her face, "Aye I feel it too. That is what I feel and that is what made me behave like an animal in the pub that night." Kitty held him tight.

"You must forget that, do you not see... I feel it too."

"God I want ye so badly." But suppressing every urge to kiss her again he opted for sharing something of his past experiences.

"I had a girlfriend at school, until we were eighteen – Rosie. I remember being desperate to get in her knickers, but that was just raging teenage hormones."

"And did you? Did you get in her knickers?" Kitty grinned up at him, enjoying teasing him a little.

"No, no she resisted all my charms with vice like thighs and immovable jeans." Kitty threw her head back and laughed. "Aye, ya may laugh but I'm sure it was not healthy for a red blooded youth. When I went to University I was so surprised that girls would have sex just because they wanted it. I spent three equally confusing years, with a string of fleeting and unrepeated sexual encounters."

"Many girls?" Kitty asked embarrassedly.

"No probably half a dozen, but most I didn't really remember. It always seemed to result from a drunken night out together. To be honest it was a bit of a haze and very confusing. The girls were always so confident and never wanted to commit, I think I felt a bit used in the end." Kitty squeezed him reassuringly; it made it so much easier to open up when he shared his feelings.

"Ya ken, I never have had a relationship. Not like you, and… Stephen. Nothing to compare to. I've had sex obviously and what I considered good sex at the time, but…"

"Go on" Kitty quietly prompted.

"I've never… made love, and I want to do that. You make me want to do that, so much it makes me feel sick, empty inside somehow."

"Well what a pair, what will we do?" Kitty looked up and pulled him in for a kiss – would she ever tire of this, Kitty feared like a drug she would very soon become dependant on it. Only the thought of facing his uncle and cousin with matted hair and puffy red lips forced Kitty to pull away.

"Lets not do it here though" Kitty smirked and they both giggled. Taking his hand he followed compliantly. The tide was out and they edged nearer the water where the stones were fewer and smaller. They continued on in silence past the farthest point Kitty had explored.

"Isle Ornsey lighthouse" Jamie stated. A pristine white round building precariously balanced on a strip of black rock. The tide being at its lowest reveals a crushed shell and coral path.

"You can only walk to it on especially low Tide's, I love this view" Kitty looked up at Jamie now, the wind buffeting his hair, the taut musculature softened by the advancing beard.

"I like this view," Kitty reached up and loved the soft feel of his soft deep red bristles. All composure lost they, embraced and kissed until the returning Tide's washed around their feet.

"Unless ye feel able to swim back round to ya croft we'd best be heading back."

With purpose in their stride they were soon passing the derelict croft and pushing ever on. Never letting go of each other's hand, Kitty realised since the first touch on the lawn this morning they had not been out of touch for a second.

Having no idea of the time they were in agreement that they were hungry and mutually relieved that Malcolm and Jeff could be seen eating their lunch in one of the vans. Scurrying into the store Kitty reluctantly let go of Jamie hand, hers felt small and very cold without his enveloping it. Jamie not able to bear the loss of contact stood behind her wrapping his arms around her waist and resting his chin on her shoulder.

"Sandwich?"

"Please."

Kitty had never had occasion to prepare food with a large man welded to her back but managed valiantly. Assisted by the occasional large hand held out, the task was soon complete. Plates on the table, Kitty extricated herself from his arms and pushed him into one of the seats. Lowering herself into the opposite chair she was grabbed mid fall and placed on Jamie's lap.

They sat eating, grinning and sipping their tea.

"Maybe if we were to make love... the intensity would lessen. Maybe it wouldn't feel so overwhelming – not so much like a ticking bomb." Jamie nuzzled her neck and in his best moustache twirling voice. "You know the horse is out of the stable anyway. By now my parents, siblings and not to mention the clan Stewart will be well aware I have been molested by an older woman – not to mention a Sassenach!"

"Oh shit! Really?"

Jamie's nodding head gave her all the confirmation she needed.

"Without doubt, Uncle Malcolm will have phoned my parents, and that is after Flo would have given them a blow-by-blow account of her meeting with you. I think I freaked them out when I shot off. They were all worried about me at the party. I was trying to put a brave face on but they would have seen right through that."

"Didn't you tell anyone?"

"How could I, I was so ashamed, so livid with myself" A dark look came over him as his brows furrowed.

"No Jamie, no, hush. That never happened, we were both confused, consumed. It will never happen again I know it, and we must forget it" Jamie kissed the hand he held.

"Well I have never been so upset, I think they thought I'd murdered someone."

"Hit and run Flo suggested. I didn't tell her any details but said it was a misunderstanding between you and me."

"Did she now! Well I'm not surprised, any way Malc will want to put my dad straight, who of course will immediately tell my mother, who will be straight on to Flo etcetera... etcetera!"

"Oh" Kitty, the woman with no family, hadn't really accounted for a clan being involved.

"Aye we will be summoned soon enough, they will be wanting to meet you."

"Oh, no pressure then. I didn't think Flo liked me that much."

"She thought you were the cause of my demise, she will love you when she sees how much I do." Leaving Kitty struggling to swallow her tea.

"I don't know how these things usually work? But shouldn't we date for a few weeks then progress to sex and a few months later we might talk of... love and meeting the in-laws."

"Aye that's the norm, but... have a care Mrs Harris. I dunna think what we have is the norm. Unless I go to Harris today I see very little chance of keeping ye from my bed" a wicked smile faded, "That is... if ye need longer… if this is too quick I could try and keep my distance."

"I think... I need to phone Amanda!"

"Oh" Pulling back this was not the answer he expected, "And who might Amanda be? And what might she have to do with us?"

"She is the nearest thing I have to family. We grew up together and she has everything to do with this." Jamie puzzled expression made Kitty laugh. "The night you undressed me, put me on the loo and undressed me and put me to bed?"

"Yes, yes and ahhh yes."

"I phoned Amanda and she changed my panic to sense, the day I flashed myself at you, she convinced me not to run away, that it wasn't such a big deal."

"I'm liking the sound of her already."

"And the day, well you know after our, disagreement, Amanda made me see it for what it was and she helped me put everything into perspective." Kitty sipped her tea and Jamie waited patiently for her to continue. "Since losing Stephen, since he ... DIED! I have functioned on autopilot, most of me turned off, on standby really. Amanda knew the real me, the prewidow me. When my brain freezes and fails to function she is there, my back up. I don't trust my own mind anymore, I've done the maddest, rashest things – like moving here."

"Oh and thank god and all that is holy that ye did." Jamie crushed her to him and breathed in her scent through her thin jumper.

"Well I think before the day is out I need to talk to Amanda. And if the offer is still there I would like to share your bed later – for more than sleep." She whispered into his hair and Jamie shivered below her.

"Mrs Harris ya would be most very welcome." Kissing her neck he suddenly stopped. "Do you think? No... no, it doesn't matter."

"What, please Jamie say it."

"Would she talk to me? Or is that just odd?"

Their eyes bored into the others as Kitty considered.

"Yes, she's not shy, in fact my only hesitation is she will say too much. That is if you feel you need to?"

"I think I'd like to Kathleen, I'm afraid of pushing ye into anything. Of asking too much of ye when it is still very soon, and very raw after Stephen. I can't jeopardise this, I will not lose thee. I will happily wait until you are ready."

Tears filled Kitty eyes and she coughed and blinked them away.

"Lets go back to yours can we?"

"Aye of course."

"Be prepared for some damage to your phone bill."

"I'm made of tough stuff, I can take it."

They kissed again, fingers knotted in hair and bodies pressed tightly together.

Malcolm's head appeared at the window and a loud tap made them jump apart. Kitty attempt to stand was thwarted by two large hands on her hips pinning her to him.

"Hi uncle, good lunch?"

"Aye can'na say I enjoyed it as much as ye did yours mind." His voice a stern Plateau but his wink a sign of approval at his nephews transformed mood – the cause very evident.

"How's my father?"

"Grand, said to say hello to ye and Mrs Harris."

Kitty groaned and lowered her head to hide in the nape of Jamie neck, both men let out load rumbling laughs.

"Your mother said to say hello and looks forward to meeting yon young lady." Another groan from Kitty caused a bigger bout of laughter.

"You can'na expect to be canoodling with a clansman an expect to keep it ta yon sel."

Looking up, flushed all over, "Yes, I see that now."

"Well good luck to ya both – but some of us have work waiting, houses ta build. Will ya be joining us laddy?"

"Not today uncle we have plans, but to be sure you'll be sick of the sight of me afore this build is done."

"Aye, suspected as much." Smiling now he winked, and was gone. Malcolm ducked out of the door and the reassuring sound of the digger starting up and the entwined couple kissed again.

"Now if I'm to face my kin I'd best do the washing up, that is unless you happen to have a cold shower? Or there will be no doubting what our plans are." Jamie adjusted his trousers as Kitty stood and she had known precisely why Jamie wouldn't let her stand in front of his uncle.

"Ye have a terrible effect on me Mrs Harris."

"I've noticed and I'm sorry. Lets get back to yours and phone Amanda... then maybe we can see what can be done about that," glancing down.

"Nothing a bit of cold water won't cure, remember I had a very frustrated adolescence. My mother thought I was just very helpful, always volunteering to do the dishes."

Kitty laughed and kissed his forehead.

"Away wi ya woman, have ye no sympathy?"

She skipped out of the shed, smiling shyly at Jeff as she rounded the corner heading for the loo. She welcomed the composure cold breeze and porcelain could bring, taking longer than she needed giving Jamie plenty of time at the sink.

When Jamie joined her in the garden they linked hands, Jamie taking a small bow at Jeff's whistle and laughed Gaelic comment. Kitty wanted to show him the work she had been doing on the wall. Expert hands ran over the stones she had placed.

"Well done Kathleen, its rewarding work isn't it?" He smiled at her proud upturned face, "When the right stone hunkers down, bedding in tight with it's neighbour."

"Yes and I really would like your help on my little derelict house. I could always pay you."

Jamie's glare shocked her, and she pulled away. She knew he drove a beaten up car and lived in his father's estate cottage. Other than working in the heritage centre she realised she had no idea how he earned his living.

"You'll not be paying me!" His voice was stern.

"Oh" was all Kitty could think of to say.

"If I want to help ye. I'll do it because I wish te. Please dunna think I was wanting any of ya money." Still stern.

"Sorry, I didn't mean to offend you Jamie" Kitty hesitantly took his hand and she could see him gradually soften.

"No, I should be the one apologising, I dunna mean to be rude. It's just something my uncle said at the party."

"What did he say?"

"Well I was interrogating him about ye." Smiling sheepishly now at her, "And he told me about all ya had spoken about. I was angry that Donald – Weasel – McDonald was sniffing around here, around you." Jamie clenched his teeth and filled his lungs, slowly exhaling before continuing. "Malcolm told me he had warned ya and that Donald had been saying things to him about ya money."

"Oh I see."

"That man is vile and it's abhorrent to me that he is ever near ya. I know his modus operandi and I, I hate him."

"You mean he couldn't just want me for my startling personality and pretty blue lace underwear" Her attempt at humour had no effect.

"For one, I wouldna blame any man for wanting ye, just the way ye are and secondly! I sincerely hope I am the only one to have seen that underwear this side of the border Mrs Harris."

"Apart from Angus of course!"

This worked and Jamie finally smiled, "Not even Angus I made him keep his eyes closed."

"More of a gentleman that you then?"

"One of us had to pull ya knickers down – and up. I happened to draw the short straw."

Jamie leaned in for a quick kiss as Kitty slapped his arm.

"Come on ya wee hussy back ta mine."

Checking Malcolm didn't need her for anything else they said their goodbyes. A fanfare of jibes and laughter and knowing looks, they were both relieved to be safely by the cars.

Jamie offered to drive and Kitty was relieved as she her heart pounded and she felt so keyed up she was sure she would have come off the road.

23

Dinner For Two

Jamie left the engine running as he leapt out and opened the cottage door.

"Why don't ye phone Amanda – only promise me ye'll be here when I come back."

Kitty grabbed his forearms, "Don't go, you can hear what I have to say" quietly then, "I don't want you to go."

"Hush lass" he lent and kissed her head, "If I'm going to woo ya with a nice meal I think it warrants more than cheese on toast."

"Oh" smiling up at him. "Can you cook?" Stephen was good at many things but it certainly didn't include cooking. Kitty's generalisation from living so long with a man, who considered cheese on toast a culinary masterpiece, was that men generally couldn't cook.

"Of course I can cook, now phone Amanda, tell her, no ask her, if it's alright for me to talk to her. And if I want privacy I will be putting you in the bath."

Kissing her now full on the lips it took all his resolve to pull away. "Duck ok?"

"Oh, um – to eat – yes."

A very flustered and slightly confused Kitty waved him off and leaned against the heavy door.

"Hello" Amanda's voice was cold and clinical.

"Mand it's me."

"Oh I was just about to hang up, and/or swear at you. Thought you were a bloody PPI cold caller, I didn't recognise the number."

"No only me."

"Where are you? And what has happened now?" Amanda in urgent assertive mode.

"Does anything have to have happened for me to phone my favourite friend?"

"No... but you're not fooling anyone, Kit I can always tell by your voice. Anyway you are lucky to get me I knocked off early and was going out. So come on, out with it! – And remember details, details. No wait, hang on." There was a knock of phone hitting hard surface, running water and shuffling noise.

"Right ready!"

Kitty could picture her friend now, legs tucked under her, cushion on lap poised for the next instalment.

"Well I've got tons to tell you and not long. I'm in Jamie's house and he's gone to do some shopping because he's cooking my dinner, duck apparently."

"Bloody hell he can cook, he wears a kilt – just cut to the chase and marry the man." Amanda laughed.

"Mand please, I need to tell you so much before he gets back. Please just let me get it out and you can question and tease me latter. And, brace yourself because he wants to talk to you!"

"Shit Kit! Why?"

"I'll explain – now LISTEN!"

Kitty started first with her meeting with Flo.

"Oh that's good Kit, at least it shows how out of character it, and - the mauling - was!"

"Amanda!"

"Sorry well you know what I mean, it's good to know."

"Then he came home."

Kitty admitted in detail the conversations, the kissing and embarrassingly the bath.

"What, he sat in the bathroom the whole time? Well at least there were bubbles."

Sharing the whole kneeling up section, Kitty shook her head as she spoke as she hardly believed it herself.

"And you wonder why the poor bugger has a permanent stiffy if you keep flashing your knockers at him all the time!"

The women laughed and Kitty only stopped as her cheeks ached.

"But we slept, yes in the same bed but nothing happened, I think it might have this morning when he stood naked in the bathroom while I was in the shower, but I remembered I had to get back for the builders and had to rush home."

"Bloody hell Kit, well?"

"Well what?"

"DETAILS – naked Scotsman!"

"Oh Mand he's gorgeous, and so big in every way, which makes the whole prospect of tonight even more terrifying. He's a good six foot four, big and muscled and toned, he's beautiful."

"Big in every way?"

"Oh yes."

"Ooh," giggling like old girl friends do Amanda tried to process all the garbled information.

"You've only slept with Stephen haven't you?"

"Yes, and for some reason I feel more like the naive virgin than I did at nineteen – although I was blind drunk the first time."

"Well if it comes to it have some Dutch courage tonight – it is going to happen tonight?"

"That's why I'm phoning you, what do you think?"

"Bloody hell you want my advice before you do the deed!" Amanda sniggered.

"Mand please don't laugh at me. That's the whole problem... since, since, you know,"

"Stephen's death – can you still not say it Kit?"

"I did, I did" proud of her achievement, "I've said it to Jamie and he's been so sweet. But it's the first time since Stephen DIED! Happy now?"

"Very good, proud of you babe."

"I don't know, I don't trust my mind. It's like I'm a clone of myself, I look the same, I even sound the same but ultimately I can't trust it is me. I'm like some confusing bloody Sci-fi film."

"You are you, babe. I know ideally you might not want to meet someone so soon or fall so fast but maybe... just maybe you needed to. To get past the place you were at, maybe this needed to happen to drag you out of the limbo you've been in. I have worried so much about you my dear, lovely friend."

"Oh don't" Kitty blurted as tears streamed down her face.

"Mum and I have been saying for months, maybe it's just what you needed to force you... help you out of the grief purgatory you've imposed on yourself."

"I didn't... don't do it on purpose!"

"Oh babe don't you think I know that. It must be some self preservation thing. You have lost too much... too much for one small soul to carry. This stifled grief could end up in a sad stifled life."

Kitty sniffed nodding, "I know."

"Well give me one good reason not to jump this Celtic stud?"

"Mand, really! I think it's just fear, fear of moving too fast, fear of ... losing him." Sobbing now, "I've lost too much for too long."

"I know that Kit, I've been with you every step of the way... and I fear that for you too. But it truly is better to have loved and lost, than never have loved or be loved at all."

"True, but I really think I am at my utter capacity for losing." Kitty blew her nose loudly.

"Why else would you not be with him? Other than the swollen red nose you're nurturing."

"Big help Mand! But no I can't think of a reason, anyway now all his family knows."

"WHAT?"

Kitty relayed the conversation with Malcolm.

"Oh so your builder is his uncle. No wonder they snapped you up, some fresh blood in the clan gene pool! Tell me Kit, is there a lot of banjo playing up there, *dada ling ding, ding ding, ding ding, ding!*"

"Stop it Mand! Well anyway it looks like its official, like we're an item. How does that work these days?"

"Well you're neither one of you a virgin – oh please god, tell me you're not about to deflower an innocent young Scot?"

"No."

"Well you are consenting adults. And you are the last person on the planet I need to tell life is short and precious babe. Tell me, do you ever look back on your marriage and think I wish we had worked more? No. Or do you think of Stephen and think I wish you had done all you had planned, all you both dreamt of doing? Of course you do."

There was silence and Amanda waited for Kitty's gentle crying to dissipate.

"Oh Mand you are so insightful and wonderful – now that is why I phoned you! Of course you are right. I wished we had taken more holidays, spent more days in bed, and just laughed a whole lot more, without letting petty things get in the way."

"Exactly! And despite what you saw in the bathroom he might be a crap lover and you'll dump him anyway for the architect."

"Oh you are incorrigible – shit I think he's back, hang on."

The key turned in the lock and Jamie entered arms full of groceries. Amanda strained at the earpiece to hear in Wimbledon what was said.

"Still on the phone then, ye were not kidding about the bill." With arms still full of bags he lent down and pinned her to the back of the seat, kissing her passionately. Taking back up the receiver Kitty struggled to regain her breathing, she asked.

"Did you want to talk to Amanda now?"

"Oh holy crap" could be heard down the earpiece.

"Can ye, do ye want to talk a wee bit more and I'll go a draw ye a bath?"

"Oh ok."

"Kit... Kit... Kitty... Kathleen!"

"Oooh hi sorry Mand," her voice was dreamy and vacant.

"Wake up, Kit, What happened?" Silence. "Did he kiss you?"

"Uh huh."

"And this is the effect on you OMG!"

Whispering now as Jamie sang softly and put away the shopping and with swift efficiency began preparing the meal.

"He's cooking now," Kitty voice like a whispered far off dream.

"Kit snap out of it, are you there? Kit, Kathleen!"

Kitty knew she was in trouble if Amanda called her by her full name. "Yes sorry Amanda! Phew, it always takes my breath away, and it's kind of hard to concentrate when he's near."

"I can hear that and I'm just amazed you two have lasted this long and not been at it like rabbits!"

"Jamie said he was going to run me a bath, do you want me to get him to ring you back in a bit?"

"Not bloody likely – leave you two alone and there will be no thoughts of poor old me, the deed will be done and no one will have the time of day for little ol me. And by the way he has the sexiest voice."

"Oh I know, isn't it though," Kitty's smugness oozed down the receiver as she squirmed on her seat. Jamie looked over from the kitchen and Kitty sighed.

"Are you looking at him now?"

"Yep."

"Well stop it! Focus. Right to the matter at hand, I can see I needed to be the responsible one. Do you still have your implant in?"

"WHAT!" Jamie stopped singing and looked over concerned.

"Your contraceptive implant, do you still have it and when is it good till?"

"Amanda James!"

Jamie took a few steps towards her so Kitty smiled and held up an apologetic hand. Smiling back he turned and carried on preparing the vegetables but it didn't go unnoticed to Kitty that he didn't resume his singing.

"Yes," she hissed quietly.

"Well that's good. Underwear good and pits shaved?"

"YES!"

Jamie walked in now tea towel thrown over his shoulder and touched Kitty on the shoulder.

"I'll run ye that bath now lass," bending again kissing her.

"Hi people, hello... hello I can hear you!" Smiling wickedly Jamie ran up the stairs two at a time.

"God, sorry Mand."

"You were kissing again weren't you?"

"Umm."

"Is he there now?"

"No upstairs running a bath, Oh Mand I feel really nervous, but excited, but sick."

"Oh babe... it will be fine, maybe a glass of something in the bath – just to take the edge off the nerves. And most very important, don't you dare forget to phone me tomorrow!"

Changing the subject primarily to kill time but also to quell the rising emotions that knotted her stomach Kitty asked about Amanda's job and love life. Jamie walked slowly down the stairs and with outstretched hand started to take the phone.

"Oh sorry Mand, um looks like I'm off to the bath." Clutching the receiver and standing as Jamie pulled it away.

"Would you like to talk to Jamie?"

"Damn straight – hand him over – love you Kit."

"Love you Mand."

Reluctantly Kitty released the phone and walked to the bottom of the stairs. Jamie waved her up the stairs.

"Well hello Amanda, I understand ye are fully abreast of our little saga" Kitty strained to hear. "Aye and lovely to speak to you to, excuse me a moment. Kathleen your bath will overflow."

Jamie laughed at Kitty's poking out tongue, and waited until she had disappeared into the bathroom. Jamie walked out to the kitchen to tend supper and confront every man's greatest fear – a woman's protective best friend.

"Well you certainly have had an effect on her." Amanda was nervous and this annoyed her and the edge was clear on her voice.

"I appreciate how special she is, and how special she obviously is to ya. That is why... if ya don't mind I thought it would be beneficial to talk."

"What can I do, or say to help?"

"What did ye say to her? I'm scared of frightening her off. Is it because of Stephen's death, or, is she always this... fragile – no sorry that came out wrong. I just mean I don't want to hurt her."

Amanda wiped a tear from her cheek. She had always been fond of Stephen and the thought of another man jumping into his bed when it was hardly cold had upset her. She would have issue with any man but hearing the warmth and genuine concern and consideration at the end of the phone gave her hope. Albeit hundreds of miles away and a few sentences Amanda was pleasantly reassured.

"It's like this... well, everyone left in the world that loves Kit, primarily me and my parents, have worried about her a lot since Stephens' death. She was a bubbly fun girl, never morose, never moody. Do you know you are one of the first people that she has actually been able to say those words to?"

"Yes she told me." Even though she didn't know him Amanda could hear the sadness in his voice.

"Well there is my worry." There followed a silence Jamie could not bear.

"What do ye worry about?"

"Like all her possessions, she has managed to sell, leave and file away her life. Bottling up her grief, putting a post it-note on in and boxed it up."

Jamie laughed – no wonder Kitty valued this woman advice and wit, he knew he would like Amanda.

"Meeting you I fear will force her hand, the lid will come off, and I will be hundreds of miles away when the bottle explodes in her face."

Jamie could hear the real love and fear.

"But I will be here."

"Yes you will, but how long have you known her. Will you still want to cook romantic meals and run her bath when she is a blabbering wreck?"

"Yes I think… no, I know I will."

Amanda didn't doubt his intentions, only doubted his appreciation of the contents of the pressure keg that was her best friend.

"Her biggest fear Jamie is loss, I don't expect you to know how you feel or if you think this will be long term b-"

Jamie interrupted, "I have never felt the way I feel for your friend. Have ye ever loved someone so much it feels like it could tear ya heart clean from ya chest?"

"Um... no I can't say I have."

"Neither had I, I donna understand it. What I do know is she feels it too. Already I can'na imagine life without her, so no Amanda, in answer to your previous question I have absolutely no intention of letting go – not in this lifetime." Both now wiped away tears.

"Well bloody hell, how long have you known each other?"

"Not long, but long enough."

"Good answer."

"Honest."

"Kit had a wonderful family and one by one they were picked off. With each one she lost a part of herself and then Stephen died. It was like she was a ghost of her fun-loving vibrant self. Like the blood had been drained and stretched too thin." Amanda sniffed but struggled on despite her trembling lip. "She needs that light put back in her life, but as you say, now, now she is fragile."

"I have no intention of going anywhere and I want nothing but her."

"Good! But Jamie if you have the least doubt, the smallest thought that this could be a casual affair – IT IS NOT!"

"No I ken, I really do."

"Any inkling and second thoughts please give her dinner and take her home." Amanda's voice had hardened and Jamie could hear the thinly veiled threat.

"I have never felt like this before so it's terrifying for me too." His strong broad voice faltered now and he coughed.

"You should be perfect together, she's frightened too."

Jamie laughed loudly, loud enough for Kitty to hear it from the deep bubbly soak. She resisted the urge to get out and only wished she had taken Amanda's advice and brought some alcohol with her.

"Well it was lovely to talk to you Jamie. Take care of my bestie. She is naturally indecisive so don't be thrown off course as I think you are just what she needs. So you know she has a contraceptive implant so you're covered. Be gentle, be kind and please be patient with her." Jamie blushed and chastised himself for not even thinking about contraception. How could he not have thought about it, it could have been a complete disaster or a mad dash to the pub toilet? He hated condoms so at least that wouldn't be an issue. Jamie didn't think he needed advice on lovemaking but was sure that was what Amanda had just given him.

"Oh thank ye."

"You had thought about that?"

"Of course, all covered" Jamie blushed deeper lying through his teeth.

"Well bye Amanda, I'm sure Kitty will phone ya" resigned to the fact that whatever did pass between Kitty and him, this woman in Wimbledon would know all the details.

Jamie walked into the bathroom after the merest of knocks and handed Kitty a very welcome glass of velvety red wine. Jamie sat on the closed toilet seat and stared down at her. Kitty was amazed as, although there was only a discreet covering of bubbles she felt no embarrassment in front of this beautiful man, yet still really a stranger.

"Amanda thought ya might need this."

"Oh... what else did she say?" Kitty face already flushed from the hot water turned positively scarlet.

"That apparently we are covered for contraception!" Kitty looked briefly into the sparkling eyes under raised brows, and dunked her head under the water. One hand gripped the wine glass and two small pink knees broke the surface. Jamie laughed and pushed the knees under the water to eject the sodden head. Eyes screwed shut, her free hand pinching her nose.

"Dinner will by half an hour," Jamie sounded matter of fact.

"Oh, are you mad?" Kitty tried to dry her eyes and looked urgently at him.

"No, I like your friend and she obviously loves you, so nothing she could say could make me mad."

"Good," rubbing her free hand through her hair. "And did it help; was it useful talking to her?"

"Yes at least it saved us any awkward conversations about family planning, I must be honest – but for god sake donna tell Amanda - I would'ne have thought about it."

"Me either, it was her that remembered I had an implant. She might have saved us from more than an awkward conversation." They both smiled and sighed, "Fancy her saying it to you though, just wait till I phone her tomorrow."

"Aye" as Jamie left with just a head visible and a hand on the door frame, "Amanda said... details!"

Jamie laughed as he descended the stairs to the sound of Kitty splashing back beneath the surface. Jamie's cottage was warm, a warmth Kitty had soon learnt to live without these past weeks. It seemed odd to be dressing in jeans a small T-shirt without layers and fleece. The blue top was tight and had lace at the collar and was the nearest thing Kitty possessed at the moment, to dressy. She was very grateful for the pretty blue underwear she had been saving for just such an eventuality.

Jamie moved lightly around the kitchen and on seeing Kitty he walked straight up to her, hugging her close and kissing her until she was breathless.

"I've been away from ye too long today." Keeping an arm around her waist he guided her into the kitchen holding her tight whilst he stirred the vegetables that boiled on the hob.

"Can I do anything?"

"There's plenty I'd like you to do but let's not let this meal go to waste, talk to me. Tell me about Amanda." He filled her glass of wine and handing it to her.

Kitty could talk easily on this topic, starting at the beginning when their mothers met at antenatal class. The fact that Amanda's mum would always pretend to be Kitty's mother if looking after them both. She would tell Kitty it was because she had blonde ringlets and was a happy giggly child, whereas her own daughter was prone to whingeing and picking her nose. Kitty had always ribbed Amanda about this and Amanda never let her mother forget the treachery. Tales from nursery and through school, Jamie was an avid listener. It was obvious this was more than a casual friendship. With all her family gone Amanda was the very essence of family, and Jamie could only begin to imagine how important she was to Kitty. He had never needed friends like that, he had friends – mates but he appreciated probably for the first time then how blessed he was with the vast Stewart clan that cared and loved him.

Jamie cleared the small oak table and lay leather mats and cutlery. The cutlery and china were old, their wear charming. Not being the best they had been given to Jamie when he moved into the cottage. Like the cottage itself, much of its furnishings were on loan from his parent's house. The vase on the table was lead crystal and distinctively deco, and Kitty was impressed with the only new item on the table – a posy of pink roses. He must have bought them while he was out and Kitty was suitably impressed.

Holding back the chair Jamie gestured to her to sit, and tucking the chair in after her he reached down and kissed her again. Whether it was the wine or the lack of oxygen from the incessant kissing she was feeling rather light headed and thought it would be very wise to eat something.

Jamie presented the meal, it looked and smelt amazing but the nagging nerves of what presumed to take place made swallowing each mouthful an effort.

"Is everything ok?" Shit she couldn't hide anything from him.

"Oh Jamie, it's delicious... it's just... well, I'm a bit nervous."

"I know me too..." Quietly adding, "But when I get ye ta bed Mrs Harris you'll be needing ya energy, so eat up."

She giggled, "Confident much?"

"Hopeful, very much."

With the tension broken and renewed enthusiasm they cleared their plates and drained their glasses.

"What now?" Kitty said playfully.

"Washing up what else."

They efficiently cleared the kitchen. Kitty washed and laughed as Jamie, his large frame no handicap, twirled and skipped around her drying and clearing. Pouring two more glasses he took her hand.

"I want to show you something."

"My mother warned me about men like you, anyway I think I've already seen it."

"Mrs Harris! If ye can just drag ya wee mind from the gutter and put on ya coat."

"Oh" disappointment obvious. Kitty was confused but put on her coat and boots, Jamie wrapping one of his scarves around her still damp hair. She pulled it over her nose and inhaled, in smelt of Jamie. Taking her hand he set off around the back of the cottage up a well worn path.

"Well we're hiking, never in all my wondering had this featured in tonight's entertainment. You have an odd style of romance up here."

Jamie smiled back at her. "Aye, not far."

She could tell he was maintaining an abnormally slow pace for her benefit but was keen to get somewhere. The evening air was reversing the effects of the wine, and she was very confused as to the meaning of all this. The light was fading but the pink glow of the impending sunset washed over them. The walk took fifteen minutes and was all uphill making talking difficult. When they reached the summit Kitty stretched and then leant over, holding her knees.

"Phew – hiking on a full stomach," Jamie rubbed her back.

"That's a wee stroll lass, but sorry, I really wanted you to see this."

Jamie stood behind her and hugged her around the waist. Leaning back into him she breathed long deep fresh breaths and took in the view. Far in the distance mountains looked like large grey folds in a blanket. Above the sky was layered with clouds, every shade of grey, edged with silver and pink. A salute to the falling sun, which still sent shafts of dazzling light through gaps in the cloud. Below stretching out was an expanse of green, broken only by meandering rivulets – black against emerald and rust, converging on fathomless pools of black. Unnoticed now, for they were everywhere, the plodding movement of countless sheep as far as the eye could see.

"It's beautiful," they had both stood for many minutes and Jamie was first to break the silence.

"Aye... my family has been here for generation upon generation. They survived the English." He winked as she looked around at him. "I wanted ye to see this, this is me. As far as the mountains over there, this is Stewart land. One day all this be will mine, mine to manage and preserve for future generations."

He looked down at the pale oval face that stared out at the sun, hugging her tighter he kissed the top of her head.

"I am solid Kathleen, as rooted in this place as those mountains. I shall not leave ye if you will have me."

The tears raced down her face, unsure why she wept. She suspected for the first time in a very long time she didn't feel alone. Jamie hushed her and kissed her head until she could bear it no more and turned, reaching up on her toes and kissed him. She kissed him with all the desperate need he had the night in the pub until she literally saw stars.

"Breathe, Kathleen, breathe lass." Kitty clung heavily to him and obeyed.

"Shall we go home?"

"Yes please."

They walked in silence back to the cottage, no need for keys Jamie pushed the door and they were home.

"Would you get us a drink? I'd like a bath."

Kitty poured the remains of the second bottle into their glasses and waited until his padding feet stopped and the water turned off.

Heading upstairs the bathroom door was open and Jamie sat in a shallow bath. There were no bubbles to conceal and he sat with arms along its edges. Kitty took his usual pew and handed him the glass.

"Would you like me to shave?"

"No I like it, its soft." She reached out and stroked his face, taking her hand he kissed the palm and Kitty shivered.

"I'll be in the bedroom." Standing at the doorway Kitty marvelled at the sight before her. A red hankerchief thrown over the bedside lamp gave a light pink subdued glow. On the mantelpiece a line of candles danced their flickering light on the wall. Kitty could see fresh sheets crisply folded and knew there was no turning back now. Kitty stepped out of her clothes leaving on the underwear Jamie had already seen, and re-entered the bathroom.

"I'm glad you have them on, that sight has haunted my dreams for weeks."

It took all Kitty's powers of concentration to brush her teeth as she stole glances in the mirror, the steam obscuring detail but showed Jamie step from the bath and dry himself. Waiting, she suspected, until she had finished, Jamie kissed her neck as she put down the toothbrush.

The charge between them had never been so strong and the hairs on Kitty arms and neck stood in reaction to his touch.

Amanda had not only discussed contraception with him but sexual technique. He had been affronted at the time but was glad of her guidance now. *Take it slow, be very gentle*. He had never been afraid of hurting a woman before but Kitty seemed so very fragile, not to mention precious.

Removing her knickers his fingers grazed her thighs, just like that first night in her cold dark toilet. But tonight he could dare to stare, to linger and do those things he had wanted to do then. Kitty took short sharp breaths and as he knelt and kissed her stomach she groaned.

She was indeed glad of the hearty meal and copious wine. Lying now on top of a thundering heart and a mat of damp chest hair Kitty smiled, totally replete and tried to stop her body's involuntary jumps and twitches.

"Well it's a good job old Agnes next door is as deaf as a post or she'd be thinking I had murdered ye."

Pushing up on her elbows she looked down and kissed his mouth, their lips sore and puffy.

"Is that why you kept kissing me?" Letting her hair fall in an attempt to conceal her blushes.

"Partly" he smiled up at her.

"Well in seven years of marriage I don't think I made more than a murmur, I'm sorry." She mumbled apologetically.

"I thought I was hurting ya lass... you're so small."

"I know there's not much of me but I'm strong enough and you really didn't hurt me."

"No, how do I say this... not your outside size."

"Oh... OH!" Kitty flushed crimson and dropped her head on his chest, barely a whisper, "Is it... was it a problem for you... d, didn't you like it?" Having only Stephen to compare it to, and there never seemed an issue before, Kitty was mortified. Holding her arms Jamie tried to free his chest of the blushing limpet.

"Kathleen please, please look at me". It was all she could do to oblige and looked up through her lashes, head hung low.

"You are exquisite, it was exquisite... I can't tell you how good is was."

"Oh... good," managing a smile at him now. "It was intense, not a hurt. Not like I have ever experienced either."

"Me too, Kathleen I told ye I had never made love. I did'na ken it could be much different – but it was incredible."

Kitty shuddered once more and kissed him again, all embarrassment gone. "I think I'd like very much to do that again but think I might need to sleep first."

"Hush then lass" Peeling their sweaty bodies apart he rolled her off him, spooned up behind her and there they slept for many hours.

24

A Moment of Panic

Dreaming she was roasting in a sauna, no handle to escape, and desperate for the toilet. Unable to find a handle, clawing at the pine walls, sleeping Kitty was contemplating relieving herself on the coals when she woke. As with all dreams there are threads of reality, and Kitty was in fact desperate for the loo and Jamie's heavy arm draped over her waist was doing nothing to ease the situation.

The clock by the bed informed her in was a little after six am. Not wanting to disturb him, Kitty lifted the dead weight of his arm and her skin felt chilled to the air. Jamie stirred but tucked his hand under the pillow and his gentle snore resumed. Wanting nothing more than to lay and watch him sleep, needs must and she exited the bed with minimal disturbance.

After much stinging relief Kitty examined herself in the bathroom mirror. Her lips were slightly swollen and although his beard was soft her face felt rough and reddened. Gently running her hands over her breasts and belly there was a gentle dull ache.

Replaying the events of last night and all that passed between them, Kitty watched her reflection as the blush extended from her checks to her décolletage. Remembering the effect he had on her - OMG the noise she had made, how mortifying. She shook her head now at her reflection.

Creeping back into the bedroom to the slumbering Jamie, Kitty grabbed her clothes and tiptoed down stairs to dress. Grabbing her coat she left as silently as she could. A fresh crisp morning and Kitty stretched and winced as muscles she didn't know she had, complained.

Getting into Pimples there was no time like the present - she would have to wake Amanda, thankful for a signal.

"Morning Mand, sorry it's early." The phone had rung for ages at Kitty had just been about to give up.

"Urm" Amanda yawned and then registered, forcing herself to sit up in bed and try to shake the sleep from her head. "Oh, no, it's fine. Oh Kit, and?"

"Well he cooked me a lovely dinner and then we went for a walk" (having the desired effect.)

"A walk, REALLY!"

"Yes it was lovely, just up the hill behind his cottage and you can look down and see for miles, lochs, mountains and sheep. And he told me, he said it all belongs to him, well not just him but his family!"

"Bloody hell, that's news, you didn't know that before did you?"

"No not at all, eldest son of the Stewart clan. I knew everything around here is Stewart land but didn't think he was that Stewart."

"Ok so he's rich – bloody marvellous, but what happened when you got home?"

"Well he put candles in the bedroom and, well, we had sex." Whispering even though she was alone.

"AND?"

"Oh Mand... it was incredible, he called me exquisite... mind blowing. Not like any thing I've ever experienced, but..." there was a long silence, "does that make me more treacherous? I feel really unfaithful to Stephen this morning"

"Nonsense, no, NO! Kathleen Harris do not bring yourself down. Now more details!"

"Well he took things really slow."

"Good boy."

"But, but in the end he did say it was a good job his old neighbour was deaf."

"What you or him?"

"Well embarrassingly... me!"

"Ooooh... do you usually? I never had you pegged as a screamer." The two women laughed until Kitty was wiping away tears and clutching her belly.

"Well it seems I am now dear" Kitty managed to get out.

"How do you feel this morning?" Physically and emotionally."

"Physically not dissimilar to the day after we went horse riding on Dartmoor."

"Ooh! Saddle sore are we?" Amanda sniggered.

"Yes very."

"Um-emotionally?"

"Very treacherous but very happy... a sort of sore contentment."

"Oh Kit, well done you. I'm so proud and happy for you, brave girl! Now no regrets or beating yourself up about Stephen, he would want you to have found some one."

"No, no regrets... to be honest I'm wondering when I'll be fit for round two." Giggling the women were once again teenagers blushing and giggling in the back of Science class with the ever-patient school nurse with her condoms and bananas.

In the bedroom Jamie stretched, coming to with flashes of memories of last night bombarding his mind. Raising himself up, was it a dream? The candles, two glasses and lying, aching and naked – this had been no dream.

"Kathleen."

There was no answer.

"Kathleen!" louder, sitting on the edge of bed, a frown now replacing the smile. Trying desperately to get his eyes to wake as fast as his mind he rubbed at them scanning the room for her clothes. There was no sign of her. Tripping and stumbling Jamie dressed as he ran to the bathroom, she was not there and there was no trace of her having been there. The wash bag was gone, the pink toothbrush, gone.

"Kathleen" his voice broke and for a minute he was glued to the spot. Regaining his senses he ran down the stairs, it was a small cottage and from the bottom of the stairs he could see its entirety. Unless she was hiding behind a chair or on the oven she was not here.

"Kathleen!" desperate now, he fell into the leather chair and held his head in his hands. Running his fingers through his hair. Had he hurt her? Had it been too soon for her? Had she regretted it?

Jamie could bear sitting no more and paced the kitchen. Thumping the worktop for the second time he tried to focus and think what to do, should he drive to hers? Hell, should he phone Amanda?

"What has the worktop ever done to you?" Standing on the doorstep was a grinning Kitty. Jamie rushed at her and picked her from her feet into a crushing embrace.

"Morning" Kitty squeezed out.

"Oh Kathleen, I thought you had left, had run away. Your things had gone."

"I just went out to the van, you looked so peaceful I didn't want to wake you... and ... I wanted to phone Amanda."

"Oh" Jamie took large deep breaths.

"It's ok, I'm right here," and hoping to distract him, "And I'm very hungry."

Pulling back he took her face in his hands now and very gently kissed her.

"I thought I must have hurt you, or upset you."

"No as I said to Amanda I'm a bit sore but very, very happy" Squeezing her gently this time he whispered into her ear.

"Come on I'll fix ye breakfast. So Amanda got her details then?"

"Only a few, but all glowing reports of you."

"Really?" He held her face and covered her face with light quick kisses.

"Positive, now feed me."

The bacon and scrambled egg was most welcome and they both soon cleared their plates. Jamie wordlessly took her hand and led her upstairs. Once in the bathroom he undressed and then undressed Kitty and the stood together in the shower. Jamie took the soap and began to wash her. Wincing minutely as he washed her breast, "Are you sure I didn't hurt ye? Are ya sore?"

"Just a bit," Kitty marvelled at how gentle a touch such large hands could afford. Taking the soap she relished the opportunity to examine those arms and shoulders and created quite a lather making foamy swirls in his chest hair.

"I like your hair."

"Was ye husband no a hairy man?"

"Stephen, no. He was very slim and about this tall" touching Jamie's eye brow.

"What colour hair?"

"Black – you are different in every way."

"But he was a Harris so maybe long back we had common ground."

"No, no... Harris is my maiden name," Jamie looked down at her waiting for explanation.

"Kathleen Vrcelj at your service." Kitty bowed her head in mock greeting.

"And ye did'na take his name?"

"I did but when I decided to come here my maiden name seemed more apt, and no one could ever say it, let alone spell it – Yugoslavian" Kitty voice trailed off sadly and tears filled her eyes.

"Aye, there is that."

Jamie guided her back under the water and ran his hands through her hair and at the same time wiped away the tears that now cascaded down her checks.

"You are so beautiful Kathleen Vrcelj Harris."

Jamie turned her so the water flushed her chest and he washed her hair. Kitty almost purred as she lent back against him gripping his thighs. Endeavouring not to be too vocal, Kitty's wobbly legs meant Jamie had to help her from the bathroom and half carry her to the bed.

After drying themselves they climbed under the duvet and cuddled. Legs intertwined Kitty couldn't feel where her skin ended and his began.

"What plans for today?" Jamie asked as he felt the soft skin at the base of her spine.

"I vote for staying right here."

"Seconded."

Kitty laughed as she struggled to stand on jelly like legs.

"Well another first. I've never had sex five times in one day. I think I might be at my limit," she said as she shuffled to the bathroom. Jamie laid back and stretched, aching in numerous places and reluctantly had to agree. Leaning in the doorway in all his glory Kitty smiled up from the toilet.

"I really am hungry now," though they had wrapped themselves in sheets and ventured downstairs at midday for a sandwich they had soon been distracted. It was late afternoon now and they were both exhausted.

"I think it's safer if we eat out" Kitty sniggered.

"Aye, ken it will at that, I'll run us a bath and we can get down to the hotel in time for food."

"Oh!" Kitty was looking at her reflection in the mirror, "Maybe somewhere no one knows us, or me any way. One look at me and they will know just what we've been up to."

"Aye" Jamie didn't argue so she really must have looked how she felt.

Kitty lowered herself into the water cautiously, "Sorry lass."

"Please stop apologising, it's all good."

They washed quickly and dressed, both determined to make it out of the house. Jamie's stomach growled loudly as they drove. Kitty's hand on his leg, she ventured up his thigh but Jamie gently but firmly pushed it back down.

"Remember the terrible effect ya have on my lass, have ye no mercy?" Kitty blushed and withdrew her hand but Jamie took it and held it tightly on Kitty's lap.

The drive wound round roads Kitty had not explored before and parallel to a vast loch that seemed never to end, the water inky and ominously still. There were few houses for the entire journey until they entered a small hamlet. By the side of the road there was a black and white pub, which Jamie slowed and drove around the rear of. There were but a few cars and Kitty was glad. The back door opened into a dingy bar, the paintwork a dull brown and a dark red over patterned carpet. The ceiling and walls had once been white but still wore the badge of years of nicotine. Kitty guessed nothing in this room had changed in Jamie's lifetime.

Walking to the bar the eyes of the four occupants followed them with unabashed interest. A pleasant looking woman in her fifties welcomed them with a dimpled smile and surprised Kitty with, "Evening James."

"Evening Margaret, are we too late for food?"

"For you, never. Take a seat Lad an I'll come over to ye" Handing him two menus Margaret's eyes didn't leave Kitty as Jamie guided them to a table at the back of the room. Jamie leant to Kitty's ear, "I went to school with her son, all the boys fancied our Margaret" Kitty's heart swelled, the snippet shared reminding her of her own mum.

"Is she still looking?" Kitty had her back to the woman now.

"Aye."

"Do you think she knows what we've been doing all day?"

"Aye" Jamie nodded and winked at Margaret.

"Stop it" Kitty gave him a swift kick under the table.

The exertions of the day had certainly given them both an appetite. They chatted in hushed tones in the otherwise silent pub, and worked their way through starters, main and pudding. As Kitty licked the last of the toffee sauce of her spoon Jamie sighed.

"What's wrong?" Kitty looked concerned but then smiled as Jamie grabbed his trouser leg and shifted position in his chair.

"Oh."

"Oh indeed. Watching ya eat has a fierce terrible effect on me. It's a first for me too – do you think you can die from too much sex?"

"Well I guess we will find out."

Settling the bill they walked full and contented to the car that had been discreetly left out side his cottage by Flo and one of his parents during the day. Once in the fresh air and under the bright stars of an unpolluted sky Jamie pressed Kitty against the car door and they kissed, hungry now for each other. Stopping only when the pub door opened, and one of the old men that had been propping up the bar came out and disturbed them.

Once in the car Kitty asked Jamie all about his time at school, and in the dark conjured pictures of the adventurous redheaded boy. By the time they reached home they were both yawning and climbed stiffly from the car.

"How about we get in our PJ's and watch some TV, I could sample some more of your famous hot chocolate."

"You don't want to be ravished?" Jamie stuck up his bottom lip.

"Have you got a good ravish left in you? Let's settle for a nice cuddle."

"Deal."

Both wearing Jamie's jogging bottoms and faded T-shirts Kitty lay with her head on his lap and legs curled up. Watching an old rerun of QI Jamie stroked her hair and they laughed easily.

"I'd better go home in the morning or Malcolm will think you have kidnapped me."

"Oh but I have."

"Come on you, bed time."

They brushed their teeth together at the sink, giggling and jostling and Jamie got in behind her in bed and pulled Kitty towards him.

"Good night Kathleen. It's the day of firsts, not only have I never had a woman to sleep here in ma bed. But ken I have never slept wi a lass two nights together."

"And how is it for you?"

"Very good, I may not let ya leave."

"Have… haven't you got to go to Harris?"

"Aye… aye one day. But dunna fret about that lassie" Jamie kissed her hair and they were both soon asleep.

Kitty woke at eight, the smell of breakfast and the sound of Jamie's deep rumbling singing was, Kitty decided, the perfect way to wake. Walking quietly into the kitchen so as not to interrupt him Jamie looked disappointed when she stood before him.

"Oh, I was going to bring ye this in bed."

"Never mind it smells great."

They sat at the table and enjoyed a leisurely fried breakfast. Kitty rested her bare feet on the small triangle of chair between his legs, absentmindedly rubbing the inside of his thigh.

"Why, Kathleen, would you be after me taking ye back to bed?"

"Oh! Sorry, no." Jamie pouted and looked genuinely upset.

"Sorry, no I didn't mean that, it's, well it's just that I really do think I should get back to Tide's."

"Ok" uncertainty on his face, "Do you mean go on your own?"

"No!" Kitty answered too quickly and assuredly for there to be any doubt and Jamie was relieved. Kitty ran her foot up and down his thigh now provocatively.

"Do you want to come and wash me?" Kitty grinned wickedly.

"You are incorrigible, that's how yesterday started. I'm game if ye are lass, but I ken we would'ne get back to your house in any fit state to be seen."

"Oh alright." Kitty hung her head and walked to the stairs, removing her top and smiling back at Jamie in the kitchen.

"Ya wanton woman, be gone wi ya!"

Kitty sang sweetly in the shower and they did their best in the confined space to wash and dress, both making great efforts to get out to the cars.

"Shall we take Pimples?"

"Aye, if ye like." Running his hand over the bonnet as he made his way around to the passenger door, "Oh I ken, I get it now" as his fingers felt the brail effect paintwork.

Jamie enjoyed watching Kitty drive, sitting with his shoulder to the window and his arm nearest her resting on the back of her seat.

"Stop looking at me" Kitty fidgeted in her seat self consciously, as she kept glancing over to his intense stare.

"You stop looking at me, you're meant to be watching the road."

As they turned down the drive Kitty was taking faltering deep short gasps of air and her anxiety was clear, Jamie watched her bite her nails as she shut off the engine.

"Dunna fret Kathleen," he reached over and squeezed her knee. As they walked across the lawn it was Jeff to see them first.

"Argh, and ya still walking lassie, I hope Jamie did'na disgrace the family name?" He smiled a shark like smile at Kitty and winked at Jamie.

"I'll thank you to show some manners Jeffrey Stewart." Jamie's voice was stern and deep as he frowned after Jeff and switched hands to stand between Kitty and his cousin. Jeff laughed, in no way threatened and walked over to his van. Kitty jumped as Malcolm walked soundlessly up to them on the spongy grass.

"Missed ye yesterday lass, I hope Jamie has been looking after ye?" Kitty could only manage the briefest of eye contact with the all-knowing piercing eyes of her builder.

"And have ye come to work today, if ye are not too tired?" Malcolm's deadpan tone and expression didn't waver. Jamie shuffled uneasily and after a brief silence.

"Aye Uncle I'll pitch in" choosing to ignore the obvious comment.

"I'll do some on my wall," Kitty added quietly, hoping the worst was over.

"Grand, come on lad we are hoping to get the roof off today and if the weather is kind we can get the new beams up this week so we'll need whatever strength ye have left."

Kitty sighed and walked to the store - obviously not then. Kitty made four mugs of tea and enjoyed the morning immensely, despite the frequent innuendos and remarks. Thankful for the foreign language, much of the banter passed between the men in Gaelic, and Kitty was privy to the sly looks and winks of the builders and apologetic smiles from Jamie.

Absorbed in her work Kitty knelt by the heap of stones. Tracing and feeling every contour in her oversized gloves. Jamie walked behind her and she lifted her head so he might kiss her.

"Planning tonight Mrs Harris? I do hope you'll be having your wicked way wi me again."

"I'll not have ye meddling with the employer lad, put the lass down." Jamie offered his uncle a hand gesture Kitty could not see but kissed her again regardless.

As always Malcolm and Jeff ate and read their papers in the van. Jamie sat at the small table and watched Kitty as she prepared them some soup and bread for lunch.

"My turn to watch you, did you enjoy watching me this morning?"

"Was it so obvious?"

"Aye, but I dunna mind."

Sitting to eat Kitty pulled her chair to be next to him. It didn't seem enough to be in the same room when there was any possibility of actually touching. The door was open and they ate and looked at the view. The temperature had dropped from previous days but he sky was clear and bright and not a cloud in the sky.

"It really is a beautiful spot." Jamie said languidly, "Before they built that great modern carbuncle over there I used to play there," gesturing across the bay to the new house. Two children played on a swing, their laughs and cries intermingled with birds and the tide washing the foreshore. The garden had a long propped line stretching from the swing framework to the house. Kitty hoped the pegs were up to the job as the shirts and trousers filled and soared like sails. Jamie sighed and continued, "The croft there behind the big house has been vacant as long as I remember. Aye, Angus and me would plan our adventures from that wee croft, it was our HQ. We would cast out trotlines and set rabbit traps. Never caught anything mind, and only old Annie would see us."

"Did you know her?" Kitty rested her chin in her hands, thoroughly enjoying listening to his gorgeous mellow voice.

"Only from across the water, she would sit on that front wall and watch us. I'd ken she was smiling but she never yelled any how."

"Who could not like you?"

"Oh, there were some, and with carrot red hair it was hard to hide in a crowd."

After lunch Kitty positioned herself on a large flat stone on the wall and watched the three burly men working in harmony. Stripping the slates, Jeff balanced on the roof and would hook them off with a strange hammer and slide them to Malcolm. As soon as they were safely in his hands he would toss them to Jamie as is if too hot to hold. Jamie caught every one and placed them in neat stacks on the lawn.

Finding small perches for her feet Kitty rested her head in hands. her elbows balanced on her knees. The front half of the roof was off and her eyes didn't leave Jamie. The rhythm of the work was hypnotic and she watched each muscle of his exposed arms as he reached, caught and placed the slates.

"Are ye enjoying the view there lassie?" Jeff called down to her.

"Do you know I really am?" They all laughed and continued to work hard into the afternoon. Only when the cold had seeped through her trousers to a level that could no longer be ignored did Kitty climb down. Pottering in the store Kitty found her book and reprimanded herself for the missing days in the building diary.

Taking her camera Kitty captured all the changes since she last photographed it. In the general playful mood there were some great pictures of the men at work. Kitty had to limit her photos of Jamie as she could have spent all afternoon looking at him, camera or no.

Back in the shed she bracketed the weekend and Monday as Jamie. There was nothing to go in the work diary since she'd driven to his house.

"Oh shit!"

Running from the store over to Jamie almost causing him to drop the slate that whizzed through the air to him.

"Whow – hang on Jeff!" Slipping off his right glove he took Kitty's hand.

"What is it lass, Kathleen, what's the problem?"

"It's Tuesday!"

"Aye."

"I've got to baby sit tonight." Kitty spoke urgently as if this was some life threatening fact.

"Aye," Jamie looking perplexed, "Aye and I have to teach tonight" Still not seeing the issue. Kitty leaned in and whispered close to his ear.

"And last time I saw Ange I was driving to yours and I was quite upset."

"Oh."

"Yes OH!"

"Oh maybe I'll have one less in class, expecting you murdered and unable ta baby-sit."

"Don't mock me Jamie."

"Go and phone her."

"Oh, um... yes, of course... I've got so out of the habit of phoning. I'll go to the phone box."

"Come on you two stop planning ya love life, some of us have homes to go to ya know." Jeff shouted down, and for his benefit she thought Jamie wrapped his arm around her, kissing her passionately. Kitty walked briskly to the lane to find the solace of the phone box. The heckling faded in the distance.

"Hi Ange, its Kitty."

"Kitty, thank goodness. I didn't know if you were going to make it tonight, and didn't know how to reach you." She sounded a combination of relief and annoyance.

"I know, I'm sorry. It's all been a bit... whirlwind and, well I've only just realised its Tuesday."

"But you're sure you are alright? you were just on your way to Ja, -you know who -when - yes that will be £4.80 Doris."

"Oh sorry Ange you're at work, of course."

"Its fine – thanks Doris bye bye – Don't go anywhere, I want to know what happened!"

"Well Saturday I did go back to Jamie's house," feeling strangely vulnerable in the glass phone box she looked around before she continued. "And well... he was home."

"Oh and how did it go?"

"Well I've been with him... ever since."

There was a short silence while Angela processed that information.

"Ange."

"Well good for you Kitty, is he there now?"

"Well I'm at the phone box, he's been helping his uncle today they are taking the roof off the house today."

"Well I'll go to the foot of our stairs! And, and are you happy?"

"Oh Ange, very."

"Oh, how exciting. I'm sorry to be boring but, can you still come tonight?"

"Yes" and before Kitty could add any more.

"Great, great, come as early as you can and we can have a quick catch up before I have to go out, ooh how exciting!"

"Yes ok, I'll get there as early as I can. Jamie will be teaching anyway. I will try to get there early."

"Afternoon Morris, yes lovely day. – See you tonight Kit with all the goss!" With that Angela was gone and so too any chance of keeping this thing, relationship, whatever it was, quiet. Kitty could picture Ange's excited little hops behind the counter and wondered who would be the first person she told – probably Morris!

Stopping in the lay-by at the high road Kitty guessed this is where Jamie saw her being kissed by Donald. She shivered at that thought. Taking in the view she could see the extent of her land. The wavy wire boundary fence running through the undergrowth at the back and the solid little wall that offered small but crucial defence from the sea. The cottage, or croft as everyone else called it looked sad. Surrounded by chewed grass and piles of building materials. A large area of the lawn was buried under the grey rectangles of stacked slate flooring and a new lower mass of roof slates.

Though virtually roofless the thick wall stood as firm and strong as ever, the grey trenches that marked the new footing marked Tide's Reach's new footprint. Looking from building to builder Kitty's eyes rested on the dark red hair she knew to be Jamie. A yearning, a dull ache in the pit of her stomach, caught her. As if the bungee cord that connected them was pulled too tight. She didn't resist it and walked briskly home, stopping only to straighten the Tide's Reach sign. The writing was almost gone, she must repaint it soon.

A very insidious panic rose in Kitty as she descended the drive. If she were to baby sit and he to teach they must spend the evening apart. Did she presume too much? Should she drive him back to his house so that he could get his car and they could drive home separately? They had not had a date as such. Were they *going out*? Was he expecting her to come back here in Pimples on her own tonight? The thought of it terrified her. They hadn't moved in together, where did she stand? Suddenly now, being apart from him for the first time in days Kitty had no idea where she stood, no confidence in herself.

The panic escalated and Kitty couldn't stop the tears that edged to overflow. If this was how she felt about being apart for a few hours, what would become of her if he went to Harris, for weeks? Unable to walk further Kitty stopped half way across from the cars to the house. A wave of nausea compounded by the frantic pounding in her chest left her gripping her knees, and trying desperately to take deep breaths when something had a vice like hold on her lungs. Her knuckles were white and her nails dug into her legs. Small flashing lights danced before her on the grass.

Oblivious to all around her Kitty almost fell as Jamie ran and took firm hold of her shoulders.

"Kathleen, what is it?" Jamie was breathless from running, his voice hoarse with worry. He had watched her walk, then pale, falter and finally almost fall.

"Are you unwell? Kathleen, Kathleen talk to me!" Pleading now, "Please Kathleen?"

He turned her to face him and straightened her, gasping at the tear covered blanched face. Hugging the limp creature to him he waved away concerned looks from the other men.

"Come with me."

Guiding her to the sliding door of Pimples he opened it and helped her in, pushing her down onto the bed. Rubbing her small hands in his.

"Ock lass you're frozen!" Picking up one of her blankets he wrapped it around her. "Kathleen are ye unwell? You're scaring me lass."

"It's" Kitty swallowed with effort her throat was raw, "It's… stupid… I don't know… I, I think I had a panic attack." Her eyes filled anew.

"Oh, do you have those?"

"No" her answer was weak.

"Um, well what?"

"I, I just … I just realised you'll be teaching and I'll be babysitting and I thought maybe I should come back here afterwards." Sobbing now, "and, and… you might want to go home on your own," Getting more difficult to understand now, "then you'll go to Harris, and, and I'll be on my own again." Kitty buried her head in the blanket and gave in to the tidal wave of emotion. Jamie tried hard not to laugh and rubbed her back. Reaching for a tissue he passed it under the blanket. A large blow and some shuddering sniffs and she seemed to settle.

"It was hard to be away from you then" sniff, "And the thought of not sleeping with you... being here on my own. I would feel more alone than ever."

"Hush, hush. I know."

"Do you, do you really, it's ridiculous! I'm ridiculous!" She shook off the blanket and slapped her chest. "We've only been together three days and I have become a strange, needy stalker" Kitty retreated under the blanket and mumbled "Leave if you want, I wouldn't blame you... go."

"Kathleen please don't make me talk to a blanket."

The blanket spoke, "I'm all puffy and horrid."

"But that is the strange thing, Kathleen... after three days I consider you *my* puffy and horrid." The blanket slid slowly off to reveal red swollen eyes.

"Now listen here Kathleen Harris, before you go terrifying me with a panic attack please be aware that these are all stupid and ridiculous thoughts you've had," Jamie held the blanket as she attempted to pull it back up around herself. "I agree it is all raving mad!"

"I knew it" Kitty began to cry again.

"But it is just how I feel too." He spoke gently and held Kitty's green-eyed gaze as he did.

"So I won't be sleeping here tonight?"

"Only if I'm with ya. And not wanting to offend ye, and Pimples,

I'd rather we were in my bed."

"Could you kiss a puffy, snotty girl?"

"I'd happily do a lot more but I'm sweaty, and ye are snotty and Malcolm and Jeff would really give us a hard time if the van started rocking." Kitty giggled and blew her nose again.

"I'll take you to Angela's house, then teach and pick you up so we can go back to mine and do what I'd like to do now" kissing the end of her nose, "And dunne worry about Harris, I dunne have to go. I will not go unless ya are absolutely alright wi'it."

Despite his words, sweat and tears there was some heated kissing before Jamie left the van. Kitty stayed behind on the pretext of tidying the van and made a show of shaking pillows and blankets out on the drive. In reality she hoped her tell tale signs of crying would have faded along with her embarrassment for the episode on the lawn.

With Jamie's help the slate was off, and quicker than seemed possible the beams and rafters were forming a high pile by the sea wall. The new roof had been delivered in the form of six large triangles.

"Best we wait till Trevor is wi' us, Jamie lad, can ye be here tomorrow? It will be a might easier wi' four."

"Oh aye."

"Grand, lets crack on and get the top ready."

Kitty was glad of their attention being so focused, and she sought sanctuary in the storeroom. She didn't know if Jamie had explained her strange behaviour earlier but she remained very embarrassed. Making the mugs of tea and carrying the biscuits out nobody passed comment but each just smiled at her. The wind had picked up now and Kitty fastened her fleece under her chin.

It was after five before Malcolm decreed they had done enough and called time on the day. The top of the walls had been strengthened and reinforced.

"Exciting day tomorrow lassie" Malcolm spoke gently at her, all teasing gone now. She wondered again what Jamie had said to his uncle in her absence. "We will get the trusses up and the walls will soon fly up. Then you'll really see it take shape."

"Oh Malcolm it's looking great and thank you again for the store room, it really is a boon."

"Our pleasure lassie, now I'll throw down the gauntlet. See if ye can finish ye wall before we get the timbers up tomorrow."

"Challenge accepted Malcolm."

Kitty reached over as he removed his glove and wrapped his rough hand around hers and shook. Her wrist, elbow and shoulder felt slightly dislodged as Malcolm gave her half a dozen sharp shakes. Her arm wobbled right down to her toes.

Pimples followed the "Stewart and Sons" van out of the drive and Kitty was happy they couldn't see how Jamie's hand wandered up her thigh, slowly driving her mad.

"I will drive us off the road, if you don't desist."

"That was very hard this afternoon Kathleen."

"It looked hard work."

"Don't be obtuse Kathleen. It was hard being near you and not being able to touch you. Like you said mid panic attack, it's like a physical need or ache – needing you."

Kitty would let the obtuse remark pass because she could sympathise with his plight.

"When I was married, you know all those years, even in the early years, in the beginning, I never knew for it to be so desperate. I don't know if I have ever felt this."

Jamie looked at her as she steered them around a bend. It never bothered him when she talked about Stephen. In fact lacking his own experience in relationships he valued her experience.

"Not at Uni? Not on your… honeymoon?" Wondering if he had crossed some personal line he kept a wary eye on her face waiting for an answer. Kitty sat quietly and frowned as she drove.

"Sorry I didn't mean to pry, you don't have to answer, sorry Kathleen."

"Oh no, its fine… we honeymooned on Crete. It was incredibly hot and the aircon in the hotel was hopeless. I think we managed to, you know most days. But I think it was because we were on our honeymoon. Truth be told we would probably been just as happy drinking on the terrace."

"That sounds sad."

"No, it didn't seem it at the time. As I've said I had nothing to compare it to. If I hadn't met you I would have considered we had a usual, a good even, sex life." Kitty sighed "But now, well!"

They continued until Kitty took the turning by his house. Before shutting off the engine Kitty continued. "When I used to have sex it was because there wasn't anything good on TV, or I didn't have to get up in the morning… but now, now!"

"Well I'm glad you feel it too. It's like I will be ill if I can't have you. Like hunger or thirst – a biological need that must be sated."

"I know, do you think it will calm down soon, fade?"

"I don't know. I hope not but then again I dunne want to be an old grey haired man still as desperate as I am right now."

Kitty laughed, "Oh so you think we will still be together when we are old and grey?" Jamie reached out putting his hand over hers on the gear stick, looking seriously into her eyes.

"Don't you?" A haunted look on his face now, he really did.

They were kissing and disrobing before the front door had closed.

"It's eat or this?" Jamie was treading out of his jeans.

"I'll eat at Angela's" Kitty shed clothes as she ran up the stairs.

25

Moving On

When she knocked Angela's front door she was agitated on two levels. Firstly she hadn't managed to get there early, instead it was a terrible rush. Secondly, they had no time to get ready properly, and she felt every inch like she had just done what she had, and what's more looked like it. Giving herself the last few seconds to gather her thoughts she filled her lungs, which felt strangely constricted, until the door opened. Jamie had dropped her and sped off to the hall before his students arrived.

"Well evening Kitty, I hear you've been corrupting our Gaelic teacher." Gavin's tone was friendly and his natural smile denied Kitty any injured pride.

"Oh I think it's the other way round Gav."

He leaned forward kissing her on the check.

"Well he's a cracking lad – good for both of ya," Gavin turned into the lounge and Kitty followed the sound of plates chinking in the kitchen to face the music.

"Sorry Ange, I couldn't get here sooner." Aware of the blush that covered her entire face she struggled to meet Angela's eyes.

"Oh look at you; I can guess why you're late. Look at you, you have got it bad haven't you?" Gavin walked in now carrying matching waterproofs.

"Come on Ange, let's go and see if Jamie blushes as much as Kitty here."

"Oh Kitty, I wanted all the details" Angela whined like one of her children and huffed into her coat. "What is your name, Amanda?" Kitty thought as she waved the couple off. Having come straight from the shower Kitty took the bread and cheese from her bag that was all that could be grabbed in the rush out. An update to Amanda was in order, and Kitty settled on the sofa once she had eaten her cheese on toast, which now sat heavy on her chest.

"Evening, is it convenient Mand?"

"Always babe, always. Remember I have no real life, guessing all the action is up there, so come on tell all."

"Well I'm babysitting, not that I need the use of their bath anymore, but Jamie teaches them Gaelic so I might as well be here."

"But Kit you don't like kids – how does that work for you? How many of them are there?"

"They are only little people Mand, I know you wouldn't want to do it but it's a doddle. There are three apparently, but two I've never seen, just lumps in the bed, but the eldest sits in bed but only ever waves me away." The friends laughed easily.

"So why don't you need a bath? Are you staying with him all the time now?"

"Well we stayed…"

"Come on details – no secrets!"

"Well we stayed in bed all day Monday and only got up and went to mine because we were done in – so to speak, if you know what I mean?" Innuendo laden in her husky voice.

"Oh, you dirty bitch!"

"Mhmm and it's so very intense – I can't tell you… it's a bit frightening."

"Why Kit?" worried for her now, "Why frightening?"

"Well we're not gliding into a relationship, we've rocketed. I suppose I'm scared it will all, you know explode – be another Challenger!"

"Kit, babe… it's just sex, and bloody good sex by the sound of it."

"That's just it Mand it doesn't feel just like sex – which is, by the way beyond incredible… but… I think I love him." Kitty voice was quiet and she could feel the creeping feeling that floored her on the lawn.

"Oh!"

"Oh, yes. That's not normal is it?"

Kitty heard Amanda sigh deeply and imagined she could hear the cogs spinning and whirling.

"Well…"

"I know, I knew it but I feel sick when I'm not with him, I mean literally. I had a panic attack today in front of the builders – his bloody relatives, as if it wasn't bad enough anyway. Because I remembered about tonight and thought I might have to go back to the van on my own!" Kitty spoke without taking a breath, her voice rising in pitch and volume – verging on hysteria Amanda thought.

"Kit breathe, breathe. I can't slap you from here, don't make me come up there for that!" Silence followed, Amanda clutching her chest willing her friend to regain some composure.

"There, any better?"

"Um."

"And, how did he react – was he freaking out?"

"No... he said he felt the same way; he said he couldn't bear to not have me in his bed."

"Well... it's not usual. Put it this way, it's never happened to me – but that's not saying anything being your most single friend. I suppose its good you are both as bad as each other. The question you need to ask, is it just how you two would have felt under any circumstances... or is it because of Stephen?"

"Precisely, that's what I wonder about, worry about."

"Slow it down a bit if you can, but really, sod it! All that matters is what you and he want. There is no right and wrong, and really it sounds very right – in the bed department anyway and why the hell shouldn't it be! As long as you are honest with each other don't question it too much babe."

"Oh you do settle my overactive mind Mand, thank you and of course you will send me your bill post haste!"

"Don't you worry you can treat me to dinner when I come up next month. Mum and Dad are getting really excited, are you sure you will be up to visitors?"

"Oh yes I can't wait for you all to see it here."

"Yes and don't think you can hide away your young man. I think my mum is that desperate for me to settle down she's hoping he has a brother!"

"Oh, of course you had to tell them all about him?"

"Only the PG rated version – So tell me the latest on the build, I don't have to edit those and then I want some real X rated details!"

They talked for over an hour, giggling and sharing a lot of very intimate details. Amanda was satisfied and quietly very envious, all joking aside she hoped there would be an available kilted man when she visited. She had no terrible yearning of potential love but definitely could do with some gratuitous sex.

When the key turned and the door opened, Kitty stayed put on the sofa as Gavin and Angela walked in together.

"They ok?"

"As usual, not a peep."

Angela was motioning with her head, eyebrows high and darting eyes much to Kitty's dismay until she heard Gavin's voice back in the hall.

"Jamie, do you want coffee?"

There was no reply as Jamie strode past the gaping mouth of Angela, raising Kitty's chin with one hand he planted a very passionate kiss on her lips then whispered into her ear,

"God I've missed you." Standing and holding both her hands, he pulled her up effortlessly right off her feet. "Oh Kathleen" his breath was hot through her hair on her neck. She remembered suddenly that they were stood surrounded by images of the smiling faces of children, not to mention the real life, open mouthed couple in the door way.

"Well!" Gavin cleared his throat, "Don't feel you have to."

"If ye dunna mind we would very much like to get home." Kitty's insides melted at the sound of his husky voice, and meekly followed him clutching his hand past the astonished faces.

"Night Ange, Gav – Ange I'll pop to the post office tomorrow for a catch up."

"Oh, make sure you do!"

"Night" Jamie swapped Kitty's hands to his left and shook Gavin firmly by the hand and reached and tapped Angela's upper arm. As the door closed Angela and Gavin giggled – not unlike their children upstairs would have.

"Well… that was intense; you could have cut the atmosphere with a spoon!" Gavin blow out his cheeks, "Come here you." Obviously the charge in the atmosphere was contagious.

The drive back was silent. Kitty rested her hand high on his thigh and he on her denim clad knee. Changing gear reluctantly they both felt keenly the relief at being back together. Becoming used to his manners Kitty waited for him to come around and open the door for her, taking his hand to stand.

"Do ye have any skirts?"

"Um, what here?"

"Aye."

"No, I mean not here but I have in storage, why?"

"I ken I would like ye in a skirt."

"Well would you now James Stewart?"

"Aye."

What was rushed and driven out of necessity earlier in the evening was savoured and leisurely now. Shaking, finally Jamie buried his face in the damp blonde curls.

"Ock, Kathleen, I…"

"What?" Kitty was breathless, and quietly, so quiet Kitty wasn't sure if she had heard properly.

"I love you Kathleen."

The tears poured like rain on a pane, each following its predecessor's track, and the coldness as they pooled inside her ears was oddly refreshing.

"Say something" Jamie's voice a whisper, pleading. As much as Kitty desperately wanted to reply, the sharp pain in her throat halted words. Slowly peeling himself off her, he saw the suddenly fragile-looking woman beneath him.

Jamie's trembling hand wiped away the tears as more rallied to find her ears.

"Too soon... too much?"

"Do you?" struggling to speak past the razor blades inside her throat. "Do you mean it?"

Looking hurt, "Of course."

Kitty raised a hand and laid it on his lips which he lightly kissed. Moving across to the bristles, tempting her to stroke them minutely.

"I phoned Amanda from Angela's."

"Aye."

"And I told her I thought I had fallen in love with you." It was Jamie's eyes that filled with tears now, and Kitty reached around his neck and pulled him back onto her.

In the morning there was an air of calm in the kitchen. The familiarity and relaxed dance around each other belied the short time of their acquaintance. Kitty handed him his mug of tea as he passed her a plate of two doorstops of toast and bright yellow fried eggs. Both leaning away from their breakfast they enjoyed a long and lingering kiss. Standing now Jamie looked quizzically at her.

"I think it's time."

"What for?" Hesitant now holding the fork of egg an inch from her mouth.

"When we finish at the croft today, I'd like to take you to meet my parents."

"Oh!"

"Would that be ok?"

"Umm, well... yes I suppose so. I, I forget other people have families. Why today?"

"No reason, but Malcolm said yesterday my mum was interrogating him about ya. They know of ya and the longer we make them wonder the more they will ken ya to be a corrupting Mrs Robinson Sassenach."

"Don't!" Kitty slapped his arm. "Will they like me?" genuinely worried.

"They will love you, just like me!" Jamie kissed her nose as she ate eagerly. Smiling and glowing throughout the breakfast – no mean feat.

There was a second van on her drive when they arrived. Walking around the strange one Jamie slapped the back that stooped into the back.

"Hey" the man stood, swung around and threw a large muscular arm around Jamie, unbalancing him and pulling him into a crushing bear hug. Kitty didn't think such a thing was possible but standing next to this man Jamie looked positively insubstantial.

"Jamie, laddie, brilliant ta see ya!"

"Aye and you Trevor, Let me introduce you to Kathleen. Kathleen Harris, Trevor Stewart, my big cousin."

"So I see, lovely to meet you."

Stepping back from Jamie, Trevor took Kitty firmly by the upper arms, turning her from right to left, and looking her unashamedly up and down. Trevor completed his inspection by planting a large kiss on the edge of her mouth. Trevor had the same features, the Viking brow and chiselled nose, but a shaggy mass of dark hair and the shadow of a beard to come that looked much more foreboding. But, when he smiled you could see he was a Stewart and Kitty knew of course, she would like him.

"Brilliant, welcome ta ya, wow, your father is gonna love her."

"Told ya!" Jamie winked at her.

"Aye, I was going to show her off this afternoon."

"Grand, aye, and dunne fret lass it's only a house!"

Trevor winked, whistled and carried a tool box as if it was a basket of eggs, Kitty guessed she wouldn't be able to move it, let alone lift it.

Jamie rolled up his sleeves and Kitty anticipated a very productive day. As they walked towards the skeleton of her house Kitty was excited to have its rib cage reinstated.

There was little for Kitty to do, and she felt even more puny and insignificant with four huge men clambering over the site. Donning her gloves, Kitty was determined to not be beaten and taking Malcolm's challenge seriously, she approached her wall with renewed vigour. Stopping only to watch, her heart was pounding as the enormous wooden triangles were winched and bullied into place, Yesterdays brick and cement pads around the outer walls provided level footings.

"Here lassie, du ya wanna help?"

"If I can Malcolm, what can I do?" Scrabbling to her feet and brushing the dust from her knees.

"Hey Trevor, take the slack and the weight lad, but Kitty could hold the other end. Here lass grab hold of the rope."

"Don't wrap the rope around ya sel Kathleen!" Pronouncing the entire name and glancing at his uncle with a frown, Kitty guessed Jamie didn't like his over familiar use of Kitty. "Holler if it's pullin toward ya and for god's sake concentrate and jump out of the way if it looks like its falling." Kitty nodded seriously.

"Jamie, stop fretting, the lass will be fine, I dunna intend dropping the thing on her wee head." Trevor winked and grinned over to Kitty. "It's like tug a war, how do ya fancy ya chances lass?"

Flexing her muscles in proud strong man stance, "Bring it on little man!"

Trevor threw his head back and roared. Four deep strong laughs rang around the build filling Kitty with joy. Two hours later Kitty was the only one of the party not sweating profusely. She suspected it was a very minor role she was allowed to take but thought it was sweet of them to include her.

The six beams were bolted and temporary straps and braces held them in place. All four men found a convenient place and sat heavily down. Kitty didn't need asking and headed for the store and filled the kettle. Coffee and a large packet of biscuits were soon demolished,

"Well done chaps! What next?" Kitty smiled happily.

"She's a demanding wee lass Jamie, is she always like that?" Chuckling Trevor rested back on the pile of floor slates and enjoyed Kitty blushes.

Malcolm smiled, "Now leave her be lads, poor wee lass. We'll get the walls up today and crack on with the roof tomorrow lass. We'll want it weather proof as soon as possible, the weather has been kind to ya so far. I ken I'll be much happier when we're covered." Looking over at Jamie now, "Donald will be paying us a visit today."

Kitty looked over to Jamie, all eyes on him now. He stiffened and put his mug down on the wall where he sat.

"What time?" through gritted teeth.

"Late morning he said."

"Great" and then mumbled something in Gaelic. Kitty hesitated, uncertain if she should. But deciding she didn't care what any one thought took her drink and went to sit next to him. Realising then that she had been in his company for hours without actually touching him she edged as close as possible. The heat of his leg and hip radiated through her trousers,

Jamie wrapped an arm around her shoulders and she encircled his back and placed her free hand on his thigh. Leaning down to her he kissed her temple and whispered into her ear.

"I might make myself scarce, would ya mind?"

Kitty weighed up her options. Keep him here which was her first instinct, or, the more sensible all-round was for him to leave and prevent scenes unpleasant to Jamie or Donald. Kitty cared very much if Jamie was upset because anything that affected him mattered. Donald was her architect and although she had absolutely no interest in his emotional well being, she didn't want to alienate him before the house was finished.

Jamie took her chin in his hand and kissed her with his hot sweet breath. Catching her breath she hugged herself to him.

"Steady lad, you'll not be on ya own now." Malcolm coughed now and Kitty pulled away, letting her hair fall across her blushes.

"Aye... I'll go and do some errands, I'll be back this afternoon." Jamie was obviously not happy.

"Still not kissed and made up lad?"

"Ya ken that will never happen!"

"Aye suppose ya right, I have to work wi the bastard. Oh excuse me lass!" Malcolm added apologetically.

Kitty got up, avoiding eye contact with the men, and went to the store and retrieved Pimples keys and together she and Jamie walked to the drive.

"Be careful with him."

"Of course, I hate leaving you, even more knowing that creature will be here wi' ye."

"Do you think your lovely relatives would let anything happen? But I understand, I feel exactly the same."

As if staking a claim Jamie pressed himself against Kitty on the far side of the pimply van. Leaving her breathless and horribly frustrated, he drove too fast out of the drive. Not wanting to face his family until she had composed herself she climbed over the low wall and combed the beach, unable to resist the best of the mussel shells.

The wind was mild but incessant and very welcome as it cleared her mind. The sea was steely grey today and a mass of small ripples. The mountains in the far distance were a misty mottled mauve and brown. Finding a large rock Kitty sat and watched the clouds - it was she concluded, her new hobby. A patch of azure surrounded a band of fluffy white cauliflower clouds hanging in the base of the sky, hugging close to the sea and mountains. Much more ominous was the high solid block of dark grey that appeared to be racing towards her.

The whirlwind that was James Stewart had totally dominated her thoughts and actions and so possessed her, she had not in days stopped to marvel at her surroundings as she did now. Looking back now to the build, she watched the flash of their bright checked shirts and listened to the whirr of the mixer and generator. Trevor fed the mixer, whilst Jeff supplied Malcolm with barrows of cement. Malcolm would frequently stop to examine the progress, smoothing and stroking his beard.

Feeling totally at home here she tried to remember her previous life. Trying hard to visualise her old house, the road. It was a nothing to her now, like a dream, soon to be completely forgotten. With the soothing sound of water circling and advancing on the stones around her Kitty allowed herself to think of Stephen, would he have believed it of her?

"I did it Stephen, I moved on." Kitty spoke to the sea before her.

26

Executor Extraordinaire

Although they had not given up hope till his very last days on earth, Stephen had insisted on talking about the possibility of his dying. It was important to him, he wanted to say it, make Kitty understand what to do if he didn't make it. Kitty smiled as a trio of ducks swam, bobbing towards her over the ripples. She smiled at the irony of the two drakes pursuing the lone female.

She couldn't remember Stephen saying, "Leave everything you know and buy a derelict house on an island in Scotland." But what did he say? She had tried hard to block these memories, but now she felt they deserved and needed revisiting so she closed her eyes and let the breeze brush her hair from her face. His words came back to her as if sailing across the water, and for the very first time since his death she could hear him. Hear his tone, his accent and recall in perfect clarity his dear, lovely face. Taking a sharp breath at allowing herself to see him again, it had been too long and always far too painful before today.

Remembering too how she had wanted to tell him to shut up; she didn't want to talk about life without him. She remembered too how angry she was with him. But knowing he needed to talk she had bitten her tongue and let him.

"Have adventures, fall in love... but only with someone I would want to have a pint with. Have babies Kathleen, why didn't we have babies?"

Kitty wrapped her arms tight around her, hugging the memory close so as not to lose it. Rocking gently on the stone seat she recalled how she had made a joke, unable to deal with the enormity of it then. A song played in her mind now, and it was a favourite track of her and Stephen, and had it played at the funeral. "On Your Shore"- an Enya song and Kitty hummed it now. The haunting melody meant even more now as she sat on her own shore, that thought made her smile. The tranquility of all around her was yet another reason she believed these thoughts and feelings were surfacing now. She was in no doubt she would never have healed in Kent. Her grief would have been permanently glossed over, left to fester and eat away from inside her until she was an empty shell of herself. A carcass, lessened with each loss and never to have been nourished or replenished.

The memories, suddenly free, flooded back to her now. The three weeks waiting for the funeral had seemed unending at the time, and now with the water soothing her soul she thought through those days for the first time. Three weeks was too long to wait, but it was Christmas. It was a blur of paperwork and phone calls, insurance to be paid out, and mortgages to be paid off. Even to this day when it was all settled, Kitty had never totally understood all the finances, Keith had dealt with all that. Keith was a strange little man and was first cousin to Stephen. She had met him twice before at a wedding and Stephens's Nan's funeral. Trying to engage him in conversation was futile and Kitty gave up after many attempts, how could you talk to someone unable to maintain any sort of eye contact?

It had been Stephen's father's idea; Kitty bristled at it but had not the energy or desire to upset the grieving father. Letting Keith into the house three days after Stephen's death, she made no effort to chat and led him straight to the study. The filing cabinet was well organised, and after two mugs of tea and three bourbons Keith had arranged everything. He may have been a loner and a personality donor but as a solicitor specialising in family law he was invaluable.

Keith's help not only arranged the funeral and all the finances, but freed Kitty up to think. The more she thought, the hours she looked at the shreds of her life, the stronger the resolve to leave it all became.

She allowed herself the time now to think back to one of the bleakest day of her life. Standing outside the crematorium Kitty felt alone. As devastated and bereft as Stephen's parents were, they clung to each other. His dad held one of his weeping wife's hands and with his other arm gripped around her shoulder – holding her, supporting her. Kitty was untouched and alone.

Where was her strong arm? Lying in the coffin covered in white flowers. Every time she glanced at it she could see the puffy grey face peering through the walnut veneer. Struggling to get her breath Kitty reached, groped for someone – anyone. It was Keith who firmly took her arm and remained there throughout the service. Unembarrassed and strong Keith was there. Kitty knew she could never repay the immense service that day and all the days leading up to it.

Kitty had written, rewritten, screwed up and cursed at attempts at a Eulogy. But as the funeral approached she admitted defeat – she couldn't do it. Couldn't condense everything she felt on a sheet of A4. Instead she sat with his parents and a stranger with a dog collar, ensuring he knew what needed to be said.

She still hoped to speak but suspected she wouldn't be able to. Her feeling of failure at not speaking eloquently at the funeral she knew threatened to eat into her, a canker to gnaw away at her and deplete her further.

The moment had arrived and taking Keith's hand she stumbled as she turned to face the room full of blackness. Waiting to go into the chapel she could look at only her hands, or the box containing her lovely, cold dead husband. Sitting in the front row she had no comprehension of how many people had filed in behind her to say their farewells to Stephen. She was amazed at the seas of faces, eyes red and the only movement hands and hankies rising to wipe eyes and running noses. Kitty passed her gaze over familiar faces and many she didn't know. Lining the aisles and out in the foyer, all here because they had lost Stephen from their lives.

"Are they all here for Stephen?" a thought rather than meaning to speak. Keith squeezed her arm and whispered, "Of course, he was loved. Are you alright? Do you want me to read it?"

"No" again her voice left her without thought. She turned to the coffin and smiled for on the large screen behind it was one of her favourite photos of her husband. For the first time since he had gone Kitty sighed and held the podium as the hideous image of him dead in the hospital bed was replaced by the face she had fallen in love with. A strength she hadn't anticipated grew within her.

"Now that's how I want to remember you." The muffled reaction from the crowd informed Kitty that she had spoken out loud. "Stephen was my best friend, he was my other half... we met at Uni and to be honest I thought he was a bit... up himself!" Kitty smiled then and closed her eyes as the image of a twenty-year-old Stephen, trade mark dark curls across his face and compulsory rugby shirt and jeans.

"But he soon wore me down," she laughed along with some of the other mourners.

"As you all know, once he'd set his mind on things..." the crowd nodded and exchanged glances.

"He was the best, he was my family, he was my best friend... I will miss him always and I will love him always."

She had done it! She said what she wanted the world to hear. Now on a beach on the Isle of Skye, Kitty realised she was allowed to have these feelings again. She could love again and no matter how different this may be, it took nothing from her love and life with Stephen. So she sat and continued to revisit her memories.

The wake was a relief, despite being hugged by everyone it was the embrace of Amanda that broke through the numbness.

"I wish you had someone... your mum, your dad, even Tommy... and it is so unfair!" Amanda struggled to get her words out. A sob escaped Kitty and she slumped into the hug.

"It's fucking unfair." Kitty whispered into her friend's hair.

"Oh Kit, I know, I don't know what to do, what to say."

"Just do this."

The two girls, women! Had been friends since infancy and held each other for many minutes until Kitty's crying subsided.

"Remember I'm staying tonight." Amanda leant back and licking her finger, wiped the smudged make up from under Kitty eyes.

"I'm glad, thank you."

Amanda's mother had prepared a casserole in the slow cooker and as Kitty closed the front door on the world and the funeral, she and Amanda kicked off their heels and against all expectations were hungry. Within five minutes they had donned pyjamas and slippers, downed a glass of red wine and were tucking into beef casserole.

Kitty had slept soundly for the first time in six weeks, and for the first time since his death, back in her own bed. Not on her side but on Stephens', burying her face in the pillow that she dare not wash. Amanda had spent a good deal of the night watching her friend sleep and aching for her loss.

The air was lighter in the morning and Kitty felt a weight had been lifted. Although the grief, the loss, the loneliness was all still as real and intense, she had a strange feeling of freedom. That although she carried them with her, they no longer anchored her to one spot.

Kitty smiled now, and turned her face up to the sunshine remembering a much brighter recollection. That was the day of the list. The napkin, which was now framed in Tide's Reach was created in Kitty's favourite teashop. Lavender tearooms with its chandeliers, leather sofas and eclectic painted furniture felt very comforting. For the first time in six weeks Kitty had an appetite. Amanda was so glad to see Kitty eating, she had watched helplessly as the weight had fallen off her friend's already slight frame... Kitty smiled up with a mouthful of breakfast and wiped the remaining bean and egg yolk with Amanda's unwanted toast.

"There's just too much loneliness here."

"I know, I know... it's just, well two things; one I'm going to miss you horribly and two, isn't it just bloody madness?" Amanda said the last words quietly, little more than a whisper and eyed her mug of tea.

"I know, but it's been in my mind since he died. That three week wait has given me a lot of time – especially with the marvel that is Keith *Executor extraordinaire!*" Kitty smiled and Amanda couldn't help but be happy for her, and delighted in her enthusiasm. After all, what did Kitty have to stay here for? Amanda knew her friend had never liked living in Kent. Maybe, Amanda hoped she may see sense and move back to Wimbledon.

"Now open mind, promise?" Kitty wriggled in her seat and pulled a well-thumbed copy of the estate agent details.

"Tide's Reach!" Kitty had said in sudden solemnity and smoothed the folds of the creased details, laying it in front of Amanda.

"Oh Kit... it's so far away." Amanda freed her phone from her jeans pocket and began tapping urgently.

"I know but you can come for holidays, hell Amanda you're a teacher – you're always on holiday!"

"Excuse me, we have planning and marking, it's hardly any holiday!" Kitty snorted at Amanda's pat defence that every teacher throws in about their endless holidays.

"You know as well as I do that you do Jack-shit in the holiday, don't you? Don't you?"

Blushing slightly Amanda nodded, "Well maybe not so much." Still fiddling with her phone Amanda stopped, slapping her hand on the table, "Ha! I knew it – see – SEE!"

Kitty took the now outstretched phone and peered at the screen.

"Look 587.4 miles and 11 hours and 9 minutes – Isle of Skye to Wimbledon. Jesus Kit I'll have to fly, you know I'm only a teacher right? I'm not a pop star more's the pity, I don't have my own jet!"

Hence the addition of private jet to the to do list.

"Don't you worry, I will slave away all year with the bloody brats while you prance about in your black cape looking all widowy and Scottish.

That goodbye was by far the hardest; the only tie that pulled her back since she had come to Scotland.

There was the promise of life here, peace, and quite unexpectedly the promise of love. She was tuned to the rhythm of the lapping and retreating waves and lost in the intensity of her long buried memories. It had been unexpectedly refreshing to let these thoughts come back to her. The year that had passed was healing her and she felt the first glimmer of hope. Hope that she could recover from all she had lost, and hope that she could once again have someone in her life.

Kitty didn't hear the arrival of the purring engine, nor the feet on the stones until they were right upon her. Startled, quickly she turned, so happy to see Jamie again, but no.

"Sorry Kathleen I didn't mean to make you jump." Donald bent and kissed Kitty's cheek. All instincts screamed to pull away but decorum dictated she graciously reciprocated.

"Just day dreaming."

"Well I must say you could waste a lot of time drinking in this view." Donald took a deep breath and scanned over the water approvingly.

Kitty looked at his profile – it was inconceivable that so much had happened since he had taken her to lunch and stolen that kiss. Donald, smug in the knowledge his companion was staring up at him, could have no idea of the true nature of all that raced through her mind, He would be most displeased.

Anxious to put an end to their isolation now, feeling strangely vulnerable in such close proximity to him, Kitty rose stiffly, her cold hips resistant, and she ached in all sorts of places. Fearful he could read her mind she roused herself. "Come Donald you must see the roof, not to mention my wall."

"Well, credit where it's due, Malcolm and his boys do work well. The roof trusses up good, good. I suppose the three of them were here for that?" Kitty nearly added that there had been four Stewarts but saved herself in time.

"Yes they had me help with the trusses, holding a rope." Kitty smiled but received a dark glare in reply and she regretting saying anything.

"Well I'll be having words with Malcolm! He shouldn't be getting the clients involved, you can have your turn when it comes to the choosing the décor." Smarmy, patronising, sexist pig was what Kitty thought, but all Donald saw was a small smile.

"I'm pretty sure I wasn't playing a real part, I think he was humouring me as I wanted to be involved. I think it was rather sweet of him, I was happy." Hoping that was enough to change his track Kitty led him to the store to show off her dry walling skills.

"Oh well done Kathleen... good job" Even when he was trying to be sincere Kitty felt his condescension waft over her like drizzle.

"Morning to ya Donald." Malcolm walked towards them.

"Looking good Malcolm!"

"Aye we had help," the blue eye winked at Kitty but elaborated no further.

"Well it must be running to plan, weather has been unseasonably kind."

"Aye, aye... if the weather holds we'll be water tight soon. It can come none too soon." Malcolm looked over the sea, squinting at the rays of sun as they bounced off the water. The white fluffy clouds Kitty had been tracking were now black edged and approaching at a threatening pace, Malcolm stroked his beard.

"Aye, yes well, I'll go over a few things on the drawing while I'm here." Donald walked towards the store, Malcolm followed raising his eye brows to Kitty. Malcolm may not be verbose, but it was clear by his expression what he thought of the architect. Lost in their discussion on the common rafter, the intricacies of the Dormer valley, Jack rafters and lintels Kitty opted to leave them to it.

Relishing the prospect of being farther from him, she walked over to watch where Trevor was making short shrift of the breezeblock wall to the front elevation. At windowsill height already the pillars between the windows grew quickly. The new shape of the house was clear to see now, the L shaped extension running the whole length of the front of the old house, past the end of the existing bedroom external wall and back to level with the back. Walking through what was to be her utility room, her long front lounge, and to the end where there would be what seemed like a huge bathroom.

"Ya could'na have picked a more beautiful spot lass."

"No, a lot of luck and not a lot of choosing. I saw the pictures on the Internet... and well just bought it."

"You'd never visited it?"

"Nope!" Kitty's chirpy reply had them both grinning.

"Well it's bonny."

"I quite agree."

Kitty sat on the small wall not twelve foot from Trevor as he returned to his work, whistling gently. Although the clouds tumbled behind, Kitty watched the patch of blue framing the stunted trees behind her cottage. There was a cacophony of bird song. Malcolm had obviously turned off the radio and the site was unusually quiet. Kitty strained to find the birds responsible, wanting to identify and locate the individuals singing the delicate tunes. Another new hobby Kitty hoped to enjoy, she promised herself to get a bird book and improve her very limited knowledge.

Her reverie was disturbed at the sight of Donald and Malcolm walking towards her.

"Come Kathleen, walk with me if you would?"

It was more of an order than a request. Taken aback Kitty unconsciously accepted, taking the outstretched hand and stood. Trevor's expressive face frowned and he threw his trowel into the trug of cement, Kitty jumped.

Kitty, quickly releasing his hand, headed off to the beach and aimed towards her little croft. Everyone else who had walked this way Kitty had been very keen to show the crumbling remains, but she was glad to pass by it now unnoticed. They walked in silence, their way easier for the low tide.

"How are you managing? I suspect you'll be glad of a decent bed and bathroom."

Images flooded into her mind of languishing in a hot bath surrounded by candles as Jamie sat close, entwined hot and sublime in his large bed. A swift blush coloured her face and she turned to face the sea and let the cool breezes refresh her.

"My day bed arrives today, I will put it in the store and it will be great to have a proper bed there."

"Yes... quite." A grinning Donald again managed to ooze insinuation from every pore and Kitty shivered.

"Are you cold, we should turn back? I just wanted to invite you to dinner Friday and I didn't want the yokels listening." Donald placed an arm on Kitty fore arm.

"Oh." Was all Kitty could manage. Scrabbling for an excuse Kitty was delighted to remember – "Darts! Oh sorry Donald, w, what a shame" but her smugness swiftly extinguished.

"Well Saturday then, Claire and Hamish will come, nothing formal."

"Oh" again!

"Kathleen?"

"Um... I can't think of a good reason why not." Kitty realised just how disappointingly rude she sounded and forced a wry smile.

"Good shall we say seven?"

"Yes, great" – Great! What was she thinking – Oh shit! Well she would have to phone and cancel later, not possessing the courage to do it now to his face. Donald reached down her arm and made to take her hand. At least in this her reflexes were faster and she turned and started to head back to the house.

"I'm sure the Duncan's would bring you, and I have a very fine spare room with an en suite you could make your own."

"Ohh, well thank you but I swim Sundays and my own bed will be here by then, I wouldn't want to put you out." She started walking purposely back to the builders and welcoming their company.

Much to her annoyance, and sure it was solely for effect Donald loudly stated. "Right, well I'll be off, until Saturday at mine Kathleen." It had the desired effect as three heads lifted and paused in their work, all whistling ceased. "And Malcolm I'll drop by to check up on Friday to see how you are getting on."

"Thanks" Sarcasm dripping off the word as Jeff spat it at him. Kitty was sure she had heard under his breath, "Like we need you checking up on us."

"Walk to the car with me Kathleen," Again Kitty found herself obeying – was she a dog? What was happening here? She looked from the frosty stares of the builders to the tall thin man giving her orders. How had she come to this?

"Grow a pair!" Kitty shouted inwardly but continued to walk across the lawn, feeling the eyes of Jamie's relatives boring into the back of her. Where was Jamie? She wondered now if it had been prudent for him to leave, would it have been better for Donald to see them together and get him off her case. Not making the same mistake as before, Kitty stood resolute on the lawn far from anything he could pin her against.

"Well it's promising work Kathleen, they are not the brightest but ye cannot fault their work."

"I'm delighted, and they are lovely men to have around."
Wanting to get that in, she hated the way he looked down his nose at the Stewarts and probably all the locals. Just because he came from Inverness he thought himself so above everyone else.

Reaching towards her Donald placed both hands on her shoulders and leaned in for a lingering kiss near her ear. "GET OFF!" She screamed inwardly but outwardly, "Bye then Donald see you... later."

"Until then, Saturday – do you like salmon?"

"Yes" Jesus Kit, get a grip and just tell him to sod off and poke his salmon where the sun doesn't shine - but she couldn't, and inanely waved as his beast of a car drove away. As it turned onto the main road and Kitty watched, a glint of red caught her eye. From the lay-by where Kitty herself had sat and watched the first deliveries, she could see Jamie looking down at her, stood in front of Pimples, (realising now, bizarrely the two most important things in her life.)

Rather than confronting Jamie here, for she felt it would be a confrontation by the look on his face, she thought it prudent to be far away from the ever-present eyes and ears of the builders. Walking quickly up the drive she found Jamie waiting for her. His face was frozen white and hard, arms folded tight across his chest. Kitty reached up to subdue the twitching muscles of his cheek. Jamie flinched back from her touch.

"Oh Jamie... no." Kitty reached with both hands but Jamie roughly took her left hand and marched away from her drive and towards the hotel and the small harbour and jetty. Jamie's breath was ragged and deep, and Kitty nervously watched the pulse pounding in his throat. Waiting for him to compose himself she looked down and played with the gravel with the toe of her shoe.

"I, I can'na bear it... to see him near ya is hard enough... but to touch ya trusdar! – Ya let him kiss ye!"

"I know he's a bit smarmy... but what can I do? He is my architect! I just need to keep him, well, sweet until the house is done." Apologetically but then angrily, "I did not asked to be kissed, I didn't want to be kissed and I certainly didn't like being kissed!"

"I appreciate that Kathleen... and... I never knew I was a jealous man, never had cause to be but I'm worried – I – I – can'na have ya near him."

"Oh" Jamie took her face and forced eye contact.

"What?" His face was so beautiful and bright with its usual smile. But this, this was very different. His frown shadowed and darkened his eyes and Kitty could have been afraid of him if she didn't know him better.

"And... I, well I, sort of agreed to go to his house on Saturday – with the Duncans for dinner," She added hastily hoping to soften the blow.

"Oh did ye now!" Holding her jaw tightly preventing her from looking away from his face.

"Ow, Jamie!"

Snapped from his brooding he released her face and pulled her in for a crushing hug.

"Why?" Jamie's voice quiet now, bluster and anger gone leaving just the fragility of hurt and fear.

"He asked me, and well... when I had dinner at the Duncans' he was there and invited me then. I think it's a regular thing for them and I think they were just being nice including me."

The silence hung around them like a shroud. Kitty tried to pull away but Jamie was having none of it.

"Not a date?"

"Of course not a date! I felt bad not turning him down, I... without doubt would have if I thought for a minute it was a date." Jamie sighed into her neck.

"I thought at first you could come," feeling him stiffen in her arms she quickly continued, "Knew that wouldn't be possible so, so... I don't want to go."

"Then don't" Standing up and holding her chin gently now he bent again to kiss her. A trace of the pent up angst in its passion. "Have you had lunch?" He asked when he finally came up for air.

"What... no."

"Come on." Holding her hand he led her back along the road, past Pimples and marched across her lawn to the house, - well, croft, - well, building site, - well, store room. Each too embroiled in their own thoughts to talk, they hovered and weaved around the small room and cobbled together lunch. The others were ensconced in their vans so Kitty and Jamie sat in silence with only bird song drifting through the open door.

After much consideration to pitch her feelings fairly and eloquently, Kitty was the first to speak.

"It's just being new, I'm aware I don't want to alienate any new friends or acquaintances – the Duncans I think could be good friends to me and well... Donald a tolerable acquaintance." Jamie made to interrupt but Kitty had to finish her prepared and honed speech. "He is building me my house, and I know the animosity between you two but I need to get the job done with as little aggro as possible."

"Aye, aye I see that, but it's terribly hard to be rational about either of ye. Ya see, I ken I hate him... almost as much, as... as I love, love you Kathleen."

Mid slurp of soup Kitty coughed, and thought it safest to forgo eating for the present. It was Jamie's turn to hold up a hand to stop Kitty talking.

"I will hate ye going and wait for ye coming back home to me, but ken I can bear it if ye wish it. But I'd ask ye to return to my house Saturday night."

"Oh yes Jamie please."

Jamie smiled and some of the tension was gone and he relaxed his shoulders for the first time since leaving the lay-by.

"And tonight I will be reminding ye of what will be waiting for ye."

"Good" Kitty reached over and squeezed his hand, issue defused for now.

27

Meeting the Parents

The end of lunch was heralded by the rising noise of approaching Stewarts. A few choice exchanges about Donald – some in Gaelic, whether for Kitty's benefit or habit. The work continued with good-humoured enthusiasm. By five, the outer walls of the extension were up and Kitty walked inside her new rooms. Block work, and dust covered the over trodden grass, but Kitty could now envisage just where her furniture would go. The right place for the old armchair to best appreciate the log burner and that view – her view.

The whistling stopped as the radio was turned off.

"See ya in the morning!" Jeff waved and headed for his van.

"Aye night lass, say hello to ya dad for me lad. Dunne fear I'll lock up when I'm done." Malcolm shot a very cheeky smile at them.

"Oh, god I'd forgotten." Kitty looked at Jamie through one of the windows – or more precisely through a gap in the wall where a window would one day sit.

"Come on." Jamie held out his hand. Kitty had been so distracted today the prospect of meeting his parents had quite slipped her mind. It had been many years since she had that dubious pleasure – meeting a boyfriend's parents.

Having only done it once the memories of it now did little to reassure her. Stephen's parents lived in Rochester and thinking back now Stephen had been in no hurry for them to meet. After six months of going out it had been a family wedding that prompted the introduction. "Well, come if you want" was the extent of the invitation. Kitty had been hurt at the time, was he embarrassed by her, didn't want to show her off to his extended family? But after meeting them she realised he had known she would be under whelmed.

Being an only child himself there was no banter of siblings. His parents had been in their early forties when Stephen was born, and Kitty suspected, not so much an eagerly anticipated arrival but a rather unwelcome and unexpected addition to their ordered life.

On subsequent visits to their bland thirties semi Kitty was always amazed, and found herself hunting for evidence of Stephen's existence. No embarrassing photographs of a gangly youth, nothing chronicling his growing. Not a trophy of achievement or broken yet cherished, crudely made pottery project.

Stephen's parents Graham and Sheila lived in a house devoid of memories. Thinking of them now Kitty felt guilty. She had not contacted them since that first brief letter on her arrival, and although they had not replied she promised - in memory of their son, to write them another long letter. The realisation was that what she had always suspected was playing out, she would not keep in touch with these people. Their only son was dead, but she would not play the part of dutiful daughter-in-law.

Since losing her own beloved father, Kitty had wondered if one day that void – if not filled, could be lined by the presence of a father-in-law. Graham Vrcelj had not been that man. Dark like Stephen but stouter in stature, he worked in London – the City. He was an accountant for a large American company and that was the extent of her understanding of him. The name was thanks to a Yugoslavian prisoner of war, who intrigued Kitty but she was soon put straight. The family didn't dwell in the past. Nor did they dwell very much in the present, or future as Kitty once remarked on their lack of interest in Stephen's life.

Sheila also in no way replaced any part of her mother. Kitty felt no maternal affection ever from the woman, and soon learnt not to comment to Stephen as she suspected he had felt quite unloved in his life and didn't need reminding of it. Kitty decided to think of Graham and Sheila no more, they deserved no such consideration, Kitty would write and send Christmas cards but there it would end.

"Come on you, I've got some people very keen to meet you." Jamie took her hand and waved goodbye to his relatives, Kitty glad to be rid of the thoughts of her in-laws.

"Are we going home? – I mean your home, sorry, to change."

"I like it very much to hear you call it home Kathleen." He smiled at her. "No we dunna have time, and anyway if I got ye home I'd not be wanting go out again." His voice husky now.

"Is that all you think of Mr Stewart?" she looked over nonexistent glasses.

"Aye, mostly. I'm sorry Mrs Harris if I've offended ye, would ya rather not do that anymore?" Jamie reached down and stroked his hand over her jeaned bottom.

"Oh I look forward to it!"

"Come on."

Pimples was still in the lay-by, and Jamie tickled and chased Kitty up the drive and they were both breathless and laughing at the top.

"Here!" Jamie took the keys from his pocket and tossed them to her. Kitty caught them but her mind had to process this innocent action. Stephen always drove if they were together, she could only recall driving him if he was ill or inebriated. Kitty suspected it was the latent sexism rather than chivalry that resulted in her always being the passenger. Kitty loved to drive, and being a slightly squeamish passenger was quite affronted at first. After experiencing Stephen as a passenger – albeit tipsy or poorly, she decided his discomfort and stress at being driven negated any pleasure she might have had. So with no negotiation or debate so it had always been that way.

The simple act of Jamie relinquishing control and being content – even happy, to sit and watch her drive warmed Kitty's heart. A heart so scarred and battered was now, since coming to this place, beginning to heal, to recover.

"Kathleen, are you ok lass? You've gone quite pale."

"Oh fine, fine. Just nervous I suppose."

"Hey, now then." Jamie strode over taking her firmly in his arms he kissed her. "They are going to love you Kathleen."

Jamie directed as Kitty drove, the roads twisted and turned. Although new roads had been added to Skye. Straighter and wider with cats eyes and white lines, they looked out of place next to the old road abandoned winding and wiggling off to the side. The terrain demanded a lot of Pimples as he bounced and hopped around the bends.

The land now was bleaker - but the joy to Kitty was its very remoteness, and therein lay its beauty. The brown and mauves Kitty knew would soon be a mass of heather and she couldn't wait. She had only seen Scotland before in the spring, and although plenty were ready to warn of the midges she was longing to see the heather.

The first sign that they had reached their destination was a pair of enormous stone pillars. Each one a good four-foot square and twelve foot high. They were bejewelled by white, green and yellow lichen. Looking as ancient as the rocks around them, they obviously had been here a very long time. Each pillar supported an elaborate cast iron gate. Arched spikes at the top, the body of each gate a mass of intertwined vines with fruit and flowers and a large oval crest in the centre.

Kitty slowed and admired the delicate pattern, and determined not to knock into them she manoeuvred Pimples carefully through. Not a good first impression she thought and smiled ruefully.

"Alright?" Jamie watched her face intently.

"Ummum." Kitty replied through gritted teeth.

"You know I have never brought anyone home before… not since Rosie. But that was different she grew up with me… but not, never as a man." The realisation was dawning on Jamie now, Kitty glanced over at him – he was doing a good impersonation of pale himself now.

"Thanks, no pressure then, I really wish I'd gone home to change first."

"No we are fine… you are more than fine."

The drive swept around a large lawn, one side edged with large Rhododendrons. Large stately trees obscured the view of the house and Kitty wondered when they were ever to get to it. When it finally came into sight she took her foot from the accelerator.

"Woah!"

Three storeys high, the grey walls and dark slate roof were brightened by white painted windows. Eight tall sash windows across and three high. To the left a smaller two-storey building extended half the size again, and where the two met a tall round tower with a conical roof. As they approached, Kitty headed for the central porch. Heavily detailed stone pillars supported a flat square roof offering protection for horse or carriage. Above this, straining her eyes to make out the detail, carved into the stone was the family crest, its details picked out in gold that sparkled in the sun.

Kitty was literally speechless and motionless as she tried to process all she saw. Jamie laughed quietly to himself as he walked around and opened her door and turned off the ignition. Still in silence he guided her to her feet. Taking her damp hand he led them along the front of the building. They crunched their way across the gravel to the far right of the frontage, through an arched Burgundy gate surrounded by a wall twice the height of Jamie.

Looking around Kitty hesitated to admire. The walled garden was the size of a football pitch. Encased on three sides by a round-topped wall that supported skeletons of roses and other climbers. On the far wall hunkered down in the shelter of the stone was a long line of white glass houses. Paths of gravel dissected the beds and no room was given over to lawn, the soil weed free and showing early signs of cultivation and the promise of many and varied shoots.

"You like to garden?" Jamie watched her face, as she took in all before her in obvious wonder.

"Well I've only ever dabbled, but I had hoped to do it more now I've moved up here."

"Well ye could'na ask for a more willing adviser, it's my mothers passion."

"I can see that."

"Come on!"

The back door opened into a boot room. Not a small excuse for a couple of pairs of wellies but a room half the size of Kitty's whole house. The stone floor was ancient, the step and first stone worn over decades if not centuries of tread. The ceiling was lined with foot square beams with an array of hooks. Kitty didn't stop to dwell on their function. A long run of pegs on the far wall held jackets and coats, all the colours of the land Kitty thought, tweeds and greens. A mass of boots and wellies underneath.

Scanning quickly as Jamie led her on through the door at the far corner into the kitchen. The cold functionality of one room immediately changed on entering the warm heart-like greeting of this kitchen. Three huge windows reached up to the cavernous ceiling. The central focus was the sprawling pine table. Jugs, bowls and kitchen clutter dotted about its top. Like the floor, years of use had curved and rounded its surface.

The original range was black and imposing. Kitty's hand traced along its mantle high above her head. Wondering if it was still in use, Kitty darting eyes found the Aga – the biggest one she had ever seen and tucked in the corner a tiny looking modern – well 1970's cooker and a large old microwave.

"Woah, you could feed an army from here!"

Jamie laughed loudly, "Well they did in the war, the house was taken over by the home office – it was full of soldiers. Don't get dad started on that tale though lass, less ye want to be up till the wee hours."

"Oh how fascinating." Jamie squeezed her hand and led her out through the hallway via a long corridor with doors all closed leading off both sides. Opening into the main hall Kitty attempted to get her bearings and realised she now stood the other side of the front porch door.

There were too many details to take in, but the most imposing was the staircase. Heavy oak, the wood had been polished and worn to its current honey warm colour. The intricately carved newel post stood as big as Kitty herself. The stairs would accommodate five or six abreast, they rose and divided at a landing to turn and turn again back on itself. Everything here was old – not twenty years or forty years but timeless. Furniture that had passed shabby and become antique, rips, wear and faded colours become intrinsic rather than unfortunate.

An imposing winged armchair sat by a large round table with an old blue and white vase filled with a mass of daffodils. Kitty let her fingers trace over the highly polished mahogany and stopped to smell the cheerful yellow faces.

"Ock, James dear, there you are."

Kitty jumped at the silent entrance of a plump woman in her sixties, tight curly greying hair and a ruddy complexion.

"Ock, well and this will be your young lassie, Aye she's bonnie, bonnie!"

Jamie leant forward to kiss the beaming woman. "Aye Maggie, this is Kathleen, Kathleen - Maggie Magee, housekeeper extraordinaire. The Stewart families' own Mrs Doubtfire!"

"Oh away wi ya. Well welcome lass, lovely to meet ya." Kitty put out a hand, Maggie grabbed it and pulled her in for a squishy hug – not what Kitty had expected, but that wasn't to say unwelcome.

"Aye, aye Malcolm said she was bonnie, and from the south he tells us."

"Yes Wimbledon, South London."

"Aye, but you'll be staying? You've no mind to go back and take our wee James now?" Although smiling throughout Kitty was in no doubt this was a threat and not an idle one.

"No, no I've bought a house, here to stay." Kitty realised she was sounding like a child trying to defend herself.

"Well good, good! Away un feed yen sels, your mother and father are already in the dining room."

"Thanks Maggie, what is for supper?"

"Lamb and tatties."

"Brilliant!" Jamie took Kitty's hand once more and led the way down another corridor, lined with portraits she assumed were ancient relatives. The door creaked ominously as he pushed it open. Once inside a slim blonde woman with Jamie's green eyes rose from her chair and stood arms outstretched.

"James darling, we were just going to start. Welcome, and this young lady must be?"

"Mother this is Kathleen, Kathleen Harris, and my mother Maureen." Maureen took a firm hold of Kitty shoulders, looked seriously at her for a second then pecked her gently on the cheek.

"And thi..." Jamie waited as footsteps grew closer and the door creaked again, "This is my father Dougal." Maureen let go and Kitty spun to see Jamie's father fast approaching. This time holding her at arms length he took his time to examine Jamie's companion. Feeling the flush in her face burn Kitty was relieved when his cool lips finally brushed them with two kisses.

"Well James, you've found ya sel a fine wee lass here. Welcome Kathleen." It didn't go unnoticed that he knew her name before Jamie had had the opportunity to introduce her. She wondered from whom he had had his information. Jamie placed a reassuring arm around her pulling her to his side, Kitty breathed.

"Come, come, have a seat, Maggie will not thank us if her supper is left to go cold."

Jamie escorted Kitty to her chair and pulled it out for her, waiting gently he pushed it in as she sat. Maureen watched on with palpable pride and love. He obviously learnt from the best Kitty noted, as Dougal did the same for his wife.

The table was highly polished, almost like glass; with seats enough for twenty people their four places occupied one end. Dougal at the head and Maureen to his right. Kitty's sat opposite his mother and between father and son. The cutlery was large embossed silver, which felt cold and heavy in Kitty small hands. The plates and tureens were gold rimmed, tarnished and worn by varying degrees. Kitty drank in every detail and traced facets of the cut glass wine glass as she sipped a very smooth red.

The four sat for a few quiet minutes, and Kitty feared she had missed some form of etiquette and they were waiting for her. Relieved when Maggie entered the room, the family picked up their linen serviettes and draped them in their laps. Keen to not embarrass herself Kitty slowly copied. Without discussion Maggie proceeded to carry the serving dishes around the table, first the lamb then an endless array of steaming vegetables.

Kitty had only ever seen this in films or period dramas but there was no pretence or state here, just relaxed routine. There was none of the haughtiness she would have expected. The genuine warmth between the master of the house and his employee was obvious, and she joked as she pottered around the room. Not a starched collar or glove to be seen, but a very comfy sweater and a tweed skirt.

Maggie's chattering relaxed all the party. "Now you'll no be eating like a wee bird lass." Kitty was struck by the authoritative tone – "You wouldn't want to mess with Maggie Magee," Jamie winked at her.

"So Kathleen tell us about yourself dear?"

"Oh um…" the mouthful proving very reluctant to being swallowed, finally. "I'm from Wimbledon, but I've lived in Kent for the past few years... I wanted a change and sold up and bought Tide's Reach and well… I've been here for a few weeks and it's flown by."

"Uh huh… and are you married?"

"Mother!" Jamie reaction was swift and fierce.

"It's a fair question laddie, the lassie wears a ring." Dougal raised a pacifying hand to his son keeping his voice calm and soothing. Kitty looked at Jamie with a pitiable expression.

"I dunna ken ye need to interrogate her." Jamie spoke through clenched teeth, his skin on his neck burning red.

"We are just curious James, it's the first time you've brought a young lady home. Would you expect us not to be inquisitive?" His mother spoke quietly but assertively.

"Can I tell them?" Jamie leaned and whispered in Kitty's ear. She didn't mind them knowing but had only recently managed to say it out loud to Jamie and certainly didn't want to do it now and he knew that, she nodded.

"Kathleen came here because her husband died last year, having lost both her parents and her only brother she wanted a new start," Jamie forced the words out and his cheeks were flushed with indignation and annoyance, "Are you satisfied Mother?"

Kitty pushed some peas around her plate with the oversized fork, and was shocked when the scraping of a chair resulted in Maureen rushing around the table to her.

"Oh dear sweet girl, I'm so sorry, how rude and thoughtless of me." Maureen hugged her from behind and planted a loud motherly kiss on the top of her head. "James I blame you." Jamie dodged out of the way in practiced avoidance of her swiping napkin.

"Why me? Why is it my fault? You've embarrassed Kathleen,

and you wonder why I haven't brought anyone home." Jamie was still angry. Maureen stroked Kitty's hair absent-mindedly as she looked at her son. Unaccustomed to seeing this level of emotion from her son she smiled over at her husband. Dougal filled the silence.

"Ye mustn't mind us lass, James is very special to us and we knew ya had swept him off his feet – and well, being the strapping lad he is that's no small feat. Our lad was very upset a few weeks ago and we were all very worried."

Kitty looked up at him and the warmth of a father's face flickered memories of her own dear dad, and she could have cried.

"Have ye quite finished mother?" Jamie still frowned at his mother who left the back of Kitty chair and ruffled Jamie's hair.

"We only ask because we care James, and if Kathleen will forgive us we will say no more on the matter."

All eyes on Kitty who was clenching every muscle trying to halt the tears, taking a large slug of wine she nodded. The meal then settled into light polite conversation. Both parents tactfully now didn't engage Kitty in conversation whilst she recovered her composure. Jamie ate one handed and held Kitty's hand until she squeezed it to announce she was once again rallied.

Dougal was the first to talk directly to her and chatted quietly about her previous occupation. Dougal's hair was a faded bleached version of his son's. He had a mellow voice, and Kitty wondered if he was a singer as it was very musical. He had a habit of pushing his round glasses up onto the bridge of his nose when he was concentrating. Unfortunately he used his middle finger and would hold it there if he was intent on the conversation. It helped lift any residual tension as Kitty tried hard not to laugh at the gesture. Kitty also noticed that the arm of his glasses were held together with tape, - the lord of the manor with Blue Peter repairs to his specs, Kitty liked him all the more for it.

Maureen was obviously delighted at Kitty's compliments on the garden. Radiant at the thought of helping Kitty with her own small plot, offering to come and help once the building work was done.

Well aided by the wine, everyone relaxed and by the time dessert was over Kitty felt very comfortable in their company – all earlier awkwardness gone.

"You're welcome to stay the night James," Maureen offered.

"Thank you mother, but we will go home," adding quickly and

noticing his parents exchanged glance, "I must get Kathleen home to hers."

Please god don't ask if I have a bed there, Kitty thought. Maggie brought in a tray of coffee and set it down in front of Maureen.

"If that's all I'll turn in."

"Aye thank you Maggie."

"Bye Maggie and thanks for supper." Jamie smiled sweetly and Maggie patted his shoulder.

"Ock, you're welcome, glad to see you and your wee lassie." Kitty smiled back, she felt very young here, like the trauma of the previous years was melting away.

"Well we'd best be heading off" Jamie stood and helped Kitty push her chair back and offering a hand, soon slipped his hand around her waist and pulled her close.

"Oh James, really, we were just getting acquainted." Maureen seemed genuinely disappointed at their going.

"There will be plenty of time mother. We're not going anywhere."

"Oh I certainly hope not, it's been a delight Kathleen." Dougal walked around and embraced her gently. Jamie reluctantly released her and went to say his goodbyes to his mum. Dougal held her head to his chest with a large Stewart hand, and it felt a very fatherly touch. Whispering in her ear, "I can't remember seeing James so happy, we are very pleased to meet you, come here whenever you would like."

Leaning back she smiled up into his pale blue eyes framed by pale gingery blonde lashes and brows, blue versions of his sons. His hair though greying, still had bright flecks of the red of his youth.

"I didn't ever imagine meeting anyone – it was never something I thought about but I am very happy and very glad to have met your son." Dougal leant down and kissed her forehead.

Maureen next embraced her and kissed her cheek.

"I'm sorry to have upset you my dear, I hope you will forgive me." The entreaty so heartfelt Kitty immediately nodded.

"Of course, forgotten."

"Bless you, welcome to our family Kathleen." Then directed at her son, "Bring her back very soon James."

"Aye, aye." Jamie said absent-mindedly as he bid his father farewell. Kitty was surprised to see the two men embrace, a big squeezing hug and both kissed each other on the cheek, and the two men had the same frame. Looking at them Kitty thought the last time she had seen a father kiss his son with such unashamed love was her own red haired brother.

Leaving by the front door Kitty pushed the keys into Jamie palm. "Will you drive please?"

"Aye, I would'na let ya anyways, how much wine did my father ply ye with?" Kitty managed a smile and looked wistfully at Dougal and Maureen. Standing behind her Dougal rested his head on her shoulder and wrapped his arms around his wife's waist. Waving and smiling broadly.

Kitty held it in until they were clear of the large gates; the tears rolled quickly down her face. Turning her head to the window she tried desperately to hold in the sobs that clambered to be unleashed, but was powerless to stem the tears and they bounced onto her hands.

"Well that could have gone better, but apart from mother – the grand inquisitor as she is known in these parts." Jamie chuckled and turned to Kitty, getting no response he reached out in the darkness and found the tense bundle of damp fingers.

"Kathleen, what is it? Kathleen, WHAT IS IT?" Look at me" As Kitty turned her head and saw his worried face in the dim dashboards light all resolve was lost, and the sobs escaped and she buried her face in her hands.

"My bloody mother, oh I will kill her! How could she upset ye like this Kathleen... I'm so sorry." Anger replaced by sympathy and concern. Concentrating on the road but all the time keeping a hand on her knee, Jamie pulled over at the first suitable space. With swift action and muttering in Gaelic Jamie cut the engine, released both their seat belts and was hugging a shuddering Kitty to him.

"Hush... hush... hush." There was little else to do or say. Kitty for her part could no sooner hush than fly to the moon. Her sobs tore at her throat and pounded in her head but she was powerless to stop. Jamie held her close and rubbed her back, legs and arms. He was helpless and her agonies cut at his own heart and he detested the feeling.

"I can'na believe she could be so cruel." Kitty struggled to speak now, holding a trembling hand to her throat.

"Come on, come here lass." Helping her out of her seat he then half lifted her into the back and sat her on the bench seat. Frantically searching Jamie finally found a carton of apple juice and fumbling with too big fingers finally managed to insert the straw. Holding back Kitty hair he encouraged her to drink and kneeling before her stroked her thighs and looking, full of concern at her.

"It's not her, it... wasn't her."

"What then, father did'na say anything did he... I ken I saw him whispering to ye?"

"No, no, god no... he's lovely."

"Oh aye, suppose he is." Looking puzzled now that only left Maggie, "Then what ails thee lass?"

"They are lovely, loving parents... it's the first time... since losing my parents – my dad. When you kissed your dad I could see Tommy... he had red hair and I was reminded..." but Kitty could say no more and Jamie rocked her as a new wave of grief washed over her. After several minutes she took some more of the offered drink and continued.

"I felt like an orphan there with your family. Worse than I ever have before. Like all the ghosts of my family had finally moved on and left me – left me all alone – bereft!" Kitty clung to Jamie and could feel the damp patch she was leaving on his shoulder. "When I lost Tommy I had my parents. When dad went I had my mum, then too soon mum was gone. But I had Stephen and for some reason never expected to lose him. But they are all gone and... and being with your family I suddenly thought about all that could have been if my family had survived." For the first time Jamie felt jealous of Stephen, was it even possible to be jealous of a dead man? What did Kitty wish for? Would she have Stephen back in place of him?

"I dunna ken how to sooth ya Kathleen, how can I make it better? Are ya not close to Stephen's family?"

"No they aren't family to me... I'm totally alone." Kitty began to sob again.

"Now I hate to point out the bleeding obvious to ya lass but there happens to be a large Scotsman on his knees before ye, and if you'll have me I've a clan the size of a small army that will take ya to their hearts – not to mention siblings, one of each just to annoy ye."

Kitty laughed through the tears and hugged him to her chest.

"I'm sorry Jamie what must you think of me?"

"I think I am at very great risk of being very much in love with ye Mrs Harris and only wished ye did'na have to suffer so much loss and heartache and pain."

Kitty clung to him and finally settled, they had sat for over half an hour and Kitty had exhausted her supply of tears. Helped by the pounding heart Kitty's breathing slowed.

"Take me home Jamie?" He leant down and kissed her head, and a long last sigh let out the last of her angst. Rebuckled in the front seat they completed the journey to Jamie's cottage, his hand on her knee.

In the bathroom Kitty splashed cold water on her swollen face. Jamie bought her a tumbler half full of whiskey, expensive, smooth and golden - smarting but then soothing her ragged throat.

"Shall I run us a bath?"

"Yes please."

Whether it was Kitty's lack of a bathroom, and the new level of appreciation that brings, or, that it had from the start, been their safe place to talk, Jamie and Kitty's relationship was founded on an inordinate amount of time in the bathroom. Kitty would have laughed at these thoughts, but now, at this moment she stood frozen in place.

Once ready Jamie undressed her. Standing like a child she stepped out of her trousers and knickers, unbidden and silent. Similarly relieved of her top and bra. Kitty stood hugging her arms around her chest, looking every inch the orphan she was. A memory of the twelve year old told her only brother was dead. The fourteen year old winded by the unbelievable fact she would never again see her beloved father. Still a child at twenty six when her mother was taken and even at twenty eight as a widow – alone - totally alone.

Jamie placed firm large hands around her ribs and guided her to the bath. Stepping into the water she was too dulled to flinch against it being ever so slightly too hot. Pushing her down by her shoulders she sat and hugged her knees. Jamie took one hand and placed the glass in it wrapping each finger onto it. Sipping and thawing as the scorching heat trickled into her stomach.

Jamie sat on his usual throne in silence watching her. After ten minutes she relaxed, the water and whiskey did their job Kitty turned blood shot eyes to Jamie and managed a weak smile.

"Would you get in?"

"Do you want me to?"

"Yes please."

Jamie shed his clothes and stepped in at the tap end of the bath – always the gentleman! Edging in slowly so as to not overflow the water he lifted her legs by the ankle and rested them on his chest.

Resting his feet either side of her hips he rubbed her prune like feet.

Kitty relaxed further from the delicious foot rub and let her legs splay and her head rest back on the edge of the bath.

"Do ya want to talk about it lass?"

"Not now, Jamie one day... one day I will tell you all about my family. I'll bore you with photos and stories." A far distant expression returned to her face.

"Whenever you're ready."

Jamie kissed her foot then continued rubbing.

"I'm sorry I'm a bit mad – it's not me – not really."

The whiskey was drained and the water had cooled. Jamie carefully exited the bath, pausing long enough to kiss the tip of her nose. Hurriedly drying himself he took the empty glass from her hand and reached under her arms and helped her to her feet.

"I feel so pathetic, I'm sorry!"

"No hush, hush now lass. Ye have right enough for sorrow but let's get ye to bed."

Jamie dried her, his large hands clumsy and fumbling but Kitty, still in the shadow of oblivion didn't seem to mind.

"Do ya want anything before bed, tea?"

"No, just you."

Jamie pulled back the quilt and naked they climbed in. Lying behind her Jamie pulled her towards him, trying hard to avoid any contact with her breasts and feeling any sexual contact would be a grossly inappropriate given her fragile state. It was no small challenge, every fibre of him wanted her but he concentrated earnestly on her loss and sadness to prevent him being ungallant.

Kitty's breathing had slowed and Jamie had hoped she had fallen asleep, but she turned and looked up at him.

"Please make love to me?" her voice frail and faltering.

"Oh... no Kathleen." He stroked her face; tears rose quickly and filled her eyes.

"Why... am I too hideous?" Jamie laughed that she could think such a thing.

"Are ye sure ya want to? You seem so terribly sad lass."

"That's why I want to... I want to feel alive. I want you, here, with me... to make me feel alive."

Jamie kissed her and moved on top of her. The tears continued to fall, cascading onto her hair and the pillow. Jamie moved very slowly, and constantly kissed her lightly, checking she still wanted this, whispering in her ear how much he loved her. Kitty's shuddering release came quickly and she clung to him. Despite his desperate urge to continue he lay still holding her tight beneath him and once again using monumental mind over matter, thought of anything and everything that would make his arousal dissipate.

Kitty clung to his neck when finally he rolled off, lying by her side. They lay there in silence with every inch possible touching.

"Thank you... I'm sorry." Kitty mumbled and was soon asleep.

28

Rafters Are On

Kitty woke with a pounding head, sore throat and mucky eyes. She lay, not wanting to move and disturb the wonderful man at her side. Jamie lay on his back, naked chest above the sheets. One arm was crooked around his head and the other across his abdomen. How on earth had she been lucky enough to find this beautiful man? The tight hairs on his chest shone in the dawn light and she checked herself from reaching out and touching them.

Remembering the night before Kitty climbed gently from the bed and closed the bathroom door behind her. It was as she suspected, reviewing the reflection in the mirror – she looked really crap!

Though still sad, the desperate loneliness was gone and the sun through the window promised a good day. Tiptoeing down the stairs Kitty pottered in the snug kitchen. Two large mugs and thick slices of toast topped with scrambled egg ready. Trying to complete the task as noiselessly as possible, whilst hunting for a tray she sent a pile of baking trays onto the floor, failing miserably. Kitty heard almost simultaneously thundering footsteps from above and the gruff call of her name.

"Jamie, Jamie... it's alright, go back to bed I'll be up in just a minute."

Pulling up outside her home the black cloud had definitely lifted. Daffodils were now beginning to open their faces and much to Kitty's delight, not just plain dark yellow ones but doubles, white, and orange. Malcolm hadn't arrived yet and Kitty and Jamie walked hand in hand around the site discussing the build and all the small details Kitty planned for its completion.

Opening the storeroom Kitty let out a very high squeal of delight.

"Jamie, look, look! It's come – when did it get here?"

"Must have been Malcolm or Trevor before they went home yesterday... what is it?"

"Tee hee!" Kitty beamed and jumped on the spot, "My bed!"

"Ock, well, whatever it is, it's grand to see ye so happy."

"Can we get it out and put it up... please, please?" like an overly excited child now.

"Aye, but I have issue wi ye purchase Kathleen, why would ye buy a single bed?"

"Well firstly it's a day bed and can act as a sofa when the office is done and ... well... in my wildest dreams I never expected to be sharing my bed with anyone, ever again."

"Oh... well better a single than no bed, I'm sure we could share it, even if not for sleeping." Both giggling they raced to unpack. Team work with a touch of competition thrown in, the job was soon finished. From the stack of boxes at the back of the room Kitty shook out new duck egg blue sheets and quilt cover. Jamie waited for her to tuck in the last of her corners then rugby tackled a squealing Kitty onto the mattress.

"Aye this is plenty big enough!" pinning her beneath him, her protestations and protests mute against his strength.

"Ye dune waste any time, I'll give ye that James Stewart!" Trevor's frame filled the doorway and Kitty quickly turned to face the back wall.

"Aye if ye keep that up lass you'll be like ma Beth in no time, any chance of a brew?"

"Be off wi ya!" Jamie growled at him before dropping his full weight on her and kissing her eagerly. When finally she was freed, "What does he mean about his Beth?"

"Take no notice Kathleen."

"No, tell me."

"Trevor and Beth have been married eight months and, well, their bairn is due in four weeks."

"Oh."

Jamie jumped off the bed and whistling, set about making the tea. Kitty was far too comfy and hadn't done testing the new mattress. Jamie stopped mid whistle, retaining the small o of his lips. Kitty smile soon morphed into a look of fear.

"Jamie... what is it? What's wrong?"

Jamie head turned slowly, his body even slower until he stood tea bags in hand to face her. He spoke slowly and quietly.

"Well... this has all been a bit of a whirlwind romance..."

"Yes."

"All this sex."

"Yes."

"No... um... this implant of yours." Slowly but the urgently, "It's still there right? I don't know how these things work."

Kitty lay back on the crisp sheets and laughed. But the shocked Jamie stood rooted to the spot and taking pity on him, Kitty stood and hugged him around the waist.

"It's like the pill, but an implant. I didn't move all this way just to steal your virtue and get myself pregnant." Looking a little affronted Kitty pulled back.

"Well... do you know, I don't even think I would mind if you ended up like Beth." Jamie quickly kissed her shocked face.

With four strong men and a willing lackey, work moved on a pace. The roof trusses for the extension were added by lunchtime. Kitty stood on the front wall and photographed Trevor and Jamie constructing the framework for the dormers that would form the windows to the two bedrooms and upstairs toilet.

Malcolm oversaw everything with an eye for fine detail, and Kitty tried to capture every new development. Progress was good and there was talk of soon getting the felt on the roof and the windows in. Three of the workforce retired to their vans as usual and Kitty threw a dustsheet over the bed. Laying her head in Jamie's lap after they had eaten, she closed her eyes as he stroked the long waves of her hair.

"What are you going to do about your friend on Harris? When will you have to go?"

"I phoned him yesterday while that bastard was here." Venom oozing from Jamie

"Oh... you didn't say." Kitty tensed and took her gaze from Jamie's face and looked out the window to the racing clouds, hoping to suppress a flicker of panic.

"Aye well... a lot happened."

Both quiet then in their thoughts until Kitty ventured, "And?"

"I'd promised him, Charlie," resuming his attention on her hair, watching the curls stretch then reshape. "We met when I went to work on the heritage Centre on Harris. He is converting an old school house." Looking down at her Jamie waited for a response but none came so he continued. "I went there recently... ye know when I was... upset with myself. I'd promised him I'd go back. Ya ken I only came back for me brothers' birthday. I had no idea... no clue... you and me, this would happen."

Jamie's mind filled the void of silence with the memory of his recent visit to Harris. His behaviour towards Kitty had been so abhorrent to him, it still haunted him. When he woke the next morning – after the coldest and most uncomfortable night of his life he couldn't face her. In complete turmoil he realised he could face no one. He felt his crimes were etched on his face, and there was no way he could see his parents as he knew what their utter disappointment would be. From an early age he was taught not to hit or retaliate to either of his younger siblings. No matter how vile and annoying Flo was as a child he was never to raise a hand to her.

But no one could have been more disappointed or upset by his actions than Jamie himself. Not only that he could have been rough and ungentlemanly, but with Kathleen – of all people. He had never felt the strength of emotion he did for her, it consumed him. The fear that he may have lost her, before he ever had the opportunity to really know her, terrified him.

Driving stiff and shaking with cold back to his cottage he remembered stumbling – probably still intoxicated, and hurriedly packing a bag. The need to flee, to get far away, but where to go? It was then that he remembered Charlie, dependable, hard working, quiet Charlie. Jamie knew he could throw himself into working on the old school house with little questions asked. He would have food and board and try to forget all about the fascinating blonde woman who had made him behave in such a terrible manner.

"It didn't really help – all I could think about was you." Jamie smiled sadly.

At the same time Kitty recalled the time he was gone and the sense of emptiness she had felt. Now the ember of fear smouldered within her and she couldn't trust her voice not to betray her fears. Could she be on her own now, she really didn't know? Did she like being so needy, so dependent, so reliant on a man she had known for a matter of weeks? - she did not!

"I phoned Charlie and explained. He was fine but I feel I've let him down."

"Jamie you must go if you need to… I hate the fact that I have turned into this gibbering wreck… I'm sure I'd be ok."

"You're not a gibbering wreck and I don't want to leave you."

"Good, so when do you leave?" Kitty smiled up at him now and they both chuckled.

"If you would be ok I would like to go next week, just for a few days and you could come with me. It's a truly beautiful place; I'd love to show it to you Kathleen."

"Oh well, I'll think about it but I don't want to cramp your style."

Gazing up at him Jamie traced the outlines of her face with his fingertips.

"Ock, Mrs Harris you could never cramp my style, and ye do have a very profound effect on me." Kitty reached up taking his hand and kissing it.

"I know, the feeling is mutual."

Whistling outside announced the lunch break was over, and Kitty sat on the edge of the bed and stretched. The afternoon was very productive and Kitty delighted as the felt on the roof transformed it back from a collection of walls to a house. Battens were swiftly nailed in place, and Kitty decided she didn't like to watch Jamie high on the roof so busied herself photographing and tidying the store. Jeff was busy barrowing what seemed an endless supply of stones to fill the void of the main two rooms. A damp proof membrane and insulation topped with concrete screed and it would then be ready for the under-floor heating and DaDaDA! The slates could be reinstated.

By five o'clock tools were being stored, and backs straightened and stretched. Once back at Jamie's a long bath helped ease the rigours of the day. Jamie's errands whilst avoiding Donald included shopping. Kitty continued to prepare spaghetti Bolognaise as Jamie replaced her in the bath. Jamie came back into the kitchen as Kitty served the salad and popped the garlic bread in the oven, his hair wet and combed back.

Sitting feet entwined they ate leisurely and finished two bottles of rich full bodied red wine. They talked and laughed and thankfully no tears were shed. Kitty shared in the briefest detail how each of her family had died. Jamie held her hand and tried his best to sympathise but only having lost two elderly grandparents he was well aware his experiences paled into insignificance.

The evening was warm and Kitty took off her fleece as the log burner glowed. Jamie had insisted on lighting it before dinner and his motives were soon clear. As the light faded Jamie closed the curtains and slowly without taking his eyes off Kitty, undressed in front of the fire. Running his hands through his now dry hair he looked truly magnificent and laying the tartan blanket on the floor he held out his hand for her to join him.

Kitty drained the very last of her wine and went to stand in front of him. She couldn't ever remember stripping like this for Stephen, and her mouth dried and she was suddenly very self-conscious.

Jamie, not similarly inhibited, moved quickly around the room. Sensing her timidity he turned off the lights and lit the two candles on the mantle place. Standing back in front of the log burner Jamie's eyes were intent and his breathing quickened. Kitty began to shed layers, eyes locked and hearts pounding.

Kitty pushed up from the barrel of a chest under her, and shook her hair back from her face where it clung to the moist skin and groaned.
"Bloody hell, Jamie."
"Happy?"
"I just don't understand."
"What... Kathleen?" he reached up and tucked the stubborn hair behind her ear. "God ye are beautiful."
"Why is it so... fantastic?"
"I don't know, is it so?" but he didn't finish.
"What?" Kitty wanted to know.
"No, no it doesn't seem ... well right."
"Please Jamie I think you can ask me anything." Kitty bent and kissed him tenderly on the lips.
"Well, is it... well it seems a bit disrespectful but... how is it different to your husband?" Looking into the soft green eyes Kitty thought how to answer. Jamie added, "Its just I have so little to compare it to – I always knew my heart was never in it before. I wonder if that is why it is so different... for me anyway it is."
"I loved my husband, very much... and we were happy and the sex... well, it was good. I thought it was good at the time – but like you I had nothing to compare it to." Kitty lay down on the blanket and cuddled up on the side of his chest, "But I never craved it, never thought about it during the day and counted down the time till I could be alone with him."
"Do you think about me then, us, during the day?"
"God yes!"
"Me too." Jamie's laughter rumbled through his chest and Kitty hugged him tighter. "If only my family weren't building ya house I ken there would be no stopping us."
"As much as I'd like to I don't know how we'd survive – sex never took it out of me like this does. I don't know why it is like it is but long may it continue." Kissing again it was nearly an hour later when they finally walked hand in hand to bed.

29

All Glass and Stainless Steel

The day had arrived, and Kitty was as indecisive as she climbed into the back seat of Hamish and Claire's car as she had been when first asked by Donald to dinner. Glad at least that her car companions had collected her – she would aim to stay close to Claire this evening.

Jamie's face had betrayed his emotion as he left Kitty's house for his own. It had been agreed that she would ask the GP's to collect and drop her from Tide's Reach. It was to be their first night apart and Kitty knew it was a wrench for both of them. Kitty reasoned, albeit unconvincingly, that it would be good for them both. A good dry run for Jamie returning to Harris.

The winding roads and smooth undulations of the car only increased the nausea she had held in the pit of her stomach since waving goodbye to Jamie, fake smile in place.

"You'll love Donald's house, he designed it himself." Hamish's eyes met hers in the rear view mirror.

"Oh yes he told me," fake smile in use again.

"He's a great cook Kathleen – I think this evening's invite is more for your benefit than ours, but I would never turn down a Donald dinner." Kitty couldn't help herself and laughed at this comment.

They turned from the main road, Kitty looking eagerly around the landscape. The sheep roamed freely here with legs too thin to support the wobbly, obviously pregnant bellies. They were deceptively agile and would trot out of the way as Hamish drove unconcerned towards them. Kitty wondered how long she would have to live here before they didn't worry her terribly. She looked, and had yet to see a dead one by the roadside so hoped it was a rare occurrence.

Two large boulders marked the entrance to the single-track lane, curving steeply back in the direction they had come. At first Kitty could only see a collection of derelict crofter's cottages, but as the road petered out her eye followed the well worn path – resting then on a grey expanse of slate.

"Ingenious isn't it, you'd never know it was there." Claire had been watching Kitty's face, triumphant now at Kitty open mouthed astonishment.

"Well... it's... is it buried?"

"Yes, dug out of the side of the hill, ecologically very green." Hamish turned off the engine and swiftly stood opening Kitty's door.

"Bugger to build mind you, but they wouldn't let him build up traditionally because of the old crofts, and there is an ancient chapel and an even older stone circle up on the high ground behind, and it would have spoilt the view to the sea."

Single file they walked in step behind Claire, walking inches from the curved worn front step of each of the sizable crofts. Five in all, the first four roofless, but Kitty stopped in front of the last to marvel at the roof. Moss impregnated thatch, ancient, green and pitted. It was weighed down by a motley selection of twine and incongruous blue nylon rope holding heavy stones at varying heights from the floor. The battered door was closed, forcing the inquisitive Kitty to peer into one of the two windows on tiptoe.

Pressing her forehead to the edges of her hands she could see the blurred interior through filthy glass. A small black stove flanked by a small wooden table and kitchen chair and on the other side a crooked looking brass bed.

"Does anyone live here?" An incredulous Kitty pulled her gaze away worried now someone might.

"No, no not any more. After years of trying we finally got old Duncan to move out." Claire answered.

"But up until recently someone did?"

"Aye, tried for ages to get him to agree to move to an old peoples home but until he broke his hip he wouldn't hear of it, no shifting him." Hamish smiled back at Claire.

"Happy now though – he loves the bath, can't get him out. Spent all his life without one, he's making up for lost time." Claire laughed.

"Did he have any water?" Kitty traced her finger over the warped glass of the window.

"No just the sea and a stream for drinking, and well, probably a hole in the ground."

"Oh, no wonder he loves his new life."

Smiling the trio headed off down the path. From an unprepossessing first view, Kitty couldn't help but be impressed as she now stood in front of Donald's house. Two storeys cut out of the slope fronted entirely with glass. As they walked along the frontage towards the door at the far side, Donald mirrored their pace on the other side of the glass.

"Welcome!" Donald smiled warmly, shook Hamish's hand and greeted both women with a half embrace and a kiss on the cheek.

"Oh Donald it smells lovely." Claire handed over a bottle of red and Kitty reprimanded herself for coming empty handed.

"Well come in, come, in. Kitty would you like a tour?"

"Oh, yes, yes that would be great." A little surprised by her own enthusiasm but her inquisitive nature getting the better of her.

"Claire, Hamish, have a seat, there are olives and bread on the table and a Chablis 59 in the wine fridge if you don't mind doing the honours?"

"Of course Don," Hamish slapped the architect on the back and led his wife to the dining area.

Donald's hand gestured to the stairs whilst the other touched Kitty lightly on her back. Regretting the tour now, Kitty skipped up the stairs. Although relieved to be free from his touch Kitty looked back at the smug smirk on his face and worried her actions had merely been interpreted as eagerness.

The house was very clinical, - stainless steel handrails and glass edged metal stairs had a distinctly industrial feel. The landing was long and barren with light oak doors leading from it, but with no windows Kitty guessed they were against the back of the hill. Opening the first door, Donald still with his hand on the handle, gestured for Kitty to lead the way in. A large bedroom dressed in shades of beige, the cushions on the huge bed, lamps and curtains. The en suite with its large cream stone tiles was spacious and spotless. Both rooms sharing the uninterrupted view of the rocky black shore and sea until it blurred with the sky.

"This is one of the spare rooms, yours for the asking Kathleen – if you ever get bored with that van of yours."

Donald leaned down to her and smiled, and not for the first time she was reminded of the jungle book snake.

"How many rooms do you have?" Kitty's cheerful question belied her true emotion as she skirted around him, back to the door and the landing.

"Um, two spares – and I mean it anytime!"

I bet you do, Kitty thought to herself.

"Another I use as a study, and then of course my room." There was something in his voice that unsettled Kitty. The other spare room was exhibited from its doorway. The study was the only room with any warmth or character. Cluttered shelves with objects and books showing cheerful flashes of colour. A large battered oak drawings chest added warmth and personality.

The last door at the end of the corridor filled Kitty with a little shudder of fear. Ceremoniously Donald pushed the door ajar and again invited Kitty to enter with long outstretched fingers.

"Had we better get back down to the others?"

"Oh you must see this Kathleen, I am most proud of this room!" Kitty's jaw clenched and she forced a smile and walked in. This room was stark with white walls and bedding and it felt cold.

"All the clutter is hidden here." Donald pushed on the mirrored wall of glass and a door opened, suits, shirts all immaculately arranged concealed there in.

"The en suite is here."

Kitty hesitated, but knew she was merely putting off the inevitable and with the best smile she could muster she followed.

"The bath and shower are designed for two." Kitty had already noticed that, twin sinks; large double-ended free standing bath and a walk in shower enclosure you could have got a small family in. Oh how his young secretary would love to luxuriate and preen in here. Kitty regretted the genuine smile this elicited, and the fact that Donald saw it – could she send him any more mixed messages?

Walking back into the bedroom Donald sat on the foot of his bed, "Join me Kathleen."

"Oh shit NO!" was her mental retort but she opted to sit as far from him as possible. Thankful for the super king sized bed, the view was quite transfixing.

"You see this is what I wake up to every morning." And there was no denying it was a beautiful view. The evening sun low and large and orange in the sky, its hue tainting everything and reflected in the crests of the small waves on the water.

"It is beautiful." Kitty added quietly.

"Yes" from the corner of her eyes she saw Donald reach across the duvet towards her – her cue – she stood and on the pretext of looking more closely at the view headed for the window.

"You must position your bed like this. The size of your windows is a little limiting, but I think if I raise the bed on a platform you too will be able to sit up in bed and see the best of the view." Had she been too harsh on him, he sounded so genuine now. But then he touched her back again and that was really starting to piss Kitty off now.

"Come on, we will eat and then I will show you the rest of downstairs."

"Oh great." Trying to curb her enthusiasm.

Entering the dining room Kitty smiled over at her doctors, she was very happy to be in their company again.

"About time you two came back, I had to move the olives or Hamish here might have eaten them all." Claire affectionately tut-tutted her husband.

"So Kathleen do you approve?" Claire smiled slyly over the table at Kitty.

"Oh, urm, well of course it's a lovely house Donald." For she could see he too was waiting for her response. Kitty didn't add that she thought it was no home, and she wouldn't want to live in it. Kitty picked at some of the bread, glad Hamish had eaten nearly all the olives, she had never acquired a taste for them and tired of people telling her she would.

Sipping the crisp wine Kitty relaxed and chatted with the Duncan's, updating them on the build. Donald whistled as he ferried bowls of salad, steaming green beans and dauphinoise potatoes. The salmon sat on a bed of watercress, and Donald soon sat and raised his glass in a toast.

"To Kathleen Harris, our newest islander, slainte!"

"Slainte!" they all raised their glasses. Whatever reservations Kitty may have had for Donald the man, there was no disputing Donald the chef.

"Donald this is delicious, thank you." Kitty smiled at him and the furtive glances between the doctors did not go unnoticed. After the main course the plates were cleared, and Donald bought in an individual glass bowls of Cranachan. The mixture of heather honey, whiskey, raspberries, oatmeal, brown sugar and cream was sublime. Resting back in their chairs Kitty was enthralled by the detailed stories of Duncan, and Donald's tales on having the gruff Scotsman as a neighbour.

"He was harmless enough but I can't say I'm sorry he has gone. He didn't really understand boundaries, and would walk in if the door was open. It's rather unnerving when you're eating your breakfast and a great shaggy face is looking in through the window." Every one laughed the easy contented laugh of sated, slightly intoxicated friends. The mood was only dampened for Kitty when Donald insisted on completing the tour.

The kitchen, dining room and lounge were open plan, so Kitty hoped it would be brief anyway. Beyond the kitchen a door opened to the utility room and Kitty was glad of the distraction of the underground source heating system. Donald was effusive on explaining how it worked and the money it had saved him. Returning to the central part of the ground floor, Kitty was heading for her seat when Donald guided her to the back wall of the kitchen, again annoyingly with his hand on her back.

Panelling along the back wall which Kitty assumed concealed cupboards, were slid open to reveal a cavern of a room. Carved from the hillside it led back underground, no windows meant only when the lights were turned on did Kitty see the back recesses. Walking away from her Donald tapped on a small keypad and suddenly the room was bathed in bright blue light.

"Whow!"

"Umm." Donald purred with pride, "This is my indulgence – do you like it?" Donald's voice had lowered a tone, and that and the odd chill in here had Kitty wrapping her arms around herself.

"It's my den; I have a projector and screen for movies, all the usual computer games and boys' toys."

"Oh and what home is complete without a full size snooker table!" Kitty sarcasm was lost on Donald who just gazed around the room he obviously loved. She jumped then, as Donald took hold of her upper arm and turned her to face him.

"You can always come over Kathleen, and I meant what I said you needn't go home tonight. I could take you home tomorrow and you could have a night in a decent bed." Not without a bloody big lock on the door, was Kitty's first thought to the kind offer.

"Oh no, no, thank you."

"Surely you don't prefer the option of your shed or van over all this?" He was frowning now and there was a subtle sulky edge to his voice. Why did she have to tread so carefully around him? She wished her house was finished as she certainly would not be in her current predicament.

"No really it's terribly kind of you," Forcing herself to pat his hand rather than fling it off her arm, "We'd best be getting back to the others. I'm sure Claire and Hamish will need to get back to their babysitter."

"If they need to go, I can drive you home later if you are determined to go home."

Knowing full well that he had matched her for wine tonight she was very relieved to have her excuse.

"Oh, that's true, if we had thought of that earlier – but how many glasses have you had? – no, no I wouldn't hear of it! Risking your licence for me." Phew that was close and she smiled at him now.

"Aye, you are good. Yes I suppose you are right, well next time, next time." Donald trailed off as he turned and led them back to the kitchen.

"Well thank you for a lovely evening and your usual tasty fare, but we really must make a move. Young Moira will be wondering where we are." Kitty was glad to follow Claire's lead and head for their coats. Eager to be safely buckled up and on the road Kitty headed outside first. Once outside the men shook hands and Donald hugged Claire and both got in the front seats. Donald held his hand on Kitty's door handle thwarting her plans to jump in. Donald moved between her and the car, thus obscuring her from the view of the couple in the car, oh crap – was Kitty's thought. Taking her by the upper arms she suppressed the inappropriate nervous giggle that tried to escape.

"It has been delightful, I have wanted to get you here to show you my home since I met you."

"Oh," was all Kitty could come up with in way of an answer; she so desperately wanted to be inside the car.

"I am very glad you moved here Kathleen, and you chose me to work on your project."

"Um," again pathetic!

"I think we could become good friends... or... or even something more."

Oh shit a brick! Every inch of her tensed and she could manage no reply. In dumbfounded stupor she watched, and was totally unable to prevent Donald leaning in and planting a cold wet kiss on her lips. Wanting to push him away and spit the taste of him from her lips, she settled on pulling away and weakly answering.

"Ahh, well, umm, thank you for a lovely evening." Holding his gaze she waited – would have prayed if she was in any way religious – until, for what seemed like forever, he released her. Only thankful Jamie wasn't here to witness it.

"I will see you Monday, I will come to yours, lunch maybe?"

"Urm, umm ok."

Even with this unconvincing agreement Donald looked pleased with himself. He was very self-assured and grinned as he opened the door and rested his hand on her back as she climbed in.

Kitty spent the drive home in quiet contemplation, wishing she could now do all the things she wished she had done to him. She felt a sense of mortification that the couple in the front seats knew what had passed between Donald and herself, so attempted no conversation and closed her eyes and feigned sleep. Once outside her van she stretched.

"Do you want me to walk you to the house Kathleen?" Chivalrous Hamish offered.

"Goodness no thank you Hamish, off you go to your poor baby sitter – remember I am one, I'm all about their rights. Thank you for the lift and a lovely evening." Claire and Hamish waved a fond farewell, and Kitty enjoyed standing in the refreshing air and the clear night sky, slowly clearing the muddle in her mind.

She had wondered, hoped, that Jamie may have broken their agreement - and been here waiting for her. She scanned the road as she driven in, full of hopes of spotting his car. Kitty stood, her hand reassuringly rubbing the lumpy paintwork of her van, taking in the large moon and the never more clear face smiling down at her. She had too much wine to risk driving to Jamie's so reluctantly made her way for the first night in her new bed.

Once inside the store – or home as she called it, Kitty pulled the curtains, glad she had got Malcolm to use the old metal rail from the old bedroom. The curtains were actually some of Malcolm's old dustsheets that he had ripped in two, but served a good purpose. Locking the door she realised that whether it was being away from Jamie, or just being with Donald, had a very unnerving effect. Soon in her nightie, and a hot chocolate in hand she was nestled in the pillows on the day bed.

Since those first few days it seemed she had not had a moment to herself. Always something to do, someone to see, builders to make tea for or errands to run. For the first time Kitty sat and thought, and wanting to rid Donald from her mind she thought about Jamie. This was no help and only made her want to get in the van and risk driving to him. Instead she tucked her legs up and cuddled her knees, and allowed herself to think about her mum.

With everything that had happened with Stephen and now Jamie, it was her mother she missed the most. Good news, gossip, men, indecisions, worries or silly facts – her first and unfaltering thought was to share it with her mum. Out of bed in a flash, Kitty opened the box and took out the photo of the two of them capturing the hysteria. In the privacy and sanctity of her shed she talked now. Fingers stroked the glass over the squinting eyes and dimpled cheeks, pouring out her hopes and fears and her dreams for this new life.

A hammering disturbed her dreams, Kitty fought off its intrusion. Her mum was stood in the middle of the derelict croft; lifting Star Trek-like boulders (obviously made of polystyrene) she raised each stone effortlessly and rebuilt the walls. Kitty - the teenage version of herself skipped and clapped at her mother's efforts. Distracted from her mother and her gangly self, Kitty looked about to see the source of the annoying knocking and slowly, and very sadly she awoke. The only mother that was really with her was the image smiling up at her from the frame she still clutched. The knocking becoming more insistent was followed by.

"Jesus… Kitty please be here!"

"It's ok… I'm coming, hang on." Kitty called back trying to wipe away the sleep and see her way clear to the door. Stumbling across the room and squinting at the early morning light. Jamie pushed open the door and scooped her up and hugged her to his chest.

"Oh, you scared me, I know I should have waited here for you last night. My minds been going wild, when you didn't answer I thought… well, I thought you hadn't come home."

Breathing in the scent of him and allowing herself a few minutes to come to Kitty nestled into his neck.

"Why would I not?" she said quietly and kissed his neck.

"Kathleen, I missed ya, I'd rather not be doing that again – it was a bloody long night without ye!"

"I wanted to drive over to you but I'd had too much wine. I'm definitely getting a landline, at least I could have phoned you."

"Yes you could have, and ya certainly are getting that phone lass."

30

The Little Church

"So is it definite? You go today?" Kitty tried valiantly to hide the sadness she felt.

"Aye, I must, but I can'na say I'm happy about it." Jamie sighed deeply.

"You've promised."

"Only because he has a job that needs the two of us and he'll be held up if I dunne go. If he could manage on his own I'd never go!" Kitty stroked the down turned face.

"Will you show me some of Skye today?" forcing a smile now.

"Aye, if Pimples is up to it, my ferry leaves at four." Sad resignation evident on his face. "I can't believe I'm leaving you, after how we felt last night."

"Yes but we agreed, if we are here we will be together, but the sooner you go and do what you have to do the sooner I can have you back." Jamie forced a one sided smile in answer.

Kitty had debated whether to go with him or stay and oversee her own project. She had frightened herself with her outburst on the lawn. Reasoning the time apart would serve her well as time to gather her emotions. Maybe let some more out while he was safely out of the way. She had, after all moved here to start her own life, not to find, and be dependent, on someone else. Further, she hoped a little time away would allow her head to catch up with her burgeoning emotions. Kitty planned to throw her efforts into the build and help wherever possible.

Provisions were quickly stowed in the cupboards, and Kitty happily relinquished the keys so she might better enjoy the scenery, outside and inside the van. In the short weeks she had been here spring was well and truly on its way. Pushing through the copper of last years fallen bracken shards of emerald rose purposefully up and out, their coiled ends reminding Kitty of calamari she had once reluctantly eaten in Spain. Primroses, violets and daffodils bright and cheerfully looking up to the sun. Although chilly, the sun shone and warmed Kitty and Jamie as they headed off to pastures new.

Jamie drove around his family's land, pointing out areas of interest, and heading away from the coast as Pimples struggled with the hills and the narrow potholed roads. The surroundings became less lush with sparser vegetation and only wizened trees braced against the prevailing wind.

Pulling into a wide lay-by carved into the side of the road Jamie parked and cut the engine.

"There is somewhere I want to show you."

"Oh ok."

Whether due to the snugness of the van or a real drop in the temperature both had to fasten the collars of their coats. Kitty pulled up her hood and pulled the drawstring tight around her face, the only way to win against a wind that tried it's hardest to rip it off her head. There was nothing to see here excepting the slight indentation of a grass path up the slope, picking its way around rocks and an occasional tortured tree.

Taking her hand Jamie led her up the incline, his excited determination had Kitty intrigued. Sheep roamed free here and although none in view, the telltale heaps of shinny currents were dotted all around. Concentrating on her footing and avoiding the heaps, Kitty looked up as Jamie stopped beside her. Squeezing her hand and standing on the brow of the hill the furrowed path continued before them, leading to a small squat grey stone building. Obviously a church, it had a small rectangular tower to one end and a lower pitched portion extending away from them. With only slits for windows it had a determined bleakness about it.

Smiling down Jamie explained it had been on the family land for as long as anyone could remember. It had survived the reformation. The Church of Scotland had long since disowned it.

"But we feel it is ours and it's the only church my family uses." His cheeky smile made Kitty smile.

"Can we go in?"

"Yes, would you like to?" serious now, "Ya not religious lass are ye? I did'na want to offend ye."

"No, no not at all. Actually I have no idea what I believe in. But I do love history and would love to tread where generations of your forebears stood." Jamie bent and kissed her on the mouth, just as she went to wrap her arms around his neck he was gone. Skipping to keep up with him, they descended down the slope together and stood in front of large double doors. The grain of the timber prominent, countless years of wind and rain had battered but not beaten them. Kitty ran her fingers along the groves and ripples in the oak. Metal strapping and large bolts encaged the door. Two large round handles tempted Kitty to try and open them but they were as unmovable as the stone around them.

Jamie's chuckle made her jump and she pulled back her hand.

"Sorry lass," placing his hand in the small of her back he bent to reach behind a large stone. Strange she thought, how that simple touch could evoke such contrasting emotions when elicited from two very different men. Jamie rose triumphant, holding up a key. Not just any key - this was five inches long, the barrel half an inch in diameter and a large row of teeth at one end. Holding it ceremonially across his hand he passed it to Kitty, Celtic knot designed handle towards her – simple but very beautiful.

Placing it in the lock Kitty turned. Expecting resistance she was surprised as it turned, heavily but smoothly. Opening the door, again expectations dashed it swung open soundlessly on large barrel hinges.

The wind disturbed a small gathering of leaves and dust that had sheltered inside. Little light was allowed access through the slit-like windows, and after a minute of eye rubbing and squinting Kitty drank in every detail. The stone floor made up from great slabs of dark greyish brown, not hewn or polished but scored and pitted. Rows of pews facing forward, and as she advanced into the chapel her hands stroked the edges of these, smooth with patination from hundreds of palms. She made her way up the aisle. A gothic carved lectern with carved spires supporting the book rest with a large crest on the front dominated the view ahead. Kitty's fingers traced this, "The same as on the front of you parents house?"

"The Stewart family crest, Great grandfather had it made, very arts and crafts but mother hates it."

"Oh no it's wonderful."

Looking now at the stone beneath her feet Kitty struggled to decipher ancient and worn lettering.

"That'll be a great, great many times over relative. Bit of a rogue from the 1760's, huge, ginger and ferocious, had sixteen bairns."

"Oh my!"

Sitting back on the front pew, surprised at how clean it was. Soon joined by Jamie many minutes passed in happy contemplation, lightly holding hands fingers entwined.

"It's wonderful that so much of your family have used this church, but really sad for it not to be used anymore."

"Oh the church may have abandoned it but the Stewarts never will. I was christened here, as were my brother and sister. Mother and father were married here. It was granted a licence so a registrar can come and conduct services here."

"Oh how lovely, you are so rooted here aren't you? I have a tenuous connection to Wimbledon but that's only from my grandparent's time." Looking into his eyes and taking both his hands in hers.

"Never leave here Jamie, this connection is tangible... it's an honour to have."

"Aye it is."

Wrapping his arm around her, there they sat. Only when a gust of wind swirled up the aisle did they stir, the ghost of a Stewart ancestor disturbing their contemplation.

"Come, I'll show ye where I will be buried."

"There! and the romance was gone!" Kitty smiled up at him.

Tucked behind the church as if sheltering, hiding from onlookers. Jamie pushed open a six foot tall elaborate iron gate. The small cemetery rose up on a gentle incline, and small stones lent back into the slope as if bracing themselves from slipping forward to the church.

"It's mainly kinsmen, some old clergy and a few loyal Ghillies and servants."

"Ghillies?" Kitty struggled to take her eyes off the stones and to his face.

"Umm, what would you say... gamekeeper?"

"Oh, right."

Jamie cut a diagonal path, zigzagging to avoid treading directly above the resting bones to an area in the lea of a large yew. The stones here were more recent without an overcoat of lichen and moss.

"My grandparents."

Jamie squatting and straightened the small vase, removing the long wilted roses and brushed the lettering reading its script.

"Euphemia Alexandra Stewart, beloved wife and mother. 18th June 1923, 9th April 2012.

Angus Malcolm Dougal Stewart. Laird of clan Stewart 2nd February 1923, 29th May 2008."

They stood in silence for many minutes.

"Were you close to them?"

"Oh, aye, aye. Granny was quite hard but Pop was gentle and kind. He loved being with us bairns and liked nothing better than building a hut or fishing in the rivers. It was like having another brother – I still miss him and I like to come here... I spent a few hours here that day after our... incident." Kitty knelt next to him and wrapped her arm around him.

"Misunderstanding!" Kitty corrected, "Did it help?"

"No as a matter of fact all I could hear was his deep voice, *tis no way to be treating a lassie!*" Kitty laughed at his impersonation of his grandfather.

The chill drove them back to Pimples and a cup of tea was never so appreciated.

"Mother called yesterday, she's busting to come to Tide's Reach and have a wee nose."

"Oh that's sweet, I don't mind."

"Can I tell her she can come over while I'm away or do you want me to keep her at bay until I get back from Harris?"

"No ask her to come this week, it will make the time pass while you are gone."

"Thank you Kathleen." Genuinely touched Jamie smiled warmly at her.

"I worry… I don't want you to be overwhelmed by my family, scared off by them. We are very close and I ken that's something you donna have."

"I know and I welcome it Jamie."

"Good I am so pleased lass, I'm sorry but we had better head off if I'm to make the ferry."

"Umm" and a shuddering sigh was answer enough to Jamie's worries at her thoughts on the matter.

The drive back to Tide's Reach was silent as neither wanted it to end, both unhappy at the prospect of being apart, but trying to conceal these feelings from the other. Inevitably it ended and Jamie's shoulders hunched as he walked to his car and drove solemnly away. Kitty bit her lip, and taking much self-control, stood for near five minutes before she could be sure of suppressing the tears and turned to walk to the site and the awaiting, interested builders.

"He'll soon be back lassie, our Jamie has it bad, he'll not stay long from ye side" Jeff called at her return.

Kitty couldn't risk talking at that moment but tried hard at a weak smile. Seeking the privacy and solitude of her store, she walked head down almost straight into Malcolm. He was leaving the store having deposited a hand full of mugs.

"Oof, lassie mind ya sel." Malcolm's cheerful rich voice was the straw to break the camels back, and she burst into tears. Unexpectedly the large man gathered her into his arms and held her tenderly to his chest. Rocking her gently he stroked her hair and hushed her with soft Gaelic as she sobbed. The crying soon stopped, replaced immediately with mortification. Drying her eyes on her sleeve, the embarrassment was trebled as she sniffed up to see Jeff and Trevor had walked over in concerned interest.

"Oh god… I'm so embarrassed, I'm so sorry." She tried to look them in the eye by the humiliation was too great.

"Hush, hush lass." Malcolm released his embrace, wrapped an enormous arm around her shoulder and guided her into the store.

"Trevor, tea" the order was quiet and the lumbering figure of Trevor obeying, selecting a mug and busying himself in her store was comical and Kitty giggled between sniffs.

"Now, that's better." Setting her down on the edge of the day bed. Kitty looked up at the concerned face of Jeff as he stood arms folded in the doorway, almost filling it and blocking the light. Furtive glances from Trevor who soon set about tea making duties, and seemingly quite at home in her small store kitchen. Malcolm stood beside her and stroked his beard, deep in thought.

"I'm alright now Malcolm… honestly. Thank you for… well your concern and... well the hug." Kitty's voice weak and small she fiddled with her fingers in her lap.

"Aye." Was all the answer she received, and silence prevailed until Trevor handed her a mug of very strong tea and a plate of beautifully arranged biscuits – who'd have thought!

"Now lass, I dunna ken what Jamie may or mayn't have told ye about life here." A pause as he pulled at his facial hair. "Maybe we live quite different to those ya used to. But here there is very little we do not know of each other. Jamie is fixing to be away for these next few days or weeks... and well, as kin you can rely on us till his return"

"Oh… thank you Malcolm… but I was just being silly, I'll be fine now. I just need to keep busy." She sighed and ate one of the biscuits to fill the silence.

"Jamie's mother is the best person you'll find and there's room enough in that rambling house if you should need it. No one wants ye to be lonely or fearful lass." Kitty guessed her story up to date was known by all these men, their wives, their mothers and quite a share of the locals. Kitty wondered what they called her – the slightly unhinged poor southerner. Well she would show them, she was made of tough stuff and would be absolutely fine on her own. But she couldn't help but feel grateful and touched by their obvious concern.

"Aye, well that's as may be, but Jamie left ye this," taking a folded piece of paper from the plaid shirt pocket and handing to her. The handwriting was fine script and contained a list of twenty or so names with phone numbers for each. A gnarled finger reached over and pointed to the top of the list.

"Obviously Dougal and Maureen at the top, landline and mobiles. There is my home number, Trevor's, Jeffrey, Lizzie – my daughter." And so the list continued. "Ye are obviously very special to our James and we are all at your disposal if ye need us." Malcolm concluded.

"He would have our heads if we did'na look after ye!" Trevor added.

Kitty was lost for words, quite flabbergasted at the concern, generosity and unity from a group of near strangers. Lightening the mood and brushing away any residual tension in the air Trevor lunged forward, patting Kitty on the shoulder.

"If ya'll be wanting to use our spare room you'd best be swift before the bairn arrives!" Kitty laughed.

"Aye well then, well then, enough said. Let's get back to work and finish the poor girl's house."

Sipping her tea and eating all the biscuits on her plate she listened to the reassuring clang and bangs of her Celtic guardians. She had often wondered in her life how it would have been to have a brother. Losing Tommy at the most irritating age she never experienced the camaraderie and friendship of an adult sibling, but guessed it would be like this. Smiling now she was very envious of Lizzie and wondered if she had any idea how lucky she was to have this father and these brothers.

Blinking against the sun Kitty made her way out to see what everyone was doing.

"Malcolm... why are you here on a Sunday?" Malcolm smiled down from the scaffold at the gable end of the new roof.

"Jamie asked us to do a few hours today to check on ye after he went."

"Oh, that's lovely... thank you so much. But you shouldn't be away from your families. I will be fine now!" Kitty knew she would and felt guilty at their being there now.

"Aye well we will be off soon, we wanted to get all the battens on. Would ya want to come back to mine, Moira can always feed one more."

"Oh no thanks again, I will be fine. Now I know I have the clan Stewart looking after me I feel very safe and happy." Beaming at them all.

"Aye well that was the aim, none of us want to face the wrath of Jamie if we did'na see you right."

Kitty waved them off when the two vans finally left the drive. Killing time she pottered around the site and made herself a large bowl of soup and wedges of bread with butter that could clog the best artery. Checking her watch Kitty walked eagerly up the drive to the pay phone to talk to Jamie.

Armed with a pocket of change Kitty dialled the number on Harris

"Hello."

"Hi... is Jamie there please?"

"Oh aye, Kathleen is it, so you are the reason, the one responsible for me losing my best worker." The strong accent concealed any trace of humour but the ensuing and colourful banter and laughter between Jamie and his friend reassured her that she was in fact being teased.

"Bugger off Charlie!" Jamie's voice was brusque but warmed Kitty to the core. More Gaelic – Kitty must learn at least the swearing she thought – a door slammed and Jamie's voice was now soft and familiar.

"Oh Kathleen, I miss you terribly already."

"Jamie, it's only been five hours."

"Five hours, twelve minutes... and probably ten seconds!"

"Not that you're counting." Kitty sniggered.

"Aye dunna laugh at me lass, I dunna like being so far."

"I know, whereas I haven't missed you so much as I've had three big burly relatives of yours hugging me and making me tea!"

A heavy silence followed and Kitty regretted teasing him, finally he spoke.

"Are the lads still there?"

"You know full well they were – at your arrangement! But no they have gone home now."

"Ye not annoyed lass? I just wanted them to see you were alright."

"Oh Jamie they were so sweet. After you left I was trying really hard not to cry but bumped into Malcolm… and well he gave me a hug. Trevor made me tea and biscuits. But I'm fine now."

"Ock lass… do ye need me to come home?"

"Jamie no, NO! This is ridiculous, I will be fine now. You do what you need to there and I will keep busy here." Jamie sighed, appreciating the logic but would have loved an excuse to drop every thing and be on the next ferry back – ridiculous or not! Kitty updated him on the build today, and was pleased to hear the enthusiasm for the work he had planned with Charlie.

"Jamie, love I must go. I'm going to run out of money, yes, yes I promise first thing tomorrow I will sort out a land line."

"And you will promise to stay in my cottage if you want to."

"Yes I am going to stop here tonight because I'm swimming in the morning. Tuesday I'll stop here as I've got babysitting but the rest of the week I think I will stay at yours... are you sure you don't mind?"

"Kathleen! How can you ask that?"

"Ok, if you are sure?"

After a juvenile waste of minutes and coin, "You hang up!" "No you". Jamie threw in I love you Kathleen and she replied "I love you James Stewart" and that ended the conversation.

Kitty leant back on the cold metal bars of the phone box and closed her eyes. Taking deep breaths Kitty concentrated intently to quell the nausea and hurt of the final goodbye. Ordering herself to pull herself together Kitty redialled and was relieved to find Amanda in and lined up a stack of £1 coins.

"So how did dinner at the architects go?" Kitty gave her all the details.

"And he's single you say?"

"Thing is Mand, he reminds me of Mr Green at school, do you remember we always thought he spied on us in the changing room."

"Oh yes, sleazy Green! I do remember, yes creepy perv – oh

that's not good!"

"Well do you remember, that look, that smile, always when he was looking you up and down."

"Yeh, yesss *just checking your uniform* checking our uniform my foot!" Amanda shuddered at the memory.

"Yeh, exactly that wasn't what he was checking." As always the two women dissolved into stomach crunching laughter.

"And how is lover boy?"

"JAMIE!"

"Yes, and wow! Thanks for the photos you emailed. Kit he's bloody gorgeous."

"I know!" smugness oozed down the phone.

"The house looks like it's coming on, are you happy with it? – and I must say his cousins are hot too, any single?"

"Very happy with the house. The builders were here today. Jamie had asked them to work as he was going away and he was worried at leaving me. And one is single."

"Good you can introduce me when I come up. Is that... well not a bit controlling?" Caution in her voice.

"Oh no, no, no... I had a bit of a melt down after I met his folks."

"What! Hold the phone! – You met his parents, tell, tell – details?"

"Ok but keep your hair on."

Kitty went on to explain in minute detail the house and what his parents had said.

"What like Downton, only all tweed and tartan?"

"Well, yes," laughing now, "But much friendlier and informal."

"Well full marks to you matey, tick V G."

"Well it made me think about you know... everything." Sighing deeply. "Every thing... well everyone..."

"Oh Kit" Amanda's eyes had filled and she tried not to let it show in her voice.

"And on the way home, it hit me... like a wave... like all the coffins had opened."

"Well I'm glad."

"Jeez, thanks." Kitty sniffed back tears, "With friends like you who needs enemies!"

"Oh you know what I mean, and I don't want to say I told you so!"

"But you will."

"Yes I will! You need to feel it babe," gently now, wishing she could hug her friend, all flippancy gone. "You can feel lonely, you can feel angry, hell Kitty, you need to feel their loss."

"I know Mand but why now? Why when I am so incredibly happy – why now Mand?" Kitty's tears fell on the dirty concrete floor and she clutched the metal cable.

"Because my dear friend, until you have let it out you can't be truly happy. Not with all that bottled up inside. You need to get rid of it to let all the good in."

"When did you get so clever Dr Amanda?"

"Listen lovey, you might have, through no fault of your own, become an expert at losing people. I, by association as your best friend have become a bit of an expert in watching people lose people."

"Yes... I can't deny that. Thank you for always being there Mand."

"Always have been, always will – even if you go and move hundreds of miles away. Still not FORGIVEN!"

"You will when you come to visit – not long now is it?"

"Only three weeks"

"Oh I can't wait." This thought cheered Kitty and she wiped her face dry on her sleeve.

"Me either, do you think you could wangle a trip to the big house. Mum and Dad would be made up."

"I'm not marrying him Mand!"

"I wouldn't be so sure!"

With that thought in mind Kitty went on tell her about the little church.

"Now for god's sake never tell Jamie this, but... well it was all I could think sitting in that cold little chapel. I've dreamt about it too... him resplendent in his kilt. But then I look back and one half of the church full of Stewarts squashed in and then... well then it turns into a bit of a nightmare. On my side are the worst images of all my dead family." Kitty let out a long sigh and buried her head in the crook of her arm.

"Well you silly bitch, of course it wouldn't be empty I'd be there! And do you think my parents would stay away. If you don't get a move on I might have beat you to it and marry that cousin of his and have a brood of ginger kids in the pews. Hell I'll be the bridesmaid, and tradition has it, you wouldn't deny me shagging a man in a kilt!"

31

Alone Again, Naturally

Kitty walked, head held high back to her store, Amanda was a tonic and she would count down the days until she arrived. But she had always had terrible taste in men, always the shiny type – all slick and vain. No doubt, yes definitely no doubt she would be attracted to Donald. She would have to work on Jamie to find someone lovely to sweep Amanda off her feet when she visited – perhaps Charlie could come over, and bring his kilt!

She enjoyed the solitude of the evening, and after supper she carried a large glass of wine and sat outside her ruin. Wrapped in a blanket she watched the sun make its slow descent. The sky grew pinker and Kitty delighted in watching clouds that had come over the mountains drift and morph out of view.

There was a feeling in this little spot she couldn't explain, Not being religious, and having always avoided anything supernatural, Kitty was never brave enough to delve into tarot cards or clairvoyants – not disbelieving but distrustful. There was no explanation but equally no denying the sense of something - a presence when she sat here. In no way scary, a little unnerving but not in a bad way. Closing her eyes she let the last of the suns rays warm her lids, allowing her mind to see the images of the past.

A small boat bobbed on the slipway at high tide. A young woman, small in stature stood where she now sat. Long heavy woollen skirts and a woollen shawl tied across her chest. What chores she would have done, what hardship to be borne. Washing billowed on a line from the croft to the small tree behind. She could imagine the comforting smell of bread baking in a small black range. Visualising the interior of this little house, Kitty smiled as she realised the image had been conjured by her peering into the croft at Donald's.

Sipping her wine, Kitty looked around her now and wondered just how difficult it was going to be to make this building, if not habitable, at least dry and useable. If Kitty was to write or pick up her brushes once more this was without doubt the best place to do so.

The sun was all but gone and Kitty took a relaxed walk back to the store. She had pasta in the small fridge but feeling confident and independent Kitty replaced her blanket for her jacket and headed up the drive to the pub.

Lilly was behind the bar and rewarded Kitty efforts with a broad smile.

"Well evening Kitty, it's nice to see you." Lilly wiped the bar in front of her with a towelling mat and patted it firmly. "Come have a seat, are you on your own tonight?"

"Yes, am I too late for food?" Kitty feeling a little giddy from the wine on an empty stomach.

"No, I'll tell Derek you're ordering, you are just in time."

Calling after Lilly as she walked to the kitchen, "I'll have steak medium and chips please."

"Sure I'll tell him." Lilly skipped out of sight and Kitty settled herself on the high stool at the end of the bar where she had first seen Jamie. That seemed like a lifetime ago now, not a matter of weeks.

"All done!" the barmaid soon back, "What can I get you?"

"Pint of bitter please."

"Soooo… is it true?" Lilly leant on her elbows on the bar opposite. Kitty wondered if the young girl knew the effect it had on her cleavage, she suspected she did.

"What?" but Kitty knew exactly what Lilly referred to and her rising blush told the bar maid she knew too.

"You and our resident red haired bachelor?"

Eyes down, Kitty waited for her beer to be served, sheepishly she looked up checking no one else in the bar was listening.

"Well… yes I suppose." Kitty drank more beer.

"Well good for you – go girl! How serious is it?" Lilly hopped excitedly behind the bar.

"God… I don't know, it's very early days but I'm very happy."

"I bet you are." Followed by a dirty laugh. "Well where is he? Not very chivalrous letting you eat alone."

"He's gone to Harris for a couple of weeks to work."

"Bummer!" Kitty couldn't help but laugh at her.

"Oh well, got a band in next weekend, you should come along."

"Great, Saturday? Will you be here?"

"Yep."

Good Kitty thought, anything to fill the time. Kitty was starving by the time her dinner came, and was pleased that Lilly was chatting to a young crowd that had tired of the dartboard. She ate greedily and finished the evening with a second pint and some girlie chatter, wending her way back to her bed very happily.

Surrounded by her boxes Kitty was very secure in her pyjamas propped up in the bed. Laptop redundant, Kitty enjoyed a novel she had owned for years but never had time to read. The alarm rattled loudly on the table and Kitty stretched and smiled after a very satisfying nights sleep. She had wanted to be ready in good time for Malcolm. She skipped her planned swim and was washed and breakfasted well before anyone arrived.

"Morning Kathleen, did ye sleep well in the shed?"

"Yes I did, slept like a log!"

"Oh good for you lass, I've had Jamie's mother on the phone today, asking for your number. I told her ya have no signal but she was keen to pop over today."

"Do you think that might be Jamie's doing?"

"Aye, but I said I'd call her if not – shall I?"

"Umm, oh no ... I'm here, why not."

"Dunna fret lass, she is a lovely lady."

"Oh I know" Kitty pottered and cleaned her storeroom. There was so little to do but she made the bed and dusted her boxes. Making tea for the men she took her own mug and paced the back garden. If Jamie's mother was coming to discuss gardening – even if that was a ruse by Jamie – she at least felt obliged to come up with some ideas. Deep in thought over what was the proper shape for a flower bed Kitty was unaware of Maureen's light steps behind her.

"Kathleen." Kitty jumped and spun to face Mrs Stewart.

"Oh sorry dear." Maureen rested her slim fingers on Kitty forearm, "I did'na mean to make ye jump."

"Oh sorry Mrs Stewart." Kitty held a still shaking hand over her chest.

"Maureen please."

"Maureen."

"Well Kathleen thank you for letting me visit, what a beautiful position. Good morning Malc, boys." The workman all called their welcomes.

"Would you show me around?" Prompting Kitty to move, as she still looked a little startled at her guest.

"With pleasure."

"And is it true you bought it without seeing it?" Maureen's voice rising incredulously.

"Yes," looking over her shoulder, fearful Maureen would think her insane, "Mad wasn't I?"

"Oh no dear, very brave, very courageous." Kitty smiled. Of course Maureen was lovely, she was Jamie's mother. Kitty's enthusiasm for the site was obvious and her guest thoroughly enjoyed sharing it. Gracefully picking up a crate, much to Kitty's dismay she carried it over to what was to be her lounge.

"Nothing beats testing out the layout." Well who would have thought? Jamie's mum sat on a milk crate testing for the optimum location for the sofa – go figure.

"Jamie tells me there is a little derelict croft around the bay."

"Yes would you like to see it?"

"Oh yes please." Kitty led the keen visitor along the path.

"You know James had never brought anyone home before." Kitty's step slowed a little.

"Yes... he told me." Feeling apprehensive now, where was this going?

"I just mention it because I worry."

"Oh about me?"

"Oh no dear, I'm delighted about you, delighted! And he is obviously head over heels for you my dear." Kitty blushed and stopped in her tracks. Maureen stopped next to her and wrapped a slim arm around her shoulders giving her a reassuring squeeze.

"I am worried that this is all happening too fast for you. I would hate to see either of you get hurt. I can't imagine what you have been through, and you are so young. I wanted you to know James' father and I are here if you need anything. You have had a startling effect on James, but if you need him to... well back off, I'm sure he would."

Kitty started walking again taking in the information, stopping again to answer.

"Thank you Maureen... I... think the world of Jamie... I never expected to meet anyone else after Ste – my husband. I certainly didn't expect to fall for someone so quickly, so intensely... he's just perfect." Kitty voice faded to a whisper and she blushed brightly.

"Oh dear, dear girl. I am very pleased you moved here – now show me that croft."

Rounding the corner Kitty enjoyed watching the agile women climb over the stones, running her hand over the moss coated slabs. She finished her inspection by sitting on Kitty's usual pew and looking out to the water.

"This is truly a special spot, a magical place!"

"Yes that's just how I feel... Oh I don't know I feel, a sense of something here – is that mad?"

"No, no I feel it too, you must get James to restore it. What a wonderful place to paint and write, and think, this will be a very reflective and creative place."

The silence that followed should have been awkward between a girl and her new boyfriend's mother but it wasn't. It was only interrupted when Kitty remembered her manners and realised she hadn't offered Maureen a cup of tea.

Sitting back in the storeroom they discussed Kitty's ideas for the garden over tea and biscuits. Kitty's lack of knowledge was well compensated for by her enthusiasm. Maureen pulled a large colourful gardening book from her bag.

"I've taken the liberty of marking the pages with good "doers", being so exposed here you will be a little limited but you could have a truly pretty garden here." Maureen laid the book on the table, and Kitty ran her finger down the edge against the array of multicoloured notelets.

"You must come to the house, why not later today if you have no plans? We can walk through the gardens and you could show me what you like – in fact you could join Dougal and me for dinner." Maureen looked eagerly across the table to her.

"Oh I don't want to be a nuisance."

"Kathleen, I'd be delighted, please say yes, Dougie will be very happy and you could phone James from ours."

Of course she knew that, Malcolm had said everyone here knows everything. She wondered if that fact should bother her, but rather than upset her it comforted.

"If you are sure?"

"Of course dear."

"Then thank you, yes please."

Winking at Kitty, Maureen added, "And we could even find embarrassing photo's of James to show you! And don't be offended my dear, but I know you don't have a bathroom here so if you would like come over earlier, say six and you can have a nice soak in the bath."

"Oh" worried she might smell.

"I know you can wash perfectly well at a sink, but every girl likes a soak!" Maureen's smile dispelled any embarrassment.

"Ok thank you again."

"Your mum and dad are wonderful."

"Aye, I know."

"We've had a lovely evening, your mum is very persuasive. I've had a bath, dinner and now I've agreed to stay over – in your bed!" speaking low and seductive.

"Oh god Kathleen, I won't sleep a wink. Promise me you'll be wearing baggy pyjamas, the thought of you in my bed, naked – hell I'm getting the next ferry home."

"Steady tiger, I've seen photos of you tonight!"

"Oh please, dunna tell me she had the kiddy pictures out."

"Oooh yes!"

"Bloody hell, not the ones by the loch – not the one with the daisy chain?" Kitty could hear the cringing in his voice.

"Ha Ha!" Kitty quieted then remembering she was in his parents hallway and had no idea if anyone could hear her. The acoustics were indeed good here and she could hear the remnants of her laugh echoing off the cavernous hall, risking offending the dower old relatives glaring down on her from gilded frames.

"You were very cute."

"WERE!"

"Are" voice husky now "Oh I do miss you." There was a heavy silence broken finally by Kitty. "Oh sorry is that too needy?" Feeling suddenly self-conscious and foolish, sitting in the grandeur of his family seat, Jamie's cough did little to allay her fears.

"I'd better go." All humour and spark extinguished from her voice.

"No god" whispering now "Nooo..." Kitty pressed the phone hard to her ear holding her bowed head.

"Kathleen I... I miss you so much I think it could make me ill. I feel positively sick."

"Oh I was worried you thought I was a bunny boiler, moving in on your family the minute you left."

Jamie's laugh was good to hear but the strain evident over the miles that separated them.

"I'm so glad you are there, and you know you can go to them for anything."

"I know." Kitty was glad to have already said her goodnights to his parents because tears streamed down her face. Relentless through undressing, teeth brushing and stopped only when sleep won out as she cuddled Jamie's quilt around herself.

It must have been something in the water but since being here she had never cried as much as she had since Stephen's funeral. Maybe that was the material point, she should have cried more the last year. Now this peace and this happiness she had found with the burly local had unleashed all the pent up emotion. Kitty hoped she could get a handle on it soon, everything was good now, now was the time to be happy.

Opening the curtains Kitty dragged the small-buttoned chair to the long sash window, taking the quilt and draping it around her shoulders to exclude the draft that rattled the old waney panes of glass. Sitting with her feet on the low windowsill she watched the dawn. It was five thirty and Kitty weighed up the option of sleeping in, but now surprisingly refreshed, there she sat.

The long drive swept off to the left and a large expanse of lawn stretched out shimmering with dew. A few steely trees, pines of some sort Kitty knew that much, stood as dark green sentries. The pink light gradually softened their outlines and the dew steamed as the sun caught it.

To the right of her view was a long bank of rhododendrons, buds full of promise - not long she thought. Memories kept her company until six; of picnics on Wimbledon common and playing hide and seek in the huge rhododendrons at the park by her school. Kitty suppressed the urge to sneak out now in Jamie's pyjamas, to rediscover the secret world that hides behind the impenetrable wall of evergreen leaves and plate sized flowers. The six year old climbing amongst the smooth twisted stems and branches, bare and clean. Like an igloo with all sky obscured by the dense outer crust of foliage, there was the secret airy open den inside. Feeling like the queen in her very special palace.

Next time she thought, next time she was here she would get Jamie to introduce her to the secret palaces here. With any luck it would be when they were resplendent with flowers.

Sitting quietly and for nearly an hour and a half although warm enough, hunger and a numb backside forced her finally to move. Peering from the doorway and ascertaining no one was around Kitty hitched up her too long trousers and rushed to the bathroom. The bath tub was enormous and large unusual taps like brass bottles filled the bath slowly. The pale brown water could have been off putting, but laying in a bath six foot long was wonderful.

Dried and dressed Kitty was momentarily confused, could she remember her way back to the kitchen or should she try to find the dining room? – oh lord was there a breakfast room? Mild panic and disorientation was soon brushed aside at the entrance of the briskly efficient Maggie rounding the corner. Without slowing in pace she gathered one of Kitty arms and towed her to the breakfast room.

"Grand timing lass, I was away to wake you, hope you like a hearty breakfast."

Kitty was released inside the room she guided her to, - there was indeed a breakfast room. Transfixed by the view from the sash windows that reached right to the floor on the far wall, she made her way towards them. Feeling her way around the carved high back chairs Kitty stood in front of the window, arms folded around herself. Monoliths of trees danced in the morning breeze and behind the earth fell away, culminating in distant azure sea and the backdrop of distant mountains.

"Not dissimilar to your view." It was Maureen's soft voice that, although startled, Kitty was pleased to hear.

"Oh not quite on the same scale." Kitty turned and smiled.

"Did you sleep well?"

"Oh yes, wonderfully."

"Ahh, good, good, have a seat Kathleen, Maggie will be in momentarily."

"Will Mr - Dougal be joining us?"

"Gracious no he was fed and gone hours ago."

Kitty tucked into bacon, eggs and fried tomatoes. The two women ate slowly, Maureen doing the lion's share of talking as she had soon finished her porridge and delighted Kitty with tales of the estate.

"If you have time we could take a turn around the garden."

"I would love that."

After finishing the second pot of tea and watching in wonder as Maggie moved silently around the room clearing and tidying, Kitty was again amazed that it wasn't strange being waited on. It was oddly comforting and reminded her of her mother.

A young Kitty would despair of her mum, who, as soon as the last mouthful was in - but not necessarily swallowed, would push away her chair and buzz around the table and ferry to and fro the kitchen until everything was efficiently washed, wiped and put away.

Dishcloth always rinsed and hung over the tap and finally and not without a little ceremony, when all else was done, her pinny shaken and hung on the larder door.

"Thank you Maggie." Kitty, shaking off the warm embrace of her mother's memory, remembered to thank the provider of a splendid breakfast.

"Aye, it's nothing lass." And with a quick smile she was gone.

"Come, Kathleen lets go and see the garden."

Both walked slowly, and the elder woman caressed each plant as they passed it, saying the Latin name and then its common name. A few Kitty had heard of and would triumphantly share the small knowledge she had.

"I know this one, it used to fascinate me as a child. The water sits on it like beads, jewels for the fairies my mum used to say."

"Yes, Alchemilla mollis – Ladies mantle, it's only just coming into leaf but this whole area will be a mass of leaves by the summer."

"A friend of my mother's had it in her front garden in Wimbledon." Kitty could visualise it now spreading over the red brick path.

"Well it made you smile and obviously remember something nice, so you must have some of this."

"I'd love some, but I'm sure I won't remember the name, we always called it Eileen's plant."

"Well it's as good a name as any!" Maureen's smile was as warm as the bright sun.

"Your back garden will be protected by the wall and the croft, so I think you could try and plant whatever you want. If it likes it there it will survive."

Nearly an hour had passed, and it was decided Jamie's mother would have her gardener lift and divide the plants they had discussed and pot them up. As soon as the building work was done Maureen and Kitty could plant them in her garden.

"Your plan with the carpet was quite inspired dear it should all come together at the right time."

"Thank you so much Maureen, for last night and today." Kitty was keen not to outstay her welcome but had to admit a reluctance to leave.

"Well you ken, we have plenty of room and Maggie is never happier than when there are more mouths to feed. So please do come back again Kathleen." Kitty turned one final time and waved from the open window of Pimples. The bath and bed had been very welcome, and time spent with his parents lovely, but she did feel the pull of Tide's Reach and was now eager to be home.

The rest of the week flowed in easy repetition. Days spent busying on site, keen to be useful she had proven herself as a hard worker and quick learner and Kitty enjoyed the manual labour. The old flags were soon to be relaid and while the men laid the foundations for the under-floor heating Kitty sang along to the ever-present radio and scrubbed the stones.

Evenings were short after eating and walking to the phone box for her daily chat to Jamie. Kitty's eyes would burn and she made slow progress with the novel, often dropping it to the floor mid sentence.

At Angela's insistence Kitty went early for her babysitting duties, and used their home internet to start the process of getting a land line connected.

"So… you and Jamie then?" Gavin grinned at Kitty despite the swift kick in the shin from his wife.

"Yes?" Kitty smiled playfully. These were good people, good friends in the making and Kitty was not about to be missish about some kindly meant banter.

"Well when did that happen? Ye did'na waste much time Kitty." Gavin asked and Kitty was impressed with Angela, she obviously hadn't betrayed her confidences even to her own husband.

"From the first time I met him really." Kitty smiled remembering the drunken carry to the toilet, but thought no one else needed that image.

"Well he's a good one, you'd have to go a long way to find a better."

32

Consequences

The weekend came and went, she enjoyed the band but being in the vibrant atmosphere Kitty missed Jamie more than ever. She half expected him to walk into the bar at any moment. Angus was there and Kitty met his girlfriend, she was younger and Kitty thought probably a little insecure. Eyeing Kitty suspiciously, she guessed this was not destined to be a blossoming friendship.

The days without builders seemed too quiet, and she had a long trip to Portree on Saturday and an extra long walk around the coast Sunday. The rigors of the week's hard work and long hours resulted in Kitty returning from the beach on the Sunday shattered. She stopped only long enough to kick off her boots before falling spread-eagled onto the day bed. The door was open to let the breeze refresh her damp skin. Laying here eyes closed, Kitty was near to sleep hearing only the pounding of her heart.

"Now there's a sight!"

Kitty leapt up rubbing her eyes trying desperately to focus on the dark shape surrounded by blaring light in the doorway.

"God Donald! You scared me."

"Sorry Kathleen, you looked like you were asleep."

"I almost was." Taking a few deep breaths, hands on hips Kitty glared at him.

"Well I'm sorry." Kitty thought he sounded offended – bloody cheek. "I said I'd be over, don't you remember?"

"Um... no, not really." Kitty rubbed at her eyes again and struggled to her feet.

"Charming, well anyway Claire and Hamish have invited us to tea. Nothing fancy, and as you still don't have a land line..." Kitty interrupted him then.

"I'm sorting it!"

He didn't acknowledge her input, "I thought I would come and tell you in person." Smiling smugly.

"Oh... well..." A mixture of confusion and agitation.

"So are you fit?"

"I've been walking, I would need to change."

"On you go then, they will be expecting us." With a slithering smile he turned, "I'll be right here."

This was in no way reassuring. Closing the door and drawing the curtains Kitty stood at the sink and undressed. As if he could see through the wall, the door or a chink in the curtain she felt exposed. Why did he have this effect on her, not only did he never fail to give her the creeps but she always seemed to meekly do his bidding.

Washing now, wondering if he was listening, imagining her there Kitty completed the task as quickly as possible and was relieved when new clothes fastened. On the walk to his Landrover they discussed the build and slowly Kitty calmed herself. She would be pleased to see Claire and Hamish and actually found herself looking forward to seeing the children, hoping a game of cards might be in the offing.

Kitty found the silence on the drive unsettling, Donald was oblivious and whistled and shot his passenger frequent smiles. Now fully awake and rational she tried to remember having agreed to this? Questions on questions – when would she be able to call Jamie? What time would he bring her home? What would happen when he did drop her home? Would she need to fend off more unwelcome kisses?

Thankfully just as a mass of panic threatened to overwhelm her they arrived. Heather and Jonty, two blonde tonics ran out to meet them and Kitty slipped from the car feeling generally much better.

"Oh good Kathleen, Donald managed to prise you out." Claire lightly embraced her and the remaining worries faded away. Entreaties for a game of fish were quickly accepted and Kitty enjoyed the familiarity of sibling bickering. The children had obviously been practising and had made great leaps, Jonty held his hand like a pro now.

Play was suspended for a batch of grapefruit sized cheese scones. All that could be heard were murmurs of enjoyment and licking of fingers as the thick butter oozed and melted its escape.

"So Kathleen, how is Donald serving you? Are you happy with the build so far?" Hamish asked.

"Yes, it really feels like it's coming together. I'm enjoying helping where I can. I'm not half as strong as a Stewart but I'm very keen." The table all laughed although she thought she saw a trace of a sneer on Donald's face. "Yes the flags are going down next week and the slate on the roof isn't far off. Soon it will be windows and doors and it will be weather tight."

"Good, that's good, you have been favoured by the weather thus far – hasn't she Donald." Claire nudged Donald who had his gaze fixed firmly on Kitty.

"Aye, aye... it doesn't matter how good your builders are, if the weather is against ye you're doomed."

The children giggled, some in-joke Kitty surmised. Another game of fish and it was soon time for the children to say their goodnights. The adults sat as the light faded, reclined on the large sofas. Having consumed a couple of large glasses of wine Kitty realised her senses were somewhat dimmed. It wasn't until it was too late that she realised that the very smooth whiskey in her tumbler was not depleting because Donald was surreptitiously topping it up.

Standing, the simple task of going to the bathroom suddenly, and embarrassingly, became very complicated. Swaying slightly Donald reached up and steadied her, her addled mind thankful for the assistance but slow to react to the fact that he held firm to her hips, his fingers pressing in to her pelvic bones.

"Ohhh, dear!" was all Kitty could manage.

"Shall I help you?" Donald stood now behind her – too close behind her and Kitty lunged forward. Taking an exaggerated step she wobbled off to the downstairs toilet.

Holding her head in her hands Kitty berated herself, when would she learn the trouble she could get into with too much drink? Tapping at the door shattered the daydream she was enjoying with Jamie, of the first time they met and he had helped her on and off the toilet.

"Kathleen... are you alright?" Claire's concerned voice was comforting.

"Yyyyyyes, fine... just coming."

Glad of the confined space Kitty rested her head on the wall whilst she fumbled with the challenge of rolled up knickers and high tech taps.

"Oh I'm sorry... I'm embarrassed." Kitty peeked out through the gap in the door.

"Don't be silly, nothing to be sorry for, anyway Donald is going to get you home."

"Oh good... good old Donny."

Smiles and over-emotional hugs completed with Claire fastening Kitty's seat belt and closing the door. The motion of the car was a greater foe than Kitty could beat, and she finally gave in and let her eyes close and gave herself to sleep.

The blast of cold air that awoke her resulted in a shiver that started in her toes and culminated in actual chattering of teeth. How had she got so drunk? She didn't know, but what was certain was the strong arm wrapped around her guiding her through the blackness. Trying unsuccessfully to get her bearings Kitty looked at the floor. She could hear the sea, see gravel and moss path, she was being taken home.

Eyes closed again and lost in complete trust of the strong arms. She thought of Jamie, Oh Jamie, wonderful Jamie, and lovely Jamie... sexy Jamie.

The opening of a door, the clink of keys on glass. The arms now turned her and picked her up, one under her legs and one around her back pressing up, uncomfortably under her arm into her breast.

Aware of the exertion her burden was having, she could feel and hear the quickening of breaths coming heavy from her carrier. Kitty nestled her face into the shoulder and took a deep breath – she wished she could focus, to open her eyes and rouse herself. The smell was wrong, something was wrong. Trying to open her eyes now but her lids were like lead, she started to wriggle.

"Steady there Kathleen."

Voices screamed in her head, who was this? This wasn't Jamie! Where is Jamie? If this wasn't Jamie, who's arms were around her? Whose fingers were digging in her side?

"Stephen?" Kitty voice sounded far away even to her and it took great concentration to get one slurred word out.

Then the arms released her, she thought she was falling. Reaching back her hands felt the cold smoothness of sheet. She lay still and was glad, she knew she was still, but the room spun regardless. Nausea rose and settled with the movement and she lay on her side clutching the sheet, thinking only about her breathing. She hoped for sleep, praying for oblivion.

The footsteps of whoever brought her to bed had faded and gone. Who was it again? Maybe it was Donald – if it was she was glad he had gone. Sleep now was the priority and she searched for it. The whiskey-fuelled stupor overwhelmed her once more and Kitty found the relief she so craved.

She was dreaming of rocking in the small boat in her bay. Aware of moving but with no thought of why, Kitty was limp and obliging.

First her arms and chest and then her legs and hips. In her mind she saw Jamie, his conker red hair blowing in the sea breeze, stroking her legs. Swiftly and efficiently Donald undressed her, falsely assuming her murmurs were for him and not the man in her mind.

One large movement as the mattress dipped and Donald climbing into the bed sparked a small light of consciousness, but before she could grasp it and pull herself free of the blur of intoxication again she was lost. A hand brushed her curls from her face and she could see Jamie looking down on her, but this was wrong – she must open her eyes. She tried for many seconds but her head, too heavy on the pillow and the room too dark to see.

The touch was pleasurable and the hand reached further, over her hair and down her back. Smooth hands on her back – on her skin – where were her clothes? Now desperate to sleep she moaned again at the touch that lulled her, the gentlest of touch, she drifted once more.

The bed heaved again disturbing her and the heat of another body, too close, the nausea deep in her stomach rising. The stroke again ran over her hair and down her back but travelled now to her hip and pushed her easily on her back. Everything spun violently and she tried to roll back to the comfort of her side but was determinedly thwarted. Her arms were being lifted above her head; she tried to resist but lacked strength and focus. Kitty tried to shake her head but this made her feel even sicker and she had to concentrate on the rising burning bile in her throat.

Small strokes of her hair and the side of her face had the desired effect and she breathed deeply, still now she could return to her dreams. This time it was the first time Jamie had made love to her. Within the dream she remembered the way he kissed her breasts, and she had looked down and felt the mop of hair above her chest. Her back arched, she had wanted him to do so much more. This dream felt so real the hand rubbing her and the hot breath, but his teeth were too rough, the fingers pinching. Kitty caught her breath and a flash of lucidity.

Pushing at the fog in her mind and her eyes now accustomed to the dim light, she forced them open. Willing them to focus and trying to still the swirling room she looked at the head leaning down over her. Not red! But black! Not Jamie! But... "Donald!" Her voice a strangled whisper, Donald looked up and smiled at her.

"No, no, no." her voice was so weak and soon stifled as wet lips too soon pressed firmly on hers. Her parched mouth was no match for his forceful tongue that probed and invaded and rendered her silent.

Struggling to breathe and panicked, Kitty tried to push herself free. The strong arms that she had unwittingly let caress her now pinned her arms above her head.

Donald was relentless, lost in his passion. His hot breath and rough kisses, sucking and pulling at Kitty lips and tongue. Her dry lips split and the scorching pain and the taste of blood caused Kitty to moan. Slowly and deliberately Donald placed one knee between Kitty's legs forcing them apart. Then both his knees spreading her legs further. She was pinned, mute and helpless as he tried to enter her. Trying desperately to prevent it her small legs were no match for his and as he forced himself inside her two things happened simultaneously. Donald broke free from his assault on her mouth to let out a great groan, Kitty, mouth free, screamed. In her mind she wanted it to be a deafening screech but it stopped in her throat and was a small gargling cry. The pain inside her was immense – searing, burning, like nothing she had ever experienced. Donald didn't move, only to lower his head on the pillow next to her. Kitty's mind raced; suddenly sober she tried to make sense of it. He had got the wrong messages, how did she let it get this far? She must make him see sense of what he was doing; surely he would stop if he knew.

"Oh Kathleen." Kitty thought she might vomit there and then.

"Donald, get off... GET OFF NOW" Her voice still frustratingly weak and sobs rose in her throat and once again she struggled, pathetic against this man pinning her to the bed.

"Oh, Kathleen... you know you want this as much as I do. Don't fight it." He kissed her neck now and very slowly pulled out of her. At least he's stopping Kitty thought, so she allowed herself to relax her many clenched muscles. All the muscles in her body that had tried to fight him off and failing miserably burnt and ached.

"I'll be gentle, you feel sooo good!" Nearly free of him the pain peaked again as he pressed hard back.

"Urgh, ow, Donald get off you're hurting me. GET OFF!" Anger was rising in her now.

Donald lifted some of his weight off her but resolutely held her wrists in one hand and spreading his legs farther cupped her backside with his free hand.

Again his mouth sought hers, putting an end to her cries. Tears poured down the sides of her face and she could feel the cold pools forming in her ears. Over and over she screamed in her head, she screamed for Jamie, where was Jamie? Help me Jamie. She was powerless to end this, her thighs burned from trying to close and push him off. Her hands numbed and her wrists stung as his rhythm intensified, he gripped harder.

His relentless kissing tore again at her mouth and lips. Refusing to stop and give her the opportunity of talking or screaming, it took all of Kitty concentration to drag enough air in. At times she saw spots dancing in the darkness as she struggled not to faint.

Waiting for him to finish – for that was all Kitty could hope for – she experienced a strange phenomenon. Whether it was a physical reaction to the incessant pain, or from the lack of oxygen and residual alcohol, or an emotional response to being violated, she had the most rational thoughts. *So this is what it is like to be raped, I must tell Amanda. Thank god I can't get pregnant I'm on the pill.*

After what seemed like hours but was nearer fifteen minutes, it was over. A few final deep scorching thrusts and he was spent. Sweaty and heavy he lay on Kitty and perversely kissed her gently on the neck.

"Let me up, please." All fight gone, Kitty sounded almost polite. Donald pulled out of her, making her shudder and wince and rolled onto his back. Taking deep satisfied sighs he reached over and patted Kitty stomach – like a dog she thought.

"Aye Kathleen... I knew you'd be good," and there he lay eyes closed and content.

Every fibre of her had fought back, tensed and aching. There wasn't a part of her that didn't hurt. One arm wrapped around her breast, she winced as she cradled sore nipples. The pain in her insides soared and tightened as she tried to stand on too wobbly legs making her bite already swollen lips.

She was in the spare room, she recognised it in the meagre light, feeling her way around the walls to the handle to the en suite. Kitty hesitated, listening to the breathing now that was deep and a hint of a snore – had he really gone to sleep?

Closing the door as quietly as she could with shaking hands, she fumbling desperately to lock it. Finding the light switch the bright spotlights hurt her eyes. When she could look out from behind her hands she examined herself in the long mirror. Her eyes and lips were swollen like she had never seen before. Her breasts and neck red from his attentions.

Gripping the edge of the basin Kitty vomited, her retching and heaving shudders hurt her all over. Once finished and her mouth rinsed Kitty's legs could hold her no more and she staggered to the toilet. Bracing herself she tried to wee. When finally she managed the pain was excruciating, white-hot knives would have been kinder. Wiping herself gingerly and flushing away the bloody semen had her retching again.

Her whole body shook, with cold and shock. She felt dirty; the smear of his sweat was all over her. What should she do? She couldn't go back in there. Kitty climbed into the bath and hugged her knees to her chest despite the pain it caused. Shaking uncontrollably and growing colder and colder there was nothing for it, she must have a bath.

Turning the taps slowly so as not to wake the monster in the next room, the water rose around her, one side of her body cold, the other scolding. She could feel it but was powerless to simply swirl the water with her hands. Nor could she cry, she was numb. Cold, shaking and numb.

The water was too hot and she watched remotely as the skin turned red under the waterline. Submerging her head the sting and prickle of too hot water was a welcome distraction from the other pains.

It was the coldness of the water finally stirred her to move. Listening constantly to the sounds emanating from behind the door, straining to hear any signs of movement. Pausing to dry, the odd loud snore freezing her to the spot and halted her breath. There was nothing for it, better to get her clothes while he still slept. It took many deep breaths, a few false starts and all her courage to unlock the door.

The moon was bright now and courtesy of the large windows, the grey light showed Kitty her clothes, neatly folded on the chair. Odd Kitty thought, he had planned to do that to her but stopped to fold her outfit. Being dressed made her feel better, less vulnerable. Kitty stood by the bed and looked down at the gently snoring man. Hair ruffled and tanned smooth chest exposed he looked, well...
handsome. "Like butter wouldn't melt in his mouth." Strange timing for one of her mother's sayings to pop into her head. And thinking of her whilst looking at him made Kitty feel sick again.

Tip toeing, she left the room and closed the door silently behind her. Once downstairs she paced the long window wall, occasionally stopping in her tracks to strain her ears for sounds from upstairs, watching the sea under the moonlight.

It was three am and the large metal clock ticked harsh and sinister. She couldn't decide what she should do. She couldn't leave, they were in the middle of nowhere. Should she call someone – Jamie? God she wanted to hear his voice. But then he would know, he would hear it in her voice she knew it. She would cry then, and he's in Harris, and she was so ashamed.

Could she call someone else? She felt her shirt pocket and there was the list of contact numbers, all of them Stewarts. She couldn't tell them, what would be her excuse? Why was she there in the first place?

"You know you want it." That had been his words, did he mean it? Could he really think that? On any planet could that have been taken as consensual? The burning pain still raw left Kitty in no doubt that Whisky or no, she had consented to nothing. Another pain persisted and would not be ignored – her throat rasped and scratched as she attempted a discreet cough.

Walking over to the fridge she took the milk and in an action she had never done before gulped straight from the carton. It soothed beautifully and filled her emptiness. Suddenly tired now but too fearful for sleep, Kitty turned the leather chair away from the view and backed it into the corner. Very thankful for the heavy throw even if it was of itchy wool, she cocooned herself.

"Morning sleepy head, what are you doing here?" The mug of coffee clinking on the glass table next to her. Waking, her mind spun to process the statement and her now hazy memories of last night. By the time her eyes shot open a bath robed Donald whistled his way back to the kitchen. This didn't equate. Had it been a terrible nightmare? Kitty reached up and felt her sore lips, and reaching for the coffee an array of stabbing pains gripped her pelvis and legs. This was no dream.

"Do you want eggs?"

Kitty was stunned, stupefied. The shaking began.

"No I don't want fucking eggs!" her brain screamed at him but as Donald looked at her for a response he just saw her frowning into her coffee.

"I'll do some." Kitty's eyes were glued to him pottering happily in his kitchen. Legs and bare chest exposed he made toast – no remorse. He continued to whistle as he scrambled eggs – not a flicker of regret or apology. Even laying the table and pouring the orange juice he smiled over to her.

"Not much of a morning person then?" He winked, he actually bloody well WINKED! Kitty tried to speak but nothing came out.

"Come on then, breakfast is served." And Donald smiled and held out a chair. Oh my god she thought, now he is a gentleman. Kitty tried to process this and struggled. Donald raised his eyebrows.

"It'll get cold." Like he was talking to a child and like a child she walked stiffly to the table.

Wincing involuntarily as she sat down Donald looked up and smiled that smarmy, sleazy Mr Green smile. Kitty thought she would vomit again. Her hand, along with the rest of her, was shaking badly now and her coffee dripped and splashed on the table.

Donald grabbed her wrist, the wrist he had bruised last night and set the cup down. Angrily now, "What is the matter with you?"

"W, wh... what's the matter?" Kitty voice was weak and hesitant.

"Yes, are you just hungover, what's wrong with you?" throwing the tea towel he was carrying into the sink. Hugging herself she looked into his eyes.

"Do you really not know?"

"Know what? Is this about last night? Don't be embarrassed I know it wasn't the greatest but you were pretty drunk." Donald rubbed a hand across his bare chest and laughed at a memory of last night. He sat at his table and tucked into his breakfast.

"Still we could always try again today now you're sober."

The shaking built and the tears rolled down her face now.

"You hurt me." She struggled to get the words out. She was scared now and was afraid of his reaction.

"Oh sorry, was I a bit rough? – You seemed up for it." Donald tapped his chin with his fork as he tried to remember hurting her. Reaching across the table he extended a long thin finger and ran it across her bruised bottom lip. Kitty recoiled and again suppressed the wave of nausea.

"I asked you to stop, I screamed... y, you... really hurt me!"

"Oh... oh." Thoughtful now.

"Well, next time I'll be gentler." With horror Kitty realised he was going to lean over and kiss her. Leaping up regardless of the pain it caused the chair clattered over behind her and she staggered back.

"Donald... you raped me." It was so quiet his quizzical look was either disbelief or lack of hearing.

"YOU RAPED ME!" slowly and courageous now she repeated it.

"Oh come now, don't be ridiculous. Are you some innocent young maiden who's virtue I've stolen – ridiculous?"

He stood and started towards her. His bare chest – the chest that crushed down on her, his obvious nakedness under the robe, transfixed kitty. She knew only too well now the extent of her own puny weakness, her complete inability to fend him off. Kitty was frozen in fear.

"Kathleen, you were very drunk and if I say so, you were gagging for it." Really, he could be smug at a time like this.

"Huh" her jaw dropped – she was speechless. The humiliation, she remembered now and a memory of being caressed, but that was the dream of Jamie. When she realised in her drunken state that it was Donald she had desperately wanted him to stop.

"I asked you to stop!" clenching her fists and trying to not cry any more so she could talk.

"Yes but all girls feign that – no stop – no don't stop!" His impersonation of an indecisive girl made Kitty's blood boil. Had he done this before?

"I don't feign anything, you hurt me... y, y, you raped me."

The silence that followed had both parties reliving last night's events over in their heads. As far as Donald was concerned Kitty had responded to his touch, she screamed and moaned with pleasure when he entered her. She was a bit frigid but she was a widow, maybe it had been a long time. Donald was first to speak.

"Well Kathleen I admit it did lack some romance, you were very drunk after all but I enjoyed it and thought you did too." At least he had the good manners to sound a little contrite.

"Well I didn't!"

"You were making all the right noises."

"Donald I was trying to scream and cry out," Kitty lifted tentative fingers and tapped gently on her lips, feeling the damage.

"Oh," looking down now Kitty watched in disbelief as he finished his breakfast and drained his mug. "Well shall we put this down to a misunderstanding?" He looked cautiously up at the pale trembling woman.

"I... I, don't know what to say" Kitty blinked back at him.

"I really like you Kathleen. I'd hoped for some time that we could be... well more. I thought last night you wanted that too?"

"Definitely not, I was dreaming, at least I thought I was dreaming until I came to and... and you wouldn't stop." Kitty lifted her fleece sleeves and stretched out her arms to reveal the red bruises around her wrists.

"Well maybe in time." He spoke quietly and rose to approach her now.

"NEVER!" her voice quivered now and she doubted how much longer she could stand here before her legs gave way. "Take me home. And if it's at all possible I never want to speak to you again." Her voice was low and resolute. Donald knew enough about women not to question this.

Donald flounced up the metal stairs, they vibrated and reminded Kitty of the stairs on the ferry, and concluded this house had just as much soul. Hugging herself to try and warm the chill in her bones, she reached and finished the coffee. Although difficult to swallow and lodging in her chest, Kitty knew she had to have something. She was ravenous and the eggs did look good, but if the coffee was a struggle she knew toast would be a step too far.

When Donald returned, dressed and composed Kitty sensed his change in tack. Speaking quietly, "If there was a misunderstanding I don't feel I was in the wrong, you were the inebriated one after all."

"You were the one holding me down against my will!" again Kitty pushed up her sleeves and rubbed her wrists.

"Well." Donald coughed and then at least had the good grace to blush.

"Please just take me home" Kitty was using her last ounce of her limited reserves and needed desperately to be alone.

"Well... I am sorry if you didn't ... enjoy it."

Kitty sighed – he would never admit it or even appreciate what he had done and she had not the energy to argue.

Climbing up onto the high car seat was painful, and Kitty sat with her hands under her thighs, clenching her legs in an attempt to brace herself against the bumps and turns as the brooding Donald drove her none to carefully home.

Relief at seeing her drive soon turned to dread as she saw two vans in residence.

"Just leave me here." She blurted out but it was too late and Donald pulled noisily onto the gravel.

"Well I am sorry you are upset Kathleen but I have wracked my brain – and I was the sober one – maybe it wasn't the greatest sex, maybe, it wasn't my finest hour but I hope you will come to see reason and will let me take you out for dinner or something soon to make it up to you."

"Really... REALLY! – just go and please don't come back, deal with Malcolm but do not contact me, or come here without me knowing – EVER!"

Kitty slid to the floor and slammed the door behind her, thankful to hear the roar as he sped off. Repeating over and over in her mind as she walked to the house, hold it together till you get in, just till you get in, hold it together. The cramping pain running up her legs and the chafing burn with each step made normal walking impossible.

33

Room Service

Trevor, Jeff and Malcolm watched her closely from the roof as she made her way to the store, head down. She dare not look up to them but went straight to the store and locked the door behind her.

"Pa!"

"I see it lad, I see it."

They went back to work, and the hammering and whistling though dimmed by her quilt were a comfort as she wept quietly under the covers. Kitty had fallen into a much-needed sleep when lunchtime arrived and Malcolm could put it off no longer. Always eager to be involved it was obvious something was amiss.

Tap, tap... tap, tap.

"Lassie are ye alright?"

Tap... tap, TAP. Louder with each knock. Kitty struggled free from her covers and wiped the tear sodden hair from its position plastered on her cheek. Resting her forehead on the door she knew she dare no let Malcolm see her in this state.

"Hi Malcolm." her voice weak and hesitant.

"Lassie, let me in would ye?"

"No... I'm not well." Her voice was distant and flat.

"What ails ye?" A mix of authority and concern.

"Nothing... I'm... just not well," she didn't even have the thought or energy to think of a lie.

"Jamie said ye did'na call last night and the lad is worried."

"I know." Malcolm could hear the pain in her voice but could not see the tears that poured at the thought of Jamie.

"Will ye be calling him lass?" Malcolm knew he would have to call Jamie himself if not, as he had already called his uncle three times today.

"Malcolm..." Kitty coughed, her voice was very shaky. "Sorry but would you phone him and tell him I will call in a couple of days when I feel better?" When the bruises had gone and hopefully the raging shame and humiliation had faded too.

"I ken he'd much rather talk to you Kathleen." Malcolm rested large hands on the door - he had comforted his daughter enough over the years to know he wished Kitty would open the door and accept a hug.

"I... I, I can't." Sobs now prevented further discussion and Kitty was relieved to see Malcolm's shadow pass the window. Dropping onto the bed she once again hid under the covers and sought refuge.

Hours passed and gnarling hunger woke her. Kitty, puffy eyed and wrung out made her way through a pack of ginger nuts. Listening then and peering out of the curtain Kitty guessed they were working on the front dormers. Short of perching on the stone sink Kitty would have to make a dash for the outside toilet. If she didn't hurt so much she would have climbed up on the sink so as not to not risk seeing any of the men.

Slipping her shoes on she unlocked the door and headed across the thirty foot to the toilet. To her horror and too far down the path to turn back, the sound of the chain pulling and the door swinging open showed Trevor fastening his flies.

"Afternoon lass..." cheerfulness replaced quickly by frown and a tone of pure concern. "Kathleen, lassie, ock will ye look at yin sel."

She turned to run back to the shed but Trevor, like his father and brother had been worrying about her all morning and reached for her hand. Catching her by her right wrist, her flinch and small cry weren't unnoticed. Trevor gently held her hand and with the other and batting off Kitty attempts to conceal it, examined her wrist. Raising the sleeve to reveal the now red, brown bruises showing the memory of fingers in shape and size. Very gently he lifted the down turned face and examined the swollen red eyes and more worryingly the swollen and cut lips.

Watery eyes blinked up at him. Trevor gathered Kitty ever so gently to his chest and whispered Gaelic words of comfort. She recoiled at first at the contact but soon melted into it reminding herself that this man would not hurt her.

After a minute, feeling her relax he guided her slowly back to the store. Pushing her very slowly onto one of the chairs, his jaw clenched as he watched her tentative lop sided descent, and the twinge as she slowly and painfully came to rest. Turning away and muttering dark Gaelic words he filled the kettle and calmly made four mugs of tea.

"Go to the toilet lass if ye need to I'll take these out... I'll not involve them in... this." Trevor eyed her up and down "I'll be back in a minute to... talk." Kitty just nodded, head bowed. Slowly and uncomfortably she stood and walked or more accurately wobbled to the toilet. Trevor took the key from the door and hurried out with the mugs, slopping as much as he carried.

Sitting on the toilet Kitty plotted her next move. She was desperate to be alone, away from pitying looks like Trevor's. Of course he would tell Malcolm, he would definitely tell Jamie. Returning to the store Kitty could hear muffled voices from the front of the house, of course bloody Gaelic! Taking Pimples keys and her handbag Kitty ran as fast as she could, ignoring the pain in her legs and glad of the spongy moss. She looked back at a perplexed Trevor, hands on hips outside the store. Leaving the driveway in her trusty van Kitty looked back no more.

Kitty had no idea where to go but drove until her arms ached. She had come across a reasonably sized town and set about her mission. A castellated large hotel set back from the road, Pimples purred to a halt in the farthest space in the car park at the rear. Kitty rested her head on her hands at the wheel and relaxed. The adrenaline of the run gone, all the aches and pains that were getting worse by the hour now overwhelmed her. All she wanted now was to be in a room, anonymous and safe.

Trevor had known she was sure, the feeling of being dirty was back, traces of him still on her. Kitty began to shake again as the icy coldness threatened to eat into her very bones again. She tried to rally herself, as taking the overnight bag she used at Jamie's she stood in reception waiting for the bell to be answered.

A nondescript man in his forties eyed her disinterestedly, "Yes madam?"

"I'd like a room please for a couple of nights."

"Are you travelling alone?"

"Yes."

"Come far?" His tone never altered and Kitty was desperate for him to just give her the key.

"Wimbledon." Was all she could think of to say, her mind was a fog.

"Oh, well ye must by tired?" He looked up then and Kitty pretended to rub her eyes in an effort to disguise her face.

"Yes I need a couple of days rest."

"Quite, and will ye require supper?"

"Yes, is it possible to have all my meals served in the room please?"

"If ye wish." He obviously couldn't care less and this guest was delighted.

After handing over her credit card Kitty walked slowly up the two flights of stairs and locked the door behind her. The room was blue and white with heavy Victorian furniture. It was crisp and clean and comfortable and Kitty had two nights, four meals and four baths without setting foot outside the room. No amount of soaking, scrubbing could erase the vile, ingrained feeling of him on her skin. Kitty watched television on a constant loop, dozing and eating with no definition between day and night, only the room service breaking up her stay.

Wednesday morning breakfast arrived, - Kitty had ordered full English, at least her appetite had returned. Today though it was not served by the young chamber maid but a middle aged woman with dyed black hair and a bosom bursting out of an ill fitting dress. Kitty took the tray and was about to close the door when a chubby hand held it open.

"My husband said ye were from down south."

"Y, yes that's right." It was the first time Kitty had opened her mouth to speak since checking in and it sounded strangely odd.

"Now it's none of our business but you've not left your room since ye arrived, and, well we were wondering if ye were alright. Wouldn't be doing me job if I did'na check ya was ok."

"Oh... thank you. No I'm fine. I was just very tired and needed a few days to just unwind." Kitty could tell this woman wasn't going anywhere without a tale told, Kitty opted for the old faithful.

"My husband died, I'm moving here but needed some time to get over the funeral."

"Oh bless ye lass, and you a slip of a thing... say no more, no more." The woman backed away and smiled apologetically. No one ever wants to hang around for that conversation. Kitty ate the breakfast and for the first time had to face facts.

1 – Donald raped her – should she see a doctor? Why? Could she be pregnant, answer no, so why bother.

2 – Should she go to the police? She was convinced Donald didn't believe he had raped her, he hadn't intended rape. She was so drunk and was probably giving him all the wrong signals, answer, no to the police.

She wouldn't press charges and the thought of telling a police man let alone a doctor was abhorrent. Her GP's would know, the very people she had spent the evening with on that day – no it was not to be tolerated. The people in the pub, the post office, Angela and Gavin would all these people know and look at her differently from now on. The dreadful thought then that the island gossip would find her dirty secret, spread to the Stewarts, lovely Maureen and Dougal. Would they want their son dating a woman like her then, damaged goods?

She knew then she had hidden too long and would have to go back to Tide's Reach. Would Malcolm have phoned Jamie, would he be convinced – OF COURSE NOT. Would Trevor have told him what he had seen? It was then that the real terror came over her. Would Trevor and Malcolm tell Jamie who dropped her off and the state of her and put two & two together?

"Oh holy crap!" Kitty realised she might be too late. Hurriedly packing her few possessions and dressing for the first time since she had arrived at her hiding place. Kitty paid at the desk only to return a few minutes later to ask where she was and directions to find her way home. Nervousness rising the nearer she got, her heart was pounding as she turned down her drive.

"Oh shit!"

There was little place to park, the vans here in their usual place, an old Landrover she didn't recognise and a police car. Pimples brakes complained at being held on the steepest turn of the drive, and Kitty settled on blocking in the vans.

The full English was sitting precariously as her heart raced and belly churned. Raised voices, a mixture of Gaelic and English was coming from inside the store. Every fibre of her being wanted to turn and run but her reasoning told her that she had probably been the cause of this gathering.

Peering in the window was a sight that any other time would have been comical. Three large builders sat in a row on the daybed looking like oversized wise monkeys. The policeman sat at the table with Maureen, Maureen! Why was she here? Standing at the back of the room, arms folded with his back to the room was Jamie.

"He's gone as well I tell you!" Malcolm growled "Been to his office, said he's gone for a holiday don't know when he will be back."

"But she wouldn't, she couldn't have gone with him." Jamie's voice was hoarse and Kitty looked at the faces of all those who now looked at him.

"Hush darling, we will find her." Maureen stood and joined her son and rubbed his back in large circular strokes.

"There's no way she'd go away with that animal, I saw her, the state of her."

"Don't Trevor please, I can'na bear it!"

Walking to the door Kitty had to cough a few times before anyone noticed her. Trevor was the first to notice her.

"Bloody hell, Kitty, WHERE HAVE YOU BEEN?"

Standing almost before anyone else saw her he reached for her hands and looked at her wrists. Holding them for all to see each finger mark was bluish black centred with faint red and green edges.

"See what did I tell ye!"

Jamie turned and Kitty was horrified to see his pale, drawn face, tear stained and shocked. Kitty and his eyes locked but neither could speak or move, it was Maureen who rushed over and hugged her.

"God bless, oh, there, there." She held her gently and rocked slowly. This warm embrace opened the floodgates and Kitty sobbed and hugged back. Jamie soon came to his senses and moved nearer but nothing was said above Kitty's crying.

"Kathleen" Jamie's voice was ragged. Kitty yearned to launch herself at him but failed even to look him in the eyes, "Kathleen, you must tell us... where have you been. I've been out of my mind. For gods sake what happened?"

Jamie tried to take one of her hands from his mother's shoulders to further examine the bruising but she pulled it away. The clamour rose, the general gist being they were going to track down Donald and do unmentionable things to him. Order was finally restored by the policeman, or Patrick as he was known. Only after eliciting promises from all the Stewarts not to lynch Donald, he insisted everyone was to wait outside.

The protection of clinging to Maureen was too valuable to be relinquished, and Patrick agreed to her staying. Kitty couldn't bear to look at Jamie, let alone talk to him, but hated herself for it. She was well aware it was he who kicked, swore and punched at everything in his way as he stormed out.

Maureen pulled Kitty down to sit with her on the day bed.

"Here darling have a sip of tea." Maureen reached for a mug and Kitty gratefully accepted. Sipping the strong tea eased her sore throat – must be Jeff's, three sugars. Patrick and Maureen exchanged knowing glances as they both looked at Kitty's bruises.

"Kathleen" Maureen's voice was smooth as honey and she

continued to rub Kitty's back, it was quite intoxicating. "Malcolm thinks he saw Donald, your architect drop you home the other morning... is that true?"

Starring fixedly at the tea Kitty finally nodded.

"Did you spend... did you stop at Donald's house Sunday night?" Kitty began to shake, Maureen held her hands.

"You can tell us darling."

Again the best Kitty could offer was a minute nod as she watched her tears drop into the mug. Maureen, gently as if touched by a feather laid her hand over the marks on her wrists.

"Kathleen... did he hurt you?" Silence "In anyway?" Nothing.

Maureen and Patrick exchanged long looks. Trying a different approach the policeman asked.

"Have you been with Donald for the last couple of days?" This did elicit a response – albeit croaky and quiet it was very definite, "No!"

"Kathleen what happened darling, please tell us?" Maureen wrapped an arm around her back now.

"A misunderstanding." The words caught in her throat like acid and she began to sob again. Patrick was no more convinced than Maureen about this, but needed Kitty to own it. Maureen hugged her tight and wiped away tears of her own.

"Mrs Harris... Kathleen do you wish to press charges or make a complaint in regards to the misunderstanding." Kitty wondered how many times she would have to hear that phrase before it stopped feeling that she had been raped.

"NO!"

"Kathleen are you sure?" Patrick had a nice smile Kitty thought.

"I'm so sorry, so sorry to have caused all this trouble." Kitty slumped into Maureen's arms.

"Patrick I think she's had enough for now. I'd like to get her home, darling can I take you back with me?"

Weighing her options, being alone here, to go back to James's house and have to tell him or – the most favourable, to go and be pampered by Maureen and Maggie and get lost in the Rhododendrons. Looking up fleetingly she managed a very small smile.

"Yes please."

"Well if you change your mind Kathleen, here's my number" lowering his voice and waiting for Maureen to get up and put the mugs in the sink. "If there was any actual abuse the physical evidence should be obtained as soon as possible." Kitty couldn't look at him momentarily, she was in no doubt to what he was referring but she had had half a dozen baths since then.

"Ok then, but if you change your mind call me." Patrick patted her arm and couldn't resist placing his hand over the marks above her hands, fitted like a glove. "Call me!"

Patrick picked up his hat and walked outside with Maureen. Kitty could hear Jamie questioning, voice raised. She desperately wanted to run out and into his arms but what would she say, how could she ever tell him. Pulling her knees up she shuffled back into the corner of the bed. The pain in her strained muscles was worse now than Sunday. She was still very sore and swollen, and weeing still very painful. In Kitty's mind women gave birth and it all recovers, and given time and hopefully no medical intervention this too would get better.

The whispered conversations outside are stifled as Patrick says his farewells reinforcing warnings to all the men about revenge. The door opened slowly and Kitty didn't look up but heard Maureen's advice follow Jamie in, "Give her time."

A large hand stroked her hair, a gesture Kitty had always loved but now she jumped away from it, shaking.

"Oh Kathleen" Desperation now, he sank to his knees before her on the floor and tried to raise her face.

"No Jamie... please don't" she mumbled into her knees.

"Christ Kathleen... what... what did he do to you?" Jamie was shaking now and taking a deep breath he gently took her hand and looked for himself at the marks. Ensnaring her tiny wrist in his hand it was plain to see how these had happened.

"I've been out of my mind worrying. Beautiful, lovely Kathleen... where have you been?"

Still muffled by her knees, "I'm so sorry... I'm so sorry Jamie." Jamie leant forward and hugged the shaking hunched creature before him.

"Hush, hush, hush now lass, ye can tell me later... but Kathleen can ye promise me one thing?"

"Anything." Came her small reply.

"Promise me ye won't run away again, I could'na stand it."

Kitty nodded and for the first time forced herself to look at him. Jamie took her face in his hands and kissed the still puffy bottom lip where the cut had been healing. Kitty tensed and he loosened his grip although already gentle and kissed her forehead. Kitty could feel his tears landing on her.

"You're safe now lass, do you want to stay with my parents, mother thinks it's for the best? But if you would like to we could go back to my cottage?"

Trying to look into his eyes she failed miserably.

"Don't be upset, but... but I think I'd like to go to... to be with your mum."

"Fine whatever you need; of course... but... Kathleen have I done anything?" Jamie so confused and desperate for answers.

"No my dear, sweet Jamie." Uncoiling herself she stood stiffly and hugged him for many minutes.

"I'll pack you a bag." Kitty nodded and reluctantly let him go. Leaving the shed she tried to look at Jeff, Malcolm and Trevor but their pitying expressions made her feel even worse than she thought possible. Trevor patted her shoulder gently as she passed,

"Dunna fear lass we will look after everything here." Attempting a small smile Kitty walked slowly and shakily across the lawn and the builders and her boyfriend exchanged dark glares.

Maureen took the keys, "James get in the back with her, the lass could do with a cuddle."

Jamie opened the door and looked on intently, desperate to help but not knowing how. As Kitty raised her leg to get in the high Landrover, her hips and legs ached terribly and she struggled, involuntarily a small cry escaped her when Jamie tried to help her second leg in.

"Jesus Kathleen, what did he do to you?" Jamie tried to keep his voice low but spat out the question through gritted teeth. Kitty buried her face in her hand, the relief of being away from everyone else she sobbed, making no attempt to control it any longer.

"Don't rush her darling, all in good time, get in."

Jamie slammed the door, and everyone jumped as he kicked the rear tyre as he walked around the car, every inch of him shaking with rage. Climbing in besides her Jamie took her carefully in his arms and cradled her head to his chest. The pounding of his heart told Kitty how upset he was, how was she ever to tell him.

34

Facing the Family

Once at the house Maureen took the bags and walked in through the open front door. Dougal stood solemnly at the entrance and exchanged knowing glances with his wife who had text what little she knew. Jamie rushed around and undid the seat belt and helped a wincing Kitty to her feet. He glared up at his father and swallowed the taste of blood from where he had been biting the insides of his cheeks.

Kitty's puffy eyes looked up at the owner of the large suede feet at the door. Dougal offered his arms but very tactfully waited for her to move in to him.

"Careful" Jamie whispered, his father smiled at him as he gave Kitty the softest of hugs, leaning down and talking quietly into her ear.

"You poor dear girl, stay with us as long as you need." Then releasing her he looked at his ashen faced son, "James take her to your room, I'm sure the lass would like a rest before dinner."

Jamie put his fingertips on the small of the back of the dazed shell of his girlfriend, even this was tainted now Kitty thought sadly. Jamie opened his bedroom door and the sea glistened in the far distance though the long window.

"Do you want to get into bed?" there was silence, Kitty seemed unable to move.

"No... I like that view," was all she could think to say.

"Wait right here." Kitty had no plans to move and if not directed wondered how long she would have stood there. Jamie kissed the top of her head and hurried from the room. Moments later the door clattered open and a pretty small floral fireside chair was hoisted in place looking out of the window. Maggie followed behind with a large soft throw and taking Kitty by the hand guided her to the seat. Wrapping her in the throw Maggie gently encouraged Kitty to sit in the snug button backed chair. Patting the gently shaking shoulder and with one stroke of her hair she left them both.

"I'll be bringing ye some nice sweet tea lass." Pausing to hug Jamie, Kitty could hear Maggie's advice, "Be patient wi her laddie, she'll be right in time."

Jamie sat on the floor by her feet and rested his head on her lap. Kitty's ran her fingers through his hair. Kitty's giggle disturbed the silence and Jamie looked up with a start.

"What?"

"After Tommy died I used to sit like this for hours... but with my cat, sorry it just reminded me." All humour gone now.

"Charming... are you that sad now Kathleen?"

"Nearly" she answered honestly.

"Fucking bastard!" The anger he had been trying to conquer exploded, "What did he do darling?"

Kitty couldn't help smiling, he sounded like his parents, she had noticed, and loved the way they used that particular term of endearment.

"Not now Jamie... I, I can't. Can't tell you..., I'm so sorry but don't ask me, not yet" Her voice was a whisper, all spark had gone.

"It's driving me mad! Kathleen... did he hurt you?"

"Yes" Her throat burned, and her heart ached.

"Did he force himself on ye?" Jamie looked up at the red eyes that filled a new. Kitty wanted to shout and scream, YES, HE RAPED ME! But once those words were out there what consequences would follow? She just wanted it to end, to move on, and to forget.

"Kathleen, did he?" Kitty looked down at the pleading eyes and pleaded right back.

"Oh, Kathleen, my Kathleen." Jamie buried his face in the yellow throw and now cried. Jamie's tears were for the days of worry, frustration at ferry operators not getting him back to her sooner. Anger at Trevor for not stopping her that day she ran. Most of all it was tears of rage for all the terrible images that played over and over in his head of what Donald had done to the loveliest woman he had ever known.

There was a soft knock on the door, Jamie wiped his face on his sleeve looking surprised at who stood in the doorway. Kitty looked around quickly at seeing his reaction.

"Now Kathleen I hope you don't mind but Maureen was so worried about you." Claire smiled at Jamie who fumed back at her, his anger evident.

"This is your fault! He is your friend!" Jamie spat the words at her.

"No Jamie, no. This is nothing to do with Claire." Reaching for his hand as he stood to stand protectively between the two women. "Could you... would you mind waiting outside?"

"But Kathleen!" Pleadingly he looked down at her.

"Please." Frail and vulnerable, how could he refuse?

"I'll be right outside." Jamie stalked out of the room glaring at Claire the entire time. Claire closed the door quietly and walked over to the window. Squatting next to Kitty Claire rested a gentle hand on her arm. The change in the young woman was very marked from just a few short days ago when she had been laughing and tipsy in Claire's house. Dark rings all around her eyes. Lank hair and sallow skin, Kitty had aged a decade.

"I'm so sorry Kathleen, can you tell me what happened? As your friend but equally as your doctor, anything you say will of course be confidential." Kitty for the first time recounted every detail. Saying it out loud made it suddenly real. She had been raped, there was no misunderstanding. Claire held her hand, horror and disbelief in equal measure.

"Do you want to press charges?"

"No... as impossible as it sounds... I think, he thinks, I really wanted it."

"That's no excuse Kathleen!"

"No... I suppose I know that. But I just want it over."

"It will be too late for a rape kit, but Kathleen I'd like to examine you... do you think you can let me?" Claire's voice was calm and assertive and Kitty stood and started to undress. Like any good professional Claire's examination had already begun, watching Kitty's hesitant and obviously uncomfortable movements. Laid on the bed covered by the soft throw Kitty removed her underwear and Claire began her meticulous examination.

"This cut lip?" Claire turned Kitty face from side to side.

"Was this a hit?"

"No just... his mouth ... and... teeth I think." Kitty could see the memory in her mind and she fought to suppress it and rid it.

"Bruising on your breasts, is that a cut over your left nipple?" Claire struggled to retain her professionalism and detach herself from the thought of her friend as the perpetrator of these injuries.

The bruised wrists received the usual treatment; fingers and thumbs lay over the long oval patches of blue. Kitty gathered the throw up around her neck as Claire looked at her thighs.

"Extensive bruising here, and here." The gentlest of touch still caused Kitty to jump.

"Oh Kathleen." Claire tutted as she slowly splayed Kitty legs.

"It still hurts to pee."

"Yes it's still very swollen, and those cuts will heal." Pulling the throw down and tucking Kitty in all around her shaking body, Claire could control her feelings no longer. Sitting down on the bed and taking one of Kitty's hands, Claire made no effort to wipe away the tears that poured down her face.

"Oh Kathleen, Jamie is right, I caused this! I encouraged you to be in his company! I knew he liked you but... believe me, please, you do believe me I had no idea he was capable of anything like this." Claire squeezed Kitty hand. "Are you sure you don't want to press charges, the evidence is quite clear."

"No, no he's gone away. If he has any sense, and someone needs to warn him – if he does come back I'm scared Jamie and his clan will lynch him – please you must make him understand."

"Does Jamie know the facts, are you two serious?"

"Yes, we are... well we were... I don't know what he will think of me! I'm too ashamed to tell him. I don't think I can get the words out."

"Ashamed, no, no! Kathleen. Nothing you could have done deserved this!" Claire gestured with her hand from Kitty head to her feet. "This was not, WAS NOT! Your fault!"

"But I was drunk and when..." Kitty sobbed, "He undressed me and put me to bed he... stroked, my, hair." Crying loudly and struggling to get the words out. "And I thought... I thought in my drunkenness it was Jamie!"

"And then what?" Claire frowned down at her and Kitty couldn't look at her.

"I realised it wasn't... before, you know, before it had got past kissing. I told him he was hurting me, I screamed when he..." Kitty voice trailed off s she looked up at the ceiling.

"Then he should have stopped – what did he do?"

"He kissed me so hard I couldn't cry out and he held me down." Kitty rubbed her wrists and then pulled up her legs recalling the pain.

"Kathleen he raped you. Never doubt that. Even if you don't press charges tell Jamie. You need to share this or it will eat you up, and do more damage than has already been done." Claire rested her hands on Kitty's twiddling wrists.

"I will record all this, so if you change your mind I have all the facts – FACTS! Kathleen this is not a misunderstanding" Kitty smiled, Maureen had obviously primed Claire.

"Shall I let Jamie in? – Please tell him." Kitty nodded, she knew she had to face that sooner or later.

"As good a time as any."

"That's a girl. I'll leave a prescription for some painkillers and some sleeping pills in case you need them. Come and see me at the surgery in a couple of days. You know you can call me anytime." Claire bent and kissed the top of Kitty head. GP's that did house visits was one thing but kissing you goodbye was something else, despite herself Kitty smiled.

Jamie and Claire whispered for many minutes, and Kitty was glad of it. Sod doctor, patient confidentiality she prayed Claire would tell him first. Jamie entered the room, the muscles in his jaw clenching furiously. Kitty could easily imagine the rate at which his heart raced now. The dark rings around his eyes, Kitty wondered how long since he had a decent nights sleep – and it was all her fault.

Sitting on the edge of the bed he looked down at the mass of blonde curls peeping over the yellow chenille.

"Can you tell me now?"

"Only if you don't speak. It's going to be terrible I don't think I'll manage if you get angry."

"That boat has long since sailed." He tried to force a smile. "Ok – I'll try."

"It was partly my fault and I'm so sorry, so sorry Jamie... I didn't realise he was topping up my glass all evening." Recounting the walk in the dark – confusion, imagining it was him and not Donald. Being awoken and undressed, having her hair stroked – again thinking it was Jamie. These were the most humiliating admissions.

"Do you hate me? I wouldn't blame you if you did. I brought this horror on myself."

"Of course I don't hate you, Kathleen, I love you." Jamie voice faltered, it was taking all his self-control to keep the rising bile in his stomach and not throw up at the images of Donald molesting her.

"I really wouldn't blame you if you didn't want to be with me any more – not now" Kitty looked up at Jamie.

"Is that why you didn't want to come back to my cottage... you thought I might not want you there?" Jamie scratched and shook his head as Kitty nodded.

"I love you Kathleen Harris. I don't know what I would have done if you hadn't come back. I would have run mad and searched the world for you." Kitty didn't doubt it, but boy did she need to hear it now. Jamie looked into her eyes and planted the most delicate of kisses then reached up and traced the healing line on her still puffy lips.

"Don't look at me while I tell you the rest."

Jamie sat slouched on the edge of the bed looking out over to the sea. Kitty reached around and he held her small hand on both of his, tracing the veins and fingernails. Then turning her hand and placing his fingers over the marks.

He shook as she told him and his tears fell onto their entwined fingers. It took monumental control to sit still and quiet and listen, not only to the horrific details of the rape but even worse to the account of Donald's attitude afterwards.

"So I'm sorry... I just had to get away – to be alone." Jamie turned and laid his face in her belly.

"No I'm sorry I should never have left you... Kathleen you must press charges." Kitty stroked his hair and at length answered.

"You are the second person I have had to recount that to, and I intend to never... never! Talk of it again."

Jamie looked up at the determined, swollen and tear stained face.

"I could kill him." Jamie's steely voice, Kitty knew he meant it.

"And I would lose you, and that would be 100 % worse than this. Claire said there shouldn't be any permanent damage."

"There is in here." Jamie placed a hand over the centre of Kitty chest, "And here!" and his other hand over his heart.

"We're stronger than that... aren't we. I know it's all new for us, it's not been long but this hasn't hurt US! You won't love me less... now I'm... damaged?" She was serious and Jamie couldn't believe it.

"I couldn't love ye more than I do now, thinking I'd lost you just made me realise how much... ye are... ye are my world now Kathleen." Jamie kissed her hair and breathed deeply, he had her back – bruised and battered but he wouldn't let her out of his sight.

"Shall I run ye a bath?"

"Please, not too hot."

Jamie busied gathering clean pyjamas from his drawers, "Ok?" Kitty nodded. Once the bath was run Jamie took his usual pew on the closed toilet and called her in.

"You don't have to look."

"Oh yes I do!" Kitty knew this was inevitable. Slowly the fleece of yellow puddled around her feet and Jamie gasped. Not wanting to look at him she closed her eyes.

"Kathleen?" His voice was hoarse as he stood and ever so gently traced his fingers over her lips and down her neck. Kitty fought the urge to pull away and in her mind repeated, "This is Jamie, this really is Jamie." Her body was not as convinced, and she trembled knowing his eyes were taking in every graze and bruise. Cupping her breast he traced above the injury. Turning her around he examined her back, dropping to his knees and with the lightest of touch he traced the painful areas in her legs. Turning her once more he laid his head on her belly, holding her hips he sobbed.

"What has he done, the BASTARD?" Kitty stroked his head.

"It's getting better."

"Oh Kathleen I really want to kill him." Jamie sniffed.

"I know, but I really need you not to." Gently he helped her into the bath and resumed his seat. His face was grey and his fists clenched as Kitty lowered her self hesitantly into the water. Donald had pissed him off when he dallied with his sister, but this, this was something else. A whole other level of anger he had never experienced.

A knock at the door interrupted the silence.

"Jamie, lad, supper will be ready soon. Do you and ye wee lass want to come down or I ken I can bring ye up a tray."

Kitty looked at Jamie waiting for an answer.

"Up to ye lass?"

"Can I eat downstairs in my pyjamas?"

"Aye of course ye can, they will be mighty pleased to see ye." Kitty giggled, the question was for Jamie – my, Maggie had good hearing.

"Nothing gets past Maggie. God, that was good to see you smile. Kathleen can I tell my parents?" Jamie reached and brushed her hair behind her ear,

"Not the details, I don't want anyone to know the details. Say he attacked me – that's easier to swallow than a misunderstanding. It's bad enough that you and Claire know what he did, I don't want anyone else to know."

"Of course, come on lets get ye dry."

Try as he might he couldn't hide the horror from his face as again he looked at the marks of her beaten body. How hard she must have fought against Donald. What chance would she have had, she was so small and delicate. Wincing as she tried to dry between her legs Jamie could literally feel his blood boil.

"Please leave him... for me, for us." Now the truth was out Kitty could finally look deep into his eyes and she hoped he heeded her plea, and for the first time she kissed him.

Feeling slightly foolish in oversized tartan pyjamas and dressing gown. She walked slowly – one step at a time down the huge stair case.

"Maybe we should have stayed in the room."

"Nonsense, you look beautiful Mrs Harris." He winked at her and for the first time she really believed they could get through this. The fear she had held that he would look at her differently, feel differently about her, were so far unfounded.

"Oh Kathleen, thank you for joining us. James, you should have asked I could have loaned the poor lass something ... well better fitting."

"Oh no Maureen," she still felt odd calling her that. "They are really comfortable." Kitty pulled the too long sleeves over her wrists and no more was said on the matter, only knowing glances between the three Stewarts.

Maggie bustled around as usual; it finally came to Kitty who she reminded her of, apart from her mother, it was Mrs Potts from Beauty and the Beast. She idly wondered if there was a disfigured young son hidden away in the kitchen.

Jamie was worried her mind was otherwise engaged and edged his chair nearer hers and reached out to hold her hand. Maureen cleared her throat and smiled.

"Now I don't want to pry, and no more needs saying on the subject but if it is better... if it's needed I have got your brother's room ready if Kathleen needs some peace and wants to be on her own."

Kitty and Jamie attempted a fumbled response but were waved away by Maureen.

"No, no, no explanations needed," and she resumed her meal. Jamie's mother really was a shrewd woman and Kitty liked her more with each meeting.

The meal was eaten in quiet conversation about nothing important. As Maggie cleared the pudding bowls she suppressed the urge to encourage Kitty to eat up, but lightly patted her hair as she reached for the untouched crumble.

"Will you have a whiskey Kathleen before you retire?" Dougal offered.

Kitty's pale face turned whiter still, and she held her stomach as the little dinner she had eaten threatened to reappear. Maggie came to her rescue hurrying from the other end of the table.

"Now what ye need is a nice hot chocolate... that'll help ye sleep."

Dougal gave an apologetic glance to Jamie who smiled sadly at his well-intentioned father.

"Great can I have one too?" Jamie attempted to lighten the atmosphere.

"Oh Maggie, make it four!" Maureen smiled at Kitty.

Kitty took a deep breath and lowered her shoulders, every one relaxed. Once the drinks were enjoyed and Maggie congratulated, gentle hugs and kisses all round and Jamie and Kitty made their way to bed early.

"I don't know the details darling but I know she won't press charges. I saw the bruises on her wrists and obviously Claire couldn't say, but I asked if her other injuries were worse and she nodded. Dougal that man must have raped her, I'm sure of it." Dougal hugged his wife to him.

"We will see to it that she never sees him again. I blame myself! We should have made his... goings on, public. When he toyed with Flo. Maybe... just maybe people round here would have seen him for what he is."

"I do pray James does nothing foolish, speak to him in the morning ... you will promise?"

"Yes darling."

"Do you want me to sleep in the other room?" Jamie took his dressing gown and hung it on the back of the door.

"Oh no, no Jamie... I'd rather be with you. That is if you don't mind?"

"Oh Kathleen." Turning now to face her. She looked smaller than ever in his clothes, young and fragile. "You must listen... this... this terrible thing! Do you think I could blame you?"

Kitty nodded and hung her head.

"Of course I don't... Kathleen... tell me please what I should do?

Is there anything I can do to make it better?" pleading for her to understand.

"Cuddle me."

The room was in darkness. Jamie's snoring was interrupted by Kitty's scream. His arm was resting across her still sore belly and even with her eyes opened she couldn't shake the image of Donald on top of her, hurting her.

Jamie bolted up and turned on the lamp. Sweat had beaded around her hairline and a terrible look of fear etched on her face.

"Hush, hush, it's over, it was a bad dream."

For the next two days Jamie didn't leave her side, even at times following her into the bathroom. Each day saw an improvement in her physical injuries, walking and sitting becoming more normal. Jamie took her on the grand tour of the house, cellars and attics with treasures and stories a plenty. The rain had finally arrived and in between showers they would venture outside.

Whilst held up in an out building, Kitty reached up and kissed the brooding Scotsman. He returned the peck but suddenly Kitty wanted more. The wall between them that Donald had created needed careful dismantling. Pulling his head down towards her Kitty tried again but Jamie tensed and pulled too quickly away.

They both stood staring out at the rain. Both desperate to talk but terrified to in equal measure. Eventually they both blurted out their feelings at once.

"Am I disgusting to you?"

"I don't want to hurt you."

They laughed – at least they could do that.

"You won't hurt me." Kitty stroked his face.

"I... I keep thinking... of that day. The day at the pub when I ... I forced myself on ye." The disgust Jamie felt for himself was evident.

"Jamie, no, god no! Don't compare yourself to him -NO!"

"I'm scared to touch you – to hurt you. Wherever he has bruised you, and the damage that I can't see – inside your head."

"Nothing we can't overcome." Kitty coaxed his head back down to her and they kissed gently until they both relaxed.

"There that's better." Kitty squeezed him and they stood breathing in unison. The first real contact they had had since they were reunited.

35

A Problem Shared

The third morning Kitty stretched and opened her eyes. Jamie lay besides her with his head propped up on his arm.

"How long have you been awake?" Kitty still bleary with sleep.

"Hours, since dawn. I've watched ye sleep."

"Riveting."

"Well no nightmares so that's good." Jamie smiled down at her.

"No." Kitty forced a smile – he didn't need to know there had been, the same dream she had had every night. But Kitty almost felt it was harder for him to hear than her to experience. No one would hear her protestations that she felt guilty and in a way responsible for what happened. She had her part to play – she had put herself in that situation making herself vulnerable. No one knew the ghastly truth that haunted her; the memory of responding to Donald's touch when she thought it was Jamie. This was her biggest shame and no one could ever understand that.

Kitty determined from that moment on, that any nightmares she might have in the future were her penance, her weight to bear as punishment for her own foolishness.

"I think I'd like to go home today."

Jamie narrowed his eyes in the saddest of frowns, "Home… as in Wimbledon?"

"No," laughing up at him, "Tide's Reach!"

"Go home for good, or for a visit?" he reached and brushed a rogue curl behind her ear, Kitty was glad at least she had stopped flinching at his touch.

"Visit, could we come back here? I know it's a bit odd, it's not that I don't want to go back to your cottage but ... I, I just feel safe here."

"I'm delighted lass, and I ken Maggie's cooking is so much better than mine, you don't have to say it."

Jamie playfully sunk down besides her at the pillow, and placed his hands on her waist to tickle her. Kitty froze, eyes wide and breath held. He immediately let go and pushed away from her.

"Sorry" all fun and joy wiped from his face.

"No, I'm sorry." Kitty rolled over so he wouldn't see the tears that threatened. Stopping himself just in time, he resisted the urge to stroke her hair. How long they both wondered, were they to suffer from what Donald had done.

Breakfast was a jolly affair. Maggie had commented that Kitty looked drawn and was making it her mission to fatten her up.

"Aye eat up lassie, plenty where that came from." Kitty sighed as the plate full of bacon, egg, sausage, mushrooms and tomatoes were placed in front of her. The daily ritual of the black pudding debate raised its ugly head again.

"Get away wi ye, It'll put colour in those pale checks." She had left the olive bullying down south only to be replaced by the black pudding brigade and its chief henchman Maggie! Mid debate Kitty was aware of hushed words between Jamie and his dad.

"Outside a minute lad."

Watching suspiciously as they left Kitty turned to Maureen.

"Dougal thinks he is protecting you, but I think you would feel better knowing. Trevor and some of the lads visited Donald's house and offices. It has been made quite plain that there will be a very unwelcome reception for him if he shows his face anywhere near here." Maureen smiled and reached out to squeeze Kitty's hand.

"Will he listen?" Kitty swallowed hard and struggled to push the egg down that now seemed glued to her throat.

"Wouldn't you Kathleen, faced with half a dozen Stewarts?"

Kitty took a swig of orange, "I almost wish he would."

"As do we all, indeed. But then it would be our kin that would be in trouble, for I doubt HE, wouldn't press charges."

Kitty guessed this was in reference to her refusal to inform the authorities.

"Do you think I am wrong?"

"What, for not pressing charges? No darling girl. You must do whatever you need to do to best get over the ... whatever happened. James told us that you had told him everything, - that he knows – that is very brave of you and good for you, good for you both. You can't hold on to it on your own. And no he hasn't told us, he would never betray a confidence. But we know enough to worry what he will do to Donald if he meets him."

"I know, me too. I didn't want to tell him – it was the most humiliating thing I've ever done, but he needed the truth." Quietly then, "It was worse than the actual ra... incident."

"Brave wee girl, how horrid for you, but James needed to know.

You know how much you mean to him Kathleen."

"I do, and him to me, I worry still that this could come between us." Kitty buried her face in the crisp linen serviette, and between small sobs. "He might learn to hate me because of it."

"Oh Kathleen, you don't know him as well as you think. I sincerely think he could think no higher of you. He loves you so much darling." Maureen stood to one side of the crying Kitty and hugged her to her chest.

Jamie and his father returned, both relieved, only to be anguished at the sight of Kitty and Maureen.

"Just getting some sadness out, hush, hush now brave wee lass." Maureen's teary smile reassurance enough for Jamie, he knew Kitty was in expert hands.

The drive to Tide's Reach was quiet. Kitty was nervous at the prospect of seeing the builders but in equal part excited at being back at her house.

"Do you think it's water tight yet?"

"Aye should be, to be honest I can'na say I'd looked at the croft since I've been back." Jamie smiled over to her, he was gorgeous and for the first time since before the rape Kitty felt desires rise in her. The thought of sex terrified her, she was immensely conflicted.

"Have you got to go back to Harris?" Kitty squeezed her hands, trying to be brave.

"I do need to go," looking back at her terrified face. "But I shall never leave ye Kathleen. If and when I go to Harris ye will be with me."

"Oh good." Relief obvious, she took some deep breaths and smiled out at the view. "A holiday on Harris. I was quite useful on the site last week, maybe I can help?" Kitty reached over and Jamie enveloped her hand with his.

"I'd like that very much."

Nervous now as the end of the journey approached, Kitty was picking at the sore fingers, Jamie taking her hand as she raised it to bite again. These men all had a fair idea of what had transpired between Donald and her. Did any of them judge her for being with him? Had any of them wondered for a minute that she was "Up for it?"

The warmth of their smiles soon dispelled any worries. Kitty and Jamie ran through the rain, thundering through the door of the house.

The roof was on and blue plastic was taped across the unfilled windows, puffing and dragging like small sails. The floor for the upstairs was in and the staircase nearly completed.

"Soon ya'll be able to check out the view from ya bedroom lass." Malcolm smiled at Kitty, and she knew they had worked extra hard in her absence.

"Did ya talk to ya pa Jamie lad?" Malcolm looked knowingly at Jamie whose face was harsh.

"Aye Uncle."

"Good so ya ken?"

"Aye Uncle." Kitty would ask the details of what passed between the Stewart men on the drive home.

"Come lass look at the back room floor." Malcolm was bright now and guided Kitty through to what had been the bedroom. Trevor was on his knees wiping the newly laid flagstones. On seeing her he sprung lightly to his feet.

"Oh grand to see ya Kitty, and looking so much better! Is she not Jamie?"

"Aye she is."

"Still want to skin the bastard?"

"Aye that I do!" Trevor thumped Jamie's arm and winked at Kitty.

"Dunna fret lass we won't let him near him."

"Good, but I'd happily skin the bastard myself!" Kitty added quickly and all three laughed loudly and it was a joyous sound.

"Can we help while we are here?" Kitty was keen to do anything and rolled up her sleeves – instantly regretting it as all eyes fell on the now green bruises.

"Skin and castrate!" Trevor growled.

"Aye to that." Jamie ground his teeth.

"Ok" Kitty felt the worst was over, she was amongst family here. She really felt that, and she no longer felt the need to hide the proof of the rape. All these men knew just what had happened and would fight for her – what better testimony to family than that.

Jamie was put to work on carpentry duty finishing the staircase. The emotions and frustrations of the last week saw him throwing himself into the manual labour. Kitty was on light duties, making tea and pottering in the shed. She guessed they all thought she was too fragile yet for work hard, and in truth she was. She found a renewed calm amongst the bustle, Kitty sat at the small table and decided it was high time to write to Amanda. A phone call was out of the question – she could hear her friend now, details, details! Amanda need only know a vague overview of the true events.

Trying to make it humorous as possible to disguise the shame and degradation she really felt. But everything she wrote that was untrue, that trivialised what actually happened squeezed at her chest – like a crushing hug. Not being honest to Amanda obviously wasn't going to be an option. Kitty angrily screwed up yet another piece of paper and threw it on the floor.

Walking on the foreshore but never out of view of Jamie, Kitty added to her collection of shells. The men all worked quietly and determinedly. When Jamie did look out and could not see the blue waterproof coat he dropped the hammer he had been using and raced out of the door. It had been a great way to vent his emotions but his uncle picked up the hammer and let out a long sigh as his fingers traced the large dents in the wooden supports. He knew plasterboard would cover this or he would never have let his nephew knock the hell out of the nails.

Looking for Kitty a wave of nausea made his feet falter, first at Pimples, but then guessing she would be round by the little croft – she had confided in him how peaceful she found it. Climbing quickly across the rocks with bounding strides he could soon see her huddled form on the door step of the croft. Quietly calling her name so as not to make her jump, Jamie approached. Looking smaller than ever, her arms wrapped around her drawn up knees. She shook as she cried, and Jamie knelt before her and rubbed her shoulders.

"It's... it's... no good. I will have to call Amanda."

"I know, I'm surprised you have'ne yet..."

There was a long silence punctuated only by sobs and sniffs.

"I have spoken to her." Jamie's voice was quiet, and he rested back on his heels and waited for Kitty to look up. Straggly hair pulled across her face and stuck in places to the tears that hadn't been wiped.

"Why... when?" She frowned back at him.

"I had to... when you disappeared." He grinned apologetically and placed his hands on her still trembling knees.

"What did she say? SHIT does she know I'm alright?" panicked now, her eyes wide.

"Aye, aye... I called her everyday. She wanted to fly up but I convinced her not to... I... I might have lied."

"Lied? Why?" Laying her hands over his.

"I daren't tell her what Trevor had seen, what we all suspected. I know her well enough to know she would have been on the phone to the police."

"Who did call the police? There was that nice man here, when... well when I came back."

"I did, when Trevor told me, he called me after you drove off." Kitty waited as Jamie swallowed hard and tried to regain his composure. "It was torture waiting to get back here, it still makes me feel physically sick thinking about it. I went straight to my place and everyone had been out looking all day." Jamie's voice was hoarse and it hurt Kitty to see his pain.

"What did you tell Amanda? I am so sorry Jamie, I... I wasn't thinking, I just had to get away." She reached up and laid a cold hand on his cheek, he took it in his, and kissed the palm.

"I told her we had an argument... she was getting more and more angry with me as the days went by." He laughed weakly. "For a lass, she has very colourful language."

"Oh, I'm sorry... again – well that settles it, I need to talk to her."

Kitty stood and he enveloped her, standing and letting the rhythm of the retreating waves calm and revive them. Wanting to waste no more time, Kitty walked back along the beach to Pimples, and waited for Jamie to make their farewells. They drove in silence to Jamie's cottage.

Once inside there was no warmth of welcome, having been left empty it felt colder inside than it had out, and certainly colder than Pimples. Jamie busied himself loading the wood burner, a shivering Kitty curled her feet under her in the old leather chair and gathered the tartan blanket around herself. Jamie resisted the urge to pour himself a whiskey but instead held aloft a bottle of red wine in one hand and the box of hot chocolate in the other.

"It should be chocolate, but I think I'm going to need that," Kitty smiled pointing at the wine. Jamie ducked back into the kitchen and soon returned with two glasses full.

"Do you want me to go away?" He asked in a whisper, Kitty hated to see him looking so drawn. In front of the flickering orange light of the now crackling fire she could see the new definition on his jaw and cheek bones. How much weight could he have lost in such a short space of time?

"If... but only if... you can bear to hear it, I think I might need you to fill in the gaps – but I wouldn't blame you if you don't want to." Tears rolled down her face, how could he deny her anything?

"Of course I will!"

Kitty drained her glass, and smiled as Jamie dialled the number from memory.

"You again! Really! And what might you have to tell me today? More excuses?" Kitty interrupted her friend's venomous little tirade.

"Mand... It's me." The emotion bubbled up and Kitty's weak voice faltered and she started to cry in earnest. Holding the phone out, Jamie took it and inhaling deeply, trying to update the screeching woman at the other end of the line. Holding their free hands tightly together. Jamie admitted his untruths, explained his motives and mapped out the whole tale - minus details of what actually happened between Donald and Amanda's friend.

After Amanda's initial shouts, mainly expletives, she finally sat quietly, hand over her mouth as Jamie told her the story.

"So, I'm so sorry, I ken that ya may be angry with me." Jamie said flatly.

"I'm so, so sorry Jamie, I've been a royal bitch to you."

"Aye, ya have."

"Well... I'm sorry."

"It's fine, she's back... a bit bruised, but I hope... alright, at least she will be."

"Can I talk to her?"

Jamie held the phone to Kitty who smiled up at him and took it, checking with him once again.

"Leave if you'd rather not hear this." Jamie leant down kissed her tears, then sat down in front of her, resting his head in her lap.

Kitty started with feeling drunk at the Duncan's. For the first time since it had happened Kitty walked back through her memories, facts and feelings. Recounting her confusion of emotions, thinking, dreaming, that it was Jamie that touched her. Blankly and composed she described it clearly and calmly. As if she was documenting a film, describing someone else being pinned to that bed and raped.

In Wimbledon her best friend wept quietly, Six hundred odd miles away, her boyfriend sobbed in her lap. It had to be said; she needed to not carry this load on her own any more. She had held things back from Jamie before, fearing it would jeopardise and alter his feelings for her. It was all out there now, for good or ill, and Kitty felt the weight of her burden shift and lighten. However it panned out, she no longer had to carry it alone.

"Then I came back and Jamie, his uncle, cousins, mother and a very sweet policeman were all there. I've been stopping at Jamie's parents since... I am so sorry Mand... But I just couldn't talk about it before now."

"Bloody hell Kit! I'm so angry, I, I know it's no ones fault but HIS! But... but I'm so sorry I couldn't have been nearer – been there for you." Amanda's voice trailed of and her friend waited until she had cried some more.

"Have they arrested him?" The thought blurted out as it came to her. "Kit, Kathleen tell me you told the nice policeman and they arrested the son of a bitch!"

Kitty could feel Jamie tensing in her lap as his arms moved around her back and held her tight. She knew this was the hardest part for him to swallow. She fully understood what no one else could, that in Donald's mind he had done nothing wrong. She had responded to his initial touch – how was he to know she was thinking of Jamie. There was little point trying to make anyone understand, that Kitty blamed herself just as much as she blamed Donald.

36

Rage

As Kitty's feet landed on the gravel outside Jamie's parent's house she reached up and stretched. Arms high to the sky she took what felt like her first proper lung full of air since the whole nightmare had begun, she smiled appreciating the twinkling stars above her.

Jamie had phoned ahead, glad that there was no one around to greet them and witness both their puffy eyes. Jamie held her hand as they walked through the boot room, kicking off shoes as they went. The large kitchen table had place settings for two, an open bottle of red wine and a note.

"Beef stew in the oven, enjoy."

The next week passed quietly and without incident. A routine of gentle conversation over breakfast and dinner in the Stewart household. Kitty was astounded at how easily she had slotted into their life, and only worried she liked to too much – she would hate to lose it now! Every day, weekends included they would set off early for Tide's and work until weary.

Everyone's focus, she was sure driven by Jamie, was to finish the build as quickly and smoothly as possible. Jamie's uncle and cousins were there as much as they were. An assortment of other younger Stewarts – "builders in the making," Malcolm called them came and went, acting as cheap labour they cleared and cleaned around their more experienced relatives.

The plasterboard was soon installed and suddenly the little shell was being transformed into a house, a home, with rooms, and Kitty was delighted. Still subdued and quieter than before Kitty wandered around the site, always sure of a smile, but the banter had now gone – everyone focussed on getting this finished.

The new windows in the rear of the rooms were, to Kitty, beautiful. Any reservations about losing the old windows were soon forgotten. As soon as they were in Kitty placed a jar on the sills and filled them with bracken and primroses. All the men thought it was madness as the green was soon caked in the dust, but of course they just smiled.

The first sign that all was not well was the thundering footsteps of someone running and stumbling past the window of the storeroom.

Kitty stood and opened the door straining to decipher the muffled shouting. Was it Jamie and his uncle?

"No lad, stay ye here!"

"Let me at the bastard!" Yes definitely Jamie, what had sparked this? Kitty walked across the back garden to the new main door to the extension. Movement on the drive caught her eye, and Kitty slowly turned to see a black Range Rover on her drive. His car! Kitty froze and forgot how to move her limbs or how to use her voice. There it was, a scene from her nightmares. The shiny black car, its driver's door open. The driver was obscured by the huge back of Trevor, who had pulled the door open and was thrusting and poking Donald in the chest with outstretched fingers.

Kitty could hear rising commotion behind her, but in the haze of her terror could no more turn to look than speak now. Into her line of sight first ran Jamie, with his cousin Jeff in close pursuit. And standing next to her was Malcolm breathing hard. It had been him trying to restrain Jamie but had been beaten by his nephew.

"Christ! The lad will kill him!" He reached and put a gentle arm around Kitty's waist but there was no guiding her.

"Lass ye need to go back in the store, ye dunna wan a see this." Unable to talk, Kitty slowly raised a hand and pointed to the escalating scene on her drive. Holding her firmly Malcolm half carried the rigid Kitty across the lawn.

"Maybe if the lad sees ya, or ye can talk some sense into him he won't murder the bastard."

"You dirty bastard, I'll have your balls for what you did McDonald!" Jamie spat the words his face flushed red and the veins in his neck and temples pulsating.

"Now hang on, hang on. What happened or didn't happen is between Kathleen and myself. What is it to you Stewart?"

Jamie lunged at the open door but Jeff clinging to his back and Trevor in front of the door was not an unsubstantial barrier, preventing contact.

"It has every thing to do with me, you arrogant fucking bastard. I love her!" tears were streaming down Jamie's face. "You dirty raping bastard!" Jamie screamed at him and looked as though at any moment he would explode.

"Malcolm, for god's sake man, call off your dogs!" Trevor reached in and grabbed a fist full of Donald's jumper and lifted him from the seat. "Dogs are we?" Followed by a string of Gaelic.

"Kathleen, ah good. If we could only discuss this rationally" Donald attempted to smile around Trevor's large shoulders, to entreaty her.

"How dare you!" It was the great booming voice of Malcolm, holding Kitty tight, not sure if she could manage to stand unaided. His deep shout vibrated through her body. "Get off this property. Your services are no longer required and should ye trespass again – as much as one toe! I will shoot ye myself!"

"Kathleen, Kathleen, what is this... wh, what's the meaning of this?" Desperation edging his voice now, "Whatever she has told you all about our... our little misunderstanding."

Jamie was trying with all his might to get free of his cousin, and was tantalisingly feet away from the man he wanted to pummel into the ground.

"There was no misunderstanding! You raped her you fucking bastard!" Jamie was beside himself, and was growling at his cousin in words Kitty could not understand, but knew were pleas to let him go and get at the man in the car. Beads of spit spraying and fists clenched Jeff could only just hold him.

"Oh come now, it was just a misunderstanding, Kathleen got herself a wee bit too drunk." Still protesting his innocence.

"Is that why she is bruised and battered? She still can't sit down without wincing, you raped her, you violated her... for fucks sake Jeff let me at him!" Both cousins fought to contain him now. Malcolm looked down at the sagging small creature in his arms.

"Is this true Donald McDonald? Did you rape this wee lass?" His words slow and pronounced.

"No, no, Kathleen tell them... for god's sake!" Donald looked with real fear at the straining man baying for his blood. "Tell them Kathleen, tell them you were drunk but you wanted it!" Donald had the audacity to smile at Kitty and she thought she was going to vomit. Her weight grew heavier in Malcolm's arms and she started to shake and dry retches convulsed her body. She wanted this to stop, wanted everyone to disappear.

The humiliation of hearing these words, the words she thought could tear her and Jamie apart. To have these men, his family, witnesses to her shame. Kitty desperately wanted them gone – needed to be alone with Jamie. She had to try and repair, to save what she had with Jamie. Donald had raped her, and now sitting smug in his car, threatened to snatch away the love she cherished.

The tension, the rage was all around her but she was powerless to intervene. Mute and unable to argue she was powerless to act.

Malcolm's words broke through the fog of her thoughts.

"Is it true lass, did he rape ye?"

"Yes" the reply was quiet but the response was not.

"Jeff, Trevor leave ya cousin be!" As always, working like a well-oiled machine the Stewart boys leapt into action. It was Trevor who ejected Donald from his car as Jeff released Jamie. Jamie struck Donald square on the jaw with a shuddering thud. Donald attempted to get to his feet with one hand holding his face. Scurrying around the car with Jamie in hot pursuit, unluckily for Donald, Jeff's foot shot out and tripped him up.

Donald landed hands and face in the soft slippery moss at the front of the bonnet, absorbing all momentum he was unable to push up. Jamie was on him and flipped him over onto his back. A constant stream of obscenities spat from Jamie, some English, most not.

With peaty water in his eyes and already at a distinct disadvantage, Jamie's rage giving him the strength of at least two men, Donald could put up little in the way of defence and there was no remission as the blows fell.

"Does that hurt? Do you want me to stop?" Again his voice dark, and lapsing into his native tongue was ferocious. Kitty watched. Looking helplessly on at the mass of swinging arms, red hair and hatred.

Donald was putting up less of a fight now, trying to protect his face with arms folded around it. A cracking right hook under his arms saw him motionless.

"Enough lads!" Malcolm shouted, and his sons primed to act, leant down and pulled a cursing and flailing Jamie to his feet, still fighting with his cousins to get at the mud and blood covered man unconscious on the ground.

"Jamie lad, your wee lassie needs ye now." Malcolm knew this was the one thing that could tear him away from the battle. Jamie's bloody knuckles rested on his knees, bent double he dragged in four deep breaths. Willing the rage to quieten, he looked slowly up to the hunched figure hanging from his uncle.

"Kathleen." Taking her gently from Malcolm, Jamie held her in a long embrace, his thundering heart pounding in her ear.

"Get her to the store room and get some spirits into her. We'll take it from here, Trevor, Jeff."

Trevor moved around the unmoving Donald and took a well aimed kick to the crotch, Donald rolled into a whimpering ball.

"Good, he's not dead – sorry, now that was a misunderstanding!" The father and sons smiled at each other, justice served a good old-fashioned Highland style.

By the time Jamie had washed his hands and wrapped Kitty in a blanket, well supported by cushions on the day bed, Malcolm was back with them.

"What have you done wi him?"

"Trevor has driven him home, Jeff followed. He's had a taste of his own medicine lad, ye can'na say fairer than that."

"J, Jamie... what if he presses charges?" Kitty had found her voice, weak and trembling but there.

"He wouldn't dare" Jamie sat next to her and rubbed her shoulders.

"Dunne fear lass Trevor will leave him in no doubt. You are family to us, you are Jamie's and he will'na dare to darken ya doorstep again."

Kitty didn't want to go back to Jamie's parents and have to explain his battle scars. He was very relieved, and neither spoke as they headed back to his cottage. Suspecting he had broken a bone in his hand Jamie kept gear changes to a minimum.

Once inside the lounge Jamie locked the door and closed the curtains. Making his way over to the whiskey, Jamie changed track at the look of revulsion on Kitty face.

"Come." Jamie's voice was flat; leading her into the kitchen painful hands guided her to a seat and made them tea. It was many minutes before either spoke. Kitty trying to quell the nausea and shaking from shock, and Jamie making an effort to calm the adrenaline fuelled rage that still simmered within him. Kitty's small voice came first.

"I'm sorry." Jamie glared at her. "Shall I leave...? I should leave." Kitty stood unsteadily and made for the door. Jamie grabbed her hand, too roughly and Kitty cried. He loosened his grip and pulled her in for a crushing hug.

"Let me go... Jamie... let me go – you don't need me in your life." The voice that had started weak and faltering now found its feet and she was screaming. "He's ruined it, he has ruined me – you would be better off without me!" Kitty pulled away and taking Jamie's swollen hands she shouted at him.

"Look what has happened to you and it's my fault!"

Jamie held her as gently as he could, but there was no way he was going to let her leave. Struggling to get a hold on his emotions, it took a few minutes of silence and Kitty feeble struggles before he spoke.

"I would kill for ye, I could have killed him for what he did ta ye – never doubt it Kathleen. But I can never hear you say again that it is your fault. You silly wee Sassenach, I love you! Do ya not ken that yet?"

Kitty stopped fighting him and hugged him back. Jamie sat the still wincing Kitty on the sofa and covered her with the tartan blanket. Jamie paced the kitchen as he held the phone close to his ear, having a long, hushed conversation in words Kitty couldn't understand. She had never been happy to be excluded by the local language but today she was glad of it. His voice changed and he reverted to English, he tried valiantly to reassure Maureen.

"Aye, aye... I will – OF COURSE!" Angrily now. "No we are fine! I don't think she wants to. She's not really talking, yes...yes I know it's probably a bit of shock... YES! – Really mother!" Jamie looked with concern at the startled eyes following his every move. Gaelic then, swearing – Kitty was starting to recognise those words, she inappropriately found that amusing. Her upturned mouth made Jamie soften.

"Mother wants to speak to you, you don't have to." Holding the phone away from him Kitty could hear Maureen's voice; "Really James" Kitty's small hand escaped the blanket and took the phone.

"Hi Maureen."

"How are you darling? And how is James, really?" Kitty could feel the concern and was genuinely happy to talk to her.

"We're alright."

"Do you need to be here?"

"No, no really I think we just want to be alone for a while." Desperate not to offend, after all this woman had shown so much affection and consideration already.

"If you are sure darling, you are sure? If you need me I'm just a phone call away."

"Thank you Maureen it means a lot." Jamie was pacing now. "Ok I, we will see you later, bye, bye." Handing the phone back to him, Jamie made impatient goodbyes and the room fell silent once more.

Both sat quietly watching inane TV. Jamie supplied cups of tea, the grumbling from Kitty's stomach saw him standing contemplating the inside of the fridge.

"I've nothing in, I'll go to Broadford." With her first animated gesture Kitty leapt to her feet and hugged his back.

"Please don't leave me, don't go." The tension that had held his frame since the fight, gave way and in the chill of the open fridge he turned and embraced her. This time it was her comforting him. A deflated mass, he sobbed and let out all the pent up sorrow for what had happened to the woman he loved more than anything.

Cheese on toast was agreed on. The squashed frozen loaf was chiselled from the freezer. The cheese was sparse as most of it had to be cut and thrown away.

The TV played, neither was really watching, but it was the excuse they both needed to not talk. Kitty's eyes were failing despite the early hour, and Jamie turned off the lights and led her to bed.

Teeth were brushed and pyjamas on and they both lay in bed on their backs. The distance between them was mere inches but to both it felt like a huge chasm. Each lay awake for what seemed like half the night, and it was Kitty who finally broke the stalemate and reached out and took his hand. Gently holding his puffy hand the pain was intense, but Jamie didn't flinch and somehow managed to join her in sleep.

The bird song and early morning sun woke them both, the coldness and distance had gone. They had reconnected in their sleep, smiling at each other now with clammy limbs entwined.

"Can we go somewhere peaceful today?" Jamie nodded in answer. They showered separately, neither one wanting their injuries on show today. Kissing her gently as they left the house they were soon in Pimples, and the world seemed a brighter place this morning.

Kitty didn't ask where they were going, she didn't mind as long as it was with Jamie – Jamie who drove valiantly despite his ever swelling right knuckle. The road was isolated and they hadn't passed a house for miles. Pimples struggled up a long steady incline, and Kitty was surprised when peeking over the brow, a small village of white washed houses came into sight. The sea danced and sparkled beyond but Kitty felt unease stir within at the sight of all the habitation.

"Elgol" Jamie announced, Kitty struggled to regulate her breathing and looked over at the profile of the man she loved but feared terribly she could lose at any moment.

Parking in a small harbour Jamie alighted and to Kitty's surprise didn't come to her door to open it for her but strode away. Was this another chink in the armour, another sign that he saw her differently now. Kitty unbuckled her belt but stayed fearfully put. Never losing sight of him she watched as he went inside a small shed and spoke for the briefest of times then walked back. But Kitty's heart plummeted further as he went straight past Pimples – ignoring or just not seeing her pleading looks; he went and stood in line at a small open fronted shop. When he did finally return he opened the sliding door behind her and stowed the supplies he had brought and then opened her door.

His eyes were still sad but he managed a weak smile and offered the less painful hand. Sitting they enjoyed the ham and salad rolls, and Kitty soon took over tea making duties as he struggled to work the stove and open tins with his damaged hands.

"It's pretty here." Kitty finally said.

"Aye, I went to school with the captain of that wee boat – Andrew."

"Oh, that's nice."

"We leave in twenty minutes, we'd best use the toilets there are no facilities where we are going." His voice was so sad it could have made Kitty cry just to hear it.

"Oh!"

Pimples was soon locked, they were fed, watered and toileted. Jamie put a sore hand around Kitty shoulders and led her down the jetty. It was a small boat holding twenty or so passengers. Holidaymakers barring two, and spirits were high with a jovial crew. Jamie bravely shook hands with Andrew and Kitty hated to see him flinch.

"Where are we going?" Kitty whispered.

"A very peaceful place."

Cameras and phones clicked, and Kitty was aware that another time she would have been hanging over the edge of the boat, drinking in the potted history of the Cullin Mountains and marvelling at the abundant seals. But all that interested Kitty today was the man at her side. Jamie remained quiet and introspective, Kitty wished she could see inside his mind and know what he was thinking. But then again, maybe she didn't, she wasn't sure she would like what she saw. Taking in every freckle and line on his drawn face she couldn't take her eyes off the jade eyes, creased and surrounded by grey shadows but still the most beautiful she had ever seen.

Andrew was a natural and compered the journey, and by the time the boat was tethered at its little mooring Kitty was anxious to be free of the fellow travellers. The joy and exuberance only highlighted their own pathetic state. Andrew announced the best way to enjoy the loch was to follow the path to the right, winking at Jamie. Waiting for the excited party to leave Jamie helped Kitty ashore. A nod to a concerned looking Andrew, Kitty tried to smile. It was obvious to a friend of many years something was amiss here, Jamie's mood and battered hands had not gone unnoticed.

The party spread off to the right and dwindled before them. Veering from the path Jamie guided her up a steep bank and away from the others, his hand on the small of her back pushing her on, firm and assertive and somehow didn't feel tender but authoritative. Breathing heavily Jamie finally stopped and placed both hands around her shoulders and turned. The view back was beautiful. The boat was now a dot of red and blue on the glistening sea, the seals small slugs on rocks and the village they had left a small collection of white specks across the sparkling water. To the other side was the flat expanse of the black loch looking fathomless, and the small dots of their shipmates scattered around its edges.

Jamie sat heavily on a slab of stone the size of a small room. Angled down and having absorbed the day's sun, it made for a surprisingly comfortable resting place. Kitty lay on her back and watched the clouds race by. Jamie pulled his knees up and folded his arms across them resting his forehead on the tense muscles. Kitty blinked up at the mass of hair jostled by the wind. A shiver ran the length of her, was she going to lose him now? The feeling of foreboding washed over her – had he bought her here to finish with her, to end it. Nausea bubbled deep within her and the breath caught as she struggled to compose herself. She had suspected that he wouldn't be able to forgive her, not be repulsed by her. If this was to be the end she dare not waste the time not touching him, sitting up she wrapped her hands around his waist and gently rested her head on his hunched back. Inhaling the scent of him and hoping never to forget it.

"I understand... if you can't forgive me... if you want to go."

He could feel the trembling of her small frame, should he ask the question that haunted him day and night. Jamie was as still and silent as the ancient rock they sat on. He had been battling with this one question since the very first call from Trevor. He despised himself for thinking it but like a shadow it was always there, lurking and nagging at his rational mind. He loved this woman, a stronger and more desperate love than he had ever thought possible – of that there was no doubt.

"Of course I forgive you, you could never be the one to be blamed for what he did." Not more than a whisper, Jamie lifted his head and the breeze chilled his face where the tears had soaked it. "But..."

Kitty tensed and wondered if she would be sick, breath held, she waited.

"There is one thing I can'na understand, why? Why did you agree to go to his house in the first place?" His voice gaining strength and momentum he carried on – now that he had said it, it was out!

"Why Kathleen? Ya know he was keen on ye – were ya getting back at me... was that it, that's it isn't it! Because I'd left ya to go to Harris – Why, WHY?"

The anger and fears Jamie had been suppressing now burst out, turning and taking her arms he pushed her away – her head falling back, the ashen face expressionless before him.

"Oh Kathleen tell me why?"

"Just go" the words came out in one breath, Kitty Harris admitted defeat and wanted the world to swallow her. All rationality lost, she would watch him leave, the bright bobbing boat could take every soul from this place and leave her to the depths of the loch. Kitty, the survivor of so much grief – the widow, the orphan, and the rape victim had just lost her last will to fight anymore. The last tattered threads of her heart cut and she didn't care – couldn't care. If she could but close her eyes and never wake, at that moment she would have been content to go.

"But I don't want to go, I love you Kathleen – so much, it is tearing me apart." Then gently and cupping her face in her hands. "Why did you go to him?"

"I didn't know I had." She said quietly. The beautiful face before her, haggard from worry and raw emotion but still with the depthless eyes that she adored. She would tell him the facts he needed to know, and then let him go.

"Donald turned up unannounced and said the Duncan's had

invited me to tea. He... he caught me off guard. I suppose I did go because you were in Harris... I, I missed you more than I can say." There was a long silence as they starred deep into each others eyes, Jamie wanting to hear it all.

"I... I think you have... had" – past tense because she feared she had now lost him. "Become my family... I shouldn't have presumed, I'm sorry. And you were gone. But I never went to be with... him. I went to play cards with Heather and Jonty." The first flicker of expression as she remembered the card game on the rug. "They remind me of Tommy, of us as children... I just wanted, needed to have..."

"Family" Jamie finished, she nodded up at him.

"I thought he was driving me home, to my house. You must believe me... I, I would never... never had agreed to go to his – even before I knew what... what he would do…" Kitty composure crumbled and the memories flashed bright and she dissolved into a wave of sobs. "By the time I realised it wasn't you, wasn't you undressing me, rubbing my back! When I looked down, imagining you kissing my breasts it... it was too late. I'm sorry Jamie I let him do that... but until that moment I had no idea where I was or who I was with." Fighting from his grasp Kitty turned and scrabbled across the rock to the grass edge and wretched, the images the memories of the pain and the monumental frustration of being too weak to fight him off.

Jamie was by her side, rubbing her back and wanting desperately to ease her pain.

"I'm the one who is sorry, I'm the one who wasn't there, and if only I had been there this would never have happened. Kathleen can you forgive me, darling please say you can forgive me?"

Turning as the last of their feelings shared, their darkest thoughts exposed - they embraced as they both cried. Both unburdened of their worries and all the pent up angst allowed out, it was twenty minutes until Jamie guided her back to their rock and they lay together. Glad of the drinks he had thought to bring.

"We will be alright, won't we Jamie?"

"I have no doubt!" Jamie's one doubt had been answered; he was a very relieved young man.

Kitty snuggled under his arm and edged her hand in through the buttons of his shirt.

"Peaceful enough for ye lass?"

"Aye" they both laughed gently at Kitty's attempt at a Scottish accent. Kitty looked now as the sun flashed bright flecks from his beard and the soft dark red of his lashes. His eyes were closed and his breathing had calmed. Kitty slowly undid the top two buttons of his shirt and traced her fingers through the soft hair on his chest. Lifting herself up she kissed first his chest and then his neck. Tiny hints of kisses around his face, on the eyelashes she adored finally finding his mouth.

Since all that had happened this was their first real kiss. No hesitation and no fear, they were lost in the moment. Whether it was the pain in his hands or the fear of taking things too far and overstepping some unknown boundary, Jamie held her to him but nothing else. Kitty's hand explored his chest and reached for his belt but Jamie's hand stopped her in her tracks.

"Not here darling." His voice was husky and tender and they continued until Kitty rolled onto her back breathless. "We will be fine Kathleen."

"I know."

The last of the crumbling wall Donald had created between them began to fall brick by brick.

37

Regaining Normality

The next few weeks saw huge progress with the build. Leaving early from Jamie's cottage tea would be ready for Malcolm et al on arrival. The staircase was in and Jeff was a very efficient plasterer. Kitty's jobs included supplying him with large buckets of water and Kitty smiled every time she heard "WATERRRR!" and always replied "COMINGGG!"

The best day was seeing the concrete screed go into the extension. All windows were in the front extension now and resplendent in muted green. Kitty removed the stickers and ignored the complaints that her vinegar window wash had them all craving fish and chips.

The dark days after both "misunderstandings" were less and on the whole everyone was jolly, and a real sense of determination had the job racing ahead of expectations. Jamie's brother was back from University for a few weeks and Kitty enjoyed getting to know the lankier version of Jamie. As was the Stewart way Alistair came and helped with the build, tidying and cleaning.

At times Kitty would slip into a quiet space. There was no reason – no cause and effect but when the need arose she found solace in one thing. All her paints were still in storage, but paints, brushes and canvas enough were purchased in the art shop at Portree. Armed with a small easel Kitty would sit in the garden or on a rock with a good vantage point and paint. Jamie knew her better than their time together allowed and would merely kiss the back of her neck and throw his own efforts into the build.

"The bathroom will be in tomorrow lass, it's just been delivered." It was Malcolm who disturbed her now; intent on getting a better capture of the lighthouse around the headland Kitty hadn't heard his approach. She stretched her arms above her head and shifted position on the small stool she used for painting.

"Oh Malcolm, I didn't hear it."

"No guessed ye were too engrossed. Well, ye should be able to have a bath by the end of the week" Malcolm stroked his beard as her appraised her latest picture.

"Wow! It won't seem real, seems a bit... well opulent."

Malcolm's deep laugh lit his face, showing his large white teeth.

Kitty realised she'd never seen it before but Malcolm was a fine looking man and had a wonderful smile. Stiff from too much sitting, Malcolm reached down and pulled her to her feet.

"Well we will be heading off soon but Jamie wanted to tell ye he's popped to town - do some errands."

Kitty frowned; they hadn't been apart in all these weeks.

"Dunna fret lass, he'll be back afore we're gone." Sensing her unease, "Still we're parched back there – you know enough about a Stewart man to ken we dunna work well dry." The wink worked and Kitty gathered her things and they walked companionably back to the house. Malcolm was more than capable of making his own tea but had become overly protective of this young woman, and in Jamie's absence was far happier having her close by. Nothing would befall her on his watch! Not again!

Stopping to admire it, Tide's Reach really had been transformed. The silver chimneystack of the log burner shone bright in the afternoon sun. The rendering of the new extension was bright white and the new windows pretty in green. The two dormer windows looked to Kitty like hooded eyes, her little croft looking out on the beautiful view.

They had discussed it over lunch yesterday, and Kitty wrapped her arms around herself knowing that soon this would be home for her and Jamie. Once completed Jamie would move out of the cottage that was owned by the estate, fortunately no sale or notice was required. They had already agreed where his few possessions were to go, Jamie had already staked a claim on where his beloved brown leather chair would sit. It was his grandfather's and Kitty thought it right that it should sit besides her granny's oak, arts and crafts chair by the wood burner.

Small embers of anxiety at Jamie's absence were brushed aside. Tea making and washing of brushes done, she examined her latest work. Maureen was enraptured by her paintings and one not dissimilar to today's effort hung now in the pretty breakfast room at the big house. Maureen had a friend who owned a small gallery in Portree and Kitty knew it was only a matter of time before she relented and let Maureen take her there and exhibit. Gazing out of the window Kitty was reminded of yesterdays visit from Maureen.

"Carla is very excited darling."

"I know, when the house is finished and I have my own paints from storage."

"I know, I know, I don't mean to pressure you." Maureen had hugged Kitty.

"Then don't mother!" Jamie's voice was stern and his mother nodded sagely.

"Yes, yes you're quite right James... but when you are ready." Kitty couldn't help returning Maureen's sweet smile, Jamie had rolled his eyes. Wandering around the site Trevor had stopped and produced his phone, and Maureen cooed over images of the new addition to the Stewart clan.

"Oh Trevor, he has grown surely?"

"By the day, by the day!"

"Argh, Beth is looking tired."

"Aye, she is, we both are. But she's a goodun and won't have me get up wi the lad at night."

"Well he looks bonnie."

Trevor had already shown Kitty the photos but he looked at her now.

"Jamie said he might pop over at the weekend, if you'd have a mind to come?"

"Oh Trevor I'd love to, I've wanted to meet Iain since he was born."

"Grand, Beth will be delighted she has heard a lot about ye." A chill rose in her spine, yet another person to know about all that went on between her and Donald.

"Everyone thinks very highly of you Kathleen." Maureen was so very insightful. She had left yesterday with promises of drawing plans for the garden as the build had come on beyond expectations. Kitty would look forward to her next visit.

"Where did Jamie go?" worries for herself should Donald appear were quickly replaced by thoughts of Jamie, hoping he hadn't gone to find Donald. Kitty had hidden the frequent nightmares from Jamie but last nights' left her shaking and covered in sweat, she had cried out and woken him. There was no hiding it, and Jamie had been more brooding than usual at breakfast.

Malcolm as if sensing her unease, "Now, no, no, don't you fret – It's all good – I have a fancy he is planning something nice."

"Oh."

Kitty realised that at five thirty Malcolm and gang were killing time.

"Malcolm you don't have to wait for Jamie, I will be quite alright on my own." She was feeling silly with her minders.

"Aye, that's as maybe but none of us want to be on the wrong side of a riled James Stewart. We've all witnessed that and don't want to be at the other end of his fists" They took the opportunity to sit in a line on the front garden wall. Content in the silence they inhabited their own thoughts and watched the tide retreat. They were, all to a man disappointed when Pimples came too fast down the drive.

"Now, I dunna think the lady pays ye to sit there on yer great arses like wise monkeys." Jamie shouted.

Jeff lobbed a stone he had been rubbing in his fingers, narrowly missing Jamie.

"Hey, be careful!" Kitty exclaimed.

"Worried I'd hit your handsome fella?"

"No, you were just close to Pimples." Three men made their way to their vans laughing loudly. Kitty was smiling as Jamie approached.

"Thanks!"

"You know I didn't mean it."

"Are you all done here?"

"Yes just waiting on you."

"Come on then," Jamie bent to kiss her and Kitty ran a hand through his damp hair.

"You've washed your hair."

"Aye."

"Why?"

"No reason."

"I sense something is afoot."

"Do ya now lassie?" Jamie led her to Pimples and opened the passenger door for her. Jamie whistled as he drove and just smiled at her distrustful looks. Opening the cottage door she was first hit by the smell, a casserole she thought – with wine – the rich sweet combination of steak and red wine. The small barley twist table was laid with a crisp white linen cloth. Heavy silverware and elaborate silver candelabra holding six tapered white candles.

Kitty's hand trailed over the cloth, tracing the intricate pattern on the candleholder and stooped to smell the fresh flowers in an exquisite crystal vase.

"You didn't have these before?"

"Maggie might have loaned me a few things."

"And these from your mothers garden?" Kitty cupped a small yellow rose in her hand.

"Aye... would you like a shower before dinner?" Jamie looked furtive.

"Umhmm." It had been their usual routine of late to shower before dinner but this seemed different – a different agenda.

Jamie kissed her on the forehead.

"I'll bring you a drink, dinner can be in twenty minutes."

"Umm...ok." Kitty walked upstairs, the bedroom door was closed and a neat stack of clean jeans, T-shirt and her set of blue lacy underwear. "Oh shit!" Kitty whispered.

Since the rape they had not made love. Cuddling, kissing but no more. Kitty could tell, there was no disguising the fact that Jamie could have done more, but always he would pull away with tender kisses and a turned back.

So this is what he had planned, she wasn't affronted – in fact she was delighted. She had wanted it herself before now but the awkward tension had thus far made it impossible.

Thinking of Amanda now - what would she say? "Dutch courage" Kitty shaved and showered quickly, paying extra attention to her grooming she creamed her legs and hoped the blush she had had since she realised the agenda for this evening would fade.

Standing in the kitchen Jamie smiled an embarrassed smile and handed her a large glass of red wine. Lifting his full glass in a toast Jamie downed his in one.

"Dutch courage?" Kitty asked.

"Exactly, drink up lass!"

The dinner was delicious and despite the nervous knots in her stomach Kitty cleared the plate. On her third glass of wine Kitty relaxed back into her chair, feet in Jamie's lap. They talked about the house and made plans about what they would do. They shared their favourite places they had travelled, and decided when the house was finished they would treat themselves to a holiday. Somewhere hot and relaxing, both thinking it but not saying, they hoped by then it could be a romantic break and make up for the lost weeks since the rape.

Jamie rubbed her feet gently but then firmly and Kitty let her head fall back and moaned with pleasure. His hands moved slowly up her thighs and she looked back at him.

"Only if you want to."

They walked hand in hand up the stairs and Jamie pushed open the bedroom door. More candles were lit in and around the fireplace and Kitty was glad when the light was turned off. More embarrassed and self-conscious than ever before Kitty shed her clothes, hesitating at her bra. Jamie guided her onto the bed and quickly undressed himself.

Lying together on the bed Jamie removed the underwear that meant so much to him.

"I'm terrified of hurting you Kathleen." His voice was rough and his breathing loud and quick.

"You won't!" Kitty rolled him on his back and it was her who dictated the pace. It was painful and cautious, whether from old injuries or just tension but they had done it. Kitty certainly was convinced it would be easier next time and they could once again enjoy the intimacy that had been sullied and taken from them.

Jamie delighted in gathering up her naked body, cuddling her and falling asleep, weeks of frustration and angst over.

38

The English are Coming

Summer was coming and so too the arrival of Amanda and her parents. Her visit had been postponed until the end of July. Kitty was in no fit state to receive visitors. Since they had broken the news of the rape, and knowing her fragile state, Kitty decided she would rather greet her closest family/friends when she was better recovered.

Amanda had wanted to fly straight up, but Jamie reassured her, and once Amanda had the facts, Kitty, on pain of death called her every other day. Long, late night calls from Jamie's cottage. Every guilt ridden detail was shared with the one person she could share everything. For Amanda wouldn't judge, it couldn't alter their relationship.

When a weary Amanda and her parents arrived, an excited Kitty jumped up and down at the top of the long drive at the Stewart house. Maureen would brook no refusal and welcomed John and Marie as guests at her house, Amanda had a room there, but a Zbed was set up in Jamie's lounge as it was suspected once the girls started talking and drinking they wouldn't easily be separated.

Face to face that first night Amanda demanded answers to many questions. A lot of wine was consumed and Jamie wondered if he could ever get to sleep with a whole new level of cackling. Dark silence then as every detail of the rape was discussed, Kitty was so pleased to share it now knowing that although it was awful, beyond awful, it had left no scars. Nothing that her and Jamie couldn't, and wouldn't overcome. Recounting it all again, it seemed each time she relived it, it drifted further away. Still as awful but less raw.

They stayed for five days and Maureen and Dougal were the consummate hosts. Jamie was their own personal guide, taking the four around the island in Pimples, picnics on beaches and long lunches in the best Hotels. Jamie enjoyed getting to know John and Marie, they were both enthralled by the countryside, having never being farther North than Birmingham before. Amanda and Kitty were inseparable and would walk arm in arm and Jamie was happy to relinquish her. Seeing her with the closest thing to family she had made Jamie happy, for she was happy.

Tide's Reach was structurally nearing completion, and though not habitable it made the perfect setting for a farewell BBQ. Bunting was hung around the front garden, candles and tea lights suspended from the small trees. Maureen loaded the Landrover with cushions and blankets from her summerhouse and they covered the low wall at the front creating the perfect seating to enjoy the view. John and Marie were now firm friends with Dougal and Maureen. Angela and Gavin, Claire and Hamish were jovial companions and their children played happily on the beach together. Malcolm and his wife arrived with Trevor, Beth and baby Iain. Alistair and Jeff arrived together and Kitty laughed as Amanda flirted shamelessly with both.

Even Flo had returned home for the gathering. Now with no suspicions pre-empting their meeting Kitty was delighted to get to know her. Their initial hug told Kitty she was well informed of all that had gone on. Squeezing Kitty, Flo whispered into her ear, "I know what the bastard did to you, I know how you feel. Don't let it spoil all you have, time makes it all better."

Kitty stood with Jamie cuddling her from behind as she watched all her friends comfortable and well fed in her front garden. For the first time this felt like her home, not a project, no longer a building site but a place to welcome friends - she had arrived. The sky was a mass of stars and the candles danced in the evening breeze. It had been a perfect evening, and Kitty hoped the start of a pretty perfect life.

Kitty and Jamie opted to spend the night in her store room in the day bed, she just didn't want to leave. They rose early, then pottered happily tidying up from last night's party. Jamie crept up behind her and wrapped her in his arms, nuzzling and kissing her neck.

"Mrs Harris I have a proposition for you."

"Do you now Master Stewart, and what might that be?"

"You are due to change your contraceptive implant next week are ya not?"

Frowning and puzzled, wondering where this had come from, "Yeeeees."

"Could I respectfully request that you don't get another one?"

"Oh" Kitty furrowed brow tightened and she continued to look out over the water.

"It's just that I ken... seeing ya with all those bairns last night and when I saw ya with wee Iain. Well it just made me think by this time next year we could have our own bairns."

"Oh" Kitty hadn't thought much about having children. She did have to admit to the odd daydream of strapping red haired sons that looked like their father – but honestly she'd sort of hoped they would be married first. Was that too old fashioned she worried now. It had only been a couple of months since she had met him, this was happening very fast.

"You dunna sound impressed Kathleen, do ye not care for children?" Jamie stiffened behind her wondering if he had moved too fast, presumed too much.

"No it's not that..." how could she say what she felt.

"And I should add there is a wee caveat to the proposal."

"Did you go and get a law degree while I wasn't watching." Jamie laughed into her neck and it tickled, relaxing her again.

"There is one condition." Jamie released her and Kitty turned to see him on bent knee.

"Would you do me the enormous honour of becoming my wife? I love you Kathleen Harris more than life itself and I... I can wait no longer to make ye mine."

Jamie reached into his shirt pocket and pulled out a worn oval green leather box. Tracing the gold etching Kitty took it and opened it, the dark green velvet interior contained a ring of three large diamonds. Turning the box to the sun its facets dazzled and she took it from its velvety bed. Covering her open mouth with the back of her hand she was speechless.

"If you would rather a new one I would'na mind... it was my grandmothers, Euphemia."

Kitty looked down at the gorgeous man before her, he sniffed back tears and his bottom lip trembled slightly, Kitty let hers fall freely. Counting the rocking pounding of his heart Jamie waited, desperate for an answer.

"No... no" a look of utter fear on Jamie's upturned face. "No I mean it's perfect, I don't want a new one... I love it!"

"Is that a yes then lass?"

"Yes, yes, YES!"

"What do ya say to us practicing the baby making side of the deal?" They ran squealing back to the store.

The local anaesthetic had worked but Claire seemed to make a meal of delving around in Kitty's upper arm to retrieve the implant.

"So you are sure you don't want another one?"

"No, we are going to see what happens. I'm not getting any younger!"

With that Claire held the implant triumphantly aloft and with the other hand hugged Kitty to her.

"I wanted you and Hamish to be one of the first to know... Jamie proposed, and I said yes – we're getting married!"

"Oh Kathleen, stop, stop I'll start blabbing, When?"

"At the end of the summer, in the Stewart chapel and a reception at Maureen and Dougal's."

"Oh perfect, PERFECT!"

The end of August saw the Tide's Reach finished in furious pace. Jamie and Kitty worked on it every day, and Stewart and sons worked above and beyond. Weekends were busy, always a gathering, Iain's christening, an engagement party, birthdays, and any excuse for the clan to congregate.

The date was set for September 29th. Amanda and Flo were to be bridesmaids. Amanda's first reaction at being told of the wedding and her part to play, "Thank god, at last I get to screw a man in a kilt, I might just deflower young Alistair."

Kitty would only finalise plans when Amanda got the go-ahead from the headmistress at work, she planned to take unpaid leave. Luckily teachers were dropping like flies, and Amanda had picked up lots of extra roles - over and above her own job. Making herself invaluable had paid off, and very reluctantly, her boss had relented.

Amanda insisted on visiting in August and joined Kitty, Maureen and Flo on a trip to Inverness. Maureen had arranged it all, the hotel far too opulent and the wedding dresses hideously expensive. Kitty's first wedding had been a small affair funded by her and Stephen. Her mother had been in no position to help, and his parents being penny-pinching accountants didn't offer.

Maureen would brook no refusal and in the end Kitty had to follow Amanda's sage advice to just not look at the price tags – it really helped.

"It's ok... but a bit French looking."

"Nice, but drowns you."

"Meringue!"

Always harsh, but honest and useful critique from Amanda, as opposed to her would be in-laws who gushed Ohh's and Arh's.

Kitty knew it was the right dress before she put it on or looked in the mirror. It was classic, with an Edwardian feel. Fitted around the bust it had small lace capped sleeves edged in pearls. It was simple yet intricate covered in fine ivory lace, with detailing of pearls around the flaring skirt. It was perfection!

Amanda, for the first time in her life was speechless. Maureen cried and Flo just held up her thumbs. Kitty felt her own eyes prickle as she looked at her reflection. The sales woman caught her hair loosely up on the top of her head with a large clip. She placed a pearl and lace comb to one side; letting a few large curls fall on her shoulders. Kitty beamed and everyone shed a tear.

"Beautiful, exquisite, perfect... now we're not in London now and we need to get every thing today so buy, buy, BUY!"

They were all shattered by five. All dresses bought – tick. Shoes – tick. Underwear, embarrassingly – tick, that was a first with a mother-in-law. Headdress – tick. Flowers, much to Maureen's obvious delight Kitty wanted to come from the walled garden - tick.

"Aren't you happy babe? Kit you've just had the price of a small car spent on you." Amanda looked at her friends frown.

"Yes... I know and I'm very grateful... but... but."

"But what?"

"It's Jamie isn't it?" Maureen lent in – Amanda embarrassed hoping she hadn't heard the money reference.

"Yes, it's silly I know but we haven't been apart since, well since... you know when."

"Yes we know." Maureen patted Kitty clenched hands in her lap as the taxi came to a halt, "Look we're back at the hotel, why don't you give him a ring?"

Weary feet dragged them to the lift. Flo pressed the button, and dared Amanda to comment as she pressed the top floor when they were only on the third. Looking between the mother and daughter it was obvious something was afoot and Amanda sensibly decided to play along. Kitty checked her phone, as she had done with frequent regularity today. Sighing she put it away, no texts from Jamie, maybe he was glad to be free of her today.

"Oh... I'm tired!" Kitty sagged back leaning on the mirrored wall.

"That's a shame." Her soon to be sister smirked and a coy glance from Maureen didn't go unnoticed by Amanda. The lift pinged to a stop and Flo gestured for Kitty to leave first. Maureen held Amanda's hand. Tired and downcast Kitty was several feet out on the landing before she noticed no one had followed. Turning she saw three grinning faces disappear behind closing doors.

"Have fun!" Amanda shouted.

"See you in the morning!" Maureen added.

"Don't do anything I wouldn't." Called Flo and the three women's laughs faded away as the lift disappeared.

"B, but!" Kitty stood, looking around her, there was no corridor as such but a small landing with six doors.

"Penthouse" she mouthed. Turning quickly to the sound of a door opening Kitty squealed with obvious delight at the sight of Jamie, tousled wet hair and wearing nothing but a bright white towel and an enormous smile.

"They know us so well and knew we wouldn't want to be apart so dad, Alistair, Angus and I came to get our suits.

Freeing her of her parcels, Jamie kissed and undressed her as he guided her through a large lounge and into an enormous bedroom.

"Let me shower first."

"Only if ye are quick." Jamie led her to the bathroom.

"Woah!"

"Exactly!" he nodded as Kitty looked around at the gilded and marble bathroom.

"You shower I'll get the champagne." Virtually undressed, Kitty removed what was left and stood under the circular head the size of a dinner plate. The water doused her and she struggled to shake off the exhaustion of the day, just standing up felt like too much effort. Returning, Jamie dropped his towel and joined her in the walk in shower that was plenty big enough for two, handing her both of the flutes full of rising bubbles.

"God I'm lucky!"

"I know." Kitty laughed and kissed his smug face. Kitty held the glasses aloft as Jamie set about washing his weary companion. Lathered hands cupped and caressed her breasts

"Ouch!"

"What - I was gentle." More a statement than a question. Since the rape Jamie had to be super careful of her breasts, a tweak too hard and she froze solid.

"No it's not you... they've been hurting all week." Kitty put the glasses on a shelf and cupped herself cautiously. Jamie's hands glided over her skin he knew every mole, freckle and contour. Standing behind her his hands rubbed her belly, her hips and back to her belly.

"When are you due on?" Kitty struggled to think but was far too tired to process this. Since losing her implant the return of normal periods had been irregular.

"Let me." Taking her hands from her breasts he tilted her back under the water to remove the suds. There was definitely something different about her, again standing back and taking a large drink of Champagne. Pulling her in for an intimate embrace he first kissed his neck then up her jaw to her ear and whispered.

"Why Mrs Harris, I think you had better not have any Champagne, I think we might be pregnant."

Kitty tried to blink her eyes open against the downpour of the shower. Reaching behind her she slapped the shower off.

"Why? How? Why would you say that?" Jamie wrapped her in a cloud of soft white towel and walked her to the bed sitting her on it.

"You've changed, your body has changed."

"Well I hadn't noticed." A little indignant now

"Ye dunna spend as much time as I do looking at ya." Jamie swung her legs around onto the bed and placed large cushions behind her and slowly removed the towel.

"Will it still be alright to do this?" Jamie asked, lying gently on top of her, "Hell yes!"

Before breakfast Jamie had found out from the front desk where the nearest Chemists was, and a long white stick was waiting for Kitty by the sink.

"As soon as ye are done."

"Alright already!" Kitty called back through the closed door.

As the toilet flushed Jamie burst in. Sitting fully dressed in front of a naked shaking Kitty, he rubbed her thighs as she sat clutching the test, both eyes fixed on the small window.

"Come on!"

"Jamie it won't work any faster if you shout at it." Jamie glancing again at his watch.

"How long, how long?"

"Calm yourself." Kitty leaned down and kissed his knotted brow. Despite his protests Kitty lifted the test out of his view.

"Well Mr Stewart... you're going to be a daddy!"

Kitty laughed as he stumbled to his feet fighting out of his clothes.

"And you my love have never looked sexier, and I'm afraid even though ye maybe with child I really must do this now!" Scooping her up he carried her back to the bed.

"Do we tell people now?" Jamie asked as he fastened her bra.
"I don't know, I'm hopeless at keeping secrets and I'm sure if not Amanda then your mother will know as soon as I see them. And one look at your face they will know something is going on!"
"It could just be all the great sex I'm having!" Flicking his eye brows and rolling an imaginary moustache.
"Oh... let's just tell them over breakfast."
"Ok!"
Grinning like two very mischievous school children they tried and failed in the long descent to the ground floor to stop smiling and giggling. Once in the lobby they walked hand in hand across to the dining room. Kitty could feel her face blush, and Amanda's reaction on spotting her told Kitty any attempt to keep their news secret would have been futile anyway.
"Well look at you two grinners!" Jamie's brother jeered and nudged Angus. Kitty and Jamie laughed.
"What?" Maureen was on to something
"We just wanted to say there is a problem with Kitty's dress." Jamie tried to keep deadpan.
"Oh no, Kathleen have you changed your mind? You're not going to elope or anything stupid like that?"
"Maureen!" Dougal held his wifes' arm. "Now what is the problem with the pair of you?" Father was taking charge now.
"You'd best go back and see if the dress can be altered..." Silence followed as confused looks flashed between all the party. "There is going to be another Stewart at the wedding." Jamie took his free hand and placed it over Kitty very slightly rounded belly.
One by one the penny dropped. Dougal was the last to comprehend but by which time everyone was up on their feet hugging, slapping Jamie's back and exchanging teary kisses.
"Darling they are pregnant!" Maureen hugged her husband who shed a few tears of his own.
"Love you Pop!"
"Love you Nana!" Everyone laughed.

39

The Big Day

Taking the brief window of quiet Kitty walked down to the lawn. The laughter and bustle faded behind her, Amanda, Flo, Maureen and Marie were willing minions to Maggie who spun and organised in preparation for tomorrow.

Thankful that the last week had seen an improvement in her morning sickness, Kitty nibbled her cracker and took great gulps of fresh air. Rubbing her stomach unconsciously she said quietly, "One day wee Stewart all this will be yours."

Large hands encircled her and rested atop of hers.

"Happy?"

"God yes!" Standing quietly for many minutes Jamie was first to break their revelry.

"Father had news today. He did'na ken if ye should be told today... I think ye would want to know."

"What?" Kitty turned and ran her fingers through his hair, loving the tones that shimmered in the sunlight. His face was stern.

"Donald?" Kitty swallowed the bitter taste the name left in her mouth.

"Aye... his house has sold. There is nothing here for him to return to. His new practice in Inverness is open and he need never return." Jamie tried to gauge her expression, frozen from the first mention of this man, but much to his relief she tipped her head back. Blonde curls suspended and moving in the wind, Kitty smiled.

"Thank goodness... Jamie it couldn't have come at a better day."

Jamie was ill pleased to be sent home to the cottage he and Kitty had called home. Tide's Reach was very nearly finished but they had yet to move in, Kitty suspected Jamie was dragging his feet on the last of the decorating. She hoped Jamie had no ulterior motives for not wanting to live there, and was sure it was no male ego issue as it was her house. Not wanting to broach the subject Kitty pushed these thoughts from her mind, she had enough to arrange with the wedding and the baby. Angus and Alistair dragged an unwilling groom to a waiting car and Kitty waved him off, a little sad but overwhelmingly happy.

Maggie and crew had been busy in the small chapel and as John took her arm and helped her from the car Kitty was keen to see the inside. Whether a local or family tradition the walk from the road featured Alistair on the pipes, playing a lilting melody. Jamie led the procession with Amanda, her hand resting on his upturned hand. Dougal and Maureen were followed by John and Marie – taking the place of her own parents. Kitty accepted Angus's hand and followed the procession of the bridal party, followed themselves by Flo and Alistair.

Amanda had been tasked with not letting Jamie turn around and seeing Kitty until she walked down the aisle. Jamie smiled at her none too subtle, "don't you friggin dare laddy!" through gritted teeth and a sweet smile.

As they approached the doors Kitty could smell the flowers even before they came into view. John had waited for her in the vestibule; he squeezed her arm under his. John went to start up the aisle to the sound of the pipes behind them but hesitated. Kitty looked up at his stern face softened through the haze of the fine veil.

"Your parents could not have been prouder of you my dear. I am sure they are looking down on you now. I know you will be happy in your choice of partner and never forget to appreciate each other."

She was surprised at first at such a sentimental speech from such a stately man, and then overwhelmed by the thought that they were there, watching. Her dad, arms folded over a cable knitted cardigan, her mum crying, no doubt. Tommy still small and freckled would have pulled on his tie, he had always hated getting dressed up. Stephen, standing now with her family and he too was smiling. Of course they would all be happy for her and she squeezed Johns' arm in return, so thankful for reminding her of them at that moment.

Determined not to ruin the make up Flo had spent an age on, Kitty reached up and through her veil kissed John on the check. There wasn't a dry eye in the pews, well at least the first three rows. At Kitty's insistence John and Marie sat with Maureen and Dougal, and bridesmaids and groomsmen on the other side. Both sides of the isle were full with all the friends she had made and the extensive family she had joined.

Amanda and Flo looked stunning in pale blue billowy dresses with pink and ivory flowers in their hair. As she slowly made her way towards Jamie, she smiled at the teary eyes of Jock's wife, the darts team and Celtic band, Angela and Gavin, Hamish and Claire and all their children scrubbed and smart. Heather, and Angela's eldest daughter Lauren - the book reader as Kitty always thought of her, had both been given a basket of rose petals and sat at the end of their respective pews excitedly waiting to follow her out after the ceremony.

All available space was full of Stewarts. Many she had met, but there were faces she had never seen but knew she would know by the end of the day, when she would surely be hugged and kissed by them all.

All the smiling faces she saw, she smiled back at, returned looks of love and approval. Only waiting until she had smiled across at Amanda's parents and Jamie's parents did she allow herself to look at Jamie. As he turned, she knew once their eyes met she would look no where else.

Jamie looked resplendent in his kilt; he was clean shaven, a sight rarely seen. The tartan was predominantly smokey blue with dark green, black and white. Long blue socks rose above the shiniest of black shoes, the glint of a jewelled dirk held on one calf caught her eye. The tweed waistcoat and fitted jacket covered a crisp white shirt, the ivory rose in his buttonhole surrounded by fine fern and heather. The sporran bearing his family's crest completed the outfit. Kitty thought she had never seen such a magnificent man, and he was all hers.

Taking her hand their eyes fixed, and didn't leave each other until Jamie had to look down to place the ring on her finger.

There had been much soul searching and debate, and Kitty had said she was happy to relegate Stephens' ring to sit on her right hand with her mothers' wedding band that she never removed. Jamie sensed her misgivings, and felt himself that Stephen should be given more consideration.

Kitty smiled and couldn't stop the large tears that fell as Jamie slipped this, her new ring in place. Jamie bent and kissed the ring now on her hand and Kitty couldn't have loved him more for this simple beautiful act.

Visiting a small dark jewellery shop in Portree, Kitty had placed the thin eighteen carat band that signified her marriage to Stephen together with her mothers ring on her right hand. Leaving her left hand free except for the inherited ring with its large diamonds. She had given up wearing her engagement ring from Stephen years ago as it was too small, and she had never bothered to have it resized. It had taken a lot of getting used to working around the big stones. Kitty adored it – even more for knowing its history. There was a portrait of a young Euphemia on the stairwell, soft brown pin curls and fresh pink cheeks, sat in a small floral chair, hands folded in her lap to show off the then new engagement ring as it was then.

"Ah, so James, lovely to see you! And this must be Kathleen... an honour!" Kitty smiled at the short bald bespectacled jeweller, bowing before her he offered her his hand almost reverently. Taken to the back of the shop, Jamie and Kitty took a seat on a low red-buttoned coach. Mr Spiegelhalter with due ceremony laid out a thick black velvet cloth on the table before them.

"Now Kathleen, James has set me a small task." An odd combination of Jew and cockney. The rotund man chuckled, and Kitty looked to Jamie for explanation but he looked defiantly straight ahead.

"Now I understand," the jewellers eyes twinkled up at her, "You have a wedding ring?"

"Well, um, yes but from my previous marriage – I'm a widow." More perplexed than ever.

"May I?" Long, surprisingly elegant fingers reached over the tips of his fingers rubbing minutely against his thumb. Kitty struggled to remove the ring from her nervous hot hands, and she reluctantly handed it over.

"Jamie?" she whispered but he just smiled.

Eyeglass clenched under a heavy brow, the little Jewish man emitted noises of pleasure and delight as he examined the ring.

"Yes... yes... it is eminently possible James, I will fetch the test piece." Scurrying away Kitty turned to Jamie as her ring vanished with the little man.

"What's going on Jamie? I, I don't want my ring melted down." Her bottom lip quivered despite her best efforts. Jamie reached out taking her hand and kissing the top of it.

"Hush darling, wait and see. But the decision is yours, all yours."

Now at the alter, as Jamie's head lifted Kitty gazed at this the most unique of wedding bands. The yellow gold of her first ring entwined and twisted around a second band. A fine band of rich rose gold a speciality of Skye. Retained inside was the engraving of *S to K 18.03.03*, and on the rose gold *J to K 29.09.14*. Perfect, and Kitty remembered Jamie's words from the day with Mr Spiegelhalter. "Stephen was lucky enough to be married to you, I can never replace him but try to be as good a husband as he was. You have given your heart twice and that should never be forgotten."

Outside the dark Chapel the sun seemed brighter than ever. The bouquet – gorgeous as it was with the double peonies, roses and lilies weighed heavy in her arms. The white heather was gathered around the bottom with ivory ribbon, Maureen had excelled, having to put some plants in cold storage to hold the blooms back. They stood and smiled for what felt like a thousandth photo and every muscle in her cheeks ached.

Jamie never let her go, and constantly told her how beautiful she looked. She was the proudest of brides and found it difficult to take her eyes off her husband. Who would ever have thought such a thing was possible, let alone in such a short space of time? But nothing had ever felt so right, so meant to be.

Finally the pictures were taken and Angus and others were tasked with taking the flowers from the chapel to transport them back to the house for the reception. Jamie held her back as she started towards the cars.

"Kathleen, mother has left these if you would like to put them around the back." Kitty smiled back at him.

"Oh, how thoughtful." Together Kitty, Jamie, Amanda and her family carried the four small posies Maureen had made. Dougal had a head stone commissioned and finished in time for this day so Kitty might have her family with her on her wedding day. A bright new stone was simply inscribed,

"Here lay the remains of Leo Harris, Lillian Harris and Tommy Harris. Beloved father, mother and brother to Kathleen Harris Stewart."

Jamie and Kitty had collected the stone only days before. Dougal had helped erect it and a shallow hole was dug to add the chalky remains of Kitty's family.

After Tommy had died her parents meant to have his ashes scattered, but Lillian could never bear the thought of letting them go. So Tommy, in his small brown plastic box, moved around the house. Sometimes in the bookcase, sometimes under the television, but always a comfort. A lot of people found it odd but to the Harris's it was normal and reassuring. And so the tradition continued, when

Lillian died Stephen accepted the three boxes in the drawer under the television, opting to avoid them whenever possible.

She wished now she hadn't agreed with Stephen's parents to have him interred at their local crematorium. It gave her solace that his mother visited him there, but today she would have preferred to have him here.

Kitty, Amanda, John and Marie laid the flowers before the stone. Kitty knew for whom John wiped his face, like her mother before her she had the privilege of two good men loving her.

Sitting in the back seat of the car they slouched down, rested back on the seat and turned, noses touching. Kitty wore her hair loosely gathered at the crown, long curls free at the back. Maureen had loaned her diamond and pearl earrings and matching necklace. Jamie marvelled at them as they sparkled, and Kitty tried hard not to think how much they were worth. Jamie reached over, outlining her face with his finger tips, stopping to pull and gently release the free curl framing her face.

"You really do look beautiful Mrs Stewart."

"No you look gorgeous Mr Stewart."

"And how is mini Stewart doing?" Jamie reached over and gently laid a large hand covering her belly.

"Oh ok, I think, just making his mum tired."

"Are you tired, poor you!"

"Not too tired." She grinned and Jamie kissed her.

The car halted and Angus coughed loudly at the open door.

"Jamie, lad, the whole party is looking!" Kitty ducked her head but Jamie merely smiled and waved.

A large marquee had been positioned on the level front lawn. Kitty hadn't been allowed in, it was to be a surprise. Every one was waiting outside and young girls, Lilly included, were weaving in amongst the guests handing out champagne. Maureen was the first to greet her.

"Before anyone else sees it come in."

Jamie and Kitty followed his parents through the door. The ceiling was draped in white muslin and every pillar adorned with six foot tall cascades of flowers. The scent was heady and strong, following the theme of her bouquet. Large round tables with crisp linen cloth, held centre pieces with heavy silver wear and swags of the family tartan. Great swathes of Tartan were draped along the top table. Kitty stood trying to take in every detail, stunned by its beauty and splendour.

"The tartan's not too much?" Maureen looked worryingly at her husband.

"Oh... no, Maureen, Dougal it's perfect. I'm so proud to be part of it, it's so beautiful!"

"Well Maggie is the one to thank really, she has really thrown herself into it."

Standing in line they were soon joined by Alistair, Flo and Amanda and her parents - all had the privilege of welcoming the guests. Maureen had thought it prudent, and had phoned all the guests to inform them about Kitty's circumstance, so there were no awkward assumptions that John and Marie were her parents.

Finally seated at the top table, Kitty was very grateful for the floor length tablecloth and kicked off her shoes. Before the meal began Angus carried the quaich (a traditional drinking cup) that had been made for the occasion, Kitty had collected it from the jewellers with Jamie only last week. Her index finger circled the fine engraving that ran around the highly polished silver rim the whole drive home. For the first time the smell of whiskey had not reminded her of that terrible night, and now that memory could be erased. When all on the top table had held its two handles and taken a sip of whiskey the marquee erupted in cheers and the food could be served.

It was delicious but fatigue was telling, and Kitty nibbled her way around the plate. Much to her delight and feeling the presence of her mother, Jamie quietly imparted snippets of information on guests on each table.

"Table two – pink fascinator – went to school with Flo – got an extra toe!" Winking down at his bride. At that moment she knew she couldn't love him more.

In truth Kitty was worrying about the speeches. Although only her second time down the aisle and each being very different occasions, the common denominator and source of much pain was the absence of her father.

Her old in-laws had said it was too far to travel, and the frosty reception she had received when she informed them of the wedding left her in no doubt they strongly disapproved. Kitty couldn't really blame them; she wasn't ignorant of the disloyalty of it. But it was as it was, and it was right and honest, and frankly she was relieved they were not here. John had offered to speak and she had no good reason to say no, there certainly was no one else. How she wished she wasn't pregnant now the nearer the time came, she could do with a stiff drink. But it was already too late, and glasses were tapped and John pushed his seat back.

"Good afternoon." Clearing his throat he paused to gulp the last of his wine. Flushed and perspiring Kitty felt so sorry to have put him in this situation.

"I stand here to represent Kitty's father. He would have enjoyed today and he and... Lillian," saying her name was obviously still tough, of course he had lost them too. Kitty reached out and squeezed his hand.

"They would be bursting with pride. Kathleen has always been dear to us, my wife and of course her best friend. We have enjoyed watching her grow into a beautiful young woman inside and out. We also have shared along the way, the loss and grief of her losing first her brother, then her father and her dear mother. It was a final blow when Stephen..." John gulped and blushed. "When Kitty's first husband was taken and we all worried about her terribly. To everyone's surprise she sold up and moved here." This was greeted with a rousing cheer from everyone.

"We worried what would become of her, but not only did she find her soul mate in Jamie but the warm embrace of the whole Stewart family. And my family thank you from the bottom of our hearts, we could not have let her go for anything less." John bent and kissed Kitty on the forehead. "So please raise your glasses in a toast to those who cannot be here."

Thank goodness for Maggie the wedding planner extraordinaire and the small lace covered boxes of tissues could be seen travelling around each table.

"To Kathleen's family, all those lost, and all those found!" John raised his glass. Kitty had managed to hold it together until then, and Maureen handed her the box.

A hush fell over the proceedings with only sniffing and nose blowing audible. Unexpectedly it was Dougal who stood next, whispering to Jamie, obviously agreeing with whatever had been asked of him.

"Well John. Thank you. As we are veering from convention I hope Kathleen and James won't mind if I make a toast today." Bride and groom nodded their assent and Dougal pushed back his chair and stood behind his son and wife and rested a hand on both shoulders.

"Thank you John for a beautiful toast."

"Hear, hear!" "Aye!" chorused around the room.

"And if you would indulge me I would just like to say a few words on behalf of myself and Maureen. They say a daughter is your daughter for all of your life," smiling along at Flo. "But a son is your son till he takes him a wife! Well I speak for both of us when I say we feel truly blessed that this brave young woman arrived on our doorstep. Rather than taking our son we feel we have been given another daughter. I know we can never replace your dear family Kathleen, but we welcome you into ours and wish to be all a mother and father can be, not to mention giving you a brother and sister – as annoying as that can be." A rumble of laughter accompanied the out pouring of tears. Well that did it, and even the toughest of Stewart kinsman were fighting over the lace boxes.

Dougal bent and kissed both of them using his serviette to wipe away the unchecked tears. Amanda blew her nose much louder than anticipated, which in a small way relieved the tension and added, again louder than she meant, "You didn't warn me! I expected the tartan but no one said about the tears."

Laughter trickled around the room and Jamie drank a tall glass of water. Drying his and then his wife's tears, he kissed her and stood to a cheer.

"Thanks chaps. I dunna know how to follow that." Joking, but then deadly serious he turned to both men, shook their hands and thanked them again.

"I no intend to make a long speech." Heckling now from various quarters, the mood was lifting to everyone's relief.

"I just want to raise a glass to my beautiful wife – Mrs Kathleen Stewart." All cheered and a sea of sparkling glasses were raised. "Now, not to have ye all reaching for the tissues – good call by the way Maggie!" Maggie took a small bow to riotous applause. "I do have just a few words I want to say. Thank ye my love for being brave enough to drive all this way so we could find each other. Thank you for giving my life purpose and meaning, and I would like to end on a traditional toast. May we be poor in misfortune. Rich in blessings. Slow to anger and quick to forgive. I love you with all my heart."

Kitty had one hand at her neck and the other in Jamie's hand as she cried. Maureen, along with all the women and well, most of the men were now blubbing, and calling over the waitress she asked that teas and coffee be served. People chatted quietly, neighbours correcting each other's makeup. Amanda hissed along the table to Kitty "Should have said waterproof mascara was a must!" This made Kitty laugh and slowly everyone gathered themselves.

It was Angus who stood next, at least this shouldn't cause tears – well not of sadness, humiliation maybe.

"Never mind the tea people! This is a celebration and I for one would like to raise a glass to the stunning bridesmaids!" Everyone in the room was relieved and lighthearted cheering and a smattering of whistling had Flo and Amanda blushing.

"Flo, as gorgeous as always, and I ken much nicer now you're not following us around wanting to butt in on all our games." Laughter from all those in the room that remembered their childhoods.

"And for Amanda who braved the six hundred and forty miles – so she keeps telling me" in mock moans, the room erupted again. "We thank ya as Kathleen's best friend and Jamie's long distance confidant, I thank ya. I do believe your very first conversation with Jimmy here was about contraceptive advice." Angus raised a glass to cheers and wide-eyed exchanges from the older guests. "Now I know how excited ye were lass, at the prospect of meeting lots of men in kilts, and have high hopes for later in the evening. I'm afraid to disappoint but I have a girlfriend, but if there is an eligible man out there?" cheers and whistles were accompanied by thumping on the tables. Amanda buried her red face in her hands, but not before seeing the disapproving glare from her mother.

"And lad, I ken ya should have taken more heed about the contraception. It is with great pleasure I have been tasked with announcing the fantastic news that Mr and Mrs Stewart are expecting a bairn." The biggest cheer yet, Angus reached and shook Jamie's hand and kissed a very flushed Kitty.

"Now when I first met our lovely Kathleen... it was band night," the band table shouted and banged their table. "Jimmy, as I remember wasn't too impressed with our little interloper, and yet, somehow, we ended up having to carry her drunken little self home – local ale a bit strong for ye lassie?"

"Oh god!" Kitty buried her face in Jamie's chest.

"Careful" Jamie said quietly and seriously to his best friend.

"And I do believe it was having to undress her and put her to bed in that spotty van of hers, where true love sprang."

"Ya bastard!" Jamie sneered.

"Now ye tell me this Angus Macleod?" It was Angus's girlfriend from the front table who called out. Great guffaws of laughter echoed around the tent.

"I kept my eyes closed, it was all Jamie!"

"Not helping!" Jamie nudged him and enjoyed his embarrassment, risking an apologetic smile at his parents and John and Marie.

Angus continued regardless, "But from very early on, I believe he said it was from the first glimpse of her blue lacy underwear – remember it was Jamie darling, not me!" aimed straight at his girlfriend now, much to the delight of the other guests.

"Our Jimmy was well and truly hooked. They have a love that is rare and real and honest and I wish them every happiness." Holding his glass up he recited a toast.

"Wherever you live in the world so wide,
We wish you a nook on the sunny side.
With much love and a little care,
A little purse with money to spare.
Your own little hearth, when day is spent,
In a little house with hearty content!
To the bride and groom! Oh and sorry... to the mothers!"
remembering just before everyone toasted again Angus fetched two bouquets for Maureen and an embarrassed Marie.

There was one final cheer and the room dissolved into animated chatter, Kitty hugged her husband.

The rest of the day was a blur of introductions and snatched conversations with all her guests. Swollen feet and rising exhaustion saw Kitty sitting, moving from table to table sat whilst Jamie stood at her side. Huge hugs were saved for John and Marie, Maureen and Dougal. Maggie, Flo, Alistair and Amanda all took their turn. If Kitty could have been crowned the happiest of brides, Jamie would have been the proudest of all grooms. As the tables were cleared before the next wave of guests threatened to arrive, Kitty pulled Jamie to the door. Leading him across the lawn, Kitty and Jamie giggled as they made their way up the staircase to the sanctity of his old room.

In the familiarity of the room Kitty flopped back onto the bed, kicking her puffy feet free from the sparkly shoes. Seeing the ridges in the swollen flesh, Jamie took her feet and placed them onto his chest and rubbed the feet of a very grateful bride.

Kitty started to laugh; holding her stomach as the laughter rose and she wriggled and squirmed on the bed. "I'm not sure this is what people think we would have snuck up here for."

"I can see how tired you are darling, let's lay here for half an hour and then we can cut the cake, have our dance and sneak off."

"You still haven't told me where we are going on honeymoon."

"No, and now it's here I'm terribly afraid you will be disappointed." Jamie took a long sigh.

"Oh how could I be? As long as I'm with you I'll be the happiest of brides." She grinned up at him.

"You must promise me, if you are disappointed we will book a holiday anywhere in the world." Kitty gestured for him to come around the bed to her.

"Kiss me husband!" Jamie smiled and bent to oblige. Kitty's hand reached up the back of his knee, passing over the fluffy hair on the back of his leg until she was cupping a naked buttock, then gave it a small slap.

Moaning he stood straight and rested his hand on his sporran. "One of the lesser known uses of a Sporran, when ya lass teases ye."

His bride grinned up at him, "What might you do about that Mr Stewart?"

"If ye would let me take that dress off I ken I have a few ideas." He ran a hand up under her dress, Kitty giggled and struggled to her feet. They returned to the party, the lights had been dimmed and pink lights now illuminated the room and the dance floor that had been installed. After their first dance they mingled, talked, laughed and hugged the night away.

Flo and Amanda had hit it off, and Kitty laughed, as Amanda was lost to her in a swirl of kilts and Stewarts. Kitty's feet hurt and her back ached, Jamie's arms encircled her and whispered into her ear, "Shall I take ye away from all this?"

"Yes please."

After running through the archway of their guests they found Charles. A life long teetotaler who lived in one of the estate cottages, he had already been lined up as chauffer. They cuddled up in the back of the car, as the roar of well wishes faded into the distance. Jamie had to remove a small hand that on numerous occasions tried to travel from his knee up under his kilt. Old Charles said nothing but Jamie often saw him glance in the rear view mirror.

"Later Mrs Stewart – a sporran can only conceal so much!" He whispered, she sniggered as his breath tickled her ear.

"Where are we going?"

"Close your eyes and be patient!"

The lack of any street lighting meant Kitty had no idea where they were when the car stopped. Rushing around to her side, one hand on her head Jamie helped his bride from the car.

"Eyes closed!" Holding her around the waist he said his farewells to Charles and waited, breathing in her scent his face resting on her neck until the car had disappeared.

"Open your eyes."

Blinking to focus Kitty glanced around; in front of her there was a strip of what looked like police tape. Reaching forward and with the help of Jamie's illuminated phone now she read out, "Keep out" Shining the light to the left the newly painted sigh shone clearly – Tide's Reach.

"Oh... we're home!" Surprised, but Jamie hoped not too disappointed. He moved her hand and shone the light on a second notice.

Danger – do not enter. Honeymooners on the loose. Do not disturb until October 5th

Kitty laughed and turned to hug her husband.

"I just thought we've worked so hard since April on the house. It's finally finished."

"It is?"

"Wait and see, what better place to stay. You're not too disappointed lass?" He took her face in both his hands.

"Oh Jamie I love it!" She reached up and kissed him. They walked carefully down the drive and across the new concrete path using the light from the phone to guide them. Tide's Reach glowed, its fresh white paint reflecting the pale moonlight. Lifting her gently Jamie carried her across the threshold. The house was filled with fragrance of the day and large vases crammed with flowers from the church.

"Maggie?"

"Aye."

"What a wonder!"

The house was spotless and on the table a letter addressed to Mr and Mrs Stewart.

"How did it all get finished?"

"Malcolm and the boys, their wives and a few others came round yesterday and went through the place like Maggie's army. Impressive isn't it?"

Kitty walked around the table, marvelling at the cleaned surfaces. No more paint brushes but a kitchen that looked like a home – her home. Kitty recognised the hand and opened the letter cautiously.

Dear Kit and Jamie,

Welcome to your honeymoon. Cupboards, fridge and freezer are stocked. No one will visit and you can come and go if you wish, but if you want to stay in bed all week – knock yourself out! It's not like you can get pregnant, that ship has long since sailed!

Maureen and Dougal – who by the way I want to adopt – have kindly offered for us to stay with them another two weeks. We have no shame and will probably outstay our welcome. So enjoy your peace, enjoy each other and we will see you next Saturday

Lots of love Mand xxxx

40

Home

Kitty still loved this room, wiping the green unit doors and wondering when the novelty of a fully functioning kitchen would wear off, if ever. Grateful for the window that looked out up the path to the drive, she could see Pimples squinting into the sun, bright silver reflecting off his visors.

Walking through the lounge she paused to look at the sea, it was her favourite colour today. Jamie's slippers were tidied under his chair and the cushions shook and repositioned, the log burner still emitting heat from last nights fire. This room had exceeded all her expectations and she could have happily loitered longer but returned to the kitchen.

She ran a finger down the calendar resting on today's date. April 14th – *"move date"*. So much had happened in such a short space of time, on this day she had left everything she knew. Embarked on her great adventure having no idea of the new and fabulous life she would find. Life before coming here was a fast fading memory. She felt so entrenched here, as if Skye was waiting for her all along – treading water waiting for this reality.

Rearranging the small milk bottle on the windowsill she removed the jaded primroses and headed out to replenish them. Slipping on her shoes she walked slowly into the front garden. Hands on the small of her back Kitty stretched backwards, her belly heavy and she smiled up at the sun as the baby squirmed and stirred inside her. "Hi you," Kitty rubbed the top of her bump at what felt like small feet trying to push free.

The wagging of a tail fanned the back of her legs and the latest addition to the family stretched and yawned, showing a mass of white teeth and splaying his huge paws.

"I've found you a puppy," Ange had said. Since being here her friend in the post office had made it her mission to find Kitty a four legged friend.

"Something small" had always been Kitty's reply. But Angus had stolen her heart and now the five-month-old Irish wolfhound was her constant shadow.

"Where's daddy? Find daddy?" And on cue Angus – named after

the best man in payment for the embarrassing underwear story – lolloped across the garden out of sight, too big feet flapping on the end of too long legs.

Rubbing her belly now Kitty spoke to the newest Stewart, "Six weeks then your time is up!" Rounding the large boulder Angus waited for her, tail wagging wildly. The path was now well trodden and Kitty approached quietly. The gable end was now reinstated to its original height but there was no window and Kitty edged round to the glass front. The door was ajar and bathed in light from the glass roof Jamie sat in the old steamer chair, surrounded by the flotsam and jetsam collected from the beach and paints and stacked canvas's of Kitty creation.

He was holding a book in one hand and with the other was absentmindedly patting the back of a pink baby gro. Looking up and smiling, he put down the book and rested his hand on Kitty's bump as she stood next to him. Reaching down Kitty kissed first her husband then the mass of pale red curls of her daughter.

"Thank you, did she get you up very early?"

"Not too bad, I wanted you to sleep in."

"Two years today, did you realise I was heading up the M1 about now. How is it possible that so much has happened?"

"I know, any regrets?"

"Oh... how can you ask? No... Definitely not!"

"No ghosts?"

"None."

She had survived her two winters and Kitty felt every bit an Islander now.

Kissing now, two years had done nothing to dampen their ardour. The intensity hadn't dwindled at all but pregnancy, a toddler and the inquisitive licks from a slobbery dog meant they had to grab their opportunities when they may.

THE END

Acknowledgements

I am constantly drawn back to Scotland ever since I first visited. Its peace, beauty and majesty never fail to strike me and focus the mind about what is important in life.

Finding a derelict cottage by the water's edge on the Isle of Skye inspired me to try and capture the healing that could take place here. Quite unexpectedly this turned into a story of recovery and the heart's ability to heal and learn to love and laugh again.

So my first thank you is to my husband Les, who first took me to these stunning lands on our honeymoon and for always being you.

Huge thanks to the patient and long suffering Les and our daughter, Lilia, who lose me for whole days when I write. Thank you for your love and support.

To my Epsom friends, Melanie, Nina and Mandi, our adventures inspire me and you were the first people I trusted to read my work.

Jill, or the grammar police as she is now known, thank you for your reading and rereading and unerring encouragement.

To Terry for the encouragement and showing me that getting my story to actually exist as a book could be a reality.

Finally to Lilia; without your IT support my books of long hand could never have been uploaded. Love you Noodle.

…,